ALDARAIA

A
Matthew Bishop
Novel by

BURT CLINCHANDHILL

ALDARAIA
Matthew Bishop - Book 1

SECOND EDITION SOFTCOVER
ISBN: 1622536088
ISBN-13: 978-1-62253-608-5

Editor: Becky Stephens
Cover Artist: Kabir Shah
Interior Designer: Lane Diamond

www.EvolvedPub.com
Evolved Publishing LLC
Butler, Wisconsin, USA

Printed in Book Antiqua font.

BOOKS BY BURT CLINCHANDHILL

MATTHEW BISHOP
Book 1: *Aldaraia*
Book 2: *Lemuria*

JAMES MITCHEL
Book 1: *Kursk*
Book 2: *47 Hours*
Book 3: *The Mogadishu Encounter*

DEDICATION

For Dad.

Special thanks and love to my wife Nathalie for her support and rereading the Aldaraia manuscript.

*As always, thanks to my mentor and critic, Andrea Busfield.
What would this novel be without you?*

Thank you Rose for re-rereading the book and keeping me consistent.

*Special thanks to all those involved who contributed.
You know who you are.*

PROLOGUE

'Qui non intelligit avt taceat avt discat.'
'One who does not understand should be silent or learn.'
John Dee, Monas Hieroglyphica, 1564

Krakow, Poland, Fall 1604

Occult philosopher John Dee walked along the dark, narrow backstreets of Krakow. At his age, the cobblestones—wet and slippery from two days of continuous rain—made walking a challenge. Using his cane like a blind man tapping out steps, he struggled to keep up with the young lantern bearer he had hired to show him the way, but then, after turning into a street so narrow it was little more than an alleyway, the lantern bearer stopped fifty feet ahead of him in front of a store window. Behind the glass there was light from a single candle. Dee looked up to read the sign above them, *'Biblioteka Łaski.'*

For a moment he thought about what brought him here. What other option did he have? The secret he carried with him was too big to be kept untold. But what was the world going to do with it? Who was ready for it? What would happen to the world if it became public? Who was to decide who would live or die? He knew he didn't have the time to find out. Someone else would have to decide for him.

Without saying a word, he reached for the purse hanging from the belt holding his leather raincoat closed. He took out a fifty groszy silver coin and offered it to the young lantern bearer who immediately snatched it from his gloved hand and ran, leaving Dee without light and standing alone in the rain. He leaned against the shop window and raised his hands to his temples as he peered inside.

Could there be anyone working at this time in the evening? he wondered. And what would he do if there wasn't? Where could he go? How much time did he really have? Suddenly, a flicker of light caught his attention as it bounced off the wall from the rear of the store. Dee picked up his cane and tapped at the glass to announce himself. When nothing happened, he tapped again, slightly harder, but carefully in case the copper head of his cane, which resembled a dragon's tail, damaged the glass. A second later, a shadow approached from the back of the store. Dee watched the hulking figure take the burning candle and hold it aloft toward the window pane. Almost immediately, Olbracht Łaski recognized his old friend and hurried to open the entrance door to the right of the window.

"Come in quickly, you're getting soaked," Łaski said kindly as he opened the door, his mind racing with questions. It had been such a long time. "Show me yourself. Is it really you?"

Łaski removed the sopping wet scarf from his old friend's neck and held the candle up to Dee's face. "I cannot believe it. It is really you. You look awful. Come, let me take you some place warmer, where you can dry. You must be freezing."

Directing Dee with a gentle hand on the shoulder, he raised his candle with the other hand and guided him to the back of the store, passing row upon row of books covered in gold leaf. There were hundreds, if not thousands, of books and the light of the candle bounced off each and every one of the gold pressed titles as they passed, like sparks playing over a campfire. As they walked, Dee stumbled several times over stacks of books piled on the floor, some so high they might be used as chairs.

Łaski opened a door leading to a backroom that was well lit by oil lamps and a huge roaring fire. "Sit, John, my friend," he ordered as he pulled a simple wooden chair closer to the fireplace. Dee glanced about him, noticing there wasn't one book in the room. In fact, the room was almost completely empty but for two chairs, one of which he was about to sit on. After taking off his gloves and coat, Dee grunted as it took a moment to kneel in front of the warmth. The book collector reached for the kettle hanging over the fireplace and poured hot coffee into a red clay cup with a shining silver edge.

"Thank you," Dee said as he took hold of the cup, cradling it with both hands so the heat might thaw his frozen fingers. "I see you still misuse the tea set I gave you to drink this filth you call coffee."

When Łaski last left England, Dee presented him with a red stoneware tea set decorated with silver. As it was the first of its kind to be fired with such detail it made the gift all the more prestigious and collectible.

"I'm sorry." Łaski gave a small smile. "So, how is it that you show up at my home with no announcement? Have you come from England?" Before Dee had a chance to answer, Łaski stroked his thick, long beard, all fifteen inches of it, and continued speaking. "No, don't tell me. That assistant of yours, what's his name, Conly? Kerry? No wait, Kelley. Edward Kelley. That's him. Did he convince you that we need to work on some kind of divine project again? Has he been speaking to his old friend the Archangel Uriël again?" Łaski laughed good-naturedly although he would have had good reason not to be so forgiving.

When Dee and Kelley last visited Łaski, some fifteen years ago, the visit had been prompted by Uriël—the angel tasked with guarding the Gate to Eden with his fiery sword. Uriël had apparently told Kelley that he should accompany Dee to Poland and share all of their possessions with Łaski, including their wives. Though it had seemed a good idea at the time, it eventually cost Łaski his marriage and sons.

Once his laughter had subsided, Łaski apologized because Dee's face made it clear he was in no mood for humor. "Okay, tell me. What are you up to?"

"Thank you, my old friend," Dee replied.

"For what?" Łaski asked as he pulled a chair up to the fire.

"For letting me in, getting me warm and finally shutting up so I might explain."

Łaski grinned. This was the John Dee he knew; a serious man with a sneering sense of humor. Ever the gentleman, he was also a man of immense imagination, more than was possibly good for him at times. It was his appointment as court astronomer, mathematician and astrologer to Queen Elizabeth of England that had made him rich enough to indulge his peculiar obsessions and since then he had traveled the world, exploring the crossroads between science and magic. As a result, he had become a believer in some quite extravagant theories surrounding a number of religious, hermetic and esoteric practices. But, by and large, Dee had been nothing but a good and sincere friend to him over the years. "I'll shut up." The big man smiled. "I'll shut up for as long as you need me to shut up."

"That's helpful because I'm dying." He paused for a moment. "I'm dying and I may not have too much time left." As Dee spoke he kept his face and voice emotionless. "I'm almost eighty-one years old and this disease within me is finally getting the upper hand. Still, I need you one more time."

"I'm sorry to hear that," Łaski replied softly.

"Do you remember our last conversation by letter?"

Łaski paused for a moment. "It must have been over a year ago, but I seem to recollect you wanting to translate some kind of secret or sacred text that apparently holds all the secrets to the universe. Do you mean that one?"

Dee replied to his friend's sarcasm with a sly smile before slowly nodding his head. "Yes, that one. And the secret text you're referring to is known as the *Aldaraia sive Soyga vocor*, or as you called it, The Book of Soyga."

"Ah yes, now it comes back to me," Łaski said. "Wasn't it some kind of manuscript by an unknown author of an unknown origin and written in code. What of it? I thought you had already decoded it?"

"I did most of the decoding, something that took the better part of two years, and from my work I would say the larger part of the text is a basic treatise about alchemy written in a Latin alphabet governed by the laws of arithmetic. Basically, they changed numbers for letters and hid the message in all manner of calculations. Then, they changed the direction of the text to read right to left, like in Hebrew writing."

"What did it say?"

Łaski was always intrigued whenever Dee dug up some weird text or ancient scripture, and he dug up a lot. When he was in his prime, Dee's library contained more than 3,000 printed books and 1,000 manuscripts, all kept at his home in Mortlake, London. A lot of the works were of an occult nature, describing various prophecies or new routes to heaven or how and when the world might end.

"The text was mostly concerned with instructions on magic. Incantations, basic astrology, demonology, that kind of thing. But nothing that really excited me in anyway except...."

"Except?" Łaski prompted when his friend fell silent.

"Except for the last pages. I couldn't figure out the last thirty-six pages. They were so different to what had gone before. Each page was made up of thirty-six rows and thirty-six columns filled with more than 45,000 letters in Latin. I had no clue as to what they stood for, well, not until a while ago."

Dee reached for his leather overcoat on the floor and from one of its pockets took out a leather-bound scroll tied together by a shoelace.

"This is it. Everything," he said, and he handed Łaski the scroll. When his friend started to pick at the lace he reached out a hand to stop him. "Please, open it later when I'm gone." But it was too late. The lace came away and as it did something made of glass dropped on the stone floor.

"What's this?" Łaski asked, picking up the diamond shaped, emerald-colored crystal.

"Please, put it back," Dee almost begged. "You'll find out when you read everything."

Łaski frowned as he looked at Dee. "Why don't you just tell me what's inside?" To please his friend, he didn't unroll the scroll and he placed the crystal back inside of it.

"A few months ago, I decided that all the standard decrypting tools were never going to solve this problem so I started experimenting with other tools, which is when I found it."

"Found what?"

"The cypher. But that's not important right now. Everything you need to decipher the last part of the book is in that scroll in your hands."

"So, what did it say? Is it another doomsday message?" Łaski looked at Dee, his eyes wide with interest as he anticipated another dark and captivating story.

"The text can be whatever you want it to be—for good or for bad, or for very bad. So, here's where you have a decision to make."

Confused, Łaski held Dee's gaze trying to understand whatever it was his friend was cryptically trying to tell him. Although Dee had always been a serious man, there was a hint of sadness in his eyes, perhaps even fear, and this scared him a little.

"I'm not going to tell you what it says," Dee continued. "Like I said, the answers to all your questions are in that scroll. It's up to you how much you may want to know."

"That bad, huh?" he asked, unable to hide the skepticism in his voice. In fact, the only thing that kept him from ripping the folder right open, there and then, was that Dee had all too often presented him with packages of intrigue only to discover they involved little more than fanciful tales built on beliefs, not facts. Łaski was a religious man, but he was also a scientist and he knew the difference between evidence-based proof and the unsubstantiated power of belief.

"What you hold could be that bad, yes, but it could also be the biggest blessing mankind will ever receive. It all depends on the hands that turn the wheel. Listen, I know you're skeptical and you have every right to be considering our past so the only thing I'm asking of you is that you keep an open mind and look at the facts when I'm gone."

"Well, I must say I'm flattered that you trust me with this, but... what do you want me to do with it?"

"As you know, ever since my first wife died, much of my family has gone the same way. For the most part, I have fallen out of grace and...."

"Sadly, the Black Death brought a curse on us all, but more so on you, my friend, and my heart aches for you."

"Thank you. I know you care and I'm grateful for that. Unfortunately, my remaining two sons, Rowland and Arthur, have both turned to a life of crime. There's also my daughter Katherine, but well...." Dee stopped talking and stared into the fire.

"I'm sorry to hear of your troubles, John. All of them."

Dee's fall from grace at the English court was no secret. Even Łaski had heard of it through the Polish grapevine, and he had at first assumed this was the reason for his friend's overly glum demeanor. Now it was clear, the sadness he had seen in Dee's eyes was more than bruised pride; it was grief. This man who had once had everything had lost everything.

"I'm okay," Dee lied, reaching over to place a hand on his friend's shoulder as tears sprang to the big man's eyes.

"This is all wrong." Łaski sniffed, resting his head on Dee's hand. "It should be me comforting you."

"Not at all. I understand too well how you feel," Dee replied. "But I've had my time and I'm ready for the next life that awaits me."

A few minutes passed before the men gathered themselves enough to sit back in their chairs, returning their eyes to the fire because it seemed easier than waiting to see who would speak first. In the end, they both spoke at once.

"What do you...."

"So, I guess...."

"Please, allow me," Dee requested. "I have come to beg a favor of you." As he paused for breath, a cough rattled his chest, leaving him gasping for air.

"Here, drink some water. It's fresh from the rain." Łaski quickly handed him a tin cup filled from a bowl standing next to the fire. "Are you okay?"

"Obviously not," Dee half-laughed. "But I'll hold on for as long as this takes. Now, that favor. I need you to keep the *Soyga* for me until Katherine reaches her twenty-first year. That's seven years from now."

"You don't trust her with it?"

"She's a child with all the naiveties that go with that age. I trust in two things. One, that she will be older and wiser at twenty-one. And two, in you and your judgment and that you will know whether she is ready or not when that time comes and act accordingly."

"When that time comes I might well be dead and buried." Łaski placed both hands on his belly and patted his large gut to emphasize his point.

"Olbracht Łaski, you're like a rat. Every time they think they have destroyed you, you come back from the dead."

Dee was alluding to Łaski's failed coup attempt on the Polish throne some twenty-five years previously. After being banished for ten years he was eventually allowed to return and a few years ago he was even reinstated as a nobleman—a count no less. Even so, after the fallout with his family Łaski preferred to live his life surrounded by books, with no one to irritate him and as far away as possible from anything that might accelerate the end of his miserable existence.

"My guess is that you will live to a hundred years enjoying optimum health," Dee predicted.

"Maybe you are right, but I'm guessing your faith in me has little to do with my potential longevity and more to do with you having no one else to turn to."

"There is that," Dee acknowledged with a smile. "So, will you help me?"

"Of course I will help you. But I cannot promise that I won't take a peek at these papers."

"I know you and therefore I trust you to do just that, and you'll see that I'm right. Also, in the folder is a letter to my daughter explaining everything."

"I'm sure there is."

Łaski rose from his chair and walked back into his bookstore. When he closed the door behind him, Dee grew curious, even more so when he heard stacks of books being dragged from one place to another. *'Do jasnej cholery!'* Dee heard Łaski shout. He didn't know the meaning, but he had heard the same phrase in other unfavorable situations. For ten minutes, Łaski disappeared and then, just as Dee decided to take a look, the door opened and Łaski re-entered the room laughing.

"Look here! I'm sure you will appreciate this." Łaski triumphantly held aloft an old terracotta jug bearing a dark red wax seal. On one side of the jug was the Star of David pressed into the clay. Łaski walked up to Dee and handed it over.

"You remember this?" Łaski asked.

Dee remembered the jug very well. Łaski had brought it back with him following one of his many travels to the Holy Land where it was probably used as a burial gift. He tried to give it to Dee when he first came to England almost thirty years ago in order to persuade the Muscovy Company to stop selling arms to Ivan the Terrible. While there, he visited Dee in London and gave him the jug. It was a bribe, of course; a feeble attempt to convince Dee to move to Poland and help him with his research into alchemy. Dee not only refused the jug, but accused him of grave robbery. Even so, he did go to Poland with him.

"You old grave robber," Dee joked. He took hold of the jug, immediately noticing how heavy it was. "Have you put something inside?"

"After you went back to England that first visit, I fermented and distilled the best sugar beets I could find and made the finest vodka possible. I filled the jug knowing there would come a day when you and I would look back at our first meeting, and here we are and here it is—thirty-year-old original beet vodka matured in terracotta." Łaski reached for two small pottery jars. "Tomorrow I'll take care of your message."

Dee nodded with gratitude and smiled as he cracked the seal from the jug. He then poured the milky liquid into Łaski's small jars.

Łaski raised his cup to make a toast. "Today we drink to all that is past and to whatever will pass from this day on, and to that which has made us who we are and who we ever shall be."

"I'll drink to that," Dee said, and they both drank their jars dry in one go.

CHAPTER 1

The Auction

London, 2008

A black cab, clearly in a hurry, passed St James's Palace, the oldest royal palace in the United Kingdom that was once home to England's royalty, including Henry III and Queen Elizabeth I.

If only these walls could talk, thought Robert Porter, watching the palace disappear from view as the cab turned a corner to take them to St James's Street. Porter gave a wry smile—St James's Palace, St James's Square, St James's Square Garden—it was no wonder he always got lost as a kid when his father was stationed there with the US military. It wasn't just the repetitive street names either; the narrow streets and tall, Georgian and Tudor-era buildings had also worked to throw him off track more times than he could remember.

After the hackney carriage turned onto the corner of St James's Street and King Street, Porter tapped on the partition to stop the driver.

"That'll be nine-fifty," the man said. Though clearly of Indian descent his accent was firmly east London. "Doing a bit of shopping, are you?"

"Who knows," Porter said as he handed him a ten-pound note.

"Can you believe that?" asked the cabby as Porter's eyes glanced at an advertisement on the divider for a movie called *Lost in Austen*.

"Excuse me?"

"The advert," the driver replied. "I saw you looking at it. That's supposed to be Jane Austen." He pointed at the movie poster. "I sometimes wonder how these great authors, who wrote such classics as "Pride and Prejudice," would feel if they saw our modern take on their stories and lives."

"You like Jane Austen's 'Pride and Prejudice?'"

"Sure, who doesn't?"

Porter nodded politely as he opened the door and left the cab, but in truth he had never cared much for the British classics even though he owned some very fine leather-bound first editions in his book collection. But reading them....

As Porter stepped onto the pavement he knew he cut a fairly impressive figure: tall, slender, athletic and dressed as only a man with money could be dressed. He glanced up at the face of the building standing on the corner. He must have passed this building more than a thousand times during his childhood as he rode his bike to and from school. The name *Christie's* was emblazoned in gold embossed letters in the window, a little below an old-looking clock that showed it was 11:15. Clearly, he would have to hurry if he wanted to be in time for the auction. As he walked up to the entrance he looked at the words carved in stone above the huge doors: King St Chambers. Porter had read somewhere that this was where the seventeenth century's most celebrated lawyers used to meet when the area became a residential favorite of the British aristocracy. As he recalled this information, his mind conjured up images of mahogany rooms filled with brown leather Chesterfield chairs sat on by men dressed in gray wigs sipping from tumblers of whiskey.

"Hurry," he reprimanded himself, cursing his easily distracted mind.

Through the large doorway Porter entered an almost perfect white hallway with wooden beams supported by white columns. A sign next to the impressive brown staircase in the center of the room read 'Olbracht Łaski.' Next to the name, a brass arrow pointed upstairs and Porter looked up to see a number of men and women shuffling around with drinks in their hands like at a reception. Walking up the stairs, he was relieved to see he was in the right place after recognizing the Spanish agent Valeria Gomez standing in the far corner. A gun for hire, Valeria was usually brought in by large bidders to act on their behalf at auctions all over the world. To Valeria's right, not far from him, he noticed Nicolas Lane. The American was a well-known collector of antiquities. Porter could almost smell the money in the room. In contrast to the others, he was a relatively small player, but he assumed these guys would be here for the bigger, more popular items up for auction.

The auction of Olbracht Łaski collectibles was the first time the property of the sixteenth-century nobleman had come up for sale publicly. This once-influential Polish family had seemingly vanished from the earth sometime in the late 1700s. Then, roughly two years ago, a farmer just outside Krakow stumbled upon Łaski's belongings when part of a cornfield caved in on his land. Once excavated, the farmer discovered six stacks of leather suitcases containing books, papers, scrolls and alchemy equipment such as Erlenmeyer-like flasks and other small distilling apparatus. The farmer brought in a local antique dealer who gave him 370 zloty for the lot, roughly $100. Two years and three sales later, the farmer's haul found its way to Christie's with an estimated price tag of £1.5 million, about $1.95 million.

Making his way to a table placed a little in front of the entrance to the auction room, Porter identified himself to the lady sitting there. He handed over a form, which she exchanged for a white paddle bearing the number 13 in red. It didn't seem the best omen, but perhaps he was being overly superstitious. Porter had always been interested in numbers and what they meant or signified in different cultures. In the realm of tarot cards, 13 stood for death, and in many western cultures it was considered bad luck to dine with thirteen people at one table. This superstition found its roots in the Last Supper. Judas Iscariot was considered the thirteenth guest, and of the twelve disciples he was the one that betrayed Jesus. Even so, it was remarkable how far the superstition traveled. At London's Savoy Hotel, a table booked for thirteen will always be set for fourteen guests. Actually, he couldn't think of even one example where the number 13 had a positive connotation. Porter looked at the paddle again, thinking there was little he could do about it now and with a resigned air, he took his seat in the auction room.

As the last bell sounded, the room quickly began to fill. Seconds later, the large, mahogany wood doors slammed shut behind him with a heavy bang. As was customary, they wouldn't open again until the last hammer fell. The auctioneer, a typical Brit with a large side parting comb-over in his hair and a tweed jacket from Cordings that perfectly complemented a pair of classic Oxford shoes, took his position on the podium at the front of the room behind the auction block. Above his head, on a large video screen, were the words *Olbracht Łaski, nobleman, alchemist and courtier.* There was also an image of Łaski's large and long bearded head in the form of a charcoal sketch.

Porter took one more look around the room, sizing up the competition. If he guessed correctly, he had a good chance of getting what he came for. He figured that most of the bidders would be looking to acquire the unique collection of first editions on sale. But not Porter; his mind was set on a small metal case containing a few old papers and correspondence from Łaski. To the best of his knowledge, the papers had been researched and found to be *'of little or no consequence'* which meant they had little or no historical value. This also led Porter to believe the papers might go cheaply.

After a short introduction explaining that Łaski was one of history's best known alchemists, the auctioneer's assistant placed Lot Number One on the auction block. It was a Wenceslas Bible, one of the earliest German translations of the Bible dating back to the 1390s, and it was in remarkably good condition. It was only the second copy known to exist in the world. As the authenticity could not be established unconditionally, the item was being sold *'as is.'*

"So, we are underway and we start the bidding on this remarkable item at £5,000." The auctioneer paused to look around the room. "5,000 over there," he said, pointing his hammer at the first bidder. "6,000... 7,000... 10,000..." As the auctioneer was kept busy, the screen above him recorded each new bid in seven different currencies including dollars, euros, yen and rubles. When the bidding reached £60,000 the room went silent. "Does no one have the common sense to further bid for this magnificent, once-in-a-lifetime item? In that case, going once, going twice..." he circled his hammer threatening above the small wooden desk before bringing it down with a loud bang. "Sold, to the gentleman in the front row."

Porter sat through the complete two hours of the auction, watching books go for amounts between £10,000 and £80,000 and at times his mind began to wander, such as the moment the Aztecs popped into his head. The Aztecs considered 13 to be sacred. For them, it was the number of time and it meant completion. This knowledge brought him some kind of relief.

"Lot item Number 212, the last item of the day." As the auctioneer spoke, Porter shifted to the edge of his seat. "A tin metal box, approximately eleven by four by one and a half inches, containing a total of six original sixteenth- or seventeenth-century documents, amongst them, handwritten letters by the count himself. The documents contain texts in Polish, English and Latin." Porter glanced to the left and right of him to see if anyone else had shifted on their seats. The room appeared calm which was in stark contrast to the tension that had thickened the air for the previous couple of hours. Unsurprisingly, Porter considered this to be a good thing and possibly advantageous. Still, he could feel the anticipation coursing through his veins as he waited for the opening bid.

"Let's open bidding on this curious item at £1,500." In a fraction of a second, before Porter even had the chance to raise his hand the auctioneer awarded the first bid to a red-haired woman in matching red dress sitting five seats to the left of him. Porter leaned forward to look at the woman. He didn't recognize her and leaned back into his seat as the auctioneer continued. "Will anyone give me £2,500?" Porter raised his arm and within a second the auctioneer confirmed the bid. "£3,500?" After a few seconds the woman raised her hand again. Porter assumed that the pause was the result of her checking out the room for other potential bidders. Since nobody reacted, Porter concluded it was going to be a contest between him and the young woman, and he considered himself lucky. "£5,000. Do I have anyone at £5,000?" Porter bid again, and before he knew it the unexpected bidding war had pushed the price up £20,000, in favor of the lady. The auctioneer looked at Porter and without saying anything he opened his arms, inviting another bid. A few seconds passed and just as the auctioneer was about to raise his hammer, Porter called out "£25,000." The screen above the auctioneer's head flashed up $33,000 and everyone's attention shifted to the woman, who after a long moment, crossed her hands, symbolizing the bidding war was over.

The auctioneer brought his gavel down on the block. "Sold to the gentleman holding number thirteen."

Immediately after the doors reopened, the room emptied. When Porter queued at the table to make payment and sort the shipping arrangements, he noticed the woman in red who had bid against him furtively looking his way. He smiled playfully and gave a friendly nod, which was met by an icy stare and an unflinching face. The woman turned and walked down the stairs, leaving Porter somewhat stunned. "Poor loser," he mumbled.

Feeling rather pleased with himself, Porter returned to his hotel. He felt that tomorrow he would have even more reason to be pleased when he would finally begin the journey back home to the US. As well as seeing his wife and daughter again, he was especially looking forward to studying the documents he had bought in London. Although he mainly collected rare books, this time he had other plans for the papers. They wouldn't simply be put on display.

A little over twenty hours after his victory at Christie's, Porter found himself sitting in another taxi, but this time he was heading up Livingston Street watching his home back in the US loom into view. Although he still enjoyed traveling he was also a family man, and the two extremes of his life often played on his mind. Whenever he was away he couldn't wait to get home to New Haven in Connecticut. But whenever he was home, after a few months, he was always looking for another excuse to get back on the road.

The taxi stopped in front 'Swan House,' the luxury home once owned by a Court of Appeals judge called Thomas Walter Swan. No sooner had he opened the door than his wife, Sylvia, and his 15-year-old daughter rushed out to greet him. Porter got out of the taxi and walked up to Sylvia, dropping his suitcase on the path to gather her in his arms.

"It's good to see you again," Sylvia whispered as they hugged each other firmly.

"It's good to see you again, too," he replied and he reached out to pull his daughter into the hug—unaware that across the street from them someone was taking photographs of their reunion through the tinted windows of a car.

"Let's get inside," Porter said as he picked up his suitcase.

"How long are you here for, Dad?" his daughter Jennifer asked.

"I don't have any plans to leave anytime soon again, dear," he replied, trying to sound reassuring.

"It's okay, Dad. I understand."

CHAPTER 2

The Legacy

New Haven, CT, USA, 2018

A young woman barged through the doors of Yale New Haven Hospital, her long blonde hair waving behind her. Clearly knowing where she was going, she raced past the atrium and the café, took a sharp right and hurried up to the Smilow Cancer Hospital, which became part of Yale University's hospital in 2009. The fourteen-story, 500,000-square-foot clinic—largely made possible by the hundreds of millions of dollars donated by former Playtex CEO and Yale alumni Joel E. Smilow—heralded a new era of cutting-edge research, advanced cancer treatment and humane patient care. Reaching Yale New Haven Hospital's north pavilion, the young woman came to a halt at the front desk. The receptionist eyed the attractive, if sweaty woman gasping for breath before her. It was a full minute before she was able to ask for directions.

"You need the third floor, room 301," the receptionist replied. "Take the elevator to your right."

The young woman immediately started running again, this time toward the elevator, just reaching it in time to throw an arm between the closing doors. Apologizing to the people inside, she joined them and pressed the still-unlit button for the third floor before urgently pressing the close door button more than a few times. Some seconds later, the doors closed and she released a huge sigh, noticing the whiteness of the finger that had been pressing so hard on the buttons.

It took only seconds to reach the third floor, but it felt like an eternity to the young woman and when the loud ping signaled their arrival she pushed through the doors even before they were fully open.

Ahead of her was a sign that read *300-324* with an arrow pointing left and another reading *325+* with an arrow pointing right. Still struggling for breath, she ran into the first room on the left where a woman somewhere in her fifties was sitting in front of a closed curtain, behind which indistinct voices could be heard discussing medical matters. The room wasn't a typical hospital room; it was made to look as much as possible like a combination of a normal living room and a bedroom. Only the presence of medical equipment—such as monitors and infusion devises—revealed its true purpose, but they were more or less obscured by an IKEA-like landscape painting of the Manhattan skyline in black and white. The walls were also decorated with wood paneling painted in pastels.

The young woman turned to the older woman in the room. "What uhhh?"

"We don't know yet," the older woman replied as she tapped her hand on the seat next to her, inviting the young woman to sit down. "This morning your dad didn't respond when I tried to wake him up so I called 911 and they brought him here again."

"Do they know anything yet?"

"If they do, they're not telling me. They ran some scans on him earlier, but they haven't revealed the results yet."

With a loud swoosh, the curtain in front of them opened and two nurses and a doctor emerged. Behind them, on a bed, was Robert Porter lying motionless, looking pale, his eyes closed.

"Is he uh...?" Sylvia Porter stammered.

"Are you family?" the doctor asked as the two nurses left the room.

"Sylvia Porter, Robert's wife," she said by way of introduction. "And this is our daughter, Jennifer."

As she nodded to the doctor, Jennifer thought back to the last time she had really felt like a daughter. She had always enjoyed a good relationship with her parents, but three years ago, at nineteen, she had grabbed the opportunity to move out of the family home in New Haven to live on the university's campus as an undergraduate in anthropology. Fascinated with languages, but even more by how language influenced social life, she had chosen to major in linguistic anthropology and right from the start of her academic career she had planned to spend a fourth year traveling in Europe. The need to travel was something she had inherited from her father.

For the past ten years Jennifer had known her father as a weak and ill man. It made her think of her father as frail and always in need of some form of medical care, a man who experienced more incoherent periods than coherent. He was suffering from all kinds of weird illnesses or new types of cancer. As the years went by it became harder for her to remember the strong father of her early teens. The father she had always pictured as some kind of Indiana Jones. At school, when she was asked what kind of work her father did, she would always describe him like the movie character. In truth, she never exactly knew what he did in those days, and when she was old enough and curious enough to ask he had already fallen ill. Jennifer shook her head to concentrate on what the medic was saying, a man who had introduced himself as Dr. Weston.

"I'm afraid I cannot give you any definitive news yet, but honesty obligates me to tell you it doesn't look good. Though I'm new to the hospital and Robert's case, I have studied his medical files. I see he's been in and out of hospitals for the past ten years and has been treated by some of the best specialists in the world." The doctor flicked through the pages of the medical file he held, his eyes alighting on one illness after another. "Is there anything you can tell me that might not be in here?"

"What do you mean?" Jennifer asked as she put an arm around her mother's shoulders that were starting to shake with the force of her tears.

"What I mean is, when I look at the chart I see your father developed a series of diseases over the years that are not really connected and can't be attributed to a single, or even double, cause. It's highly unlikely that such a diversity of illnesses would develop in just one person. So, it might help us find a cure if we knew what could have caused this. Like, did he work in a hazardous environment or a foreign country? Did he work with certain chemicals?"

It took Sylvia a few moments before she felt able to shake her head even though she realized she had no real idea what Robert may have got up to whenever he was away. When Robert was at home he lived a fairly dull life, working from his desk in the study. But the rest of the time he traveled as a cultural anthropologist conducting research into how language organizes large-scale cultural beliefs and ideologies. He was convinced that the modern world had been shaped in Europe because their linguistic influence on modern-day life was clear to hear. However, Robert rarely spoke about his work at home and much of the time, his wife and daughter were only aware of the countries he had visited, not the purpose of those visits.

"My father traveled the world as a scholar, looking at how different cultures develop in relation to their environment," Jennifer told the doctor. "He read books, mostly. He read them all over the world, but I doubt he came into contact with many dangerous chemicals or such things."

The doctor nodded and turned to Sylvia. "I noticed one more thing, if you don't mind me asking. In his file there is an extensive list of medication your husband used over the years, from fairly standard radiation and chemo therapy right up to the most advanced and target-specific treatments here at Smilow, all of which have been accompanied by a huge variety of pills and other medicines. Yet on the chart there are almost no painkillers mentioned. Why is this?"

Jennifer knew the question would come because it had come from many doctors previously and she would once again explain for her mother who had long ago grown tired of the same old questions. So, she told him that despite the catalogue of illnesses that had plagued her father, he had never shown any sign of pain, not even after the most intrusive and harrowing treatments. It was a mystery, so much so that one doctor conducted research on her father's resistance to, or rather absence of, pain. However, in one of his more lucid moments he made it clear he had no interest in being a guinea pig.

A nurse entered the room and handed a file to Dr. Weston. "You wanted these as soon as they became available."

"Thank you," he replied. Taking two X-rays from the brown envelope he clipped them onto the lightbox in the room. They showed Porter's head and neck and as he took a moment to look at them so did Jennifer and her mother.

"Here you see Robert's head and neck taken less than a month ago," Dr. Weston told them, pointing to the X-ray on the left. "On the right is a picture we took today which clearly reveals the brainstem glioma tumor in Robert's neck has failed to respond to the experimental treatment here. In fact, rather than shrink, it actually grew."

The response to the X-rays was a stunned silence, but then Jennifer swallowed hard and spoke up. "What does that mean? What's the next treatment?"

The doctor breathed in deeply before replying as gently as he could. "I'm afraid there will be no next treatment. Your father has had every treatment possible, as he did for every disease he developed in the past ten years. Neurosurgery isn't an option; the operation would kill him before we even reach the tumor. We've already tried chemo and radiation therapy as well as dendritic cell immunotherapy, the highly experimental treatment that works with the tumor and white blood cells to produce a chemotherapy that should have had a direct impact on the tumor." The doctor paused for a moment as if he was gathering courage to give his conclusion. "So, I'm really sorry, but there's truly nothing more we can do for him here."

For a long moment the room stayed silent. "How long?" Sylvia asked, breaking the silence and wiping away the single tear that rolled down her cheek. "Will he regain consciousness?"

"The answer to both your questions is that there's no way of knowing. As you know, we have him on a drip that keeps him asleep to prevent any seizures that could rupture the tumor, which would be fatal."

"And if we take him off the drip?" Jennifer asked.

"Like I said, there's no way of telling what will happen. I have given Robert something that will hopefully stop the tumor from swelling and this might be enough to allow coherent consciousness for a time, but should he have another seizure...."

Jennifer looked at her mother, knowing she would have to make the call. She herself had made up her mind the moment the doctor gave his prognosis. In truth, she would give anything for one more moment with her father. There were so many questions left unanswered and so little time and, subconsciously, it was killing her. There was a need she had to satisfy. She needed to know what her father had been up to all those years he spent abroad. She needed to know why her mother refused to speak of it, always changing the topic should she bring the subject up. Maybe she didn't actually know. Maybe she too had been kept in the dark. Whatever the truth, she only hoped her mother would agree to bring him back, no matter for how short a time.

"Okay, let's try it," her mother said softly, sniffing back her tears. Jennifer glanced at her mother, surprised she had made the decision without looking for support first. She then nodded to the doctor to show she agreed and watched him as he walked up to the IV drip to clamp the valve, closing it off.

"It's done," he informed them gently. "Now all we can do is wait. It will be at least an hour before we see any change. Naturally, you can stay here or you can wait in the atrium cafeteria and check up on him from time to time."

As the doctor left the room, Sylvia and Jennifer stood next to the bed, holding tight to each other while Sylvia also held her husband's hand. After five minutes passed, Jennifer broke the silence between them all.

"Do you want to get a cup of coffee?" she asked, no longer being able to stare at the lifeless body in the bed.

Still overwhelmed with emotion, Sylvia shook her head.

"It's half past three now. Let's come back here at four," Jennifer gently persisted. "We'll be back well before he wakes and it'll be good for us to get out of here for a while."

Sylvia stared at her husband's gaunt face. She didn't want to leave him, but she agreed to visit the cafeteria, more for Jennifer's sake. So, she followed her daughter out of the room and spent the next thirty minutes staring at the clock, as the coffee in her hands slowly cooled. As she watched the clock, each minute passed by like an hour.

"Shall we go back?" Jennifer finally said, and Sylvia couldn't have been more relieved. Without a word, she rose from her chair and started heading toward the stairs while Jennifer quickly laid ten dollars on the table next to the bill before rushing to catch up. By the time she reached her mother she had already ascended the first staircase.

"Slow down," Jennifer begged. "Dad isn't going anywhere."

Two minutes later, they reached the door to room 301. It was open and ahead of them they saw shadows moving in the background. Jennifer was the first to enter the room only to see two nurses making up the empty bed. Coming up to Jennifer's side, Sylvia gasped.

"What's going on?" Jennifer asked, as a dozen different scenarios crossed her mind. "Where's my father?"

"Mr. Porter is your father?" asked one of the nurses.

"Yes."

"The duty nurse asked us to clean the bed while she took him to the rooftop healing garden."

"The rooftop healing garden?" Sylvia asked.

"Yes," the second nurse answered. "On the seventh floor. I heard Mr. Porter clearly ask to be taken there."

Sylvia and Jennifer looked at each other in shock.

"He's awake?" asked Jennifer.

"Sure," the nurse replied, clearly unaware of what was going on.

"On the seventh floor?" Jennifer asked. As the nurse nodded she grabbed her mother's hand. "Come on."

Almost dragging Sylvia to the elevator, Jennifer impatiently pushed the top button on the panel and in the forty seconds it took to reach the seventh floor, both women remained too anxious to speak. As the elevator doors opened, Jennifer sprang out, heading for the frosted glass doors of the entrance to the *Betty Ruth & Milton B Hollander Healing Garden.* The garden, a relaxing oasis filled with trees, shrubs and plants as well as a small stream and several benches, was created for patients and family members to meet in. The garden was designed to pay homage to nature's healing qualities featuring all the sights and sounds that were supposed to have a positive effect on the physical and mental health of patients.

As the glass doors to the garden opened, any sense of being on a rooftop disappeared. The scene was simply amazing with paths leading through the forest before them. Although the plants were all carefully selected, the overriding impression was one of a natural landscape right down to the fallen leaves of autumn. The garden was immense and dense, and there was no immediate sign of Robert Porter.

"You wait here for a minute," Jennifer ordered her mother who raised her collar to protect her neck from the cold. Although the floor of the garden was heated, most of the warmth dissipated in contact with the open air and it was a brisk fifty degrees outside.

As Jennifer turned a corner, she noticed a small wooden gazebo in the distance. Below the open roof of the gazebo she saw a wheelchair with its back to her and immediately recognized her father's head, despite the woolen scarf and hat.

"Mom!" Jennifer cried out as she walked up to the wheelchair, noticing for the first time the nurse sat opposite her father. As she came around the side of the wheelchair, Jennifer saw that her father's eyes were open, staring at the view of the harbor in the distance. "Dad?" Jennifer kneeled before him and took his hands. But there was no response. "Dad?" she tried again, just as her mother approached.

"Nurse, please," Sylvia called out, and the nurse rose from the bench to gently shake Porter's shoulders.

"Mr. Porter," the nurse said firmly, but there was no reaction. The nurse next placed two fingers against Porter's neck. "I'm sorry," she said turning to Sylvia who immediately started crying. Jennifer turned to comfort her mother, not noticing the white envelope that fell to the floor as she let go of her father's hands. She put her arms around her mother, holding her tight as they moved toward the bench and gently wept.

"I'm so very sorry," the nurse said after a minute passed, "but is one of you Jennifer?"

Jennifer nodded and the nurse handed her the envelope that had fallen to the floor. "Then this must be for you." She handed over the wrinkled envelope that had "J'fer" written on it, the way her father had always written her name.

"Do you want to go inside?" the nurse asked.

"Just give us a moment please," Jennifer replied as she looked at the envelope for a moment. She then slowly tore it open and took out a single sheet of paper and started to read.

CHAPTER 3

Yale

The Present

The majestic Sheffield-Sterling-Strathcona Hall—known locally as the SSS—glowed golden under the beam of halogen lamps that lit the gray-bricked building. Built in the 1930s as the Sheffield Scientific School in order to compete with the Yale College Academic Department, the SSS educated a number of famous Americans including Harry Guggenheim and Francis du Pont, when annual tuition fees were a mere $30. Then, in 1945, it became part of Yale University.

Matthew Bishop had agreed to give a special guest seminar for potential undergraduate students at Yale's Department of Mathematics and Philosophy. Bishop had been a professor at Yale for a little over ten years now. Bishop was twenty-nine when he became the second youngest professor at Yale, after the scientist Oktay Sinanoglu, who was only twenty-eight when he became a full professor at Yale University in 2006.

Having studied at the University of California-Berkeley, gaining a first-class bachelor's degree in 1998, Bishop got his master's a year later at the Massachusetts Institute of Technology (MIT) where he was awarded the Sloan Research Fellowship. He completed a PhD in mathematics at the University of California-Berkeley in 2001.

Despite his qualifications and experience, and the playful accolade of Yale's Most Eligible Bachelor by his students, Bishop considered himself a part-time teacher. Tall and slender with steel blue eyes, he worked out three times a week and was considered a charismatic man, and yet Bishop felt most at home at the research table in his office or in the field. The fact was he had never completely lost his fear of speaking to large crowds even though he continued to lecture. That day, he had an audience of more than 400 people eager to hear what he had to say about mathematics and philosophy during the time of Plato. In fact, the lecture was so popular that both students and parents of students had packed the auditorium to listen to the 'internationally acclaimed' author and professor.

The auditorium's high beams, substantial wood paneling and large stained-glass windows, rising from floor to ceiling, gave the theater a church feeling. The only thing missing was an altar. At the end of the auditorium there was a small stage on which was a lectern. A large video screen made up the backdrop. Behind the lectern stood Bishop. He had short, reddish hair with a slight wave in it and a three-day-old beard. He was dressed in blue jeans and a gray sweater with a big capital Y on the front. The lights in the auditorium had been dimmed to better show the screen behind the professor, which displayed a stone bust of Plato. As Bishop began the final part of his lecture, his voice resounded around the hall, coming across loud and clear from a number of speakers.

"This will change the history of western thought, specifically the history of ancient science, of mathematics, music and philosophy."

On the screen behind him, a portrait appeared of a man with dark hair, somewhere in his forties. Bishop paused a while before continuing.

"What do you think when you hear these words?" he asked, stepping out from behind the lectern.

From the room a number of skeptical answers rang out.

"It's a bold statement."

"Crazy."

"Implausible."

"Very doubtful."

"And now?" Bishop asked as he pressed a button on his remote to reveal the text beneath the portrait: *Dr. Jay. Kennedy, University of Manchester, UK.*

"Delusions of grandeur!" someone shouted from the back of the room.

"Could be, could be." Bishop smiled. "Anyway, I think we can agree that it's a big claim, but let me explain more. For years, scholars and other followers of Plato have believed that there's more to his work than you can read on the surface. For decades, people have searched for hidden messages, almost desperate to give more meaning to the texts. No one ever found anything, not even a theory, until in 2010 a professor from the University of Manchester—who specializes in the philosophy of science and is an expert in music and mathematics—took a computer and the best and most accurate modern versions of Plato's manuscripts and restored them back to their original form. He then found out that every line consisted of thirty-five characters, without spaces or punctuation. Plato's dialogues had line lengths that were all based on round multiples of twelve hundred, all within the margin of error of just one percent. According to Dr. Kennedy, this is a pattern and no accident. Take a look at what he found."

Above the professor's head appeared some statistics.

Plato's work -	**30 books**
The Apology of Socrates	: 1,200 lines
The Protagoras	: 2,400
Cratylus	: 2,400
Philebus	: 2,400
Symposium	: 2,400
The Gorgias	: 3,600
The Republic	: 12,200
Laws	: 14,400
Total Pages	: 2000 pages

"So, what did Kennedy see?" Bishop asked, and the room erupted.

"A code!"

"Division by twelve!"

"Stichometry!"

"Coincidence!"

Bishop had anticipated the many reactions. He also knew that these were the kind of stories that got new students interested in the field; an ancient text, hidden messages and a big earth-shattering discovery.

"All just about correct, as far as I can understand you," Bishop replied and the room fell quiet in response. "Kennedy was convinced that Plato used the line counting not only to keep track of where he was in his text, but also to embed symbolic passages at regular intervals. Now, all he had to do was find the key to crack the code. Coincidentally, I believe he was listening to a classical piece of music at the time—it came to him. In those days, the Pythagoreans used a twelve-note musical scale. Convinced that this pattern somehow corresponded to the scale, he divided the texts into equal twelfths and found that, like in music, positive notes lodged at the harmonious third, fourth, sixth, eighth and ninth 'notes' were considered to be most harmonious with the twelfth. Negative notes were found at the more dissonant fifth, seventh, tenth and eleventh." Bishop looked around to make sure the audience was still following him. "Are you still there, and awake?"

"Still here!" someone shouted.

"At least we have one awake." The professor smiled. "I'm sorry; force of habit. For the parents in the room, your children will understand all of this should they attend my classes and they can explain it to you later." In the auditorium most of the youngsters now laughed while their parents clearly weren't sure what to make of such a remark. "What I meant to say was that Professor Kennedy found that every twelfth line, depending on its place on the musical scale, contained a positive or negative message, together forming a new text. A new text that after translation, of course, needed new interpretation. And as we all know, interpretation leads to new discussion. With the press of the remote, Bishop changed the image on screen behind him.

> *This will change the history of western thought, and specifically the history of ancient science, of mathematics, music and philosophy. – Dr J. Kennedy*

"So, what do we think now?" Bishop pointed to the screen, pausing long enough to let the message sink in. On the front row, a young man shifted in his chair.

"Dr. Kennedy sounds like an arrogant man who is very happy with himself?"

The auditorium burst into laughter and Bishop couldn't hide a small grin himself. "This may very well be so. I don't know him personally, but I saw some interviews with him and he came across as a very decent, down-to-earth person. You must not forget that Dr. Kennedy is a very well-respected researcher in his field; a historian and philosopher of science and an expert in music and mathematics at the University of Manchester with degrees from Princeton and Stanford. His breakthrough regarding the hidden messages in Plato's work in 2010 was published in the then-leading U.S. journal *Apeiron*. So, maybe Dr. Kennedy's way of bringing what he calls a true discovery, not simply a reinterpretation, may sound a bit pompous to us, but that doesn't mean it isn't true." Bishop walked from the left to the right of the stage, giving the audience time to think. "Remember, Plato was like Einstein in Greece's Golden Age and his work stood at the base of western science and culture. This is a man who died almost 2,500 years ago and many of Plato's scholars feel there is something to be read between the lines. Why is that? Anyone have an idea?"

"Wishful thinking?" said a voice from somewhere in the back.

"Ah, we have a cynical audience today," Bishop replied, to some laughter. "Don't get me wrong, cynical in this case isn't, by definition, bad. As long as you keep asking the right questions. So, 'wishful thinking,' you may be right. Humanity tends to search for more meaning to life than can be seen on the surface. Some seek truth and meaning in the past and some in the future."

"But if Plato had some kind of important message, why didn't he just write it down in plain text instead of in some secret code?" another voice asked.

Bishop looked into the audience, trying to see who had spoken, but the stage lights made it impossible. "That's a very good question. Why does it seem that the best and juiciest secrets are always hidden away so nobody can find them? Well, in Plato's case, it seems simple. Plato's teacher Socrates was executed for his beliefs. Plato himself fled the country for some time fearing for his life. You must realize that in that day and age, the world, and especially the Greeks, ruled through religion, yet here was a new generation that thought of science and philosophy as the cornerstone to all life, even while power in the country was determined by people who believed that Zeus ruled from the clouds while other gods such as Apollo, Atlas, Dionysus, Ares and Eros meddled with humans on Earth. For those of you who don't know what I'm talking about I can recommend some fairly decent superhero movies from our past history."

"*Clash of the Titans*!" someone shouted.

"Correct!" Bishop shouted back pointing in the direction the voice had come from. Away from his work, Bishop loved to spend what little free time he had in the cinema watching thrillers, mysteries, fantasy and science fiction movies. While many of his colleagues thought movies were a complete waste of time, Bishop believed that any creative process that could put a person's mind into an alternate state was good for imaginative development.

"Now, back to your question." Bishop swept a hand over the auditorium. "Why would Plato hide his secrets? Fear. Fear is the answer to your question. Plato kept his secrets for his own safety. His ideas were a threat to the Greek religion because he claimed that it wasn't Zeus or the gods who controlled the universe, but the laws of mathematics that made the planets revolve around the sun. The pioneers of this new philosophy had already revealed to Plato the dangers inherent in such thinking. Pythagoras was chased through the country and eventually killed for his beliefs, and Socrates, Plato's teacher, was executed for being a member of the Pythagorean sect. So, what would you do?" Bishop stopped talking for a moment, opening his arms to welcome a reply, but none came. To keep the shadow of his stage fright at bay and his concentration on point, he drummed his fingers on top of the lectern for a few seconds, until a female voice spoke up.

"So, I take it you agree with Plato?"

"Wouldn't you?" Bishop replied, relieved the silence was broken.

"Probably, yes. But what did the newly discovered text say?"

"That's a good question." Bishop nodded thoughtfully. "Kennedy claims that all 2,000 pages Plato wrote contain secret messages and that it will take a generation to work out the implications. But he does give us an example of a piece of translation. Many of you have probably heard of, or may even have had, a platonic relationship—although I guess many of you wouldn't be here if your parents had enjoyed such relations...." As Bishop's joke didn't get the reaction he had hoped for he quickly moved on. "It was long thought that Plato was a cold fish who favored love without sex, something we now know as platonic love. From only a small part of Kennedy's translation, we've discovered that Plato wasn't the prude we all thought him to be. The decoded text shows, in fact, that Plato didn't invent platonic love. What he advocated was morality through moderation, without abstinence and promiscuity. He actually had and loved sex.

"Plato is often described as the man who pushed western culture away from poetry and toward logic, reason and mathematics. According to Dr. Kennedy, through the parts he translated, Plato looks very different and not so much of a cold fish, but rather a writer who was also a member of a radical, persecuted, political movement known as the Pythagoreans who had to resort to coded texts to hide his 'dangerous' views.

"The Pythagorean sect believed that everything in our universe could be comprehended in terms of numbers. They founded this belief by looking at mathematics, music and astronomy. Let me give you an example. The Pythagoreans observed that the vibrating strings from musical instruments produced harmonious tones with the proportions of their length representing whole numbers. From this discovery to explain the universe in terms of numbers, the concept that everything could be understood through mathematics began to take shape. It was a new, central concept in the development of science. So, even though on the surface we still see Plato as an advocate of reason, through greater decoding of his texts it is now believed that in years to come we'll learn more of Plato's more mystical and romantic side."

Bishop glanced at his watch; it was time to wrap up the lecture. He pressed the remote to switch the image on the screen behind him to a single word: 'Conclusion.'

"Well, I guess that has to be it for today," he said. "I'm sorry to say I took a little too long explaining the last section so I only have time left for one or two questions."

From the center of the room, a male voice immediately spoke up. "If I understand it correctly, thanks to Dr. Kennedy, a platonic relationship can now involve sex?"

As laughter rippled through the audience, Bishop smiled. "If that's what you've learned from this class, I'm proud that I've been able to teach you something today."

"Why should we believe anything Dr. Kennedy claims?" asked a female voice, one Bishop recognized from a few moments earlier.

"That is probably the question of the evening and the answer is: you shouldn't. In our academic world every answer should be questioned, even when it comes from a respected professor. Dr. Kennedy's work has already been subject to lots of follow-up research which has raised as many doubts as Kennedy's revealed truths. Even Kennedy himself admits there are some flaws in his theory. So, I guess the correct answer is 'research,' not only original-source research, but research based on the work of others. We can't all be original because, quite simply, there are not enough secrets left in the world to discover.

"And now, we've really come to the end. If you were my class I'd send you away with a few questions, but as this is not yet a university class I won't send you away with homework. Even so, I'd like you to think about the following simple question."

On the screen, the question automatically appeared.

What will be the implications of Dr. Kennedy's work?

A low rumble sounded across the room as the discussion started and Bishop nodded with satisfaction.

"Right, I hope to see many of you back here after the summer. Until then, thank you and good night."

As the lights of the auditorium turned brighter, the audience applauded loudly for a minute or more before readying to leave. As people made their way toward the various exits, a young woman pushed against the tide. Looking up, Bishop immediately noticed her as she walked purposefully up to him.

"I'm sorry, but I've somewhere to be and I'm already very late," he apologized.

Ignoring him, the woman took out a wrinkled envelope from her purse. "If you could have a quick look," she said, and Bishop glanced at the name written on it.

"I suppose you're J'fer? Jennifer?"

"I am." She opened the envelope and took the letter from it.

Despite being pressed for time, Bishop took the letter and pressed it flat in front of him on the lectern. It looked recent and he noticed the paper had a watermark in the shape of a star, which was unusual nowadays. He put on his reading glasses. "Please, don't tell anyone," he joked, before starting to read.

The first part of the letter was some kind of excuse from a father to his daughter for not being there when she was growing up. Bishop skipped over the text until his eye dropped on his name.

> *Please, take the contents of the box to Professor Matthew Bishop. He can help you find the truth....*

Bishop skipped the rest of the text to find the signature, which he read aloud.

> *By the length of time all wounds will be healed....*
> *Your father, Robert.*

Bishop immediately connected the dots. "You're Jennifer Porter. Robert's daughter." Bishop recognized Porter's flair for the dramatic and Jennifer nodded. "I'm so sorry. I heard what happened to him."

Bishop hadn't spoken to Robert Porter for more than a decade. Though he always admired his work and his tenacity regarding ancient papers, the two had often discussed, but rarely agreed on various theories or interpretations of translations. Bishop often found Porter's conclusions vague and of little scientific substance. He contributed their differences to their different approaches. Whereas Bishop researched old text based on proven scientific theories, philosophy and mathematics, Roberts expertise was in astrology and ancient history, both directions filled with assumptions, and Bishop wasn't keen on assumptions.

"He was a good man," Bishop told Jennifer. "I hadn't seen him for a while but I missed our occasional debates. He was ill for a long time, I hear."

"He was ill for most of the time I can remember, and I barely got the chance to speak to him in his last years," Jennifer admitted, picturing her father in the bed they had placed in the living room of their home to make it easier to care for him. "So, what do you think of the letter?"

Although Bishop thought it was typical of Porter, full of drama and mystery, he kept his answer kind.

"I think it's interesting, but I really have no idea what your father is talking about. Did you recover the box he mentioned?"

"I did."

"And?"

"I didn't bring the box, but I can tell you that it's a box filled with old texts."

"That's no problem. I don't have the time to look at it anyway." Bishop thought for a moment, which allowed his curiosity to get the better of him. "Look, maybe you can show me tomorrow, perhaps? Say, at twelve, lunchtime, at my office?"

"That would be great, Professor Bishop." Jennifer retrieved the envelope and letter from the lectern and put them back in her purse.

"Perfect. And please, call me Matthew." Bishop handed her a business card. "So, tomorrow for lunch. Please bring your own sandwiches."

"Will do." Jennifer smiled, and the two of them walked off the stage together toward the exit just as the lights switched off.

"I guess the mystery begins...." Bishop joked in the dark.

CHAPTER 4

Creating Malkuth

The room was dark and silent except for the labored breathing of a young man kneeling on the ground. In his late twenties, his head shaved, he was blindfolded and naked. From one corner of the room, a match was struck to light a candle on the floor. Someone dressed in a white hooded robe then continued to light more candles along the walls, and the room began to reveal itself: the floor was tiled like a black and white checkerboard, there were no windows, and chairs lined the walls that were papered sepia, the same color as two doors. The room was no bigger than thirty feet by thirty feet. As two big candles placed next to the man were lit, a three-foot marble altar took shape behind him. A draft caused the candles' flames to flicker and lick the kneeling man's naked legs. He didn't flinch.

Embossed in gold upon the altar were the two Greek symbols for Alpha and Omega—the beginning and the end—pictured intertwined.

Two more large candles lit up a golden image of Isis, the Egyptian goddess of nature and magic with her wings spread wide. On either side of the altar stood two floor-to-ceiling pillars, one black, one white, both engraved with ancient Egyptian symbols. Once the last candle was lit, the hooded figure left the room, leaving the kneeling man alone again.

The hooded figure moved through a narrow hallway and nodded to a man dressed in a red velvet robe who was waiting. As they passed each other, the man's cellphone rang. Searching through his robes, he found his phone, looked at the screen, and sighed softly before answering it quietly.

"Yes," he half-whispered. "It's me."

For a minute or more, he listened to the voice on the other end before answering. "I understand, sir. Officially, from today, but depending on the job it might be too soon to put him on a solo assignment."

The voice on the line grew louder, and the more he continued, the more upset he sounded. The robed man took a few steps back to stop anyone else from overhearing the conversation.

"Yes, but... No, I understand... You're the boss."

At that admission, the voice on the other end of the line calmed down, allowing the robed man to speak again.

"I can have him standing by in a few hours," he said, his voice taking on a more compliant tone. "I'll be awaiting your orders, sir."

Placing his cellphone back within the folds of his robes, he tried to accept what he had been told to do. He always knew this moment would come. So, taking a deep breath, he turned to the white-robed figure standing a few feet away and nodded.

Back in the room, and no longer able to ignore the candles scorching his sides, the blindfolded man panted in discomfort as the door at the back of the room opened, bringing soft, indistinguishable chanting. After a short moment, a line of white-robed figures entered, winding along the walls like a snake. Their faces were hidden beneath deep hoods and masks depicting different mythological figures. There was the animal head of Seth, the Egyptian god of chaos; the Ibis-beaked head of Thoth, the god of wisdom; and the pretty face of Hathor, the goddess of love. The last figure to file into the room was falcon-headed Horus, the god of war.

Lining up against all four walls, each person stood still in front of one of the chairs placed between the burning candles. When the chanting stopped, an eerie silence filled the space and the man dressed in the red robe entered the room. As he stepped into the light, the full splendor of the blood-red velvet robe that draped majestically around his body was revealed. The man was large and his unmasked face was pale. He was in his forties with a dark unibrow and black goatee. Upon his head he wore a nemes, the traditional gold-and-blue striped headcloth of the ancient pharaohs that once ruled the 'new kingdom' from 3100 BC until approximately 500 BC. The nemes was worn with lappets flanking the man's face. Holding the nemes in place was the golden figure of a rearing cobra, Uraeus, the symbol of the pharaohs of lower Egypt. In one of his hands the man held a five-foot-long gold painted wooden stick on top of which was a small golden statue of Horus, the falcon-shaped god. In his other hand was a short wand that he used to slowly draw circles in the air. The wand was engraved with the symbols of the '*Tria Prima*,' the three primes of alchemy: mercury, representing the mind; salt for the body; and sulfur for the spirit.

After a few moments, the man set aside both the wand and scepter and positioned himself behind the altar where he opened a thick leather-bound book. Looking up, his dark brown eyes signaled to the others that they should now be seated.

"Brothers and sisters, welcome," he said. "It is my great honor and pleasure as Kether and Imperator to officially open this convocation of the adepts of the order of Alpha et Omega." He kept his face unreadable, masking the pride and joy he felt in his role. "Today, we initiate our new member and neophyte so that he might take the rank of Malkuth and begin his education into the techniques of practical mysticism."

Around the room, the robed figures began to chant. When they stopped, Kether sounded the word 'Atheh,' prolonging each vowel as he touched and covered his forehead with his right hand. Once he had finished, the white robes rose from their chairs to repeat the word and actions of their leader before retaking their seats so Kether might continue.

"Malkuth," he said, releasing the vowels in a moan that lasted 15 seconds as he placed a hand on his solar plexus. Again, as he finished, the room repeated the word and movement. It was a pattern that continued until each separate word combined in an ancient prayer and each action appeared to make up the sign of the cross.

"Atheh malkuth ve-gevurah ve-gedulah, le-olahm. Amen."
"Thou art kingdom and power and glory forever. Amen."

As they finished, Kether folded his hands in front of his chest with both thumbs pointing upward. "Thank you, my brothers and sisters, for this lesser banishing." Stepping away from the altar, he picked up the wand and went to stand in front of the kneeling man, whose muscles glistened with sweat. "Neophyte," he commanded. "Today, you will become an associate of a very elite cluster of individuals who are dedicated to the deeper understanding of western mystery." The man put the tip of the wand on the head of the blindfolded man. "All the mysteries are intended to provide you with the necessary tools to develop complete self-mastery in every aspect of your life." As he spoke, the room began to gently hum. "This won't be an easy task, nor can it be completed overnight, but we are convinced that with dedication, determination and persistence our universe will reveal itself to you in an infinite number of self-enhancing ways." Kether kneeled in front of the neophyte. In the room, the people added to building a climax by softly tappping their knees with their hands leading to a soft rumbling sound filling the room. "Our system is the crowning jewel of all mysteries. In the system and order of which you are now a part, you will learn skills that are practical and usable on a regular, daily basis. More importantly, you will learn about the greatest mystery of all: yourself." Kether continued for some five minutes describing all kinds of wonders that the young man would experience now as part of a clearly divine assembly. "We welcome you in fraternal love, in truth and knowledge, and remind you that your fellow members and your personal adept stand ready to assist. Now stand up, neophyte!"

As the room fell silent, all attention was directed at the taut young man still kneeling naked on the ground. As he got to his feet, his flesh shined in the light of the candles. Though a little unsteady at first, he stood before the Imperator who removed his blindfold before nodding to the side of the room. At his command, two hooded figures picked up a folded white robe waiting at their feet. Then, going to stand on either side of the neophyte, they carefully unfolded and lifted the robe above his head and waited for instructions. When the nod from the Imperator came, they slowly lowered the robe over the neophyte's head until it covered his body, hiding the burn marks scarring his legs. Finally, they took the hood from the back of the robe and carefully placed it over the Neophyte's head before returning to their seats.

Taking his position behind the altar again, Kether stretched both arms toward the fresh-robed man before him. "I now invite you to proclaim your pledge," he said.

The neophyte went down on one knee, picked up the wand waiting in front of him, also decorated with the three prime alchemical symbols, and held it out in front of him. "I, in the presence of the Lord of the Universe and in the presence of my higher self, the divine guardians of this order and this assembly in this hall of the neophyte, do of my own free will, hereby and hereon most solemnly promise to keep secret this order, the names of its members, and any and all proceedings that take place at its meetings from every person in the world who has not been initiated into it."

As he finished, the others began to softly chant.

"Very worthy exponent!" The Imperator's voice roared over the chanting men and women. "Having satisfactorily labored to diffuse the light, what is our reward?"

"The consciousness of having performed our duty to God and man, and more particularly to our fratres of our brotherhood," replied the man.

"With this guerdon let us be content. Aid me to create and dissolve the mystic circle and hermetically seal our secrets in the chamber of our souls." As Kether paused, the others rose from their chairs. "All join now and form the mystic circle."

At the words everyone came together to form a circle around their newest member.

"Let us pray," Kether commanded. "In the light of thy countenance, Oh Father of angels and men, we rejoice and are glad." The men and women in the circle bowed. "May we leave thy footstool with purer hearts and clearer consciences, and may we be spared to assemble again in this temple of truth. Hasten, we beseech thee, the coming of that day when thy knowledge shall cover the earth, and the fullness of thy glory be revealed to all mankind." Everyone bowed twice and uttered amen before Kether officially welcomed the neophyte to the order under his new name.

"By the mystic word I N R I, and by the authority vested in me by the Lord of the Universe himself, I hereby declare that you should no longer be addressed as neophyte but as Malkuth." The gathering broke into applause. "May we have your motto, fitting to your new name and rank of Malkuth?"

Malkuth lowered the hood from his bald head before speaking, keeping his voice emotionless.

"Latet enim veritas, sed nihil pretiosius veritate."

"Truth is hidden, but nothing is more beautiful than the truth."

The crowd applauded again, but with greater vigor, making it difficult for the Imperator to make his voice heard.

"Then I hereby dissolve this mystic circle and declare the chain of union imperfect until we are again united by the power of the mystic word."

CHAPTER 5

451 College Street

As Jennifer Porter passed Beinecke Plaza on Wall Street a small crowd of men and women chanting and waving banners turned the corner from Rose Walk, and moved toward her.

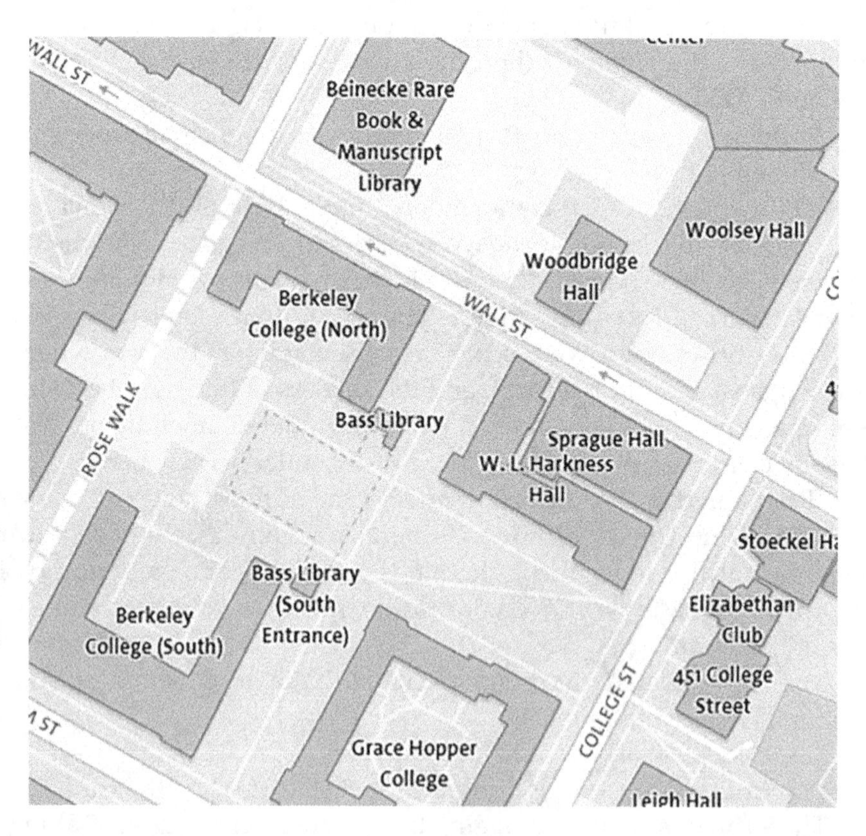

As the crowd neared, she was able to read some of the signs: 'Yale on trial, end racism;' 'Yale, stop insulting the New Haven community;' 'Shame on Yale, down with racism.' Amid the chanting she heard the phrase 'I Can't Breathe' repeated time and again. She recognized the words as the last ones spoken by Eric Garner seconds before the black man died in the chokehold of a white police officer in 2014. Over the years, Garner's last words had become a national symbol of anti-racism appearing in print and in songs. Unsure what had brought on this latest demonstration, Jennifer searched for a sign that would lead her to 451 College Street, home of the Department of Comparative Literature and the Department of Religious Studies. As she walked, she was reminded of how the campus was like a small village in itself and easy to get lost in.

Shortly after Jennifer found the sign for College Street, she almost immediately found the address she needed after glancing across the road and finding 451 written on a blue plaque by the door of a large red-brick building. The arched portico hid the entrance that stood behind five columns, and the building reminded her of a smaller version of the White House in Washington D.C., albeit in red brick with white columns.

As Jennifer walked past the small lawn, the door suddenly opened and a young man flew down the three steps of stairs, racing past her in such a hurry he grazed her arm. Taken aback, she watched the young man run before turning to the doorway where she saw Professor Matthew Bishop standing before her, his hands on his hips, shaking his head.

"It's clearly a busy morning," Jennifer greeted in a playful tone as she walked up to the casually dressed professor.

"Your meaning?" Bishop curtly replied, and Jennifer was taken aback a second time within as many minutes.

"I'm sorry, but I was almost run over by a group of protesters on my way here and now a young man leaving this building has nearly done the same."

"But at least you are here on time," Bishop replied as he pointed Jennifer inside. If there was one thing he disliked in modern youth, it was their lack of respect for time or, rather, being on time.

Leading the way through the hallway to a small office at the back of the building, Bishop pointed to a chair behind a spotless desk and invited Jennifer to sit. He then took the seat opposite. As she sat, Jennifer glanced around the white, sterile-looking room; it was nothing like she had anticipated. She had expected the office of a professor located in the comparative literature department to look like a small ancient library with stacks of old, dusty leather-bound books and scriptures hung up on the walls. But this place was nothing like that. The glossy desk she sat at only supported an Apple MacBook, neatly centered next to a small aluminum tray holding pens. On the other side of it, papers were stacked neatly together next to a dispenser holding hand sanitizer. Behind Bishop an Ikea-like bookcase displayed both modern and classic volumes carefully arranged by size and color.

From his desk drawer Bishop took a carefully wrapped sandwich.

"You brought your own?"

"What? Uh? Oh yes, thank you. I'm not hungry," Jennifer replied as she watched Bishop take a bite from his BLT. "I attended your introduction to a new understanding of Plato," she said uneasily, feeling lost in such a sterile environment and desperately seeking a way to break the ice. "Do you really believe Dr. Kennedy's discovery to be authentic?"

"Well, in answer to your question, I believe that everyone who is interested in the subject should make up their own mind."

"I guess that's true," Jennifer replied and the conversation once again ground to an awkward halt. "So, what's with the protesters?" she eventually asked.

Bishop sighed. "That's a good question." He gave a wry smile and Jennifer softly laughed with something close to relief before he continued in a voice that sounded pretty uninterested in the matter. "A black, thirty-eight-year-old former Yale dining hall employee took a broomstick and broke a stained-glass window depicting slaves working in a cotton field in the Calhoun College building."

"And you think that is a bad thing?"

"Oh no, sorry, that's not it. On the contrary. The building has been the target of students for some time now because it's named after U.S. Vice President John C. Calhoun, an ardent nineteenth century defender of slavery. It's just that on campus it's sort of old news. Yale knowingly carries the weight of its questionable history. It hardly needs reminders. Anyway, today the man will be in court facing a felony charge of criminal mischief and a misdemeanor charge of reckless endangerment. Ironically, Yale had already agreed to change the incriminating windows and even rename the college from Calhoun to Grace Hopper, a female trailblazing computer programmer and rear admiral in the U.S. Navy."

"Ironically?" Jennifer asked.

"Well, it's kind of ironic, I guess." Bishop rolled back his chair until it stopped with a soft bump against the bookcase behind him.

Walking his fingers over a row of old books in front of him, he selected a thin book and searched through it for a second before rolling back to the table to place the open book in front of Jennifer. '*Elihu Yale and the Madras connection*' was printed on the open page below a picture of a seventeenth-century painting showing Elihu Yale proudly posing on the porch of his home in Madras, now Chennai, in India. When Jennifer started reading the text, Bishop closed the book.

"Let me help you," he said. "It's something of a public secret not often taught at the university that Elihu Yale, the seventeenth-century benefactor the university is named after, wasn't only the president of the East India Company, he was also a British merchant and slave trader. As the self-appointed president of Madras at Fort St. George the corrupt Elihu Yale bought private land with East India Company funds. He imposed high taxes leading to revolts by local Indians whom he ordered to be viciously slain by his garrison soldiers. The Indians who survived were arrested and tried by his own personal court, usually resulting in public hangings."

Bishop searched through the book again until he found a page with a picture of a town square showing a row of Indians hanging from five scaffolds while white aristocrats watched.

"I think I understand where you're going with this," Jennifer said, turning her head away from the gruesome image.

"Indeed," Bishop responded. "It wasn't until he was in his late fifties, in the late 1600s, that Elihu Yale was finally charged with corruption and replaced. Though he subsequently lived without status, he enjoyed a long and wealthy life before dying of old age at seventy-two, some fifteen years later."

"Maybe you should start a petition to change Yale's name," Jennifer suggested and Bishop smiled at the suggestion.

"So, what is it you do?" he asked. "Are you planning to step into your father's shoes and pick up where he left off?"

"Well, not exactly," she answered after a short pause, her mind still grappling with the knowledge of Yale's historic slave trader. "I study linguistic anthropology here at the university. Through my father's travels and stories, I got interested in both languages and cultures so, I figured...."

"You figured, 'let's find a study that combines both and see what comes of it?'"

"Something like that, yes."

"I understand." Bishop put the book back. When he returned to the table he pressed the top of the sanitizer and cleaned his hands. "Actually, it's not very different from how I got here." He smiled. "So, did you bring it?" he asked enthusiastically.

Jennifer picked up her backpack, took out a small tin box and placed it in the middle of the table. Bishop put on his reading glasses and took the box between two hands and brought it closer to his steel blue eyes, carefully rotating and inspecting it. Despite its small size the gray box made of tin felt surprisingly heavy while looking a little battered. There were two hinges on the long side and two rings opposite, probably once used to lock the box with a small padlock. Bishop couldn't find any significant markings on the outside and he put it carefully back on the table.

"Let's see what you can tell us," he half-whispered as he put on a pair of white cotton gloves. Carefully, with little force, he flipped open the lid. For a long moment he looked at the small stack of papers that lay neatly folded at the bottom of the box. The papers looked old, but completely intact. He took a corner from the top paper between two fingers and rubbed it softly to see how frail it was and whether it might fall apart should he handle it.

"It's okay," Jennifer assured him. "You can take out the papers. They're completely intact and sturdy."

"You read them?"

"As far as I could read and understand them."

Bishop carefully took out the top paper, unfolded it and placed it in front of him. The text was handwritten and there was a seal. For a moment Bishop examined the piece before taking out the other six papers and gently positioning them from left to right on the desk. "Do you also have the letter your father wrote you?"

Jennifer reached into the backpack, retrieved the envelope and took out the letter.

"Thank you," Bishop said politely before placing the letter in the middle on the table on top of the six other documents.

The professor leaned, several times, from left to right and back over the table, examining the documents from every angle, sometimes grunting as though he recognized something. All the while Jennifer waited patiently. After a few minutes he picked up two papers and switched them on the table, looking at them again before repeating the movement like in a three-card monte, only with six cards.

"That's better," Bishop stated after spending a minute shuffling around and leaning back in his chair, before shifting his eyes to Jennifer.

"You found something?" she asked.

"Something," Bishop answered hesitantly. "Yesterday, when you showed me the letter your father wrote to you I just took a quick look at it, but I knew there was something familiar about it." Bishop pointed at the signature below Jennifer's father's letter.

"By the length of time all wounds will be healed.... Your father, Robert," Jennifer read aloud.

"That's what you see, but it isn't what it says, exactly. I didn't recognize it before. I thought it was just your father's idea of a dramatic ending."

"It isn't what it says?"

"I don't think so, no." Even as he spoke, Jennifer saw the dawning of a new understanding appear on Bishop's face. "'By length of tyme, and heale the woonde againe.'"

Jennifer questioned the professor with her eyes and he replied by rolling back to the bookcase to pick out another slim book that looked like a new copy of an old manuscript. When he placed it in front of her, Jennifer silently read the title.

> *Theatrum Chemicum Britannicum, Severall Poeticall Pieces of our Famous English Philosophers who have written the Hermetique Mysteries in ther owne Ancient Language.*

"Around 1650, Elias Ashmole, a renowned English antiquary solicitor and freemason, compiled several works of alchemical literature," Bishop explained. "Previously, these works could only be found in private collections. The book features manuscripts of famed alchemists like Geoffrey Chaucer, John Gower, John Dastin, William Backhouse, Edward Kelley and John Dee. It's that last name that hit me." Even with the book upside down he easily turned the pages to find the one he needed—*Testamentum Johannis Dee to Johannem Gwynn*. It was a one-page verse that was a short rhyming letter. Bishop pointed his finger about half way down the verse.

> *By length of tyme, and heale the woonde againe.*

Jennifer looked at the sentence. "John Dee, the sixteenth-century magician?" she asked, somewhat disparagingly.

Bishop recognized her reaction; he saw it almost every day in his students. It was as though the young simply didn't have the time or didn't want to make the time to look beyond the obvious.

"What do they teach you over there?" he asked with a frown. "John Dee was much more than a magician or advisor to Queen Elizabeth I. Arguably, he was one of the greatest thinkers of his time. He was fluent in Greek, Latin and Hebrew and studied and mastered astronomy, astrology, philosophy, cartography, mathematics and medicine. Admittedly, after all that knowledge it still wasn't enough to straddle science and magic and he eventually gave in to the occult. But nobody can deny he was a great scholar whose many books and diaries still speak to many people's imaginations nowadays."

Jennifer's face showed the guilt she felt at her thoughtless remark. "But why sign the letter to me with a quote from John Dee?" she asked, trying to sound more interested in order to correct her earlier mistake.

"Well, that is the big question, isn't it? Let's see." Bishop rose from his chair and bent over the desk to point at the first letter. "I arranged the letters," he said, pointing at the letters one by one. "These first two are in Latin and are actually not letters, but pages from John Dee's diary. I recognize them from hundreds of pages like these I have seen before. For about thirty years he kept extensive reports of his travels all over the world. Many of them are preserved in an excellent state."

"Okay. When I found the box, I looked through the letters, but the parts I could read or translate meant little to me, with the limited knowledge I have of Latin."

Bishop smiled. "The third letter is in English and addressed to Olbracht Łaski, a Polish nobleman and alchemist who befriended John Dee in England somewhere around 1575. But the letter is dated 1604. The fourth one was also written in 1604 by Dee, but addressed to Katherine, probably Dee's daughter, and the fifth page is written by Łaski a year later." Bishop pointed at the letterhead in the top right corner. The date read May 1605. "This one is also addressed to Katherine."

"I see I've come to the right place," Jennifer said, impressed.

"Wait for it," Bishop replied. "From here on it gets a bit trickier. Now, this sixth page is something completely different." He turned the page toward Jennifer.

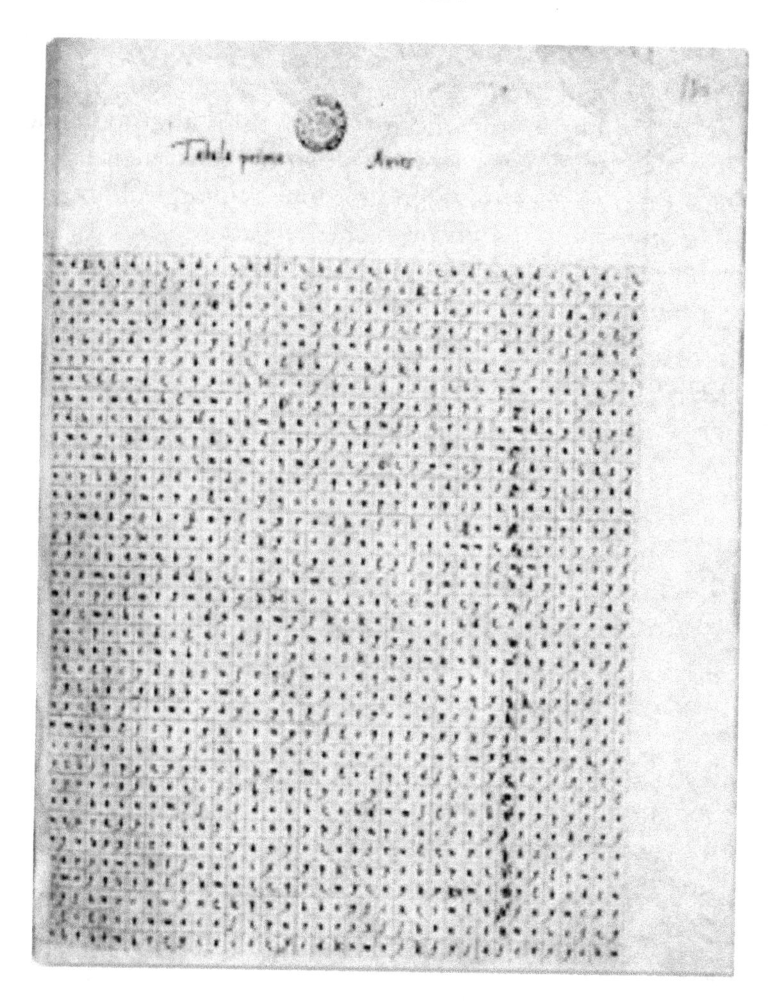

On the page, almost filling it completely, was a large square divided into a smaller grid holding seemingly random letters in each square. Above the grid was a faint oval-shaped form.

Jennifer glanced from the paper to Bishop's questioning face and back. "You have no idea?"

"I do have an idea," Bishop replied, "but I want to check something out first before I can comment on this one."

Looking at his watch, Bishop apologized before explaining he actually had to hurry. Removing his gloves, he gave the hand sanitizer another pump, then picked up a scruffy looking leather bag from the floor. Taking some papers from the aluminum tray on his desk he neatly tucked them away.

"That's it?" Jennifer asked, somewhat disappointed.

"Nope," Bishop replied while packing. "But I'm pressed for time. I have a meeting in ten minutes. Can you meet me here this evening? Let's say at seven? I have a few hours to spare this afternoon and if you agree to leave the documents here I'd love to study them and let you know what I find." Bishop saw Jennifer looked doubtful about leaving the letters unattended. "It's no problem. The room stays locked when I'm away and nobody comes in," he assured her.

After a moment or two, Jennifer gave a hesitant nod. "Seven, you said?"

Bishop nodded. "Seven it is."

CHAPTER 6

The Assignment

The Imperator left George's café at 36 Blythe Road looking like any other well-dressed Londoner in his dark blue Tom Ford suit and tie. But, of course, looks can be deceiving.

Blythe Road snaked its way from Shepherd's Bush Road all the way to the back of Olympia, the nineteenth-century event hall well known for its horse shows, industry fairs and, more recently, dinner shows. In the last decade, Blythe Road had gone up in the world with a change in postal code elevating it from the more down-at-heel suburb of Hammersmith and Fulham to part of West Kensington. The move naturally had an enormous effect on house prices with postcode snobs now able to boast about living in Kensington without having had to pay for the privilege. But that wasn't the most interesting fact about Blythe Road; one of the homes on the village-style street hid a mysterious secret.

Passing the grocery store, the Imperator turned up his collar to guard against the wind.

"Nasty weather we've got coming up, Mr. Simpson," the grocer called out in a broad Scottish accent as he smoked a cigarette in his doorway.

"I'm afraid you're right, Mr. McKidd," the Imperator replied in a friendly manner. "Best get inside fast."

Heeding his own advice, he picked up the pace. At the end of the street, as he neared a parked Bentley Continental GT, he reached for a key in his pocket and flicked the switch, causing the alarm lights to flicker before the doors unlocked. After the Imperator got in, he started the car and drove off; the low rumble of the V8 engine thundering through the street, turning the heads of the few people who hadn't yet escaped the rain.

Turning the corner from Blythe Road into Hammersmith Road, the Imperator's ringtone suddenly sounded through the speakers. It was Summer number one, the second movement of Vivaldi's Four Seasons as played by Nigel Kennedy. It was a personal favorite of his. He looked at the display which said *Main office* and pressed the green button on his steering wheel.

"Simpson here."

"Can you talk?" a man asked in a low, gravelly voice.

"I'm on my way home and alone in the car." As he spoke, he pulled over to the side of the road, knowing he was easily distracted while phoning and driving.

"Good. Regarding what we talked about earlier today, I'm afraid the time has come." The voice sounded almost apologetic yet demanding at the same time. "I have just received the message confirming they have met. After all these years this must be the break we were waiting for, so I need you to deploy our man."

Simpson paused for some time, thinking about his response. "He's not ready, sir," he eventually said. "You know I'll do as you ask of me, but I want you to hear me when I tell you this."

"I hear you, but you've had him for over a year," the man on the other end of the line snapped. "You said it would take between six and twelve months. You've had him for thirteen. He's ready."

"But are you sure we need to intervene? I mean, this soon? We have no idea yet what will come of the meeting. The professor could still turn her down." Simpson felt himself teetering on the edge of dangerous territory. His boss wasn't one to tolerate any form of dissent.

"I'm not asking you to intervene," the man replied tersely. "I just want twenty-four-hour reports for now. I want to know when they meet, where they meet and wherever possible to know what they're talking about. Now, this Malkuth of yours must be able to do that."

Simpson fell silent again. In his heart he felt what he felt, but he also knew when to quit. The only reason he was now Imperator was that his boss trusted him to make the hard decisions when necessary, but most of all to blindly follow orders when told to.

"All right then, sir. Consider it done."

"Thank you," came the reply before the line went dead.

The Imperator gave a deep sigh before banging his fist against the steering wheel. Staring into nothingness for a second, he knew he had become a slave of sorts to a man he'd never even met or seen. He also knew that this day had been coming and he now searched his feelings, wondering if it was all worth it. Then, like snapping out of a dream, he shook his head a few times and turned a knob on the dashboard until the LCD screen showed *Malkuth*. He then pressed the green button that appeared and the phone rang.

CHAPTER 7

The Box

When Jennifer walked the streets of the Yale campus in the twilight, the diversity of architectural styles she saw reminded her of Epcot. As a kid she had loved the yearly visits to Epcot she made with her parents, and she had been especially charmed by the display of eleven different countries, each with their own specific architectural looks. It had felt like she was on an adventure around the globe. As she passed the Georgian and Gothic building styles on her way to Matthew Bishop's office, she almost felt like a child again.

As she climbed the three steps leading to the building's entrance, Jennifer noticed the door was ajar, though there was no light she could see coming from inside. She slowly pushed the door further open. The hallway and adjacent rooms were dark and empty, but a small beam of light escaped Bishop's half-open door on the right, in the back of the building. As quietly as she could, Jennifer tiptoed through the corridor, coming to a stop some three feet away from the door. She reached for the door.

"Is that you?"

Caught by surprise, Jennifer gasped as her heart skipped a beat at the loud voice breaking the silence.

"Will you please never do that again?" Jennifer begged, still struggling to catch her breath as she walked into the room to see Bishop sitting behind his desk.

"I left the door ajar for you," Bishop said, clearly not aware of the scare he'd given the young woman. Jennifer was ready to say something but changed her mind. "Is something wrong?"

Jennifer shook her head. "No, nothing. Absolutely nothing."

"Good. Sit down." The instruction was abrupt, but there was no hiding the excitement in Bishop's voice as he pointed at the chair next to him. The six letters from the Łaski box were laid out in front of him. On the edge of the desk Bishop had clamped a large magnifying glass on a swing arm.

"So how did it go?" Jennifer asked. "Did you find anything?"

"I think I did." Bishop shifted to the edge of his seat. "I spent a few hours digging around and I think I found out what your father was trying to say to you, and to me for that matter."

Jennifer frowned.

"Let me explain."

"Please do." Jennifer waved her arm over the letters.

"Now, I translated the Latin of this first letter here on the left." Bishop pointed to the letter. "It was written by John Dee and addressed to his good friend Olbracht Łaski in 1604. Dee apparently knew he was dying and the letter talks about Dee trusting Łaski with a great responsibility. He talks about a folder he entrusts Łaski to hand over to Dee's daughter Katherine on her twenty-first birthday. From what I could find out, Dee's daughter must have been fifteen or so at that time. The available records are not clear about that. So, it's an inheritance, if you will."

"Does it say what was in the folder?" Jennifer asked, her curiosity piqued.

"Unfortunately, Dee doesn't say. What he does say about the contents of the folder is that its knowledge could be *prodesse omnibus hominibus,* of benefit to all mankind, or *orbis terrarum finem malum,* a world-ending catastrophe. Or here...." Bishop pointed at another Latin sentence. "*In eventus vertit,* with dire consequences. And, finally, I especially like this one. *Orbis terrarum et afflicta.*" Bishop pronounced the words as if announcing the trailer for a movie epic. "A world without suffering."

"Okay," Jennifer replied, not feeling any the wiser.

"A secret that could be a blessing or a disaster?" Bishop asked. "But let's keep that in mind and move on to the next page. A letter, written by Dee addressed to his daughter Katherine." He pointed to the relevant letter. "This one starts with an apology from Dee to his daughter. Basically, it's the same letter your father wrote to you; apologizing for not being there. After that the letter reads like the first, mentioning the secret that can either spell doom or prosperity."

"That's all?" Jennifer asked somewhat disappointed.

Bishop raised his finger. "There's one more to make this little soap opera complete." He moved his finger to the third letter on the table and tapped it hard a few times.

"Please be careful," Jennifer said.

Bishop gave a soft laugh. "I made copies this afternoon. That's why

I'm not wearing gloves. By the way, the originals from the box were also copies. High quality prints made recently."

"I see, but I thought you wore gloves because of your... uh...." Jennifer paused, unsure whether to say anything more. In a recent interview she had read, in which Bishop had talked about his latest book, *Science and the Greek Gods,* it was revealed that he suffered from mysophobia, a pathological fear of contamination and germs.

"My fear of germs?" Bishop finished the sentence for her. "No worries there; it's common knowledge I don't like bugs. No matter how big or how small they are. It's a long story." Bishop paused for a short moment before picking up where he left of. "So, back to the final part of your soap opera." Bishop returned his attention to the third letter on the table. "A year after the previous two letters, Łaski wrote his own letter to Katherine. Now, I figure that Dee must have thought that because Łaski was almost ten years younger than him he would live long enough to hand everything over to Katherine. Unfortunately, Łaski himself became sick and died a year later, so...."

"He wrote the letter to Katherine."

"Indeed. I don't know by whom or how the package was meant to get to Katherine, but I assume it never did. Actually, I never did ask you. How did your father come into possession of this box?"

"My mother thinks he bought it at an auction. But what I don't understand is, why give the box to Łaski in the first place? Why not someone even younger, or to his wife or one of his closer friends?"

"Probably because his wife had died and he had fallen out of grace in England," Bishop explained. "When his closest friend Edward Kelley betrayed him he had no friends left at all, and his children were either criminals or minors except for...."

"Katherine," Jennifer said. "And the rest of the letter?"

"Oh, uh, nothing of consequence. Just Łaski describing Dee as an honest and decent man, though he may not have been much of a father. So, that concludes our drama here and we still have three papers left. You remember I told you that the first two papers were from John Dee's diary?"

"Yes."

"Well, I was wrong. Or rather, not completely right. You see, the first letter is indeed a page of a diary, describing a short trip to Poland. On the page it talks about John Dee and Olbracht Łaski traveling from Lubeck to Rostock and on to Szczecin before finally spending Christmas in Poznan. On its own, it's not very interesting."

"Okay."

"Now, the second letter from Dee is, in fact, written as a diary piece, but on this page he makes an attempt at some kind of alchemical verse, a rhyming poem. Remember I spoke about the final sentence of your father's letter?"

As Bishop spoke, Jennifer thought he sounded like the typical professor he was. *By length of tyme, and heale the woonde againe,* Jennifer thought as she pointed to the sentence on her father's letter.

"That one," Bishop confirmed. "The sentence from Dee's Testamentum Johannis Dee to Johannem Gwynn." From a stack of papers on the desk, Bishop took a copy of the original verse and put it next to the diary page from the tin box. "Now, on this second diary page, which is also not an original but a copy by the way, Dee wrote a draft of this testament, probably when he was on the road in Poland. Now, I have compared the draft with the final version and guess what?"

"They're different," Jennifer answered, even though the question was rhetorical.

"Uh, no," Bishop said after a slight pause. "But, also, yes." The professor shook his head, knowing he wasn't making much sense. "The final version contains fourteen sentences," he explained. "Now, these are almost the exact fourteen sentences we find in the draft." Bishop pointed at the two copies. "But in your father's version, there are sixteen sentences. Two completely different ones that are not on the original and, frankly, they don't quite fit in with the other ones." Bishop put the magnifying glass over Jennifer's father's version of the text. "Read it," he commanded and Jennifer started to read, softly mumbling the words.

"Alloweth's taketh the path returneth to the cathedral ion the east,
Whe'r to findeth Uriël in the color'd glass."

Bishop nodded. "Now, where both versions talk about nature, time and God, the two extra lines of your father's version talk about a journey, a search. And the strangest part is that the old, or to be more precise, the old modern English seems to be out of place as if written by someone else. And look closely. Do you notice anything else?"

Jennifer looked at the poem for a long moment before answering excitedly. "It doesn't rhyme! But what does that mean?"

"I have no idea other than someone made it so that the two lines might stand out, and if so, it worked."

"So, we have, 'A secret that could be good or bad. A journey to the east in search of an angel.' It's all bit vague if you ask me. Actually, it's a lot of vague whether you ask me or not."

"You must be the product of your mother," Bishop replied.

Jennifer gave him a questioning look.

"I mean, your father was a true believer of...well... of everything, I guess. And here's you, frowning at great historical figures like John Dee and decrying whatever you don't understand as vague. Well, did you think that maybe it is vague by design?" As Bishop spoke, he recognized he'd said the same thing so many times to his college students. Young and restless was how his mother had described him when he was little. *If only his mother could see the youth of today,* he thought.

"I'm sorry," Jennifer said. "I guess I'm somewhat disappointed. I don't know why exactly. Maybe I was expecting some big treasure or something."

"And just maybe, with a bit of patience, creativity and inspiration...." Bishop didn't finish his sentence. It was up to her if she wanted to hear more.

"You're right. I'm sorry again. If you please, we've one more letter to go and maybe then you can tell me what to think of it all."

"Okay." Bishop let the matter go. He knew when his point had been made. "The final page. The mystery page." He placed the paper in front of them and positioned the magnifying glass over it.

"You had to check something?"

"I did. Although I immediately recognized its origin." Bishop took a folder from the stack of papers. As he opened it, Jennifer saw a number of copies of old papers bound together with a simple metal clip. Bishop opened the folder to the first printed paper and Jennifer read.

"Aldaraia sive Soyga vocor."

"The book of Soyga," Bishop explained. "Or, as many scholars and researchers have named it over the years, Aldaraia. Written in the sixteenth century, only two copies are known to exist. One of them was once in the possession of John Dee. Then, after being lost for four hundred years, both copies were recovered in 1994."

"Lost and found? Where were they all that time?"

"We don't know. We only know they were found by a young woman named Deborah Harkness—now a European History and History of Science professor at the University of Southern California. She's also a fiction writer who, at the time, was working on a dissertation about John Dee. She read Dee's diaries and found out that Dee prayed—or, rather, talked—to the archangel Uriël, asking him for help in translating the book. Up until then the book was known under the title *'Book of Soyga.'* From the diaries, Harkness came up with the other name *'Aldaraia sive Soyga vocor.'* When she started her search, she soon found it under its alternative title in the British Library, which arguably holds the largest collection in the world with over 150 million books. The other one was discovered shortly after in the Bodleian Library, which is the main research library at the University of Oxford. And that's all we know. The theory is that Dee, who ended his life as a poor man, sold it for cash shortly before his death. Anyway, the book is still generally considered to be one of the most mysterious and astonishing works from that era."

"But who wrote it and what is it about?" Jennifer asked as she leafed through the pages while peering through the looking glass.

"Both good questions. The first answer is short. We don't know who wrote it. The larger part of the book is written in what looks like Latin, and it basically is, but it also has a code worked into it. We do know Dee translated a large part of it. The complete work consists of several smaller books, *The Liber Aldaraia, Liber Radiorum* and *Liber Decimus Septimus* as well as a number of others. Together, they form a treatise of magic and alchemy. It discusses Renaissance magic and it also talks about and classifies several angels and demons. Additionally, it is filled with numerical and logical symbols that have lead many researchers to believe the book is also related to the Christian Cabala, a Christian derivation of the Jewish Kabbalah." Bishop paused for a moment. "Anyway, the most recent—and in my opinion best—translation was made in 2014 by a Jane Kupin who started her version with *'Scientia non habet inimicum preter ignorantem,'* meaning 'knowledge has no enemy other than ignorance'."

"And how did John Dee get his copy of the Aldaraia?" Jennifer asked.

"Nobody knows. Or at least it isn't known to be documented anywhere."

"All right." Jennifer took a moment to process all the information, trying to think whether she had missed something. If everything was as clear as Bishop made it appear, why was he so enthusiastic? She felt as though she were being tested in some way. "But if everything is translated, why is it still considered mysterious?"

"That is the real question." Bishop waved his finger ecstatically in the air. "And there's a simple answer to that question and that is because not everything is translated." Bishop pointed to the last paper on the table. "At the end of the book, the last thirty-six pages were never translated and they all look something like this."

Bishop picked up the final page from the table. He then flipped open the folder with the Aldaraia inside, finding the last chapter, and he put the pages side by side on the table. Jennifer leaned closer to inspect them carefully.

"They're identical?"

"They are," Bishop confirmed. "The book contains thirty-six of those pages, each of them made up of thirty-six rows and thirty-six columns totaling more than 45,000 characters. Latin characters all, seemingly, randomly positioned and not a clue what to make of it. When Dee wasn't able to break the code in 1582, he and his scryer Edward Kelley...."

"Scryer?"

"A scryer is someone who gazes into crystal globes. A seer."

Jennifer gave a cynical smile and Bishop continued.

"Anyway, Dee and Kelley were known to be in direct contact with Archangel Uriël. Dee asked the questions, and Kelley would rub a special mirror and answer the questions through his own body and voice. The complete conversations were written down, word for word, and survived the ages." Bishop took a small stack of papers from the pile on the desk and handed it to Jennifer. On the paper was a transcript of the complete conversation Dee and Kelley had with Uriël.

Δ — ys my boke, of Soyga, of any excellency ?
VR — Liber ille, erat Adae in Paradiso reuelatus, per Angelos Dei bonos.

While Jennifer started to read, Bishop started explaining. "The delta sign represents Dee, asking the questions in English, and the VR stands for Archangel Uriël, answering in Latin."

Jennifer's fingers leafed through the sheets of paper. "They must have talked for hours."

"They talked for days, and if you believe it, Uriël helped Dee a long way with translating the book, but when it came to translating the last thirty-six pages...." Bishop paused.

Jennifer, suspecting he was doing it for dramatic effect, waited with anticipation.

"When Dee asked Uriël to translate, he said the book had been revealed to Adam in paradise—before the creation of Eve—and could only be interpreted by Archangel Michael. Then the rest of the text in

Dee's diary is vague at best. It talks about a secret to be revealed in *a hundred and od yeres."*

"Meaning?"

"Your guess is as good as mine."

"So that's it?" Jennifer knew she sounded disappointed again. "Sorry."

Bishop gave a wry smile and pointed at the four corners of the page. "There's one last thing that stands out on the page of the Aldaraia. Do you see?"

"They're circled?"

"Correct," the professor replied. "And reading clockwise from the top left they read 'one, five, nine, seven'."

"One, five, nine, seven," Jennifer repeated. "1597. A date?"

"One might think so as it's about the same time this all played out, but I'm not sure. Maybe it isn't related at all." Bishop stopped talking.

Jennifer had to fight the urge to ask the obvious—an effort that wasn't lost on the professor.

"Well, that brings us to the end of our exploration. So, what do we have? I'd say it's clear that John Dee had a secret in a folder that he entrusted to his best friend and his daughter. Unfortunately, Olbracht Łaski—the man who was to give the secret to Dee's daughter, Katherine, when she became old enough—died before he could pass it on. We don't know what then happened to the folder, but your father bought the letters that came with it as well as some other papers. We know that the folder contained a big secret that could be used for both good or bad purposes. We have diary pages that describe Dee's travels to Poland, ending in Poznan, and two added sentences added to a poem that Dee wrote. Finally, there's the Aldaraia page with numbers one, five, nine, seven." Bishop thought for a moment to mentally check whether he had missed anything. "That's about it."

"What do you make of it all, professor? Does this mean anything to you?"

"Please call me Matthew."

"Sorry, Matthew."

"First, you have to think about the tin box your father bought at an auction. Apparently, someone, before your father, or maybe your father himself bundled the papers into a volume in the box so, to me, it would seem they have some kind of significance kept together. It took me some time, but when you look at the whole, I think the papers are sending a clear message."

CHAPTER 8

Uriël

2009

The driveway at Swan House resembled a parking lot with cars taking up every inch of space, as well the road in front of the house. Coming from the back garden, a number of voices could be heard singing "Happy Birthday."

"Happy birthday, dear Jennifer, happy birthday to you."

Loud applause and cheering broke out as the newly-sixteen-year-old Jennifer stared, somewhat uncomfortably, at the crowd. Standing next to her father, Jennifer gratefully followed him when he walked away to attend to the steaks on the barbecue.

"How do you like your birthday so far?" Porter asked his daughter.

"It's great, Dad. Everyone is here."

"Isn't it? Even your Aunt Becky from Florida drove all the way up here to witness your sixteenth. Wait a second, I have something for you." Pausing to check the pockets of his pants, he presented his daughter with a square, black velvet pouch. "Happy birthday, my little girl."

Jennifer allowed a small sigh to escape to show she was uncomfortable being called her father's "little girl." She then opened the pouch and took out a golden coin, a Krugerrand. When she sighed again, it was accompanied by a smile.

"You know what I always say?"

"I know, Dad. And though it's a replica, I know you give it to me with love as it's meant to represent my 'golden heart'."

On one side of the golden Krugerrand was a portrait of Paul Kruger—the last president of the Old Transvaal, the former South African republic. On the other side of the coin was a springbok antelope. A genuine golden Krugerrand contained one troy ounce of fine gold and carried a street value of more than $1,000. Before the invention of Bitcoins, the Krugerrand was highly prized by rich investors and money launderers.

Robert Porter always carried a pouch with replicas of old coins with him that he would fiddle with when he was restless or bored. Up until recently—because Jennifer now considered herself to be too grown up to play games with her father—she and her father often played hide and seek using a replica Krugerrand, with her father giving her cryptic clues as to where she should look for it. Whenever she found the coin, he would let her keep it. Over the years, she had collected a fairly big bag's worth.

"This one's different, dear." Porter winked at Jennifer, who took a closer look at the coin.

"I don't see it," she said with a shrug, before almost immediately changing her mind. "Really?"

Robert Porter nodded. "To help you save for your setup when you move out."

Jennifer threw her arms around his neck and kissed him on both cheeks. "Thanks, Dad. And is this a hint that you want me out?"

"You know, dear, that you can stay 'til the end of time, but to be honest, I don't think you'll make it that long."

Jennifer's eyes glistened. "I know, Dad, and thanks again. So, anyway, I'm going to get a beer now."

Jennifer marched off toward the bar, but she was clearly joking.

"Don't you dare, young lady!" Porter shouted after her.

"Robert? Robert?" Porter took a quick look as he turned the steaks on the grill and saw his wife Sylvia waving her arms, gesturing that he should join her.

"I can't. What do you think...?" Robert began until he realized his voice couldn't be heard over the noise of the crowd. Gesturing wildly, Porter tried to convey to his wife how busy he was, but she continued to wave. In fact, she was no longer beckoning him over, but ordering him to come. Robert spoke to the man standing next to him. "John, would you be so kind?"

Before John could answer, Robert handed him a large fork and walked away, taking off his apron and telling him he would be back shortly. He then crossed the garden to Sylvia, a feat that wasn't as easy as it looked because every couple of yards Porter was accosted by almost every one of the guests eager to tell him what a great party it was and how impressed they were with Jennifer, so it took more than a few minutes for him to finally reach his wife.

"And what's so important it couldn't wait for a perfectly cooked steak?" he asked, panting a little from the exertion of getting to his wife.

Sylvia pointed toward a woman with red hair standing on the driveway in front of the house.

"Who's that?"

"I'm not sure," Sylvia replied, "but she said she had to speak to you immediately, that it's a matter of life and death. Do you not know her?"

"I don't recognize her from the back," he said sarcastically. "Stay here. I'll check it out."

As Porter approached the driveway, the woman turned to face him. He looked at her carefully, thinking she seemed familiar, but he couldn't fit her face to a place or a time.

"Alice Hartman," the red-haired woman said by way of introduction, as she held out her hand.

"Robert Porter, but I guess you already know that." He reluctantly shook her hand. "Do I know you? You look familiar."

"We met once before in London though we were never formally introduced."

Porter took a moment to place her. His face then changed as he remembered. "The sore loser from the auction a few months ago!" As he spoke, his mind was already wondering what the hell she was doing in his driveway. His next thought was that he needed to get back to his daughter's party. "I'm sorry. I'm not sure what you're doing here, but as you can see we're having a party and I need to get back to it."

"This will only take a minute. I'll be brief," the woman replied, employing a tone of voice that matched her business suit. "As you now recall, I bid on the item you took home with you from London."

"You should have offered more," Porter said bluntly. "So, what on Earth are you doing here?"

"I would have offered more, but my employer gave me explicit instructions not to bid any higher. That has now changed."

Porter tilted his head a few degrees, revealing his surprise.

"All right then. If I remember correctly, you paid £25,000 for the item. My employer would like to double that amount for the box plus any research you might've done."

Porter didn't immediately answer the woman because he heard his daughter calling. "I'll be right there, dear," he said as he turned around and saw Jennifer behind him.

"Who is that, Dad?" she asked, looking at the red-headed lady.

"No one, dear. Please go back and join the party. I'll be back soon."

Jennifer hesitated for a second before returning to the garden.

Porter turned his attention back to the woman. "I told you I needed to return to the party in a minute and I'm afraid that minute is up. Please tell your employer I'm not interested. Not even if you triple the amount. Now, if you'll excuse me."

The woman looked at Porter, appearing to weigh up her options. As he turned to walk away she asked, "What if we make it a nice round number? Say, £100,000?"

Porter turned around in surprise. He then walked up to the woman, stopping only inches from her face. "Why is this tin box of such importance to your employer?" he asked quietly, looking directly into her eyes.

The woman didn't flinch. "Let's just say that my employer has followed your work on the contents of the box over the past few months and he's started to believe you might be on to something."

"What do you mean, 'followed your work?' My work isn't public. There's nothing to follow."

"It's like I said. We are very impressed with your previous work and can offer you a substantial amount of money for it. We would have no problem with you keeping copies of the original documents if you wish to continue with your work. In this way, we'd have two parties researching the papers. I figure you probably wouldn't want the research to stop if—God forbid—something happened to you, your house or your family."

Porter tensed at the woman's indirect threat. Bullied as a kid because he was a late starter and small of stature in those days, he was no stranger to standing up for himself and he had decided long ago that he would not put up with any form of bullying behavior.

"I don't think you understand me, lady." Porter took a big step backward and raised his hand along with his voice. "My work and the box are not for sale. So, tell your employer that should something come of my research he'll be able to read it when everyone else does."

"I think you're making a mistake," the woman replied icily as she handed over a business card.

Porter gave it a quick glance and turned it over to see if there was more, but the card only read:

Alice Hartman
0131610812927

Porter grunted. "It's my mistake to make," he said as he walked away. Once he was at the garden he turned and added, "My wrong choice to make," but the woman couldn't hear him over the noise of the party.

Back in the garden, Porter approached his wife to tell her he would be back in a minute or two. He then went inside, ascended the stairs to his study and checked the window to see whether Miss Hartman had left the premises. He was just in time to see her get into the passenger side of a dark blue Lincoln Continental before it drove away. After closing the curtains, he walked up to his desk and looked at the Łaski papers spread out on the desktop. He quickly stacked them before depositing them in a small safe embedded in the wall. Shaking his head as he tried to make sense of what had just happened, he threw Miss Hartman's business card on top of the papers, closed the safe and gave the dial a big spin.

"My mistake to make," he repeated to himself before rejoining the party.

The Present

The professor's revelation that he had a good idea as to what the papers were trying to say lingered in Jennifer's mind as she tried to second-guess what that explanation might be. The thought of her father leaving her a secret message made her feel both proud and angry; proud that he seemingly trusted her with a secret, and angry that he had to die before finally speaking to her. Ironically, the more interested she had become in her father's work, the more he had deteriorated, to the point of catatonic. Now, she realized that her decision to study linguistic anthropology was most likely triggered by the secrets that lay behind his unresponsiveness. Could this provide the connection with her father she so desperately sought? Of course, having become expert at hiding her enthusiasm to guard against disappointment she frowned as she waited for an answer. The stern face wasn't lost on Matthew Bishop and he walked to a corner of the room where a large bookcase stood. Taking hold of an old book, he opened it to reveal pictures of plants and herbs and strange letters.

"You know this one?" he asked, closing the book to show Jennifer the cover, which was made of thick leather and bound by four flat leather straps. In an ancient font, the words on the front read *Voynich.*

"I've heard of it," Jennifer replied. "The Voynich manuscript. Carbon-dated to the early fifteenth century and discovered by the Polish librarian, antique bookseller and collector Wilfrid Voynich around 1900. As I recall, the book is written in a language no one has been able to translate so far, and the illustrations of plants and animals have not been identified as having any relation to modern-day specimens."

"That's correct. A close friend of mine who works at the Beinecke Library here on campus gave me this copy. The original is kept at the library. He figured the translation of the book would not only involve mathematics but also philosophy."

"And how is this connected to our mystery?"

"Every word or sentence can, theoretically, be translated into mathematics if you know the cipher. To understand the mathematics used to formulate a word or a script without a Rosetta Stone we must understand the philosophy behind it, behind the writer, the rhyme and reason, so to say. There are those who say that even in these modern times, poems can't be translated solely with mathematics; we must understand the philosophy behind them."

"And?" Jennifer asked. "Could you make heads or tails of the Voynich manuscript?"

"Absolutely not." Porter laughed. "But I thought you could use some distraction. Are you ready now?"

The professor walked back to the desk and Jennifer thanked him for the bizarre distraction he had offered. They both then turned to the papers on the desk.

Bishop pointed at the first row of letters again. "So, the initial letters are of no consequence except to reveal some big secret lying in a scroll that is lost, and now probably hidden somewhere."

"But where?"

"That is the big question. All the evidence points to a specific location in Poland. There are the diary pages that refer to Poznań, where Dee traveled to and where he talked to Archangel Uriël. The two sentences added to the end of the poem talk about a return to the cathedral in the east where Uriël is to be found in the colored glass."

"A stained-glass window?" Jennifer suggested.

"I think so. I did some digging and the church Dee talks about must be the Archcathedral Basilica of St. Peter and St. Paul. A simple Google search reveals the church to be the oldest one still standing in Poland." Bishop opened his laptop and after a few seconds the website of the cathedral came up with a gallery of pictures. The professor swiped through the images.

"That's a lot of stained glass," Jennifer noted as she looked at the pictures showing the full gothic splendor of the big cathedral.

"It is. So, I took the liberty of calling the office of Archbishop Golecki to see if they have a window picturing Uriël. I told them I'm investigating the role of Uriël in the Roman Catholic Church."

"And?"

"They have such a stained-glass window, but when I asked for more information they were reluctant to give me any, which seemed strange. They did, however, invite me to come and see it for myself."

Jennifer thought for a moment. "And what about the numbers one, five, nine and seven?"

"Good memory," Bishop said as he closed the laptop. "I have no idea... yet. I researched the date briefly. In 1597 the Dutchman Frederick de Houtman discovered the spice islands in the West Indies; in Japan, Christians were slaughtered by the new government for being a threat to Japanese society; and about a hundred other facts of varying interest occurred on that date, if it is even a date."

"So, what do we do now?"

"That depends. What are you doing next Friday?" Bishop asked, catching Jennifer off guard. He picked up a folded piece of paper from the desk and waved it in front of her face. "I have two tickets on standby to Poznań, courtesy of the university."

"We're going to Poland?" Jennifer asked excitedly, hardly believing it could be true.

"Pack for chilly weather," the professor teased. "It's a sixteen-hour flight with a layover in Munich, Germany. We're flying economy class, so I wouldn't get too excited."

Jennifer smiled. "Gives us plenty of time to get to know each other."

CHAPTER 9

Poznań

"I think we're landing." Jennifer poked Bishop's shoulder with her elbow. He had slept through almost the entire journey, waking up only for a thirty-minute stopover in Munich where they had to run for their connecting flight. *So much for getting to know each other,* Jennifer thought. She concentrated on clearing her ears as they began to pop on the descent into Poznań- Ławica Henryk Wieniawski Airport.

"Huh, what?" Bishop asked in panic as if waking from a nightmare.

"Are you okay, professor?"

Bishop often woke up distressed when in unfamiliar surroundings. It was something he attributed to his childhood. Being an only child in a single-parent family, he had traveled all over the world with his father who worked as a sales rep for Boeing business jets. From as far back as he could remember, he would wake up anxious if he didn't immediately recognize where he was. Of course, it was an anxiety that only lasted minutes, if not seconds, and he quickly told Jennifer he was okay.

"We're landing."

"Oh, great." Bishop shook his head a few times before glancing out of the window. "Poznań," he muttered as the plane flew over the densely populated city.

The airport lay in the heart of the city district of Ławica, which had led to many discussions between city officials in the past decade.

"So, tell me, what was your father like?"

Now he wants to talk, Jennifer thought, feeling slightly annoyed. "What do you want to know?"

"I knew Robert in better times," Bishop revealed, not completely deaf to the tone of her voice. "When he disappeared from the professional playing field there were wild rumors about the circumstances. Some said he got ill and others spoke of him not returning from some kind of treasure hunt."

"Both have a bit of truth in them," Jennifer admitted. "I don't recall exactly, but somewhere around 2009, when I was in my teens, he did come back from what my mother later called 'a treasure hunt' and within weeks he got very ill. First in his mind—losing his memory to the point where he didn't even recognize us—and soon after that his body began to degenerate." Jennifer paused.

"It's okay," Bishop said tenderly. "We don't need to talk about it if you don't want to."

"I'm good. It's just that sometimes I blame myself for not trying hard enough to get in contact with him in those days. Up to the end there were moments of clarity when he remembered everything. But they were brief and I never witnessed one."

"He must have been clear at some point when he wrote you the letter."

"We believe he wrote the letter in the hospital right before he died. We're just glad he never suffered."

"I guess that's a positive thing when you've been sick for such a long time." Bishop reached for a folder in the pouch attached to the seat in front of him, clearly uncomfortable with the topic of conversation. After leafing through the folder, he took out a copy of the Aldaraia page illustrated with the 36 × 36 square of letters.

"So, no one found the meaning behind the thirty-six tables?" Jennifer asked, though she knew the answer.

Bishop shook his head. "No one we know of." As a strong believer in everything can be true until proven otherwise he always chose his words carefully. "We know that the first twenty-four tables of the book are named after the constellations of the zodiac, two pages for each sign. You see?" Bishop pointed to the faint text at the top of the page.

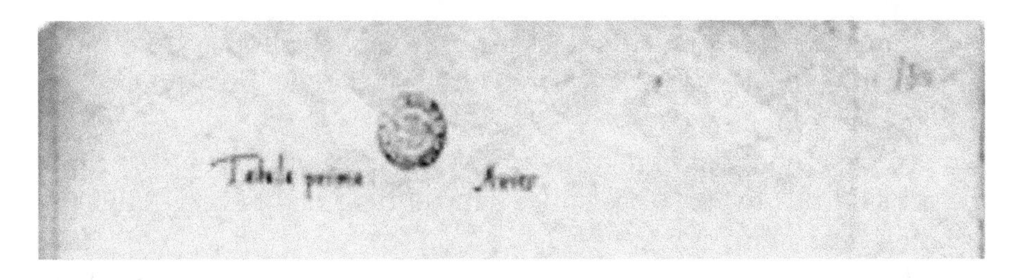

"*Tabela primera,* the oval seal and then *Aries,*" he pointed out. "And this continues for seven pages, all named after the planets. After that, the pages are named after the four basic natural elements and a final page, strangely, is titled *Magister.* Like I said, the final thirty-six tables aren't translated, but in 2006, Jim Reeds, a mathematician, published a paper called "John Dee and the Magic Tables in the Book of Soyga,"in which he claimed he had discovered the secret of the Aldaraia. Reeds is a mathematician from Princeton who also tried to translate the Voynich manuscript."

"And failed," Jennifer interrupted bluntly.

"Correct. Hence the fact that the Voynich manuscript remains a mystery. Anyway, after studying for two years, Reeds found a mathematical structure, a rhythm if you will, to the thirty-six tables. With this structure he was able to mathematically prove every next letter in each table on every page. He himself called it 'order to the chaos.' But he never found the meaning, no words. He tried to explain it by calling the Aldaraia a faithful representation of the universe. He found the structure of the code perfectly mimics the creation of the world from a word and a mathematical rule, and could unendingly go on forever and ever."

"That's more a philosopher's reasoning than a mathematician's," Jennifer noted.

"That's true, and it doesn't explain why the tables were created in the first place," Bishop replied just as the wheels of the airplane hit the ground.

Both Bishop and Jennifer reacted with a soft gasp of surprise. As the plane rolled along the tarmac to park on the runway both of them stayed silent.

Some fifteen hours after leaving the U.S., Bishop found himself standing at an empty taxi rank, stretching his body. "This can't be good for you," he complained.

"At least the wind helped us claw back an hour during the flight," Jennifer said positively. "Now all we have to do is find a taxi and go to the hotel, freshen up and...."

"Hmm." Bishop looked at his watch. "If you don't mind, I'd like to drive by the cathedral first to take a quick look. It closes to the public at five so we have about an hour left."

Jennifer thought for a moment. She was tired and feeling dirty from the long trip, so she would have preferred a warm shower rather than a visit to a musty old church. But who was she to complain? The professor had brought her to Europe and paid all of her expenses.

"Sure, no problem," she replied.

A second later Bishop stepped onto the road to hail a passing cab.

"You speak English?" he asked as they got in.

"Little English," replied the middle-aged Polish man.

"Can you take us to the Poznań Cathedral?"

The taxi driver looked into his mirror. "Little English," he reminded.

Slightly annoyed, Bishop mumbled as he searched in his coat pocket for a small oval-shaped black glossy device that was smaller than a cellphone. He pressed the button on the back and a small circular screen appeared with the English flag on the left side flanked by the white and red Polish flag. Bishop pressed the screen. "Can you take us to the Poznań Cathedral?" he asked again, and a moment later a clear female voice said, *"Możesz zabrać nas do poznańskiej katedry?"*

"Ah, *Katedra Poznańska,* cathedral," the driver replied.

"That's what I said," Bishop answered. "Yes."

"Nice," Jennifer said by way of compliment as the driver put his car into gear.

"Meet Travis." Bishop handed her the gizmo. "You can instantly translate eighty languages and even have a two-way conversation translated on the fly."

Men and their toys, Jennifer thought. Normally she was impervious to men and their gizmos, but in this case even she had to admit this one might come in handy since neither of them spoke Polish.

After fifteen minutes of the taxi snaking its way through the many small, cobblestoned streets in the larger Poznań metropolitan area, Bishop had Travis translate what was on his mind. "Isn't there a faster way?"

"I'm sorry," Travis said as it translated the words of the taxi driver back to him. "There's a big pile-up on the highway so this is the fastest route. But we'll be there in about ten minutes. Did you know that Mieszko I, the first ruler of Poland, lived here and is buried at the cathedral you are going to?"

"I didn't," Bishop replied.

"True story," the driver said, and the conversation died again.

Ten minutes later the car drove onto the highway, which almost immediately crossed a wide river.

"The Warta river," the driver informed them via Travis. "Your church is located on Cathedral Island, an island enclosed by branches of the Warta. It was the location of the first ruler's palaces. Now, most of the ancient buildings are destroyed. The cathedral is one of the last remaining original buildings, I believe."

"Lucky us," Bishop responded.

After crossing the river, the cab immediately left the freeway again.

"*Ostrów Tumski,*" Jennifer said, reading from a street sign.

Bishop looked at her in surprise.

"I remember the name from the cathedral's website. It's the cathedral's address," she explained.

At that point the car turned and two large domes over a small church appeared. Bishop saw the mishmash of architectural styles combining Romanesque, Baroque, Neo-Classical and Gothic to create a monster as history's successive rulers sought to leave their own mark and preferences on buildings they inherited. It was the same the world over. He'd most recently seen the evidence of it at the Hagia Sophia in Istanbul, Turkey—once a Christian church then an Imperial Mosque, and now one of Europe's most intriguing, architecturally interesting and cultural buildings. It seemed that over time even the world's greatest architectural monstrosities could become its biggest attractions.

"Are U.S. dollars okay?" Bishop asked as the cab stopped at the side of the building.

"Twenty-five, or fifty if you want me to wait."

Bishop paid the man $50 partly because Jennifer was already out of the cab and on her way to the front of the cathedral. Racing to catch up, he joined her in front of the enormous wooden doors standing below a single gray-colored stained-glass panel that covered almost two-thirds of the front façade. Jennifer gazed upward, straining her neck to take in the two huge towers flanking the sides of the building.

"Impressed?" Bishop asked.

Though she hadn't heard him approach, Jennifer didn't flinch. "I think I am," she replied. "Impressed, but also a bit...."

"Oh no," Bishop interrupted, looking at the big clock on top of the right tower. "Ten to five. We need to hurry." Without any more discussion, he walked up to the closed wooden doors with Jennifer now trailing behind him. In front of the carved doors Bishop stopped and searched for a handle, but found none.

Jennifer shrugged her shoulders as Bishop looked at her. She then stepped forward and pushed the right door, and it slowly swung open.

"That works too, I guess," Bishop said as he pushed on the left door. Immediately, the sunlight poured in, illuminating the dark cathedral from the front to the back as the doors opened further. As the light moved over the floor, Bishop noticed large golden letters carved into the black-and-white-checkered marble floor. The letters spelled the names of former rulers of Poland as well as bishops from Poznań. Bishop recognized the name of Bolesław Pobożny, the first name engraved in gold on the floor. Pobożny, nicknamed Bolesław the Pious, was a duke of Greater Poland in the thirteenth century who—ironically in a Catholic church—granted the first written privileges to the Jews of Greater Poland giving them judicial authority over the Jewish population and trading activity. Bishop gazed at the list of names that rolled all the way to the front of the cathedral.

Stepping inside, Jennifer was surprised to see there wasn't a soul in sight and as she walked the click of her heels on the marble floor echoed around them. The center of the church was surprisingly small. On either side of the aisle there were twenty or so dark wooden benches, but they couldn't have held more than five persons each. A series of archways flanking the benches revealed six small chapels and at the end of the aisle stood a large golden pulpit that appeared to be floating ten feet from the floor. On its roof was a large golden statue of Jesus. As Jennifer imagined one of the bishops preaching from the pulpit before a packed church, a loud bang from the back of the church broke the silence, followed by loud footsteps. As the footsteps neared, Jennifer moved closer to the professor.

"*Co mogę podać*?" asked a voice to their left, startling them.

When they turned, they saw a man stepping out of the shadows into the light. He was dressed in jeans and a turtleneck sweater.

"I'm sorry," Bishop said. "Do you speak English?"

"I do," the middle-aged, gray-haired man confirmed. "I'm Father Matula, a priest and one of the caretakers of the Archcathedral Basilica of St. Peter and St. Paul."

"Just the man we're looking for," Bishop told him. "My name is Matthew Bishop, professor at Yale University, and this here is Jennifer Porter my, uh, research assistant."

Jennifer gave a tight smile to the stranger.

"Ah, yes, Professor Bishop," Father Matula said. "Excuse my attire. I was closing up. It's almost five, you see."

"Do we know each other?" the professor asked.

"No. Your name came up at a meeting at the archbishop's office yesterday. I was told you wanted to visit us regarding your research on the role of Uriël in the Roman Catholic Church."

"Wow," Bishop reacted, genuinely surprised. "That's what you talk about at the archdiocese?"

The priest grinned. "Within the greater scheme of archdioceses, we're only a minor one and command little international interest. An American professor interested in our humble surroundings will quickly attract attention. Besides, I Googled you and read some of your work."

"You find anything you like?"

"My interest was drawn to your research into the theory that the Dead Sea Scrolls prove the non-existence of Jesus Christ. I haven't read the complete research yet though I think I can guess the conclusion because if you had proved the theory I'd probably have heard about it from my boss and I'd be out of work by now."

"You may have a point there," Bishop said, recalling that research paper and cringing a little because it wasn't one of his finest. It almost dragged the university into a big brawl with the diocese of New England. After publishing the paper, the diocese had decided Bishop was trying to disprove the very existence of Jesus Christ and they demanded his resignation from Yale. They later conceded this wasn't what Bishop was trying to achieve or had even achieved. They apologized when the findings were pointed out to them saying the exact opposite to what they had claimed; basically, Jesus could have existed.

"But seriously," the priest continued while glancing at his wristwatch, "what can I do for you?"

"I know it's almost closing time, but we've traveled a long way and Jennifer here couldn't curb her enthusiasm. She insisted we try to visit you today."

Jennifer glanced at Bishop, eyes wide.

"Not a problem," the priest replied turning to Jennifer. "I can spare you a few minutes. I understand you were specifically interested in a stained-glass window picturing Archangel Uriël?"

"Uh," Jennifer stammered, struggling to find her bearings in her new role.

"I understand," the priest said kindly, just as lights at the front of the cathedral came on, lighting up the sanctuary like it was bathed in sunlight. Almost immediately the nave, vestibule, porches and aisles followed. "Let there be light," Father Matula joked as he showed Bishop the remote in his hand. The priest then turned toward the back of the building and stretched out an arm toward the highest point above the altar.

Bishop's eye was momentarily caught by the sight of a bright red braided band on the priest's wrist, before looking to where he was being directed and seeing four glass-stained mosaics.

One by one Father Matula pointed at the mosaics. "Saint Michael, who is like God; Saint Gabriel, God's strength; Saint Raphael, whom God healed; and Uriël, God's light," he explained.

"Do you have a pair of binoculars?" Bishop asked, semi-seriously. He looked around noticing that none of the stained-glass mosaics were anywhere near the floor.

"I'm sorry," the priest apologized. "But maybe I can do better. One second, please." With big steps, Father Matula disappeared between one of the arches on the right side. Seconds later, just as Bishop was about to address Jennifer, the priest walked back, leafing through a thick book. Stopping in front of Jennifer, he turned the book toward her and pointed at a picture on the open page.

"Did you know that it is generally believed that Uriël was added later to the other three as the fourth archangel representing the four cardinal points?" He looked at Bishop. "But, of course, you do. You are researching Uriël's role in the Catholic Church, so you must know that already. What do you think, Miss Porter? Is this the Uriël you're looking for?"

Jennifer took the book from his hands to inspect the mosaic more closely. It showed Uriël, complete with halo, as regent of the sun, holding the sun in front of his chest. At the bottom of the mosaic was "ST. UR-IEL.".

"Nothing especially stands out," she said as she handed the book to Bishop who also failed to find anything special in the picture.

"Do you mind?" Bishop asked as he took his camera phone from his pocket and pointed it at the page.

"Be my guest," the priest said, opening his arms in invitation. "Is there anything special you are looking for?"

"We're not sure yet," Bishop told him. "We hope we'll recognize it when we see it. Was the mosaic always placed where it is now?"

"I don't think so," Father Matula replied, explaining that although the cathedral was originally built in the second half of the tenth century it was ravaged by fire in the fourteenth and fifteenth centuries and rebuilt several times. Pointing at another picture in the book, showing a sketch of the cathedral in flames, he explained that the last major fire broke out in 1772 after which it took on a more neo-classical style. Then, during the Second World War, the Germans tore a lot of the church down and most of the original mosaics were lost.

"Do you know if there was anything unusual about the original mosaic?" Jennifer asked.

Father Matula leafed through the book again, stopping at a page showing pictures of two of the chapels in black and white. "These pictures of the chapels were taken during the Second World War under the orders of the Führer himself. In 1943, Hitler ordered the registration of religious heritage throughout the Third Reich. Despite his actions, Hitler was a devoted Christian who was known to thank God for giving him the opportunity to do what he did. But anyway, that's another topic. However, from the photographs that Hitler had demanded, they were able to restore the saved mosaics and recreate new ones."

"And the Uriël mosaic?" Bishop asked. "Is it an original or a remake?"

"Couldn't say," Matula replied. "But here, on the left, you can see the first original chapel." The priest pointed in the book and then to the left where the chapel was. "You see?"

Bishop and Jennifer looked from left to right comparing the two. Where the stained-glass used to be, the book clearly showed mosaics of the four archangels. Below the mosaics, on the floor, were two large, highly decorated caskets, whereas now that alcove only possessed two benches where people could pray in private. Bishop took a closer look at the caskets in the book.

"Bishops," Father Matula explained. "In days gone by, the bishops were buried above ground, in caskets which were then placed in the chapels."

"And what happened to the caskets?" Jennifer asked.

"Good question," the priest answered. "Before the end of World War II there were plans to modernize the place, creating more room for churchgoers who visited during those hard times. They moved the caskets to the underground tombs where most of them still reside untouched. But I'm afraid they're absolutely not open to the public; we had some problems in the past."

The priest pointed to a big black wooden door at the side of the church that read, '*Prywatny*.'

Bishop took out his camera phone again and glanced at the priest who simply nodded. He first took a picture from the page in the book followed by one of the modern chapel before taking several more snapshots of the cathedral's interior.

"I really need to close up now," the priest said, looking at his watch again and seeing it was past five. "You know what?" he said, handing the book to Jennifer. "Keep it. The gift shop is already closed and maybe this will help you with your research."

"We're sorry for taking your time," Jennifer told him. "And thank you for your hospitality and the book."

"Yes, thank you," Bishop repeated.

"No problem. Did you get enough for now?"

"You were more than generous," Bishop told the priest.

"Please, come back tomorrow if you need anything else. I'll be here."

"We'll be back, for sure."

After shaking Father Matula's hand, the two of them walked up to the large doors where they had entered, noticing they had copper handles on this side. Bishop pulled at one of them and they walked outside. The heavy door automatically closed behind them with a bang followed by two loud clanks as a deadbolt locked the entrance. On the steps of the cathedral, Jennifer looked at Bishop.

"'Jennifer couldn't curb her enthusiasm?'"

"I'm sorry," Bishop answered with a smile as he took out a small bottle of disinfectant that he then sprayed onto his hands.

"Was it worth not cleaning up first and getting some rest in the hotel?"

"I believe it was, my dear Watson," Bishop joked.

With a click of the remote, Father Matula returned the cathedral to a state of near darkness. From a pocket he pulled out a cellphone and dialed.

"James here," replied a dark voice on the other end of the line.

"Your friends just left," Father Matula said.

"And what did they want?"

"It was like they explained. They're researching the Archangel Uriël. They were particularly interested in the Uriël mosaic, but didn't say why."

"Did they take anything?" the voice calmly asked.

"Nothing more than a few pictures, but I believe they'll be back. It's closing time here so I asked them to leave."

"All right. Thanks for telling me. Will you keep me informed if they return?"

"Will do, but if you were to tell me what this is all about maybe I could help more," said the priest, failing to keep the excitement out of his voice.

"Thanks for the offer, but you're doing great as it is. I already owe you many thanks. But take it from me, the less you know, the better. Please keep me informed."

The line went dead and Father Matula grunted with disappointment.

CHAPTER 10

The Scarlet String

The room in the Novotel Poznań Malta was small and simple, but adequate. There were two queen-size beds separated by a nightlight with only three feet of space between the beds and the wall-to-wall desktop that functioned as both coffee bar and bureau. It was spotless, but then Matthew Bishop had selected the hotel precisely because of the cleanliness it was praised for on TripAdvisor.

"I don't understand," Bishop complained as he sat at the desk and looked for the umpteenth time at the pictures of the stained-glass window of Uriël in the book they had been given.

"What I don't understand is why we couldn't get two rooms," Jennifer muttered as she sat on the bed facing Bishop, his back to her.

"I feel—no, I know—there's a clue in here somewhere, but I can't seem to find it."

Jennifer took another bite from her *zapiekanka*, a pizza-like open sandwich, typical Polish fast-food dish, ordered from room service. "How's your *zapiekanka*?"

Bishop's food lay untouched on the plate that he had shoved aside the moment it arrived. "I can't stand it," he grumbled.

"So, what did you think of Father Matula?" Jennifer asked trying to shift the professor's focus.

Bishop grunted before he put the book down and turned to Jennifer. "Did you notice something about him?"

Jennifer heard the strange tone of Bishop's voice. "No. Should I have?"

"Well, it's probably got nothing to do with our search, but I noticed the priest wore a crimson braided string on his left wrist. It was hidden behind his sleeve most of the time, but visible when he stretched."

Jennifer's furrowed brow revealed her confusion.

"The scarlet string is traditionally worn as a talisman to fight off bad luck. Customarily, it's made of wool, needs to be knotted seven times and is worn on the left side—the side that, according to Kabbalists, is the receiving side of the spiritual body. In more modern times it has become a symbol of sympathy for the modern Kabbalah."

"The Kabbalah?" Jennifer asked, surprised. "Isn't that a form of Jewish separation—in a Christian church, worn by a Christian priest?"

"Maybe. Admittedly, it's not very common nowadays, but the Christian Kabbalah has been going since the renaissance around the sixteenth century. Our own John Dee, a devoted Catholic, made Kabbalah sorcery popular in England and many feeble minds in those days were captivated by the cheap tricks it supplied and the promise of ultimate knowledge, giving the Kabbalah an almost romantic, uh... appearance."

"That must be a coincidence," Jennifer stated.

"In relation to our search about Dee and a priest with a red ribbon?" Bishop laughed out loud. "I should think so."

"Saying that, it is interesting. A few years ago, many celebrities started wearing scarlet strings: Demi Moore, Ashton Kutcher, Madonna, Paris Hilton, Lindsay Lohan, Nicole Richie. Come to think of it, I haven't heard any news about it lately," Jennifer said.

"Well, I must admit I have no idea who most of those people are, but you're probably right. Many people have claimed to be scholars of the Zohar, the Kabbalist's foundational literary work and mystical guideline." Bishop realized he had been distracted and his head felt more relaxed as a result. He glanced again at the book, then turned to Jennifer.

"Perhaps you should eat something," she said. "Let me have the book for a few minutes so you can eat and I can examine it."

"No, thanks. Here." Bishop took his phone from the desk and threw it onto the bed where it bounced.

Jennifer managed to grab it before it fell onto the hard floor.

"Use the pictures on the phone," Bishop said smiling.

Jennifer scrolled through the photographs taken inside the cathedral.

As both of them stared at their own sets of pictures, the room fell silent. Bishop leafed through the pages of his book and Jennifer's fingers swiped the small screen she held.

"1597!" Jennifer cried out.

"What?"

"One, five, nine, seven. Wasn't that the combination of numbers we didn't know the meaning of?"

"You found something!" Bishop turned to Jennifer to find her waving his cellphone at him. He quickly rose from his chair and excitedly moved toward the bed to sit down next to her.

"I think I did. In fact, I'm sure I did." Jennifer sounded proud and excited. "I couldn't find anything by just looking at the pictures so I downloaded a few apps to the phone to edit the pictures. I placed the pictures you took from the book next to each other. Here on the left is the mosaic as it is now and on the right the picture of it made by the Germans." Jennifer showed him the image on the phone.

Bishop took a quick look, expecting Jennifer to tell him the results. When she didn't, he gave her an impatient look.

"Well, look who's impatient now," she teased. "At first, they looked exactly the same, then I increased the contrast which gave little result, used some filters, nothing—until, that is, I changed the image to a negative." Jennifer swiped to the next picture and handed the phone to Bishop.

"On the left you have the original German picture and on the right.... Well, you get it."

Bishop put on his reading glasses and with the phone almost against his face he focused on the picture on the right. "One, five, nine, seven," he said softly and slowly. "You're great! The numbers were in the mosaic." He pointed at the corners of the image. "When rebuilding the original mosaics from the pictures they never noticed the numbers because they didn't have your tricks with my phone. That's fantastic!"

"But what does it mean?" Jennifer asked. "We knew about the numbers so it doesn't give us any more of the information we need."

"We also know John Dee was here in that year. But you're right. The numbers don't actually tell us anything. So, the answer must be at this location and, if so, the answer must be in the old image of the chapel."

Bishop opened the page with the old image of the chapel.

"We focused on the mosaics. Now we must focus on the surroundings." From his pocket, Bishop took a small pouch and from it he took what looked like a clip from a clipboard mounted onto two small tubes. He clipped the gadget onto his phone exactly covering the camera lens, flipped a small switch and a blueish light came on beneath the gadget. "Sixty times zoom macro lens," he said proudly. "You have your apps. I have the toys to match."

Jennifer smiled as Bishop slowly moved the phone over the picture, the screen now functioning as a giant magnifying glass.

"Nice," she said as the professor began to scour every inch of the picture.

After five minutes, he took his eye off the screen and tilted his head thoughtfully.

"That must be it," he half whispered.

"Must be what?" Jennifer asked, throwing her hands in the air with impatience.

"Look." Bishop showed Jennifer a photo of a more detailed scene, as seen through the magnifying glass. "On the left wall of the chapel is an old gravestone carved in marble. In between the Polish text you can see the name of the deceased, Łukasz Kościelecki. My eye was drawn to it because I recognized it as one of the names that was engraved in gold on the floor of the cathedral. Take a look at the date."

Jennifer peered closely at the picture because, even magnified, the numbers were barely readable, but with a bit of concentration she saw them. "One, five, nine, seven," she said. "We're looking for the bishop?"

"I guess we are."

"But why and where?" Jennifer asked, puzzled.

"Regarding your first question, I have no idea. Your second question is easy to answer. You see here?" Bishop pointed again at the enlargement of Kościelecki's gravestone in the wall. "Here, below the date, there's an image of a family coat of arms."

Bishop swiped to the next image. "You see the two caskets in the old chapel?" With two fingers Bishop now zoomed in on the left casket, which was rectangular, without any text and looked more like a bookchest. The casket was covered with what looked like leather, embossed with an image.

"The coat of arms," she said. "So, that must be the casket Kościelecki was buried in."

"And we heard what happened to the caskets," Bishop added.

"So, what do you suggest?" Jennifer asked, almost afraid to hear the answer. And because Bishop saw by her eyes that she had already guessed the right answer, he remained quiet.

"Okay. Well, I guess we could ask, but I don't think they'll let us examine the casket," Jennifer finally said. "Hell, they won't even let us near it if the priest is to be believed."

"That's oh so true," Bishop said in such a way that Jennifer was in no doubt he already had a plan. A plan she was probably not going to like.

The rental car, which was more than ten years old, was a white Mercedes Benz E class, which made it quite conspicuous as it made its way through the dark city.

"Take the next left," a woman's voice commanded through the speakers and the driver did as he was told before continuing to sing along to the Bon Jovi track, "Wanted Dead or Alive."

Ever since his transition from a Neophyte, Malkuth felt a better man, more self-conscious, more self-aware and more secure. More of a man in body, mind and spirit. It was a strange sensation. Maybe, for the first time in his life, he felt recognized. With both hands on the wheel his eyes were drawn for a second to the scars on his wrist, showing beneath his rolled-up sleeves. He grinned. It was unimaginable now to think he was once so desperate for attention he could only seek it that way. His thoughts then wandered back in time to the period a little over two years ago when he met Kether. He could no longer remember the true name of the man who had convinced him in a bar to check out his organization and beliefs.

Malkuth felt his phone vibrate in his pocket and he shifted in his seat to reach for it. He quickly pressed the fingerprint scanner.

Please let me know when you're at your destination. K.

Malkuth tossed the phone on the passenger seat.

"Turn right after one hundred yards," instructed the GPS voice. Malkuth did as he was told almost immediately. The faceless voice then informed him, "You will reach your destination in five hundred yards. Your destination will be on the left." Malkuth followed the road. Within a minute, he saw what he was looking for and stopped the car. He stared outside before putting the car in reverse and driving back some one hundred yards to get out of sight of the target. He parked the car in a dark spot alongside the road. *I guess this is it,* he said to himself as he picked up his cellphone and started typing.

I have arrived. Please send confirmation. M.

Malkuth sat in the dark waiting for the light on the cellphone's screen to light up again.

Your assignment cleared. Good luck. K.

Malkuth read the message and released a small sigh, realizing he felt a little nervous. They had made him one of them, which offered feelings of worthiness, and now he needed to prove their confidence was well placed.

He grabbed a black training jacket from the back seat and got out of the car. Covering his bald head with the hoody attached, he started walking.

The line of sight on his target was blocked by a large building that ran along the entire street up to the corner of the building. He saw the words '*Pałac Arcybiskupi*' on the face of the tall construction as he walked alongside it. At the end of the building, the light from the street outside bounced off the cobblestones. After taking his final turn he stopped for a moment, looking on in awe as the Archcathedral Basilica of St. Peter and St. Paul appeared, reflecting yellow and red light from the bricks and green from the dozen or so copper rooftops and towers on top of it. In this light, the cathedral looked even more majestic.

CHAPTER 11

The Break-In

A small desk light was all that illuminated the hotel room where Jennifer Porter—sitting on the bed—looked Professor Matthew Bishop straight in the eye, trying to work out whether he was serious.

"Breaking in? Into a church of all places? Are you absolutely...?" She swallowed the last word, thinking she might regret speaking it. The professor gave a wry smile.

"You said it yourself. There's no way the priest will allow us to visit the catacombs. Besides, you thought your father was some kind of Indiana Jones and you wanted to be like him when you were little. Well, this is your chance. It will be a neat break-in."

Though Bishop tried to sound reassuring, Jennifer wasn't convinced. She slapped her hands against her head in exasperation. "What the hell is a neat break-in?"

"What I meant to say was, we go in, do our thing and we get out again. Nobody will be any the wiser."

"How are we going to break into the church? You heard the doors being locked by deadbolts."

Seeing Jennifer was calming down a bit, Bishop sat next to her on the bed. He took her hand in his own. "We won't have to break in, as such. Like the Passetto, the secret passage between Vatican City and Castel Sant'Angelo in Rome, the cathedral has its own passageway from the Pałac Arcybiskupi, the Archbishop's Palace. It was a way for the priests and bishops to safely—and I guess dryly—move between the two buildings."

"We still need to get into the palace." Jennifer sounded smug.

"That's the easy part. Please, trust me on that one. That solution is only a phone call away."

Jennifer took a deep breath. She didn't like where this was going but, on the other hand, if she backed out now she would never get the answers she so desperately sought regarding her father. Without saying anything more, she nodded.

"Great." Bishop immediately got to his feet, picked up his coat and walked to the door. "Be ready in the hotel lobby at 8:30. I'll be back before then."

"Where are you going?" Jennifer asked, but Bishop was already out of the door and it slammed shut behind him.

The Poznań Novotel lobby was strikingly furnished with purple and pink seats and sofas that had been carefully positioned in an otherwise empty hall. A small reception desk tucked away in a corner was the only real reminder to visitors that they weren't in some kind of minimalistic lounge club. Just as the attendant offered Jennifer a cup of coffee or tea while she waited, Bishop wandered into the lobby carrying a small backpack.

"Are you ready to go?" he called out, clearly in a hurry.

Jennifer thanked the attendant for his kind offer, picked up her coat and went scurrying after Bishop, who was already halfway out the door.

"Wait a minute. Slow down. Where are we going?" she cried out.

Bishop didn't slow. Instead, he made a gesture with his arm inviting her to come closer. As she reached him at the end of the walkway to the hotel, a small group of tourists passed them.

"Come on. This is our tour. I made reservations."

Jennifer looked amazed as she fell into step with the group who were led by a guide speaking in three different languages as he explained the origins of the Park Tysiąclecia that faced the front of the hotel.

"We're on a tour?" Jennifer asked.

"The Royal Imperial Route," Bishop confirmed. "It goes from the old Miłostowo cemeteries in the east to the old city center in the west."

"And why are we on this tour?"

"Did I not mention that the tour takes us to the Archbishop's Palace?" Bishop flashed a bright smile. "Relax. Enjoy the walk."

It took a little over ten minutes for Jennifer to realize she hadn't taken in any of the information the guide had given the group. Her mind was too preoccupied with not knowing what the professor's plan was. By the time she realized she was missing the details of the tour, they had passed the Jordan Bridge—named after the first Bishop of Poznań in the tenth century—and the fully-lit palace appeared, a three-winged building built by Giovanni Battista Quadro and Pompeo Ferrari in the eighteenth century. As the group crossed the street leading up to the palace, a white car turned the corner with a screech of tires, scattering the group. After some colorful shouting in Polish, with hand gestures to match, the tour leader quickly gathered everyone back together before picking up the pace. Seconds later they were at the palace entrance, flanked by two large statues of the saints Peter and Paul that had once flanked the entrance to the cathedral itself.

"We must be on the right tour then," Bishop joked, but Jennifer didn't respond.

Once inside the building, the group snaked their way along the hallways with the guide explaining which bishops had once occupied which offices they passed. As the tour took another turn, Bishop took hold of Jennifer's hand to slow her down until they came to a complete stop. Once the last person in the tour group had disappeared from view, he opened the door right behind them bearing a sign that read, '*Biuro finansowe*.' Pulling Jennifer quickly inside, he closed the door behind them. After a brief search of the wall, he switched on the light using a finger wrapped in his sleeve. The room was small and the centerpiece was two modern desks facing each other. Bishop took some latex gloves from his backpack and handed Jennifer a pair.

"I don't have mysophobia," she said.

"Fingerprints?"

Embarrassed by her own stupidity, she took the gloves and put them on. Bishop took a piece of paper from his pocket and examined it closely, comparing it to the room. He then walked toward the wall to their right.

"Look," he ordered, pointing toward a large closet against the wall, "over the top." Just above the closet was a crack in the wall shaped like the top of an old door frame. "Help me. We need to push it that way."

Bishop pointed to the right and got into position. With Jennifer's help, the closet quickly moved sideways and the wall instantly revealed the full contours of an old door, with no handles or any other protrusions. Bishop scanned the room and noticed a shining chrome shoehorn carefully placed next to a pair of shoes. Only in Poland, he thought. The shoehorn fit neatly between the door and the crack in the wall and with a little force the door gave way. Bishop and Jennifer then stared for a few seconds into the darkness before them. Taking a flashlight from his backpack, he aimed it into the dark hole to reveal a narrow corridor filled with dust rags and cobwebs.

"After you," Bishop said to Jennifer.

"Thank you, but that honor is all yours," Jennifer replied.

Bishop took another look around the room and armed himself with a large black umbrella from an umbrella stand.

"Let's go," he said, waving the umbrella in front of him as he entered the corridor. The floor looked like old marble, the walls finished with wooden planks. Along the sides hung old oil lamps once used to light the path. After some 100 feet, another door appeared. Bishop gave Jennifer the flashlight and pushed, but the door wouldn't budge. More force, Bishop figured, as he put his shoulder to the door. Still no movement. "This could be a problem," he said with a sigh.

"May I?" Jennifer asked, handing back the flashlight.

"Be my guest," Bishop said somewhat condescendingly. The young woman pushed and pulled on the iron ring that hung from the center of the door.

"I told you...."

Jennifer gave the ring one more pull and the center plank fell, immediately followed by the other parts of the door, leaving a completely open space.

"Pull, not push," she said.

"I knew you'd be a valuable research assistant," Bishop joked.

Behind the opening, three wooden steps led down to a small alcove leading to a dimly lit room. Bishop descended first, Jennifer fast behind him.

"Wow," she said in awe as she turned the corner into the room.

A modern iron walkway ran around, above and across the room. It was some 150 feet long and 60 feet wide. Below the walkway, in white sand, were the foundations of the original cathedral. Around the sides, remnants of the old stone and marble carvings were displayed, as well as signs next to the walkway revealing the brickwork's 1000-year-old story.

"Wow indeed," Bishop agreed. "This way." He pointed to the other end of the walkway.

"How do you know all this?" Jennifer asked as they walked. "I mean, the tour, the door to the tunnel?"

"I have a friend at UNESCO who works in the archives of the world heritage list. Now, while the cathedral is not on that list, he did know how to get me some old blueprints so...."

At the end of the walkway, a small iron staircase took them to a marble-floored room, at the end of which was a small altar in front of a large sculpture of Jesus on the cross. To the left and right of the crypt, two rows of coffins were placed on brown marble platforms.

"Look at all those coffins," Jennifer said.

"Technically, there are no coffins here," Bishop replied, sounding smug. "Traditionally, a coffin—from the Greek word *kophinos*, meaning basket—refers to a hexagonal funeral box, tapered to fit the human body. These are caskets and sarcophagi, basically straight boxes or ornamental cases made from wood, iron, marble and sometimes...." Bishop paused to point at a brown casket.

"...finished with leather," Jennifer said, recognizing the brown leather casket from the pictures.

Bishop went to the casket, took a piece of cloth from his backpack and wiped the dust from the front panel.

"The coat of arms," Jennifer muttered, looking at the embossed emblem on the front. "This must be the coffin of Bishop Kościelecki. Sorry, casket."

Below the coat of arms was a banner that had once borne a name that was now unrecognizable after being weathered by the years. Bishop continued to scour the casket.

"Did you know that the Holy Roman Emperor Joseph II ordered his people to use reusable caskets to save the trees? True story. The man was way ahead of his time. The caskets had a trap door at the bottom and once the mourners had left the party, the door opened, the body fell out and the casket was lifted again for the next funeral."

"Very interesting, but can we please quit the lecture and move on?" Jennifer said tetchily, feeling a sudden sense of unease at the thought of being surrounded by so many dead people. "This place is giving me the creeps."

"Sorry. Sure we can. Please help me. The casket is covered by a weighted wooden lid recessed within the side panels so we need to lift it before we can move it." Bishop pointed at the top left corner of the casket. "When I give it some room I need you to help lift it. When it's high enough we can turn it a little. From there it should be easy."

"Okay. Let's make it quick." Jennifer put her fingers on the lid where Bishop was going to lift it.

"Here we go."

Bishop's fingers almost immediately turned white at the knuckles from the exertion of trying to lift and push the casket. Releasing a small grunt, he closed his eyes, but just as the lid seemed to move a fraction and Jennifer tried to prize her fingers in between, he had to let go. The lid fell back with a soft swoosh and Bishop blew air through his tight lips.

"That's heavier than I thought," he admitted. "Give me a second and we'll go again." He wiggled his arms by his sides, releasing the tension from his muscles.

Jennifer glanced around the room feeling more anxious by the minute. In her mind, she asked herself if she realized she was collaborating in a grave robbery. Before her mind had chance to answer, Bishop tapped on the casket and gestured for her to get into position. Jennifer nodded and Bishop started pushing and lifting, giving it his all right from the start. Almost immediately, the lid moved and Jennifer was able to get her fingers under it. Now wiggling four hands between the casket and the lid they slowly turned the lid to the point where it couldn't slip back. Bishop released a sigh of relief whereas Jennifer frowned.

"What is it?" Bishop asked.

"I don't know. I guess I didn't know what to expect."

"Did you expect a waft of air and eerie sounds? Let me assure you, that only happens in the movies." Bishop chuckled at his teasing. "Now, let's see what we have here."

Putting his full weight against the lid, he turned it until the top of the casket was fully open. Jennifer turned her head away, but it was too dark to see inside anyway. Switching on his flashlight, Bishop directed the beam into the casket. A few seconds later Jennifer managed to bring herself to look. The casket was about thirty inches deep and gray pieces of disintegrated cloth covered the bottom. Bishop handed the flashlight to Jennifer and from his backpack he took out a small brush fitted with bellows. Bending over, deep into the casket, Bishop tried to move the cloth aside, but it crumbled between his fingers and a small cloud of dust particles appeared in the torchlight, chilling Jennifer's heart as it pounded in her chest. Using the brush to move the pieces of cloth, more dust blew up, obscuring the bottom of the casket. Bishop cleared a large part of it before retracting himself to give the dust the chance to dissipate. As the two looked into the chest, with some anticipation, the heavy dust quickly settled and the casket revealed its secrets.

Bones were scattered throughout the casket.

"Is it supposed to look like that?" Jennifer asked.

"The casket has been moved several times over hundreds of years so the bones would become dislodged with nothing there to tie them together anymore."

Bishop leaned into the casket again to sift through the bones, putting them aside, one by one, as Jennifer's eyes widened.

"What are you looking for?" she asked.

"I don't know. I'm hoping I'll recognize it when I see it," Bishop replied, his voice muffled as he leaned further into the casket, making it near impossible for Jennifer to light his way. As he balanced on the lip of the casket, Bishop suddenly tipped forward and he would have certainly fallen in had Jennifer not grabbed the back of his coat quickly and pulled him back up.

"Thank you," Bishop said before immediately going back in. Suddenly, he saw a shimmer of reflection from the torch light. "Can you shine it a little bit further here?" After a moment his wiggling body was still. "Aha! Can you please help me back up?"

Jennifer pulled Bishop's jacket and he quickly came up to stand on his own two feet again. With his hands still in the casket he brushed something he was holding. Jennifer pointed the light at it and gasped.

"Is that...?"

"This must be him," Bishop answered, showing her the dust-covered skull that must have once been Bishop Łukasz Kościelecki. Jennifer slowly exhaled while Bishop continued to clean the skull.

"Is there anything special about it?" she asked.

"Maybe. Let me get this dust off and...." He didn't finish his sentence as his attention was caught by the left eye socket. Brushing and blowing the last dust particles away, he found a glass-like object stuck inside of it. "If you please." Bishop indicated Jennifer should shine the light on the object. As she did so, she was startled to see the object reflected a bright green light, reminding her of an eye opening. If Bishop was also startled, he didn't show it. Instead, he stuck his gloved fingers into the socket to remove the object. With some wiggling, it finally gave way and Bishop took it out slowly. The emerald-colored crystal-like form was shaped like a stretched diamond, about four inches long and an inch wide at the bottom before tapering into a spike. Wrapped around the crystal was a small scroll that looked like a papyrus roll, tied with a tiny string. As Bishop touched the string it crumbled beneath his fingertips, releasing the scroll. Bishop put the scroll gently on top of the lid and took a closer look at the green crystal.

"Glass?" Jennifer asked.

Bishop put on his reading glasses, took the flashlight and examined it closely. "I don't think so. You see, looking through it there are tiny flaws and irregularities. Glass or other artificially-created compounds would be much more perfect on the inside. And look, when I shine the light on it, it doesn't reflect an array of rainbow-like colors like it should. I think this is a real gem."

"It's an odd shape," Jennifer noted. "Have you ever seen something like this?"

"Not really, and I have no idea as to the significance." Bishop took a piece of cloth from his backpack and carefully wrapped the crystal in it.

"Now, what about you?" Bishop picked up the scroll and slowly unwrapped it. It felt sturdy despite its apparent age. He thought it must have been prepared with something to withstand time. On the brownish paper, written in black ink, Bishop recognized a few lines of text. Examining the words closely in the light of the torch, Bishop hummed to himself.

"What is it?" Jennifer asked.

"I don't know. It's clearly written text, but I don't recognize any of the characters." Bishop took a Tupperware-like storage container from his backpack and put the scroll and crystal inside.

"We're taking it?"

"We are. They must have some significance to our mystery. We can check it out when we get back to the hotel. Now, let's get out of here."

"Thank God." Jennifer sighed in relief.

After Bishop carefully placed the skull back where he had found it, they quickly closed the casket.

"We can't go out the same way we came," Bishop said. "The palace will probably be locked now. They have an active security system. Thankfully, the cathedral doesn't have such a security system, but it does have cameras outside. I checked them out. I found a blind spot that we can use if we simply leave through the front door."

After a few seconds, the crypt again looked untouched and the two went on their way. Small nightlights placed along the paths and the stairs within the church made it easy for Bishop to navigate their way to emerge from behind the altar. Despite the dim lighting the front doors were clearly distinguishable.

"This way." Bishop took Jennifer's hand, leading her to a passageway next to the chapels. As they were about to pass the last chapel, Jennifer flinched from Bishop's hold, gasped in shock and stopped dead, as if nailed to the ground, as she peered into the chapel's alcove. Bishop took a step backward to see what she was looking at, and he, too, stopped in surprise. Inside the chapel, over a dark brown wooden prayer bench was a lifeless body. The head was covered by a jacket.

"Is that...?" Jennifer asked, her heart beating in fear as she pointed to the scarlet string on the corpse's wrist.

Bishop didn't answer. This was a first, even for him. Carefully, he took a few steps into the alcove and kneeled next to the body. No blood, he thought as he inspected the motionless figure. Hesitating for a minute, he thanked his luck that he was wearing latex gloves and raised the jacket covering the body's head.

Jennifer gasped as Father Matula was revealed. His pale face looked gray, even blueish.

Bishop lifted the head a little with the jacket, and it lifelessly bounced back with the pull of gravity. Bishop rose to his feet and quickly took a few steps back.

"Is he dead?" Jennifer asked.

Bishop nodded.

"What do we do?"

After thinking for a short moment he said, "There's nothing we can do for him. We need to get out of here as quickly as we can and take it from there."

Jennifer hesitated, but then agreed. As they moved away, she took one last look at Father Matula's body. It reminded her of her dead father, sitting in his wheelchair in the hospital's rooftop garden.

Getting to the front door, Bishop quickly unlocked the deadbolts, opened it a little and checked the surroundings.

"We're clear." Bishop signaled that Jennifer should follow as he stepped outside. "We'll be okay if we go left and stay close to the walls."

Jennifer obeyed the order. "How can he be dead?" she asked.

"I don't know," Bishop replied. "But what I do know is that if we stay here we don't have a very good story about why we are here."

Jennifer shook her head in disbelief, and as they inched their way along the walls of the cathedral, they failed to notice a car parked on the dark street opposite them. Inside was a man talking into a cellphone.

"We're too late," he said.

CHAPTER 12

The Cipher

The impressive Beinecke Rare Book & Manuscript Library at Yale is the largest building in the world entirely dedicated to rare books and manuscripts. Built with Platonic mathematical precision—one for height, two for width and three for length—the building has been called the 'jewel box' because of its precious contents. Through the thin, translucent, gray-veined marble panes covering the windowless building, daylight illuminates the six-story-high, glass-enclosed tower of book stacks. More than 180,000 rare volumes are able to be displayed without damage because the marble panels filter the otherwise dangerous sunlight leaving just enough light to dimly light the library. In the underground book stacks, another million rare volumes are preserved for posterity.

On the mezzanine, Walker Monroe looked through the showcase glass protecting one of the finest copies of the remaining 48 Guttenberg Bibles. Only this early in the morning, when the first rays of filtered sunlight hit the Bible, could the true splendor of the first book ever created on a moveable-type press, be captured. Rightly or wrongly, Monroe considered the Guttenberg Bible to be almost a part of him, so deeply did he value its history.

Since his appointment as curator of early books and manuscripts, Monroe watched over the collection as though it were his own, and he treated it like he might have treated his children, had he ever had any. As the only black man on staff, and a Brit nonetheless, he was particularly proud of his commission four years ago. Given an office in the basement of the building, Monroe spent most of his days sitting behind his laptop at a small desk sandwiched between the Guttenberg Bible and the glass tower filled with 'his' books. This early in the day he felt he did his best work with no one around to distract him. But then his smartphone alerted him to a call. In just a few steps, Monroe returned to his desk to see the name on the screen: *Matthew Bishop*. The curator smiled as he picked up the phone.

"Matthew Bishop. As I live and breathe. What are you up to this early in the morning?"

"What do you mean early in the morning?" Bishop said, even as he realized that there was a six-hour time gap between them. "Sorry," he corrected quickly, "I forgot my time zone. I'm in Poznań, Poland."

"Poland? What the devil are you doing there?"

"I'm afraid that's a simple question with a long answer. I'll explain later. For now, the shorter version is that I'm researching a theory about the Aldaraia and I could really use your help. Can you switch on your video screen?"

"Sure."

Monroe put the phone on the desk in front of him and switched on the holographic screen. The RED Hydrogen One smartphone displayed 3D images and videos in a manner that appeared to have them floating in midair, enabling the viewer to see an object from different angles and also interact with it—all without the need of specially-designed glasses. Bishop and Monroe were amongst the first to experiment with the technology.

"You have an image?" Bishop asked.

Above Monroe's smartphone, the image of Bishop sitting behind a hotel room desk materialized. "I have an image of a Polish hotel room with an ugly American in it. Is that correct?"

"While I have an image of a British bald guy sitting in a dark library," Bishop replied, laughing. "I guess there's no accounting for taste." He paused to point the camera of his phone at his desk. "Are you getting this?"

Above Monroe's phone the image of an unwrapped brown paper scroll appeared accompanied by a crystal.

"Can you please record this?" Bishop asked.

"You found something?" Monroe inquired as he pressed the record button on his smartphone.

"A crystal and a scroll, and that's where you come in." Bishop put his phone back on the desk. "As you can see on the paper there's written text—"

"And you want me to tell you what it says?" Monroe interrupted, rotating the floating image while occasionally zooming in with a spread of his fingers.

"I do. What can you tell me?"

Monroe enlarged the image until it was a single letter on the screen and scrolled along the text. Although some of the text was barely readable, he nodded. "I think you know what this is."

"I knew I came to the right place." Bishop laughed. "So, you agree and think it's Enochian?"

"I'm almost sure it is. Of course, the characters are faded for a large part so I'll need to make a computer reconstruction to be sure, but from what I see here there's enough to work with." Monroe switched his phone back to camera view, and Bishop floated above the screen again, in his hotel room, allowing Monroe to see the enthusiasm on his old friend's face.

"You think you can translate it?"

"I'll do what I can," Monroe replied. "Not all signs look recoverable, but I'll see what I can do. Do you have any context to go with the scroll?"

"Very little, I'm afraid. We found the objects in the ancient grave of a Polish bishop after following a clue from documents related to the Aldaraia. That's about it."

Monroe noticed someone move behind Bishop. He enlarged the image to reveal the silhouette of a woman lying in bed, stretching out her arms as she clearly woke up. As she moaned, Bishop turned to the bed.

"Who's that behind you?" Monroe teased.

Bishop quickly turned back to his phone and switched off the video. "That, my friend, I'll also explain later. But, please, get back to me sooner rather than later."

"I can't wait to hear this story, my friend," Monroe said with a chuckle. "It's still early over here, so I'll see if I can squeeze some time in today and have a look. And as I said, I look forward to hearing what you've been up to. You owe me dinner when you get back."

"You have a deal. Talk to you later." Bishop turned off the phone and looked toward Jennifer. "Good morning, sunshine. Or should I say good afternoon?" Bishop poured her a cup of coffee from the thermos on the desk. "Black okay?"

Jennifer stretched out her arms, yawned and accepted the coffee. "What time is it?"

"It's almost twelve. You've slept through the entire morning." Bishop opened the curtains, forcing Jennifer to squint in the bright sunlight.

"Sorry. I kept them closed as long as you slept, but I could use some daylight now." Switching on the television, he turned to Channel 88, *Poznaj Lokalne Wiadomości*. "This is the Poznań local news channel. That much I found out last night before falling asleep. I'm curious to see if there's any report from the cathedral."

"And is there?" Jennifer asked still squinting while sipping her coffee.

"Nothing so far. Did you finally get some sleep?"

"I recall the alarm clock reading five before I fell asleep. You were comfortable enough, snoring your way through the night."

"I'm sorry. Did I keep you awake?"

"No, not really. It was the image of Father Matula's dead body that kept me awake. I still can't believe it."

"I know. It was a gruesome sight. I don't know what to say. Thankfully, I'm blessed with the ability to sleep no matter what. But I empathize with your feelings."

"Remind me again why we didn't call the police?"

Before Bishop could reply, a picture of the cathedral appeared on the TV. *Okropna śmierć w katedrzesee*, gruesome death in cathedral, read the caption below the image. The church was cordoned off with yellow tape and a small fleet of police cars guarded the perimeter. Along the yellow tape a number of reporters were doing pieces into cameras while others were interviewing anyone who had anything to say.

"That is why," Bishop finally answered. "It wouldn't have changed a thing if we'd called the police. We would only be part of the investigation and we have nothing to say. We don't have a clue as to what happened; it could have been a crime, an unfortunate accident or even natural causes that caused the Father Matula's death. And if we'd reported it we wouldn't be leaving Poland anytime soon."

Jennifer nodded reluctantly. She knew there was some truth in what Bishop said, but her heart didn't agree. Every time she blinked, the image of the priest's lifeless body hanging over the bench appeared and sent a chill running up her spine.

"Can you please turn off the TV?"

"Sorry, of course." Bishop picked up the remote control to switch channels when a fully-robed priest appeared on the screen. Bishop pressed the pause button." You see that?" he asked, pointing the remote at the screen.

Jennifer raised an eyebrow. "I don't see anything. Just a reporter interviewing a man—a priest, I think."

"Look closer." Bishop pointed the remote closer to the frozen image of the priest. Jennifer crawled over her bedclothes to get closer to the TV before sitting up straight.

"Ah, now I see it." She pointed at the priest's arm which clearly displayed a scarlet-colored string tied around his wrist. "What does that mean?"

"I guess it could mean anything but it's a hell of a coincidence. The simplest explanation is that they have a lot of Christian kabbalists in Poznań, meaning it indeed is just a coincidence." Bishop frowned.

Jennifer noticed the crystal and the paper scroll sitting on the desk next to the copy of the Aldaraia page. "Did you find anything?"

"What? Oh sorry, well, uh, nothing conclusive." Bishop picked up the crystal from the desk and stroked it with his fingers. "It's definitely a real emerald, cut in a way I've never seen before. Six uneven, but perfectly cut faces. Nearly flawless. I haven't a single clue to its meaning or purpose."

"And the text on the scroll?"

Bishop placed the emerald back on the desk. "I had my suspicions and I've just had them confirmed by my good friend who's a curator of early books and manuscripts at the Beinecke."

"Walker Monroe?" Jennifer asked. "Tall, dark bald man. Early fifties and thick British accent?"

"The same one," Bishop replied. "How do you know him?"

"I once followed a summer school he did on hagiography, the biographies of saints, spiritual beings, religious icons and the miracles they allegedly performed. What did he confirm?"

"That the text is almost certainly written in Enochian."

"Enochian?" Jennifer frowned and picked up the emerald from the desk.

"An obscure angelical and divine language said to have been sent by angels and received by John Dee and Edward Kelley in the late sixteenth century. It's supposed to be the language God used when he created the world and was spoken in the Garden of Eden. When Adam was later banished from paradise, he supposedly lost the language and created Hebrew from what he could remember. Dee initially called it 'Angelical,' but somehow the name later changed to Enochian after Enoch, the great-grandfather of Noah who, according to the Bible, lived 365 years before God took him."

"I thought it was Methuselah who lived for so long," Jennifer remarked.

"Actually, a lot of people in the Old Testament lived to be really old, but Methuselah was the oldest. He died when he was 969 years old. His father died a young man, at 365, the same age that Enoch died. But who's counting? Anyway, ever since its existence, there have been many doubts about Enochian, and in the late sixteenth and early seventeenth centuries, the language was considered to be the language of demons. In more recent studies, they discovered that the language has syntactic similarities to English instead of Semitic languages like Hebrew and Arabic, like you would expect. Both languages, according to Dee, were derived from Enochian. So, nowadays, most theories say that the entire language was Dee and Kelley's creation."

"But you can you translate the text?" Jennifer asked.

"I can't translate it, no. But, if anyone can, it's Walker Monroe. He's trying as we speak." Watching Jennifer roll the emerald between her hands, he added, "Can you please not break the emerald?"

"I'm sorry." Jennifer placed the emerald back on the bureau, noting the sun's rays reflecting the shape of a green irregular hexagon on the white desk.

Bishop also noticed and took the tip of the emerald between two fingers. Slowly, he turned it.

"Curious," he muttered.

"Curious?" Jennifer asked, but Bishop didn't answer her.

Completely zoned out, he kept spinning the emerald slowly, focusing on the shape reflected on the desk.

"Professor?" she tried again. Nothing. Finally, she placed a hand firmly on his shoulder and called his name. "Professor Matthew Bishop!"

Startled, Bishop returned to reality. "What? What is it?"

"You were completely gone for a moment. You had me worried. For a second, I thought the emerald had some kind of power over you."

Bishop laughed out loud. "Sorry about that, but there's nothing to worry about. I sometimes zone out when I'm really focused. Even though an emerald crystal is formed under pressure over hundreds of millions of years and many cultures attribute all sorts of power to them, they're nothing more than unique works of mother nature's artistry and, basically, they're only stones, polished to give a nice shine. Though I must admit this one intrigues me."

"How so?" Jennifer asked out of curiosity.

Bishop turned the gem between his fingers. "See that shape?"

Jennifer took a closer look at the irregular green shape on the desk.

"Tell me what you see."

Jennifer raised an eyebrow.

"I know I sound like a teacher, but please indulge me."

As Bishop turned the emerald, Jennifer examined the shape on the desk closely.

After a long moment she sighed in exasperation. "I'm sorry," she finally said. "I don't see anything."

"And I guess that's just it," Bishop said with a smile, the excitement showing in his eyes. "You see, the sides are irregular, so when you turn it you'd expect the reflecting light on the table to change." Bishop paused to watch Jennifer think about what he'd said.

"Yet it doesn't change," she said hesitantly.

"That's exactly it. Look!" Bishop turned the emerald again yet nothing changed in the reflection. "But," he next moved the crystal a few feet to the left on the table.

"Now it does change," Jennifer remarked.

"It does. And that got me thinking. Obviously, the emerald is cut in a very specific way. I don't know how they did it, but the shape only changes when you change the position of the light that shines onto it." Bishop moved the object over the table from left to right and back again and Jennifer watched, intrigued.

"So, what does it mean, other than someone probably went to a lot of effort cutting it like that?"

"I think it means the emerald isn't just for show, that it's a utensil, a piece of equipment, if you will. We have to use it somehow. I believe it may be some kind of cipher."

"A key to a coded message?" Jennifer clapped her hands in excitement.

Bishop replied with a simple nod.

CHAPTER 13

The Monas

2009

Robert Porter's desk had always been a mix of papers and weird looking antiquities. Fighting for space between stacks of documents was a scary-looking wax moulage of a dead person's head sitting within a glass bell. There was also a 3000-year-old Ushabti statue, once buried with an Egyptian nobleman, and a small Keichousaurus fossil estimated at around 200 million years old. As for the rest of his study, the room could easily have been mistaken for a small museum. Objects from all over the world covered every bit of floor space. There were antique weapons, dishware, statues, paintings and books—lots of books.

After clearing a little space on his desk, Porter turned to the wall behind him, opened the safe and took out a small stack of papers. He spread them out in front of him just as his cellphone rang. *Unknown.* Curious, as it was fairly late for phone calls, he answered.

"Yes?"

"Mr. Robert Porter?" a woman's voice asked.

"Who is this?"

"It's Alice Hartman again, Mr. Porter. You remember me? From the auction and the visit to your home?"

Porter knew immediately who the woman was, but didn't feel compelled to answer.

"I guess you know why I'm calling."

"Again, and at this hour?"

The door to Porter's study opened and Sylvia walked in having heard her husband speaking. Porter's face revealed his exasperation as he moved the phone from his ear for a second.

"I'm sorry, I'm not quite used to dealing with the time difference. My employer instructed me to contact you again, one last time, and double the standing offer for the items. I think—"

"One last time?" Porter interrupted, a little agitated. "What do you mean one last time?"

Sylvia tilted her head in response to her husband's raised pitch.

"What I'm trying to say, Mr. Porter, is that my employer thinks the offer is more generous than it should be and that this is the one and only time that his offer will stand. There will be no more offers."

"So, there is good news," Porter said glibly. "Please, thank your... uh... employer one more time and tell him his offer is turned down again and for the last time. Thank you, Ms. Hartman, and please don't call again." Not waiting for the woman's reaction, he hung up the phone by firmly pressing his screen.

"Again?" Sylvia asked. "Who are these people and what's so special about the papers they keep asking about?"

"These are the papers," he said, pointing to the small stack on his desk. "I bought them at the auction in London last year. You remember?"

"Vaguely," Sylvia replied, coming to stand next to him. Her husband had been on the road a lot and often brought back trinkets. In the early days, she had tried to embrace what she called 'his curiosities,' but when their house started to look like a pawnshop she banished him and his trinkets to a single room. "What are they?"

"Basically, they're letters from old English and Polish noblemen. But somehow, I feel there's more to these seven documents than meets the eye. Like this one." Porter picked up the page from the Aldaraia showing the table filled with letters.

"Looks like an ancient crossword puzzle to me," Sylvia joked and her husband replied by pinching her leg.

"Don't you dare, you old hoarder," she cried as she backed away.

"Hoarder?" Porter replied with mock indignation, though he knew full well how his habit of collecting things drove her insane. He knew she was okay with it as long as he kept the clutter to his study and cleaned the room himself. But she still didn't understand the passion. As far as she was concerned he was simply holding on to stuff he didn't need and to illustrate this thought she turned to look at all the collectibles fighting for space in the room.

"Point taken," Porter replied, and his wife walked up to him and kissed him on the forehead.

"Come to bed soon," she told him. "You could use more sleep. And wash your hands before you get into bed."

"Yes, ma'am," Porter playfully replied and Sylvia left the room.

Before putting the page down, he took another look at it. *There had to be a clue to all this. It had to be here somewhere,* he thought.

From under his desk, he pulled out a small camera backpack holding his new toy—as his wife would call it—a Leica M9 full frame 18-megapixel camera he'd bought secondhand earlier in the week. Proudly, he blew a speck of dust from the top of the otherwise pristine camera. It had been the best $2,500 he'd ever spent. With its ISO 1250 setting, he should be able to capture a crisp image even in the dim light of his study. It was time to put it to the test. Standing up, he carefully centered the first letter from Łaski in front of the table. Pointing his camera at the document, he pressed the shutter button. He missed the traditional sound of the mirror clapping up and down, but as he looked at the image taken on the small LCD screen on the back he released an impressed whistle. The image looked perfect. Even when zooming in on the smallest detail, it looked perfectly clear.

Satisfied, Porter continued shooting all the documents front and back before putting the camera away and restacking the papers. The top paper showed a charcoal sketch of an old church, above which were the words, *Sanctum lavacrum loco nativitatis,* "A holy place of birth and rebirth."

Then, as he straightened the stack of papers, his eyes were drawn to the bottom right corner of the document. A small symbol, partially hidden in the sketch, caught his attention.

Porter's eyes scanned the study, searching. It must be here somewhere, but where? He thought the image looked familiar to him, but he needed to be sure. After a short while, he turned in his chair and bent down to a crate on the floor. "It's almost always in front of you," he mumbled as he took hold of a number of copies of old documents and put them on his lap. One by one, he took a document from the pile and tossed it back into the crate. *No,* he thought as he took a close look at every front page of every document until the stack slowly diminished. About two-thirds of the way through, he suddenly stopped as he was about to toss the document in his hand. Quickly discarding the rest of papers, he turned back to the desk to put the document under the light.

"Monas Hieroglyphica, Ioannes Dee Londinensis," Porter read to himself from the cover of the document.

Quickly, it came back to him. *The Monas* was a short text explaining a symbol or hieroglyph with the same name created by John Dee in the sixteenth century. Dee was believed to have written the paper in twelve days while in a peak mystical state, claiming the symbol itself contained the possession of the most secret mysteries. Claiming it had been written with the pen of God, Dee said the document would revolutionize astronomy, alchemy, mathematics, medicine, magic and adeptship. The document had been translated more than once, but Dee's wordplay in Latin and Greek became lost in the translation of modern English. Though it had been suggested that his capitalization of certain words and the strange arrangement of text around graphics and randomly inserted word accents were a way of hiding the fact that the words didn't have any real meaning. Porter didn't actually agree with that and he found that many of Dee's texts coincided with the Hermetic tradition, also known as the Platonic dialogues; a literary genre of texts written by Plato, among others, that philosophers discussed through the ages.

What is the *Monas* doing on a sketch of a church? And how does it fit in with the rest of the documents?

CHAPTER 14

Beinecke

The Present

Thirteen hours had passed since Bishop talked to Walker Monroe on the phone. Bishop and Jennifer now boarded a taxi at Tweed New Haven airport. After touching the cab's door handle, Bishop squirted more sanitizer on his hands and rubbed them together.

"Do you know what I noticed?" Jennifer asked. "You have mysophobia yet you're not afraid to get your hands dirty."

Bishop smiled. "As long as I know that I'm within seconds of cleaning my hands again, somehow I know that I'm okay. Trust me, it gets a lot trickier when I can't clean up."

Jennifer chuckled as she wondered what exactly would happen, but she didn't ask.

"121 Wall Street," Bishop told the driver who immediately set the car in motion.

After a fifteen-minute drive, the taxi stopped in front of the Beinecke Library. Jennifer must have passed the building hundreds of times as she walked between classes, but she had never visited it before.

The security measures in the library were fairly strict, thanks to the antiques dealer, Edward Forbes Smiley III, who was caught cutting maps from the pages of rare books with an X-Acto blade in 2005. Smiley was busted when he dropped the blade in the reading room. He had cut out 97 rare maps, and it cost him three-and-a-half years in prison and $2 million in damages. Since then, security in exclusive libraries all over the world had tightened. At the Beinecke, every inch of the library open to the public was now under constant video surveillance. There was also *Controlled Access*, meaning visitors needed a personal invitation to come and they had to enter through metal detectors. They also had to hand in coats, hats, briefcases and any other personal belongings not essential to their work. This meant visitors could only bring in paper and books that were essential to their immediate research. Pens and indelible pencils were not allowed inside, let alone blades.

Jennifer felt privileged as she entered the small glass hallway to the library.

"Coming or going?" a voice sounded from behind the security check, and Bishop immediately recognized the British accent. Monroe pointed at the travel bags they dragged behind them. "You can leave them with security," he said before turning to the guard. "Please let them through."

The security guard gave a friendly nod and pressed a button on the wall. As the glass barrier opened, Bishop raised his backpack toward Monroe.

"Bring it," Monroe told him before turning to Jennifer and shaking her hand. "Welcome. You must be Robert Porter's daughter."

"Jennifer," she said by way of introduction. "You knew my father?"

"No, I'm sorry to say I never met him, but I know of him. And now, thanks to my dear friend Matthew Bishop, I get to meet his daughter."

"What brings you up from your dungeon?" Bishop joked while Jennifer gazed in awe at the six-story glass tower before her filled with ancient books.

"I was just passing through as I saw you exit the taxi," Monroe answered. "Besides, you know I hate the dungeons."

The offices and reading rooms at the library, tucked away in the basement of the building, some of them completely deprived of sunlight, were commonly called 'dungeons' by those who frequented them.

"Are you coming?" Bishop called to Jennifer as he and Monroe made their way to the staircase.

Jennifer snapped out of her trance and quickly joined them. "Sorry."

The wide, straight concrete staircase took them two floors down into the basement where Monroe's office was located.

"Please enter," Monroe said after unlocking the first door they came to and pointing inside.

His office was just big enough to hold a small desk and a small conference table with four chairs. The only light in the room came from a window in the ceiling allowing the daylight in from the library above. Along the walls were shelves filled with books behind large glass doors giving the room a look of a library within a library.

"Sit down," Monroe said, gesturing toward the conference table. "How was your trip?"

Both Jennifer and Bishop nodded and mumbled their replies.

"That good, huh? So, tell me again, Matthew, what happened. You get a visit from a total stranger with a stack of papers and you jump on the first plane to Poland?" Having teased Bishop, Monroe turned to Jennifer. "No offense."

"You know me," Bishop replied, the corners of his mouth turning up.

"Maybe better than you know yourself." Monroe shook his head. "Which is why, the moment you return, the first one you visit is your old friend."

"Who, if he did his homework like he promised, has something for us," Bishop said playfully.

"And here I was thinking it was I who gave out homework around here."

"Am I the only one curious about the text?" Jennifer asked with a small sigh.

"Impatient? No problem. I have something for you, but after that, you have to tell me what you're up to." Monroe stretched backward and took a folded piece of paper from his desk. "First, I can now say for sure the language is Enochian. Now, you have to know that translating Enochian isn't an exact science. It's what we call a poor language. Although we can translate every character into an English one, Enochian has only twenty-two characters, like Hebrew, and each character can have more meanings with different sounds. It has no nouns and very few adjectives or adverbs, and it shows phonetic features that don't appear in natural languages. What you are left with, after translation, is a bunch of words to select and construct a sentence from. And finally, I had to fill in some characters due to the withering of the paper."

Monroe paused to check they understood all the potentials for inaccuracy, and Jennifer and Bishop both nodded.

"Tell us, please," Bishop requested.

"Here we go." Monroe unfolded the top of the paper and placed it in front of them.

ABRAMG AR GONO IPAM CICLE OL OIAD IADNAH CAPMIALI GIGIPAH HOMIL ANANAEL

"Abramg ar gono?" Jennifer asked, as she tried to pronounce it.

"Sounds like Klingon," Bishop joked.

"It does, doesn't it?" Monroe replied. "This is how you might say the words, but without any living reference there's no way to know for sure how the words of a dead language are pronounced. So, if there's any truth to legend, this is how Adam and Eve once spoke to each other in paradise. Now, the next part I'll show you is my interpretation of these words."

Monroe laid before them another sheet of paper.

I have prepared new faith beginning mysteries. At the Hekhál successfully of living breath of true aging secret wisdom.

Bishop read the translation out loud.

"It's pretty much a literal translation," Monroe said.

"This is it?" Jennifer asked. "Not to be impatient," she added as the two men looked at her.

"Two sentences to go. Keep in mind, it's the best I can make of it. I was kind of hoping it might make sense to you."

"Not yet," Bishop replied.

"What is a Hekhál?" Jennifer asked.

Bishop and Monroe looked at each other.

"Be my guest," Bishop said.

"Okay," Monroe replied before turning to Jennifer. "Hekhál in Hebrew means 'holy place,' but it's generally referred to in relation to the Aron Kodesh or ark. It's most commonly used by the Sephardi Jews to describe the ark in a synagogue or on a rabbi's grave. It's usually some kind of receptacle or ornamental casket, which contains the Torah scrolls, sometimes held in a chest or a jar."

"A Torah scroll," Bishop added, "is a long roll of paper containing the entire text of the five books of Moses, handwritten in the original Hebrew. Four times a week, on Shabbat morning, Shabbat afternoon, and on Monday and Thursday mornings, the complete work is read out loud."

"And the cabinet containing the scroll always points to Israel," Monroe added. "If you've ever seen pictures of the inside of a synagogue, it's usually kept behind a curtain, a parokhet, usually a red or blue one."

Jennifer frowned realizing she knew very little about Jewish tradition. Her parents were atheists and as such they had never made a point of teaching her other beliefs, though her father often worked with religious books and relics. 'If God created the world he would have made sure we all would believe in the same thing,' her father liked to say to her.

"So, what about the next sentence?" she asked.

Monroe unfolded another piece of paper revealing the next part.

The stone has the truth when the sun is highest over the mountain.

Monroe looked at the two visitors to see if they recognized anything. Jennifer's face had a large question mark written all over it while it was clear Bishop's mind was working overtime. Both remained quiet for a moment before Bishop pointed at his backpack, gesturing to Jennifer to hand it over.

Bishop reached inside and took out the crystal and papers. With the crystal in his hand, he pointed at the second sentence.

"Remember what we saw in the hotel room?" he asked.

Jennifer stammered a negative response while Monroe shrugged his shoulders as he leafed through the papers.

"All right, well, starting at the second sentence, which I believe to be the actual first sentence, I think I have some idea. The only difference between a stone and an emerald is that emeralds have repeating crystalline molecular patterns. Not for nothing, we say things like 'that's a nice stone' when we talk about a diamond in a ring. Then there's the sun, coming over the mountain."

"The light on the crystal," Jennifer interrupted now seeing where Bishop was going.

"Exactly," Bishop replied. Turning to Monroe, who was still in the dark, he took a small flashlight from his bag and pointed the light directly at the crystal. On the desk, the irregular green hexagon appeared. Bishop turned the crystal and the shape kept its form. "Nifty, isn't it?"

"May I?" Monroe asked, and he took hold of the flashlight to repeat the action. "That's odd, indeed. The shape only changes with the angle of the light, but not when rotating the crystal. Must somehow be the way it is cut."

Bishop nodded. "I bet we have to use a light source in combination with the crystal to reveal something. But what and how?" Bishop turned his head away, distracted. He then mumbled the first sentence again. "I have prepared...."

"What about the last one?" Jennifer asked pointing at the paper.

"Ah, yes, the last one." Monroe unfolded the complete paper.

The start to secret wisdom miceth reveals itself in the graves three all-powerful men in the holy land god.

"This was the easiest one to translate," Monroe revealed, still fascinated by the light and the crystal. "I mean, the one with the least interpretation possible."

"So, what do you think it means?" Jennifer asked glancing at Monroe, whose experiments were reflecting shards of green light throughout the room.

"Do you want to answer your friend?" Monroe asked Bishop.

"Sure," Bishop replied. "The holy land of God usually refers to the promised land—Israel—although the borders of that land have been highly disputed over the years, centuries for that matter. Apparently, we start by finding three graves to gain... um... something eternal, I guess. Or something forever, for all time, in perpetuity, eternally, and so on. The word *miceth* can mean a lot of things, but most meanings have something to do with a very long time."

"But a very long time what?" Jennifer grinned. "So, we need to travel to Israel and find three graves to reveal our mystery? But isn't Israel kind of a big country?"

"We don't know the exact age of the document," Bishop replied. "But given the date of the other documents from the box, let's say 400 years ago. At that time, Israel didn't exist. It was part of the Ottoman empire of Syria. At that time, the Ottoman empire was vast and it consisted of parts of what we now know to be Yemen, Jordan, Cyprus, Israel, Palestine, Syria, Lebanon and even parts of Egypt."

"I get it," Jennifer said. "It's an even bigger place to look for three graves."

Bishop conceded after a small pause. "I think we may need some time to mull this over. What do you think?" he asked Monroe, who didn't immediately reply. "Walker?"

Monroe was completely fixated on the green light shining from the emerald onto the Aldaraia papers. Bishop and Jennifer gazed at the librarian and followed the shards of light as they danced around like green fireflies upon the letters on the table.

"What—"

"Do you see that?" Monroe asked, interrupting Jennifer.

"Indeed, I do," Bishop replied, leaving Jennifer lost. "What was that second sentence?"

Jennifer picked up the text from the desk. "The stone has the truth when the sun is highest over the mountain."

Monroe ran his fingers along the oval sides of the crystal's bottom. After finishing rotating he repeated the movement on the oval shape at the top of the Aldaraia page showing the table filled with letters.

"They're identical," Bishop said as Monroe placed the object on top of the shape on the paper. Pointing the flashlight at the crystal, six shards of light pointed directly at seemingly random letters.

"When the sun is highest over the mountain?" Monroe asked.

"Must be a time," Bishop answered. "Noon."

Monroe now moved the flashlight exactly to the top of the crystal. They all held their breath as the six shards of light moved over the paper to stop on six individual letters.

"I-L-U-R-I-A," Jennifer said, spelling out the letters. "Iluria. Does that word mean anything to you?"

"Not as a word," Monroe replied as he fired up the laptop on the table. On the opening screen, he typed *Iluria* into the search box and a page of results immediately appeared concerned with e-commerce programming tools.

"That's probably not it," Bishop said.

"You think?" Monroe quipped while typing in *Iluria* again. The next result on the page gave details of a neuropsychologist named Aleksandr Loeria. "Nope," muttered Monroe before pointing the mouse to the next name on the list. "Isaac Luria," he said. "Of course, that's him. That must be our man. Stupid. I should have recognized it immediately."

"Who is Isaac Luria?" Jennifer demanded.

"Aren't you glad you came to me?" Monroe asked Bishop.

"Yeah, yeah," Bishop answered. "We're very glad we came to you. Now tell us who this is."

"Thank you," Monroe said smiling before turning to Jennifer. "You see, this subject is right up my alley. I wrote several papers on the region and the Kabbalistic school of Safed. Safed is considered to be, by many, the birthplace of the Kabbalah and also one of Judaism's four holy cities along with Jerusalem, Hebron and Tiberias. It is thought that when in Matthew 5:14, Jesus says, '*Ye are the light of the world. A city that is set on a hill cannot be hidden,*' he actually talks about Safed. At 3,000 feet, Safed is the highest city in Israel."

Bishop nodded his head toward Jennifer. "It's true. We came to the best. I'm afraid I must admit it."

Monroe wrote 'Isaac ben Solomon Luria Ashkenazi of Safed' on the paper beneath the translation and turned it toward Bishop and Jennifer. For a moment they both read it.

"Also called *Ha'ARI*, Holy Lion, Luria was a mysterious sixteenth-century rabbi," Monroe continued, clearly reveling in his expertise. "He was born in Jerusalem and grew up in what is now Egypt. He spent most of his life there studying the Talmud and the Zohar. When he was thirty-five he returned to Israel—Safed to be precise. That was two years before his death."

"And what made him so mysterious and special?" Bishop asked.

"Luria was a mystical poet who, later in life, taught the Kabbalah. In his last years in Safed it has been said he revolutionized the Kabbalah—until then it had been taught to only a small group of insiders for the past 1,500 years—making it accessible to the masses. He also founded a new school in Kabbalistic thought, known as 'the system of the Ari.' Though he didn't write much down, his followers created scriptures from his teachings. Some of them considered him to be a saint while others thought him to be the *Mashiakh*, the Messiah."

"A Jewish Messiah?" Jennifer asked, looking puzzled.

"Ah, you thought only Christians had a Messiah." Monroe shook his head. "Though the Torah doesn't speak directly of a Messiah it does contain several references to the *acharit ha-yamim*, the 'end of days' at which the time for the 'world to come' starts. A new world ruled by the King Messiah."

"Didn't know that," Bishop admitted. "So, three graves hold an eternal secret, starting with the grave of Luria?"

"It does seem so." Monroe started typing on the laptop again. On the screen, a picture of a blue concrete sarcophagus in front of a gray concrete wall materialized. The base of the sarcophagus was filled with burning candles next to kneeling and praying rabbis.

"What's that?" Jennifer asked pointing to a large metal chain wrapped around the grave.

"According to the Talmud, when someone dies, their soul continues to dwell for a while in the grave he is buried in. Putting on a chain symbolically keeps the soul tied to this world to comfort the living."

"Sounds a bit selfish. And uh, what about uh... what was it called?" Jennifer asked. "The Hekhál?"

"Very good. The ark," Monroe replied, scrolling down the image on the screen to the top of the gravestone where a small glass cabinet with what looked like a small chimney on the top appeared. Behind the glass was a cylindrical object about a foot high and four inches in diameter.

Both Bishop and Jennifer leaned toward the screen. "The Ark," they said simultaneously.

Monroe nodded and smiled with satisfaction. "And now that I've done my part, are you going to fill me in?"

"What do you mean?" Bishop asked glancing away from the screen.

"What's this all about? What happened in Poland and what am I helping you with?"

Bishop looked at Jennifer gesturing she might like to explain.

"He's your friend," she replied.

Bishop took a deep breath. "All right, but for now I need you to keep everything we tell you under wraps. We have no idea what we are dealing with yet."

Monroe nodded and Bishop explained from the beginning, starting with the Łaski papers bought by Jennifer's father at auction, the clue that led them to the cathedral in Poznań, the bishop's grave in the stained-glass window and, finally, the dead priest.

"Wow," Monroe replied. "And you think this man was linked to the Christian Kabbalah?"

"The priest, Father Matula," Bishop answered, "wore a scarlet string. A similar looking string we saw later on a different priest being interviewed about Matula's death."

"That's some coincidence," Jennifer added. "And especially interesting given our latest findings in regard to Isaac Luria."

"A bit too coincidental for my tastes," Bishop said.

"Which is all well and good, but do we have any idea what this is all about?" Jennifer asked.

"That is a good question, if not the only question," Monroe told her and both of them looked at Bishop.

Raising his eyebrows, Bishop took a deep breath. "Well, there's no way to know for sure at this point," he said opening his hands in apology. "But reading the text, I would think the secret revolves around the words living, breathing and age or aging."

"Sounds like an Oil of Olay commercial," Monroe joked.

"Everlasting beauty?" Jennifer said, finding common ground between the joke and a sincere question.

"Who knows," Bishop answered smiling. "It could mean a lot of things. I don't think that whoever wrote the messages wanted us to know. At least not now and not with the information at hand."

"I could always use a better day cream," Jennifer said playfully. "So, what do we do now?"

"Now we rest," Bishop answered. "We get a good night's sleep and then we decide what to do."

"Not so easy for me," Monroe said. "I'm drowning in work preparing for the new season so I'll be here when you need me."

"Understood. We'll talk again in the morning," Bishop replied.

"I'll walk you out," Monroe said.

On their way to the exit, Bishop tore the paper with the translated sentences in three equal parts in between the sentences and handed them out.

Jennifer raised an eyebrow at Bishop.

"Just in case," he told her. "It's symbolic. We all carry an equal piece of the puzzle now."

CHAPTER 15

Demon Est Deus Inversus

Jennifer's apartment was actually a garage converted into a guesthouse in the back of her aunt's garden, but the white-painted conversion had all the comforts she needed: a living room, bathroom and kitchen on the ground floor and a bedroom attic beneath the slanted roof. At the back of the house was a small river where, in the summer, she loved to watch the pleasure boats pass by.

Waking with the first rays of the sun as they seeped in through the two skylights, Jennifer was always quick to begin her daily routine. With close to military discipline, it never took her more than thirty minutes to get ready, from waking up to closing the door behind her as she left for the day.

As she put on her jeans, she felt a piece of paper in her back pocket and took it out. While drinking her morning smoothie she read the lines to herself. "The secret wisdom eternal reveals itself in the graves three all-powerful men in the holy land god. Isaac ben Solomon Luria Ashkenazi of Safed." Jennifer hummed to herself as she lay the paper on the coffee table then, looking at her watch, she stood up with alarm, grabbed her coat from the rack, put in her earbuds and, as the first hip-hop beat by The Black Eyed Peas sounded, left her apartment, jumped on her bike and rode away at speed.

As Jennifer cycled, she didn't notice the car driving up to the house. Once she'd turned the corner, the car stopped in front of the driveway.

"Professor?" Jennifer called out as she opened the door to the office only to be met with silence. As she walked into the empty room she realized that they hadn't actually agreed on a time to meet when they last spoke. *It could be a long wait,* she thought. Sitting down behind Bishop's desk, she took out her cellphone and texted.

Am at your office. Where are you?

Finished, she stared at the screen for a minute. There was no reply and, just as she released a huge sigh, the door to the office opened and in walked Bishop.

"Matthew, what happened to you? And by the way, you left your door open," Jennifer said as she looked at his unshaven face, the unkempt mop of red curls and the clothes that looked suspiciously like the ones he was wearing the day before. "Rough night?" she asked.

"And an early start," Bishop answered. "I slept upstairs. Or, rather, I didn't sleep much because my mind was constantly trying to work out what to do with the information at hand."

Jennifer waited a short time to see what was coming, but Bishop was struggling to keep his eyes open and looked like he might doze off any minute. "Please sit down." She stood up and offered him the chair.

He took a deep breath as he sat down. "I think that I've found a way—if you want to, that is—for us to check out Safed."

Jennifer could hardly contain her enthusiasm. "We can go?" she asked, trying not to smile.

"This morning I talked to several of the university's departments looking for acknowledgment and funding for our project."

"And?"

"Let me start off by saying that not everyone at Yale is a morning person and my actions won't win any popularity contests in the near future, but...." Bishop paused and Jennifer raised her hands, beckoning for more. "After an hour or so I received notice from the departments of anthropology, religious studies and mathematics, all granting a small budget that should be enough providing we don't travel all over the globe pursuing this quest."

Jennifer walked up to the professor with her arms outstretched. As she neared, he pushed his chair away and raised a finger. "There's one more thing. Linguistic Anthropology has agreed to a four-point course credit should you write a paper about the subject and get it approved."

Jennifer felt excitement surge through her body as she finally lost control over her enthusiasm. In two big steps, she reached the professor and hugged him tightly.

"We're going!" she cheered, making a small dance through the office before abruptly stopping. "When are we going?"

"We can leave as soon as we make travel arrangements. So, I guess I don't have to ask if you want to go?"

Instead of answering, Jennifer resumed dancing.

Demon Est Deus Inversus

"The Devil is God inverted." Kether spoke to Malkuth as he read from the brass plaque on the wall. "William Butler Yeats took on this motto when he was initiated into our order in 1890. Good and evil, spirit and matter as separate conceptions can only exist by their mutual conflict."

On the plaque below the motto was the inscription *1890* instead of a name. The order had always kept the identity of their members secret in order to protect them from the prejudices of the public, and also each other.

Not completely understanding Kether's explanation about the plaque, Malkuth stroked the sign in admiration before looking at the rest of the plaques on the wall. It was next to the room where, just a short time ago, he himself had been initiated into the order.

"I remember now," Malkuth said. "There is no evil per se. Our concept of pure evil comes from our own inability to take in the whole at a single glance." Malkuth gave his own interpretation of Yeats's words from the plaque. "You taught me well, and I'm still grateful, master."

Five years ago, the young man now known as Malkuth ran into a packed bar after a failed heist on a post office. With just about every cop in London searching for him, he had stumbled into the bar backward, facing the door and expecting the police to follow. Seconds later, he stumbled over a chair, fell flat on his back and looked up and into the face of this man he now admired so much. He had introduced himself as Simpson, stretching out an arm. "You're lost?" the man had asked as he helped him up, just as the silhouette of a police officer appeared on the frosted glass of the door to the bar. After a quick nod to the barkeeper, Simpson pulled the young man into a back room. In silence, they waited there until the barkeeper had convinced the policeman he'd seen and heard nothing, and everyone else in the bar confirmed that fact. From that moment on, the young man knew Simpson to be a man of influence. "I don't know what kind of trouble you're in, but I think I can help you," Simpson had told him as he stroked his goatee. It would take another year before he revealed himself as Kether. From that moment on, the teachings on the ways of the order had kept him on track, away from his drunken mother and his abusive father and their premonition that he would never achieve anything in life.

"What was it you wanted to see me about?" Kether asked.

Malkuth reached into his pocket and took out a folded, wrinkled piece of paper. After carefully unfolding it, he ironed it on the altar with his hands before handing it to Kether.

Kether read the text on the torn piece of paper.

> *The secret wisdom eternal reveals itself in the graves three all-powerful men in the holy land god. Isaac ben Solomon Luria Ashkenazi of Safed.*

"Israel," he mumbled. "Thank you. You did good."

"Thank you, master. But I'm afraid I failed you on my last assignment. The priest was fragile, more fragile than I had anticipated. I never meant to hurt anybody. I never hurt anybody in my life."

"I know. I understand, and according to our tradition, you choose your own path of punishment. For now, I need you to continue your assignment and follow the message on the paper."

Kether put his hands on Malkuth's shoulders, pushing him down onto his knees in front of him.

"Long has thou dwelt in darkness, quit the night and seek the day of a new golden dawn." As Kether spoke he placed his hands on the younger man's bald head. From the altar he picked up a paper bag and handed it to Malkuth who replied with a simple complying nod.

"I won't let you down again."

"I know," Kether said. "Now, rise." And Malkuth, being a head taller than Kether towered over the man again. "I have something else for you," Kether said, handing over a heavy object wrapped in brown cotton. Malkuth unwrapped the cloth and a bright shiny brass plaque revealed itself.

> *Latet enim veritas, sed nihil pretiosius veritate.*
> *Truth is hidden, but nothing is more beautiful than the truth.*
> *2018*

Unable to hide his emotions, Malkuth shed a tear as he rested his head on his master's chest.

"It's okay, my son," Kether replied, realizing the truth of his own words. Malkuth was like a son to him, the son he'd never had. In some ways it felt like compensation for the loss of his wife and unborn son who perished more than fifteen years ago. It was a case of wrong time and place when the Real IRA, a splinter group of the provisional IRA, exploded a 100-pound bomb in a gray Saab 9000 on Ealing Broadway in West London. Though he had found his way back to the order following the tragedy he knew he would never find his way back to a normal life and normal family. But now he realized he had a son again who loved him. "I'm proud of you, my son," he said, taking back the plaque. "When you return from your trip, your motto will be up on the wall. Now go, and may Isis guide you on your way."

On the corner of Blythe Road and Hazlitt Road, Kether had rented a single room apartment for Malkuth just above an Indian restaurant. Though he didn't care much for the smell, Malkuth appreciated it as the home he never had. The fifteen by fifteen-foot room was furnished to a basic level: a bed, a desk and a dining table all previously owned and in various styles and colors. They were the only items in the room.

As Malkuth walked in, he placed a paper package next to him as he sat on the bed and started to undress. Once he was naked, he unwrapped the package and took out a brownish piece of cloth, about six by three feet tall with a large hole cut in the center, big enough for a head to go through. From his studies with the order, Malkuth recognized the cilice, also known as a hair shirt. The cilice was an undergarment made of goat hair and burlap that was worn to mortify the flesh in either atonement or simply to strengthen the spirit. Charlemagne and Ivan the Terrible were buried in them to repent for their sins in the afterlife.

Malkuth put the cloth over his head and tied the burlap rope around his waist. He knew he had to atone for his sins in Poland and would not remove the cloth from his body before his assignment was finished.

With his head lowered, Kether finished his prayer in front of the statue of Isis.

"...Oh, Heavenly Isis, in sending us your spirit you open the way to eternal life. May my sharing in this gift increase my love and make my belief grow stronger. Give me your spirit to cleanse my life so that my offering to you may please you and reward me with the eternity of heavenly life. Thou art the kingdom and the power and the glory, forever. Amen." Crossing his heart, he walked away and took his cellphone from his pocket, quickly punching in numbers.

"You have news?" demanded a gravelly voice.

"Yes, sir," Kether replied obediently. "We've learned that the trail to our destiny leads to Israel. We have a location, but no specific details yet."

"Good," the man replied. "You see, I told you your boy was ready."

Kether fell silent for a moment wondering whether or not he should tell his employer about the incident in Poland. He held him responsible for the death because he had said Malkuth wasn't yet ready and killing the priest was proof of that. On the other hand, telling him such a thing might lead to unwanted attention.

"You were right, sir," he finally said. "And we'll continue to follow any leads."

"Do so and keep me informed. Whatever they find we can't allow it to go public. Not at any cost." He then reiterated the comment. "At any cost."

"You've been clear on that many times, sir. We'll do our job. You just keep your promise."

CHAPTER 16

The Ark

The airplane suddenly dropped thirty feet and the cries of shocked passengers rang around the cabin.

"Hello, this is your captain speaking," a calm voice said over the intercom. "We're very sorry for the inconvenience. We're flying through some air pockets due to the extremely warm weather below us and the cold weather above us. Please remain seated with your seatbelts fastened as we'll be landing safely in a few minutes at Rosh Pina airport. Thank you."

Immediately after the announcement, the plane dropped another ten feet or so and the nineteen passengers on board the small Beechcraft 1900 propeller plane strapped their seatbelts even tighter and clung on to their armrests and, in some cases, other passengers. The domestic flight from Tel Aviv had taken only thirty minutes—thirty sweaty minutes, according to Bishop.

"Take it easy. We'll be on the ground in a few minutes," Jennifer said, trying to reassure Bishop, glancing at his white knuckles as he gripped the armrest between them. Turning to the window, Jennifer saw the green of the Meron forest broken by a brown sand hill upon which the city of Safed was built. Minutes after passing the city, the plane made its final descent.

"I'll never get used to these small airplanes," Bishop said as the wheels hit the ground. Five minutes later, the plane was parked, the door was opened and he released a huge sigh of relief as he prepared to disembark after cleansing his hands with sanitizer. "Now, let's get a taxi and go to the hotel."

With 30,000 inhabitants, Safed was a relatively small city that grew exponentially in the summer thanks to tourists seeking any kind of enlightenment. Although Safed's Kabbalah background was world famous, few of the tourists could fulfill the long-term commitment the study demanded. And yet they kept coming. However, as it was now late in the year, most tourists had left and everyone working in the tourist industry had either gone home or taken up their winter professions.

The taxi took them to 11 Simtat Yud Zain, stopping at the door of the hotel Azamra Inn Tzfat located in the Old Jewish Quarter of Safed and only a fifteen-minute, half-mile walk through the hills from the old Jewish cemetery. It was a narrow street and the building was made of Meleke stones, a cream-colored, coarse crystalline limestone found in the mountains between Jerusalem and Safed. Once inside, Bishop and Jennifer found their room was also finished with Meleke, giving it an ancient look.

"One room again?" Jennifer observed.

"But much more classy and spacious," Bishop replied. "Are you wearing that?" Bishop pointed to her T-shirt as he unpacked before pausing to hand her a scarf from her own case. "I know the weather is warm for this time of year, and while your jeans may be just about tolerated, your naked arms may present more of a problem. You better cover them up when we go."

Jennifer took the red scarf and draped it over her shoulders. "Better?"

Bishop nodded as he put on his backpack. "Shall we go?"

As the two left the hotel to begin their half-mile walk downhill, Malkuth stepped out of a car from across the street. Keeping some distance between them, he followed on foot.

"The Kabbalah keeps coming up," Jennifer observed as they walked the narrow streets of the old city.

"It sure looks like that," Bishop replied. "Though Monroe is more expert on the subject, I've never heard of anything like the lost secrets of the Kabbalah. Kabbalists are usually known as a peaceful people who keep to themselves."

"I always thought the Kabbalah was a Jewish splinter group that practiced some kind of witchcraft."

"Well, that's both right and wrong. The ecstatic Kabbalah is all about finding wisdom and the true meaning of God through meditation. It has an occult aspect, but it's almost always of a peaceful nature. The theosophical Kabbalah is more associated with violent rituals and black magic. A very well-known example is the ritual of

Pulsa Dinora, meaning Lashes of Fire. Basically, it's a ceremonial prayer invoking angels of destruction who are asked to forgive a sinner his sins. The drawback to this forgiveness is the death of the subject. The performing of the *Pulsa Dinora* is prohibited by the *Halacha,* the Jewish Law and yet it's believed to be practiced in military disputes and politics. But more generally, the Kabbalah were of Judaist origin. They studied the deeper thoughts behind the Torah, the first five chapters of the Tanakh, the Hebrew Bible.

"The five books of Moses," Jennifer added smugly.

"I see you paid attention. Indeed, you're right. The five books of Moses are comparable to the first five chapters of the Old Testament. That's Bereshit for Genesis, Shemot for Exodus, Vayikra for Leviticus, Bemidbar for Numbers and Devarim for Deuteronomy." Bishop suddenly stopped walking after turning the corner onto HaAri Street. "There it is," he said, putting a hand on Jennifer's head, turning it to the left, facing downhill.

Jennifer's eyes widened. "Wow."

A huge wooden staircase snaked through the downhill landscape for hundreds of yards. All across the terrain, as far as the eye could see, the flanks of the staircase were filled with graves. Although tradition forbade above-ground burial, the traditional Jewish graves were simple concrete or brick layered sarcophaguses that stood above ground simply because the rocky soil on the mountain was too hard to dig graves below the surface. Some of the graves had large matzeivah's, the Jewish variation of headstones, others bore simple plaquettes on top of the sarcophagus while others had been weathered by time and the elements to a single stone, some of them more than 2,000 years old and hidden between large thistle fields. Between the graves, upon the footpaths, a few men and women walked and prayed.

"That's good," Bishop said. "It seems to be a quiet day."

"There must be more than a thousand graves," Jennifer said in wonder.

"There are," Bishop replied. "Jewish law prohibits cremation or any other kind of desecration of the body. All the dead should be buried."

"Why are some of them painted blue?" Jennifer pointed at the blue spots on the terrain.

"In Jewish, and more specifically Kabbalah, tradition, blue is considered a 'low color.' The Zohar teaches that all colors are a good omen except for blue. Blue is considered a bad sign. The working theory here is that by painting the tomb blue it filters out the blue, or bad influences on the grave."

"This is turning out to be quite an educational trip," Jennifer joked before pointing at two large, decorated, brick-layered, arched gateways halfway down the wooden stairs. "That must be the entrance."

"That would be *my* entrance." Bishop grinned as he started descending the stairs. "Yours will be over there." He pointed at the right side of the arches.

In the distance, Jennifer noticed a small iron gate designated for female visitors.

"I know. I'm privileged," he said with a smile.

As they made their way to their own entrances, Bishop pointed to a corner in the distance where they would meet again. "See you in a few," he said.

Meanwhile, from the top of the hill, Malkuth watched in confusion.

Having reached their rendezvous point, Bishop and Jennifer headed for the grave of Isaac Luria.

"I'm afraid we'll have to split up again," Bishop said, nodding at a sign showing two arrows pointing to different sides of the road. Under each arrow was a word in Hebrew.

"You can read it?" Jennifer asked.

"Men, women," Bishop confirmed, pointing to the left and right of the sign. "I can read some Hebrew, but don't expect too much. Just follow the path and it should bring you to the back of the grave. My path will lead to the front. We won't be able to see each other, but we should be able to talk to each other. Please wait for my call and when you hear me you can join me at the front."

Jennifer nodded and continued on her way. As Bishop walked toward Luria's grave, a small group of people wearing tallits—Jewish prayer shawls—passed him.

"Shalom," the men mumbled.

"Shalom," Bishop mumbled back, giving a small nod just as he felt his cellphone vibrating in his pocket. After unlocking it with his fingerprint he read the message from Walker.

The word from Poland is that the priest's death was no accident but murder.

Bishop sighed. It was clear it couldn't be a coincidence, meaning they were not the only ones looking for answers to this mystery.

Wondering whether or not to tell Jennifer, he walked up to Luria's tomb. The grave was nothing more than a blue painted stone sarcophagus about two feet wide, five feet long and two feet high. On top of it was a large, blue bulb, like a hood scoop on the hood of a car. Less than two feet away from the next tomb, the grave was hidden among dozens of similar graves. Behind the sarcophagus was a black tombstone engraved with silver letters. Bishop's knowledge of Hebrew was just enough to translate small pieces of it, including a mention of the Holy Lion, which was Luria's nickname.

Some thirty yards further up the hillside, Malkuth watched from behind a large tombstone. Raising his head just over the stone, he lifted a pair of digital recording binoculars to his eyes. With the sun descending behind him, he had a perfect view of Luria's grave and of Bishop's back bending over it.

The sarcophagus was almost completely covered with spent tealights. If this was the product of one day's devotion, Bishop could only wonder how the grave would look after a week. Bishop checked if the coast was clear before calling out to Jennifer. "Are you there?" Except for some birds chirping in the distance, the graveyard remained silent. Louder now, Bishop called again. "Are you there?"

"Yes," came the hushed reply from behind and slightly above the grave. "I'm here."

"Can you see anyone near you?"

"There's no one here."

"Good. Can you come over here?"

"I'll try, but I need to find a way to get down from here."

Bishop heard the crunch of footsteps on the graveled path.

Despite nearly losing her footing on the pebbles, Jennifer turned the corner of Luria's grave. For a moment she thought she saw something moving in the near distance and stopped to look up at the hillside.

"What is it?" Bishop asked.

Stupid, Malkuth berated himself, wondering whether the woman had seen him. Panting with adrenaline, he decided to stay out of sight for the time being, knowing that if the two of them decided to take a closer look there would be no place to hide.

"I thought I saw something moving," Jennifer told Bishop who also cast his eyes over the graveyard.

"I don't see anything. Must have been a bird or lizard or a desert lynx. Maybe even a snake."

"Snake?"

"Sure," Bishop teased. "Didn't you know that Israel is home to ten different types of viper?" He rolled his eyes.

Jennifer responded by punching him in the shoulder.

"Ouch," he said, feigning pain. "That doesn't make it any less true." Turning back to Luria's grave and spreading his arms he told her, "Here we are."

"It looks a lot... um... what's the word?"

"Simpler, smaller?"

"Yeah, I guess that's it," Jennifer said. "It looked much bigger in Monroe's picture."

"You must keep in mind that although many of the Jews buried here became famous for their beliefs and research, they were essentially poor men who chose to live a life of poverty."

Jennifer nodded "Are those...?" She didn't finish the question, pointing instead to three padlocked candle boxes, each housing a metal canister.

"The Ark," Bishop confirmed. "Only there are three instead of one."

"Which one do we need and how do we open it?" Jennifer asked, pointing to the padlocks on each ark.

Bishop ran his hands through his hair. "I actually have no idea which one we might need, but I don't think opening them will be a problem." He tapped at his backpack before taking it off. "May I suggest you just choose one."

"Me?"

"Sure, why not? Your guess is as good as mine."

Jennifer nodded, thinking Bishop was probably right. The ark on the left was the only one painted blue and it was weathered by age while the other two looked like they were made of stainless steel now reflecting a bronze glow from the setting sun. "I'd go for the left one."

"Any particular reason?" Bishop asked while searching in his backpack.

"It looks like the oldest."

"That would have been my guess too," Bishop admitted as he took a small leather etui containing a set of metal pins from his backpack.

"You pick locks too?" Jennifer asked, stupefied.

"Fifteen dollars on a Chinese website for the tools and a fifteen-minute course online, courtesy of WikiHow." Bishop smiled.

Walking up to the ark he put on his gloves and took a good look over the valley of the graveyard where the light-colored graves now glowed orange. "Can you please stand guard?" he asked before turning to inspect the padlock.

Jennifer immediately turned around to survey the graveyard as Bishop inserted two metal pins into the padlock and started tinkering. When Jennifer heard the lock spring open after just a few seconds she turned around in amazement.

"Please keep watching," Bishop told her as he took the lock off, opened the door and took out the canister. With a grunt, he tried to unscrew the top lid but his hand slipped. After drying it on his jacket he tried again. Another grunt followed as the lid came off only to slip from Bishop's hand and fall on the ground, rolling a few yards down the stony hill. The clatter of metal on stone echoed loudly through the valley and as the lid rolled past Jennifer she immediately put her foot on it. Startled, she looked back at Bishop who was busy checking their surroundings to see if anyone had heard. There was nothing to see and his heart hammered with relief.

"You opened the middle one," Jennifer noted.

"Sorry," Bishop replied. "I had a hunch."

"What kind of hunch?"

"Well, the blue one is probably the oldest, but it's not old enough to contain the original contents. The one in the center is probably newer but I'd say the center place will undoubtedly be the one containing the most important, original content."

Jennifer shook her head in exasperation.

"Spur of the moment choice," Bishop added, smiling.

"So, what's in it?"

Bishop kneeled down, took a flashlight from his backpack and lit the inside of the cylinder. "Papers," he said, using a finger to carefully check for signs of deterioration, but it felt pretty sturdy. He then turned the cannister over. Cautiously shaking it, a roll of paper slowly slid out. Jennifer came to sit next to him. The gray scroll felt heavy, like a stack of papers rather than the single-sheet scroll Bishop had expected to find.

"And?" Jennifer asked. "What do you think?"

"There must be more than fifty documents here," Bishop answered, leafing through the stack of paper. "We'll need to go through them one by one and see if anything stands out.

"Looks like Hebrew," Jennifer said after glancing at the papers.

"So?" Bishop asked.

"Well, maybe there's a quicker way since the first message was in Enochian."

"You're right. Of course, you're right." The corners of Bishop's mouth turned up. He put the stack of paper on the sarcophagus and rapidly leafed through them again. After a minute or so, at about two thirds of the way through the stack, he suddenly stopped and returned to the previous page. Quietly, almost without breathing, he stared at the paper.

"You found something?"

Bishop stayed silent as he took a page from the stack and put it on the grave. Jennifer looked at it and though she couldn't read any of the words, she knew this wasn't Hebrew. She'd seen these strange scribbles before.

"I think that qualifies as standing out," she said with a smile.

The paper was divided into three parts. The few lines of Enochian were followed by what looked like sketches of plants, herbs perhaps, and other symbols. At the bottom of the document were rows with Roman letters and numbers.

"That looks like Latin," Jennifer said.

"It sure does," Bishop confirmed, grabbing his cellphone. "Here, hold it for a second."

Bishop pointed his phone at the paper Jennifer now held and took a few snaps before putting the paper in a tubular case and then in his backpack.

Meanwhile, in the distance, Malkuth followed their every move through his binoculars, also taking pictures. But as he moved, he scraped his binoculars along the tombstone and the sound carried over the empty graveyard.

"Did you hear that?" Jennifer asked.

The two kept absolutely still. With the birds and most of the wildlife gone for the evening, the graveyard was quiet.

"I didn't hear anything," Bishop replied while scouring the surroundings. With the sun now pretty much gone the graveyard had an eerie look about it with single candles here and there burning in the valley.

"I think we better get out of here quickly," he said, rolling up the other documents and returning them to the metal case and back into the ark, which he then locked. He quickly sanitized his hands, threw his backpack over his shoulder and tilted his head to Jennifer. "Shall we?"

CHAPTER 17

RX

From the top of the hill they took a last look down into the valley just as the floodlights came on. The amber lights reflected off the light-colored graves, making it look like the place was on fire. Jennifer stopped for a second, soaking up the scene.

"What are you thinking?" Bishop asked.

"That it's impressive," Jennifer replied. "Such a wide area, so many people, all of them dead and buried. I was thinking about the knowledge all these people once had. Now gone."

"Why did you think about that?" he asked as they walked away.

"Well, I was thinking about my father and all the knowledge he had before he died. Only parts of that knowledge survived in his writings." Jennifer teared up.

"Is that why you're here?" Bishop asked. "To gather the knowledge that was lost with your father?"

Jennifer thought for a long moment. "I'm not sure. Maybe. That and the fact that he died mysteriously. For those last years of his life he was barely reachable as there were so few lucid moments. I always had, and still have, the feeling there was more to it than simple bad luck that he fell sick."

"Well, it's entirely plausible we'll find out more about his unfortunate circumstances on our trip and, if it's any consolation, Kabbalists believe only the body perishes. Knowledge is forever."

Jennifer looked at Bishop in disbelief.

"Don't dismiss it out of hand. I can't tell you the specifics. You need Monroe for that, but the Kabbalah theory isn't just based on faith, but also on science. You should talk to Monroe some time."

Jennifer gave a sad smile and they continued to walk up Simtat Yud Zain toward their hotel. Due to the lack of streetlights, the hotel stood out even from a distance, especially as the street was deserted. As they neared the hotel, a taxi drove away leaving a large, dark-skinned man standing at the curb with a single suitcase next to him. Bishop recognized the posture immediately.

"As I live and breathe, Walker James Monroe!" Bishop called out and Monroe turned in their direction to watch two silhouettes approach him.

"I'm glad to hear you're still breathing," Monroe called back and within seconds, the two friends came face-to-face, happily shaking hands. As they pulled a way, Monroe acknowledged Jennifer by name with a polite nod of his head.

"What are you doing here?" Bishop asked. "I thought you couldn't leave, snowed under with work, I thought you said."

"Well, that's true, but we also have another beetle infestation in the library, which is one of the biggest threats facing libraries all over the world. Did you know that in the late seventies the death watch beetle ate a serious part of our collection?"

They both shook their heads.

"So, what do you do?" Jennifer asked. "Use bug spray?"

Monroe laughed. "We found a less toxic way to deal with it. After the last infestation, we devised a way to eradicate the paper-eating bugs by freezing the books at minus thirty-three degrees for a few days. They do it all over the world now. That being said, it's a good excuse to be here with you, where the real fun is. So, what have you guys been up to?"

"Have you eaten yet?" Bishop asked.

Monroe shook his head.

"Well, get checked in and we'll order something to eat in our room and fill you in.

Monroe nodded. "Sounds like a plan."

Emerging from the shadows, Malkuth walked past the hotel entrance. At the side of the hotel, grunting like an old man, he sat down on a large Meleke stone clearly feeling uncomfortable in the cilice he wore. Taking out his cellphone, he punched the large K on the home screen.

"How are you doing?" came the reply almost as soon as Malkuth put the phone between the hood and his ear.

"Master," Malkuth said. "I believe they found the second document at the graveyard. I'm not sure if they took it with them. Also, they have just been joined by the Beinecke professor. What do you want me to do?" For a long moment there was silence until Malkuth broke it. "Do you want me to recover the document?"

"No," Kether answered. "How many graves did they visit?"

"Only one. I watched them the whole time."

"And they didn't see you?"

"No, sir. There has been no contact whatsoever."

"Okay, that's good. Now listen, only if there's absolutely no risk of exposing yourself, I want you to photograph the document, but don't take it. They don't need to know we are watching, so don't get seen."

"I understand, master," Malkuth replied before releasing a low grunt.

"Are you okay?" Kether asked. "Are you still punishing yourself?"

"It's nothing, sir. I'll be fine."

"You need to stop punishing yourself."

"But you taught me...."

"You need to stop right there," Kether interrupted. He knew what Malkuth was going to say. In the order, they taught their followers that taking responsibility and punishment for one's actions would reveal the true soul. "If you punish yourself now it could disrupt your mission, which means you would effectively put your soul before the mission."

Though there was some truth to this, Kether had made it up on the spot. He felt his son's agony. Both men fell silent for a moment.

"I think I understand, Father." Malkuth finally replied and Kether gave a huge sigh of relief as a sense of pride washed over him. He had long called Malkuth 'son' but this was the first time Malkuth had called him 'father.'

"That's good, son," he said, struggling to hide his emotions. "Now, find yourself a comfortable place to rest and we'll talk later."

Malkuth pressed the red button on his phone, rose in agony from the stone and walked into the hotel.

Bishop removed a chess set from the small table between the two couches in their room. He rolled out the document from the graveyard on it, weighting the corners with chess pieces.

"Boring game anyway," he grumbled.

"That's because you never win," Monroe told him as he entered the room, admitted by Jennifer.

"Sure," Bishop agreed with a smile.

"Is that it?" Monroe asked, approaching the table with the paper.

"No, this is our travel itinerary," Bishop joked.

Monroe rolled his eyes.

"Gentlemen, behave," Jennifer told them. "Yes, this is the document. We've only had a minute to look at it ourselves so you know just as much as we do. Sit down. Let's talk and eat." Jennifer directed Monroe to another table offering a variety of Israeli finger food. "Date truffles, latke waffles, spicy jalapeño hummus, fried chicken and deep-fried matzah balls."

Monroe glanced at the spread but didn't sit down, instead opting to circle the table, hovering over the document.

"It's quite different from the last one," Monroe stated. "That bit is definitely in Enochian again." He pointed to the top six lines of text. "Shouldn't be much of a problem translating it. I brought some gear with me."

"And what do you make of the plants and symbols?" Bishop asked.

"They're plants, indeed. But I don't recognize any of them."

Both men now looked at Jennifer.

"Don't look at me," she replied. "Wrong study. This next part though." She pointed to what looked like a listing in Latin. At the top left of the message were two letters intertwined.

"Rx?" asked Bishop.

"Rx," Jennifer confirmed firmly. "It stands for the abbreviation of the second person singular imperative form of the Latin word *recipere* which means 'to take.'"

Both men nodded their heads, saying, "Wow."

"I have an uncle with a pharmacy and used to temp there during my holidays. He taught me some history about the business." Jennifer smiled, feeling valued for the first time around Bishop. "Should I go on?"

"Please do," Bishop invited, spreading his arms.

"After the world stopped understanding Greek at the time of the Renaissance, medical linguistics were translated into Latin. From that time, prescriptions always began with the Rx intertwined, 'take thou' followed by the ingredients one would have to take."

"And is this what I think it is?" Monroe asked pointing to the list on the lowest part of the document.

"I don't know what you think, but I can tell you it's a prescription in the form of a recipe. You see, here are the ingredients: *hydrargyrum drachmas quinque*, five drachms of mercury and, here, *tincturae digitalis drachmam unam*, one drachm of digitalis tincture." She then read the other five ingredients on the list.

Bishop looked at Jennifer proudly. "Good job."

"Thank you."

"I think I now understand the pictures on the page," Bishop said, pointing to one of the images.

"Mercury," Monroe revealed.

"They're pictures relating to the ingredients. I bet one of these plants is a digitalis," Bishop said. "In medieval times, digitalis was considered both wonder drug and poison.

"Nice. We need the Enochian translation," Jennifer said, surprising the two men as she now took the lead in their discussion.

Monroe nodded slowly. "You're right, and when you're right, you're right. I'll get my laptop and get to work on it straight away."

Monroe took a few pictures of the text with his cellphone and hurried out of the room. "I'll be right back."

CHAPTER 18

Now, It's My Desire

"Finally, he's gone so we can eat," Bishop joked, taking a date truffle from a plate. "You seem to be having fun."

"I am," Jennifer admitted, her eyes glistening. "You must admit you, too, enjoy fitting together the pieces to an ancient puzzle."

As Bishop smiled in response, Monroe stepped back into the room carrying what looked like a bulky laptop. Bishop looked curiously at the machine as Monroe placed it on the desk.

"I see you looking," Monroe said, noticing Bishop's interest. "The Rocky RF10. Military grade, complete in a NATO green color scheme, well known for its use during military operations for mapping terrain where there's no Internet available."

"Wow, you came prepared then," Bishop replied, helping himself to the abundance of finger food—something that slowly diminished over the course of the next two hours as Monroe clicked away on his machine.

As they waited on the couch, Jennifer dozed off while leaning her head against Bishop's shoulder. She suddenly woke with a start and sat up, noticing Bishop had also fallen asleep. Understanding he wouldn't be stirring any time soon, she placed her head back on his shoulder and nodded off again.

"Now, it's my desire to reveal secrets!" Monroe bellowed exactly as the clock struck twelve.

Without moving an inch, Bishop slowly opened his eyes. "I anticipated a bigger return, but this will do."

Suddenly aware of the weight on his shoulder, Bishop turned his head to see Jennifer sleeping there. He wiggled to let her know it was time to get up.

She grunted, opening her eyes to feel a trail of spittle at the corner of her mouth, which she quickly wiped away.

"I'm sorry," she said as she sat up.

"No problem," Bishop replied, handing her a napkin from the table. He yawned before turning to Monroe. "I gather you finally translated the text?"

"Well, to be precise, I finished some twenty minutes ago, but saying the words exactly at midnight gave it some extra, uh, gravitas, don't you think?"

"What in the world are you talking about?" Bishop asked.

"All right, all right," Monroe said, tempering his enthusiasm. "Not only did I translate the message, I also think it leads us to another place. And I know where that place is."

Bishop and Jennifer, still drowsy from sleep, stared at Monroe.

"Seriously?" Jennifer asked.

Monroe nodded theatrically.

Both Bishop and Jennifer leaped from the couch to flank Monroe at the table.

"Speak," Bishop ordered.

"Okay, first the translation...."

Monroe pressed a key on his laptop and the message appeared on the screen.

> *Now it is my desire to reveal the secret, ending the premise that pain is the sensation of the absence of the upper light.*
>
> *The route to the second point of the Magen David shall be found on the final month of the year at the final hour of atonement.*
>
> *When the house has filled with visitors who entered without my permission follow the line to the truth that's hidden in the sand behind the Luchot HaBrit parokhet.*

"I had to interpret some of the words," Monroe explained, "but I'm sure this translation is as close as can be to the writer's meaning."

Both Bishop and Jennifer mumbled as they read the text.

"You get it?" Monroe asked smugly.

"Sure, we do," Bishop replied, rolling his eyes. "But why don't you tell us just to be sure we're on the same page."

Monroe smiled and raised his eyebrows. "I take it you brought the Aldaraia and the crystal?"

Jennifer and Bishop nodded.

"Great. I don't think we really need them to get to our next location, but it can't hurt to verify a few things. Now, first of all, the opening sentence—'Now it is my desire to reveal the secret'—immediately triggered something in me. Does it ring a bell?"

Bishop and Jennifer shook their heads and Monroe lifted his arms as if preaching.

"Now it is my desire to reveal secrets. The day will not go to its place like any other, for this entire day stands within my domain."

Jennifer looked at Bishop to see if he had any ideas.

"Nothing?" Monroe asked.

They shook their heads again.

"All right then." He sighed. "Shimon bar Yochai."

Monroe paused and Bishop nodded in recognition of the name. Yochai was a second-century rabbi and generally accepted as the author of the Zohar.

"The Kabbalah writings on mystical explanations behind the Torah," Jennifer said as if reading his thoughts.

"Yes, the Zohar, among other writings. Clearly, someone has paid attention in class and done her homework. Written in medieval Aramaic it's also a guidebook on mystical psychology and cosmogony, but it also discusses the nature of God, as in what is or was God. It's not one book, by the way, but a series of books. Yochai is said to have written the books with his son Eliezar, studying the Torah in a cave for thirteen years. For more than ten centuries the book was lost until it was finally recovered by a thirteenth-century rabbi named Moses de León. Some say de León wrote the Zohar himself. But the theory about Yochai is much more romantic I think."

"And what was Yochai's secret?" Jennifer asked. As Monroe looked puzzled, she elaborated. "Now it's time to reveal the secret?"

"Good question, and probably one that has puzzled many for a long time," Monroe answered. "Legend suggests that all the secrets are somehow in the Zohar. It was evening when Yochai spoke the words on his deathbed. The story goes that as he was still finishing his work, daylight mysteriously extended for him so he could complete it. Nowadays, its customary that on his *yahrzeit*—his dying day—all over Israel and also the rest of the world Jews light large bonfires symbolizing the lengthening of daylight on a national holiday of celebration."

"And our next location?" Bishop asked. "You said you already found it?"

"Okay, back to the text," Monroe replied. "The second sentence—'The route to the second point of the Magen David shall be found on the final month of the year at the final hour of atonement.' If you would please take out your copy of the Aldaraia and also the crystal."

Jennifer took the objects from a suitcase and placed them next to Monroe's laptop. Bishop joined them bringing a flashlight.

"Now," Monroe continued. "I'll bet you a month's salary that when you turn to the thirteenth page of the Aldaraia, put the crystal on top and light it with the flashlight at a one o' clock angle we'll see the next grave to visit is Yochai's."

Jennifer quickly leafed to the thirteenth page with tables and placed the crystal on top. Bishop turned on the flashlight and six specks of green light moved on the page as he positioned the light at a one o'clock angle. All three now held their breath as they read the green highlighted letters.

Jennifer read the letters one by one. "Y-O-C-H-A-I."

Monroe sighed in relief, which made Jennifer and Bishop smile.

"Smart work," Bishop told him. "And all that from, 'Now it's time to reveal secrets?'"

"Not exactly. The final sentence starting with, 'When the house has filled with visitors who entered without my permission...' is also a reference to Yochai. Another theory about the lengthening day is that in his final moments people gathered from all over the town to visit his home—believers and unbelievers. He kicked them out and no one without permission was allowed back inside. To prevent people from coming in they lit fires in front of the entrances."

"Hence the bonfires," Bishop concluded.

"Indeed." Monroe looked around the room. "Is there anything stronger here to drink besides this Limonana?" he asked pointing at a carafe holding green liquid made up of lemon and mint juice.

Bishop immediately disappeared for a moment, emerging with a bottle of Macallan double cask, 18-year-old highland whiskey.

"Ah, you brought the good stuff," Monroe said as Bishop took three glasses and started to pour.

"You?" Bishop asked, pointing the flask at Jennifer who shook her head. "Ice?" he asked Monroe.

"No, of course not. You're a barbaric whiskey drinker."

Bishop opened the ice bucket, but it only contained a small pool of water at the bottom.

"Shall I?" Jennifer asked as she stretched out her arm.

"That would be great." Bishop handed her the bucket.

"Be right back," she said.

Once she left, Monroe turned to Bishop. "Did you tell her?"

"Tell her what?"

"About the Polish priest, how he died?"

"Not yet. I didn't see any reason to upset her. We have no idea what it means."

Monroe frowned. "No idea what it means? What else can it mean other than we're not the only ones looking for this secret?"

Bishop squinted and sighed.

In the hallway, Jennifer opened the lid of the large icebox oddly positioned in the hallway, which meant no one could get past as she filled the bucket. When she was done, she stood on her toes to reach for the lid handle, grunting with effort as she finally grabbed hold of it. As she pulled the lid down she was startled to find a man, naked from the waist up, watching her.

"Oh, sorry," Malkuth apologized.

As the lid fell shut Jennifer took a second to get her breath. "No, problem. I just didn't hear you coming."

"Again, I'm sorry. I didn't mean to startle you."

"You're British?" Jennifer asked responding to the accent. "Tourist?"

"You could say that," Malkuth answered cryptically. "You have a good night now."

"Uh, you too," Jennifer replied as she slowly turned away. Walking back through the hallway she waited to hear the man go on his own way, but there was no sound. When she looked behind her the hallway was empty again. *The strong, silent type*, she thought, still overwhelmed as she returned to the room.

Standing behind a corner, Malkuth waited until Jennifer was out of sight before sighing deeply and taking out his cellphone. With a trembling finger he started typing.

Accidentally made contact with the Porter woman. She doesn't know who I am, but saw my face. Please advise. M.

As Malkuth calmed down, his fingers stopped trembling and within a minute he got his answer.

I understand. Don't worry. Just take extra precautions to stay out of sight and don't take unnecessary risks. Just keep an eye on them from a distance. K.

"Ah, ice," Bishop said as he took the bucket from Jennifer. "Something wrong? You look pale."

"No, nothing," she answered. "I just ran into someone in the hallway who startled me."

"Okay then," Bishop said. "Where were we? Oh yes, I think you were about to explain how you knew which page of the Aldaraia we should use and how you found out the correct time for the flashlight."

"Simple," Monroe said. "'The route to the second point of the Magen David shall be found on the final month of the year at the final hour of atonement.' The Jewish calendar has twelve months, but they're completely different from our Gregorian calendar—their months are based on the phases of the moon, and a new month starts every crescent moon. When you add up twelve lunar months you're eleven days short every year so every three years or so they add a thirteenth month to keep in sync. Page thirteen."

"And one o'clock?" Jennifer asked.

"Simple again," Monroe replied. "The time of atonement in Jewish tradition, or Yom Kippur, as they call it, is a period of twenty-five hours of fasting. Twenty-five on a twenty-four-hour clock makes one o'clock.

"Wow," Jennifer said. "I'm truly impressed. And what about the route to the second point on the Magen David?"

"The star of David," Monroe answered. "Not sure about that one. All I can think of is that the star has six points. We already passed one point right here when we found this message. So perhaps the second point on the star represents the second grave."

"But the first message spoke about only three graves," Jennifer recalled.

"That's true. So maybe there's more than just the three graves to the secret." Monroe shrugged his shoulders.

"So, what now?" she asked.

"We go to Meron," Monroe replied. "The grave of Yochai. We get a few hours of good sleep and, in the morning, we drive up there. It's, at most, a ten-mile drive."

"Do we even know what we are looking for?" Jennifer asked.

Bishop read from the laptop screen. "Follow the line to the truth that's hidden in the sand behind the Luchot HaBrit parokhet. Luchot HaBrit must refer to Moses's stone tablets."

"So, we look for stone tablets behind a curtain?" Jennifer asked.

"Not sure what it means exactly," Bishop answered. "But I hope we'll recognize it when we see it."

"We're going?" Monroe asked. Without waiting for an answer he walked to the door. "Around ten?" he asked, leaving and shutting the door behind him before anyone could answer.

"No choice, I guess." Jennifer smiled.

"Would you have it any other way?" Bishop smiled back.

As Monroe walked to his room, he took out his cellphone and dialed. "Hi. Yes, it's me. It seems we were right."

Monroe listened attentively for a moment. "I helped them determine what it is they're looking for."

The voice on the other end grew louder.

"I don't think they do. And besides that, I promised to keep you informed, but I don't answer to you."

The voice on the other end of the line sounded somewhat agitated before softening again.

"I'll do as promised. Trust me, I know what the risks are. I'll stay with them as long as I can. Talk to you later."

CHAPTER 19
Livingston Street

2009

With no streetlights on Livingston Street, Swan House was only visible in the dark because of a single bulb at the door that lit part of the porch. The lack of lights had never bothered Robert Porter, possibly because one of the reasons he had chosen to live in the area was its low crime rate.

Livingston Street skirted East Rock Park and, as usual at that time of night, it was deserted with no cars parked along the curb. A dark sedan emerged from East Rock Road and drove slowly up the street. After some thirty yards the car stopped, park side. A minute later, a male figure dressed in black exited the car from the passenger's side. After mumbling something to the driver, he walked up the street, using the park's trees and bushes as cover. Opposite house number 300, the figure stopped and squatted among the shrubs. After checking out the neighboring homes he ran across the road and over the lawn up to Swan House. Passing the driveway, he snuck up to the side entrance and glanced into the kitchen. Taking a small flashlight, he lit the door lock and inspected it before taking a key ring from his jacket pocket. Silently, he took a single bump key from the ring and inserted it into the lock. From his other pocket, he took a small piece of wood and placed it against the key. With a firm, but not too loud blow, he hit the wood, driving the key into the lock. With a simple twist, the lock clicked open.

For a moment, the figure waited to see if he had woken anyone inside, but there was no sign of movement or lights. The figure quickly went inside, moving through the kitchen and up the stairs. Looking left and right at the bedroom doors, he paused for a moment to check that all was quiet. Clearly knowing his way around, he entered the study and moved toward the safe located behind the desk. He rotated the combination lock: 70 left, 90 right, 62 left, 80 right, 60 left and, finally, 71 right. A click followed. He opened the safe and balanced the flashlight in his mouth as he looked through the contents. After taking out a piggy bank and a metal rectangular box, he picked up a small stack of papers and shone the light on them briefly. A brief grunt followed as he rolled them up and put them in his inside pocket. Leaving the safe as it was, he quickly returned to the hallway, but then just as he put a foot on the stairs he heard a door opening behind him. Glancing back, he saw a young woman staring at him. Startled, the man thundered down the staircase.

Jennifer stood there in silence, frozen to the spot.

"Dad! Dad!" Jennifer cried as Robert Porter, wearing blue striped pajamas, entered the hallway from his bedroom.

"What is it? What happened?" Her father asked, still drowsy from sleep. By the time Jennifer regained her senses, her mother had also joined them, dressed in her nightgown.

"What happened?" Sylvia asked, confused by all the commotion.

"There was a man!"

"What?" her father asked.

"A man!"

Porter hesitated a second before running to the stairs. He only got as far as the first step when he heard the kitchen door slam shut followed by footsteps on the driveway. On pure adrenalin, Porter ran downstairs, almost tripping over himself in his hurry, and sprinted out onto the driveway. Looking right and left, there was no sign of movement along the dark street, but then a car's headlights turned on, an engine roared to life and Porter saw a figure jumping into a vehicle on the passenger side. The door slammed shut, the car shot forward, made a sharp U-turn and sped away in the other direction. Everything happened in seconds and the street was again quiet.

Porter stared ahead of him for a minute before slowly walking back to the house as a light switched on, illuminating the garden. From the kitchen door, Jennifer and Sylvia watched Porter approach.

"Dad, are you okay?" Jennifer cried, pointing to a trail of blood on the path. Porter looked at his feet, seeing the cut on his right foot.

"I'm okay," he said, unaware of any pain. "I must have bumped my foot somewhere."

"Was it a burglar?" Sylvia asked.

"I think so," Porter replied. "I only saw the car drive off in the distance. Are you okay?"

Jennifer nodded.

"He didn't touch you?"

Jennifer shook her head.

"What did you see?"

"Uh, nothing," Jennifer said, still clearly overwhelmed. "A dark figure on top of the stairs. It all went so fast."

"Did you see a face?"

Jennifer thought for a second, almost feeling guilty. "No, nothing."

"Not a problem," Porter reassured her as he grabbed a dish towel and wrapped it around his injured foot. He then turned to Sylvia. "You call the police and check down here. I'll check upstairs."

After hobbling back up the stairs, Porter first looked inside the first door to the left, which was the guest room. Nothing. The next door was Jennifer's. Her room was as messy as ever. Then, as he turned, he saw his study door ajar, and felt a knot form in his stomach. Carefully, he opened the door and switched on the light. At first glance everything looked okay, but as he approached the desk, he saw the safe was open and some of the contents were on the floor. He knew then what had happened. "Shit," he whispered as he stared at the open safe for a long moment. Then he glanced to the side of his desk, sighing in relief to see his camera bag was still there.

Two blocks away, the dark sedan stopped at a small parking area on Farman Drive, in the middle of East Rock Park.

"Why are we stopping here?" the man in the passenger's seat asked.

"Do you have the envelope?" the driver asked.

"Sure but—"

"I have a feeling I don't want to hang on to these goods any longer than is absolutely necessary."

"You're being paranoid."

"Sometimes that's a good thing. We'll deliver it to the 24/7 post office, collect our money and be done with it." The passenger handed him a large yellow envelope from the back seat. "And the documents?"

Reaching into his inside pocket, the passenger handed over the stolen papers and the driver quickly put them in the envelope, licked the adhesive strip, pressed it shut and handed it back. As the car started, the passenger read the address label.

Culver BioPharma
11 Canefield Road
Los Angeles, CA 90762

Three days later, the Porters's doorbell rang and Jennifer ran downstairs to answer it.

"I'll get it," she called out. A minute later, she slammed the door shut and walked into the living room to hand her father a large yellow envelope and immediately ran upstairs again.

"What is it?" Sylvia asked.

Porter opened the envelope and took out a set of prints of the old documents taken on his Leica camera. He held them up to his wife.

"Your lost documents," she said and Porter nodded. "I thought maybe it was the police with news."

"I wouldn't count on any news, dear. They have nothing to go on. No witnesses, no cameras."

Sylvia sighed as Porter took the empty tin box from the coffee table next to him. Carefully inspecting the documents he was thankful he'd had the foresight to photograph both sides of the originals. Even the paper felt original. One by one he folded them the same way the others had been folded and carefully placed them in the tin box.

Later that evening, Porter sat in his study and asked himself what could possibly be so important about those stolen documents. Having paid out £25,000 for them, he almost wished he hadn't, but he was also intrigued, and certainly curious, to know what secrets they held. He looked through his magnifying glass at the charcoal image of a church and John Dee's Latin text known as The Monas. What was Dee trying to say? *Sanctum lavacrum loco nativitatis,* a holy place of birth and rebirth. Perhaps he needed to find the church. But where to start? He moved the magnifying glass back from the paper and inspected the picture inch by inch, working from left to right.

The pole on top of the bell tower revealed it was a Christian church, but where there should be a cross was some kind of banner pointing east. If this was a clue he couldn't think of any significant meaning. The church tower was covered in ivy, which didn't seem especially unusual. Porter rubbed his eyes. The time on the clock appeared to be either twenty past eleven or five to five. Again, he could think of no great significance attached to either time.

For almost an hour Porter played with the numbers; he created dates of birth, dates of deaths and even used the Elizabethan cipher method that John Dee demonstrated in his Monas Hieroglyphica. Nothing made sense. As his eyelids grew heavy, he looked at his watch. It was 2:15 a.m. With a sigh, he stretched his neck to ease the stiffness. He took up the magnifying glass again and moved on from the church to the graveyard scene in the picture. At first, he found nothing as he methodically worked his way along the rows of gravestones. In his mind, he began counting them, simply to keep himself awake.

After counting seven graves on the second row, his eye was suddenly drawn to a headstone in the bottom right. Though he couldn't read any text, he noticed a pattern drawn in pencil and tried to make sense of it by moving the magnifying glass back and forth but he couldn't make heads or tails of it. *This has to be the clue,* he thought. He looked over his desk, searching for something else he could use. Suddenly his eyes stopped on the camera bag next to the desk and he smiled. Focusing the desk light on the page, he took the Leica and made a macro shot of the drawing's lower part. He then opened his laptop and connected a cable between the computer and the camera. After clicking a few buttons, the screen read, 'Do you want to import the images from your device? Yes/No.' Porter clicked hastily and images appeared on the screen, like a roll of film. Porter clicked the last image and it opened to fill the screen. Zooming in on the headstone, he squinted as he tried to make sense of the pattern. He also thought he saw letters. And then it suddenly clicked. Opening his eyes wide he sat up straight and smiled. Could it really be that simple?

CHAPTER 20

Lag B'Omer

The Present

"Where's your car?" Monroe asked.

"Over here." Bishop smiled and pointed to the side of the curb. "And since you're the last one here you get the back seat."

Monroe frowned as he looked at the tiny red two-door car that looked like a bowler hat. It wasn't just the size of the Fiat 500 that concerned him; as he looked around it, there wasn't a single panel undented.

"It has a two-cylinder, twin air, 85 horsepower engine," Bishop joked. "It even has windshield wipers." He took hold of a wiper and moved it up and down the window. "Hey, we're on a budget and we didn't know you were coming, so...."

Bishop opened the passenger door for Monroe and lifted the front seat so he could get into the back. It took a lot of effort for the big man to lower himself into the car and he grunted as he climbed into the back. Jennifer took the front passenger seat. Bishop got in and they drove off.

From the other side of the street, Malkuth started his black rental and as the red Fiat turned the corner ahead, he followed.

They passed the Safed city border less than a minute later and drove onto Highway 89 and the first green areas of the Meron Forest.

Monroe leaned between the two front seats. "It's surprisingly comfortable back here," he said before pointing at the view ahead of them. "Mount Meron."

"I know," Bishop replied. "Almost 4,000 feet above sea level and known for its hiking trails."

"And kosher wine," Monroe added, glancing at the grapevines adorning the passing hillsides.

"So, Yochai wrote the Zohar and now he's like a saint to the Kabbalists?" asked Jennifer.

"Well, not only the Kabbalists," Monroe replied. "Also, the majority of Orthodox Jews."

"But—" Bishop interjected.

"Yeah, yeah," Monroe said, cutting him off. "I know what you're going to say. But his reputation isn't without controversy. One of his quotes is often cited by anti-Semites—'even the best of the Gentiles should be killed'—basically, kill all the non-Jews, which is grist to the mill of those advocating the Jews as a lesser people. Did you know Isaac Luria himself thought he was Yochai's *gilgul*, his reincarnation? It's been said that through his reincarnation he got his calling to create his new Kabbalistic system and spread it across the masses."

"Do you believe in reincarnation?" Jennifer asked Bishop.

"I really don't know," he answered after a few seconds. "What I do think is that if it's true then what good is it to me? I mean, I don't recall any past lives so what's the added value?"

"What if it made you a better man?" Monroe asked. "Maybe without your past lives you wouldn't be the kind, handsome, caring man we know today."

Jennifer laughed.

"The Kabbalah also believes reincarnation can be a way to complete a prior life's task or correct a particular sin."

"Well, I wonder what my prior self did to deserve you in my luxurious rental car today?" Bishop said, turning slightly to Monroe and they all laughed.

"But seriously," Monroe said as the laughter faded. "As people, we only perceive or understand things through our five senses. Sure, scientific advancements like telescopes, X-ray machines, microwaves, high-frequency microphones and smoke detectors can complement our natural senses. But all these devices eventually have to translate back to the basic five for us to understand them. You can record a sound that you can't hear, but you need to use your eyes to understand a dial or number showing that sound, or your ears once we enhance the sound somehow. Thus, we can't escape our basic limitations. Kabbalists believe that through their teachings we can develop a new sense that could perceive a broader, all embracing realm of reality. You can think of it as the soul. But in this case, it works just like any of the other senses. It's just there. Isn't that the best way to grow to have insights into your own soul? Anyway, that sixth sense could be the one that survives traditional death and reincarnates into a new body, added to the five at birth, so to say."

"Forgive him," Bishop said to Jennifer. "He sometimes switches to blabber mode."

"I think it's an interesting thought," Jennifer replied and Monroe smiled.

"Thankfully, we're almost there." Bishop sighed as he pointed to a road sign written in three languages, the last of which read, 'Rashbi Tomb.'

"What's that?" she asked, pointing at the barren landscape where a number of tents of all colors and sizes had been erected. "Roadside tourism?"

"Seems like an odd place to go camping," Monroe joked.

"Take the next right," ordered the GPS, and Bishop turned up a narrow concrete road where they were surrounded on all sides by traditionally dressed Jews.

"What day is it today?" Monroe asked.

"Wednesday," Jennifer replied.

"The date!" Monroe snapped.

When Jennifer threw him an icy stare he quickly apologized.

"It's the second," she told him and Monroe took out his cellphone and tapped at the keyboard. "All righty," he said a moment later as he read from the screen. "Today is Lag B'Omer."

"Lag B'Omer?" Jennifer asked.

"Remember he told you about the national holiday when Jews all over the world light large bonfires symbolizing the lengthening of daylight?" Bishop asked.

"Lag B'Omer?" Jennifer replied, and the two men nodded.

"That's not good," Bishop said. "The place will be crowded with people. There must be thousands of pilgrims all over the tomb today and tomorrow."

"Not the best day for a covert operation," Monroe admitted.

"So, what do we do?" Jennifer threw her hands in the air while Bishop slowed the car to a walking pace.

Without answering Bishop continued to drive slowly. The roads were filled with people talking and chanting. Carefully navigating his way through the crowds he stopped behind a wooden roadblock in front of a crossing.

"I must have missed a road sign," Bishop said as he searched for a way out. "Oh, there it is." He pointed at two, large arches made of Meleke stone. "I recognize this from pictures on the Internet."

Monroe and Jennifer moved their heads to get a better view between the hordes of people.

"It sure looks like it," Monroe confirmed as a policeman walked up to the car.

Bishop gestured that he was already turning.

"We need to find a parking spot," he said to the others. "Be on the lookout."

Driving slowly and carefully, they struggled to find a space to park, but then a hundred or so feet ahead of them, a man waved them toward what looked like a residential garden. As they looked at him, a black sedan drove straight up to them.

Malkuth looked through the Fiat's window straight at Bishop and Jennifer, desperately hoping they wouldn't see him if he was forced to pass. The men wouldn't be a problem, but the woman would surely recognize him. If she saw him, she might consider it a coincidence or it could make her suspicious. Slowly, he slid lower in his seat. He took the hoody from his jacket and put it over his head, covering his features as much as he was able without inhibiting his ability to drive. But then he noticed that everyone in the Fiat was intently looking at a man waving at them, so he was able to drive past without being noticed. Malkuth sighed in relief.

"250,000 shekel," the man said to Jennifer through her open window and he pointed at his garden.

"Parking?" she asked the man as she turned to Bishop.

"That's $75!" Bishop said, displeased.

Jennifer held up her hand. "You want to drive around here all day looking for a parking space? Or maybe we could drive back to the woods and park with the tents."

Bishop grunted as he took out his wallet. "Dollars?" Bishop shouted out of the window as he handed Jennifer a small stack of bills. The man nodded as Jennifer took the money and handed it over. After counting the notes, he stepped back and opened the gate to the garden. Bishop continued to grumble as he parked the car and they got out.

"Let's stay close together," Bishop said as the three fought their way through the immense crowd.

"We picked a great day to go unnoticed," Jennifer said. Despite their casual dress, nobody seemed to be paying any attention to them. Within a few minutes, they stood beneath the Meleke stone arches leading to the burial site of Shimon bar Yochai.

"This is as far as you can go," Bishop said to Jennifer.

"Again?"

"Although the Kabbalah teaches that men and women are equal, the more orthodox Jews aren't as broadminded," Monroe told her. "I believe that sometimes they allow female visitors to look around, but I don't think today is a good day to challenge Jewish tradition."

Jennifer frowned and theatrically leaned against the wall.

"Sorry. We'll just take a quick look," Bishop said, and he and Monroe walked to the entrance of the site that housed Yochai's tomb.

Inside, the music and singing were deafening. Even the guards at the tomb cheered and played with the automatic weapons on their hips. A narrow passageway led from the first Meleke stone arch to the other some thirty feet ahead. At the top of the arch, Hebrew text was painted in blue. Monroe tilted his head, gesturing that Bishop should translate it. Bishop stood on his toes to get a better look over the heads of the hundreds of people in front of him.

"It's something like, 'Behold, a watcher and a holy one came down from heaven. May it not be forgotten by his descendants.'" He then turned to speak loudly in Monroe's ear. "I think it means his teaching shall never be forgotten. Isn't it time you learned some Hebrew yourself?"

"Go, go, go!" Monroe shouted as a small passage through the crowd emerged. They snaked their way through the masses quickly and with remarkable ease to pass underneath the arch and into a courtyard, again filled with people. The people here were quieter than those outside. In fact, most of the men whispered or prayed in silence.

"Follow me," Bishop whispered as he made his way to a door on the left that most people seemed to be disappearing through. The two of them then stepped inside the tomb's building.

A narrow, dimly lit hallway with an arched ceiling gave the passage a cavernous look. Turning left and then right, past some closed doors and a few bookcases, they arrived at a large white room with more arched ceilings. Everywhere they looked, men swayed while praying or sitting at the tables that filled the room. According to the Zohar, when a Jew utters one word of the Torah the light in his soul is kindled and it dances like a flame on a candle. This is what the swaying signified.

The walls of the room were decorated with traditional Jewish drawings and every few feet there was a parokhet attached to it. The alcoves were used as bookcases, filled from top to bottom with scriptures. The alcoves that didn't contain bookcases led to other rooms with more arches, tables and people praying.

"This place is like a labyrinth," Monroe whispered.

"We'll have to check out all the rooms," Bishop whispered back.

"You lead the way," Monroe said and Bishop walked into the first room on the left.

To Bishop's eyes, the room looked exactly like the first one. There were parokhets hanging on the walls depicting texts and figures such as chalices or the menorah—the seven-armed chandelier Moses used in his desert sanctuary—but nothing stood out. Walking through the central room, they inspected the second room again. Nothing. After searching four rooms that all looked somewhat the same, they passed a red velvet curtain hanging from the ceiling. Monroe looked at Bishop and he responded by quickly glancing around before pulling the curtain aside to reveal a small ten by ten-foot white-plastered room. On the right side of it a large tray filled with small burning candles hung from the wall. The back wall was covered with frames filled with Hebrew text and the left wall was covered by a large blue parokhet decorated with gold embroidery. In the center was a small table with stacks of texts, bottles and pottery. There was also a plastic plate containing coins and paper money.

"The local shop," Bishop whispered, looking at two men praying and swaying in front of the parokhet. Monroe shrugged and smiled, and the two of them turned to leave the room. But then Bishop tapped Monroe on the shoulder.

"What is it?" Monroe asked, looking at the blue curtain.

"Over there, between the two candles."

Monroe took a look and shook his head.

Bishop walked up to the curtain and slyly pointed at the golden image embroidered on it.

"You think that's it?" Monroe asked. "Doesn't look like the Luchot HaBrit to me."

As Bishop took Monroe by the arm and back through the curtain, three men walked inside.

"I expected the tablets to be round-topped stone engraved rectangles," Monroe said.

"The round-topped rectangles are a medieval invention," Bishop replied. "In early scripture, Rabbinic tradition spoke of them as rectangles with sharp corners. Like Michelangelo's statue of Moses in the San Pietro basilica in Vincoli, Italy."

"I know that one. I always figured he got it wrong." Monroe smiled. "So, what now?"

Bishop slipped his fingers between the curtain and the wall and pulled it a few inches forward. The wall behind the parokhet ended to reveal what looked like a large opening. A cough startled him and he let go of the parokhet.

"We have to take a closer look behind that parokhet," Bishop said with a sigh. "But not in this crowd." He tilted his head toward the way they had come and started walking. It took about five minutes to wrestle through the crowded rooms before they entered the courtyard again. Both men felt their breathing steady as they crossed the courtyard to walk under the first arch and finally through the second one returning them back to the street. Bishop looked around. At the corner of the street he saw Jennifer, her red curls bouncing as she danced with a group of traditionally dressed Jews. Bishop walked up to her and placed his head by her shoulder. Jennifer turned as she danced.

"Hey, you're back!" she called out and Bishop gestured her to follow him.

Jennifer gave a small bow to her group and followed the men to a slightly less crowded part of the street.

"You're having fun," Bishop said.

Jennifer smiled. "Can't a young woman have some fun while the men go out and play? Did you find anything?"

Bishop nodded. "Possibly. We found a parokhet picturing the Luchot HaBrit and there seems to be an open space behind it. But the place is packed so we couldn't take a good look without being noticed."

"So, what do we do now?" Jennifer asked.

"We wait," Monroe answered. "As the legend goes, Yochai kicked everyone out when he was dying, so they will empty the place near the end of the day before lighting the bonfires."

"And that will be our moment to sneak back in and hide until the place is empty," Bishop added.

"And what do we do in the meantime?" Jennifer asked.

"That's a good question." Monroe turned to Bishop, but he was already walking down the street toward a small stall.

"What's that?" Monroe asked catching him up. Bishop took three small plastic drinking bags, complete with straw, from the table and handed one to Jennifer and Monroe.

"Choco," he said. "Free drinks. I say we celebrate while waiting."

Bishop shook his hips awkwardly and while taking a sip of his drink he danced his way over to the sidewalk.

CHAPTER 21
Bonfire

Six hours of dancing, chanting, drinking and talking had passed when Jennifer, Bishop and Monroe sat down on a terrace offering a view of the tomb's entrance. On the square next to it the crowd had only grown bigger with barely room for anyone to move.

"I'm beat," Bishop said with a sigh.

"I'm with you," Monroe replied, checking his watch. "They should start clearing the tomb in fifteen minutes or so."

Bishop also checked his watch and nodded. "Yup. It's probably time we went in before they close up. You wait here again?"

"Do I have a choice?" asked Jennifer.

Bishop shrugged as he grabbed his backpack and rose from the table. "Sorry. You enjoy the festivities and we'll be back as soon as possible. And if there's anything important, you can reach me on my cellphone. It's on vibrate."

"Take care," Jennifer said before the two men walked off to weave their way through the crowd.

Fighting against the tide, it took Bishop and Monroe a few minutes to get back into the tomb's central room. Only a few men remained, finishing their prayers and closing their books. At the back, Bishop carefully opened the curtain to the room with the Luchot HaBrit on the parokhet. He peeked inside. The room was empty and after looking back to see if anyone was paying attention he quickly tilted his head to Monroe.

"Let's go," Bishop whispered and the two disappeared behind the curtain.

Taking his flashlight, Bishop directed the beam behind the parokhet as he lifted it from the back wall. A ten-foot-square of empty space was revealed. Bishop shined the flashlight into the far corner of the alcove. Nothing. Just sand and a rough brick wall. Both men went down on their knees and crawled along the edge of the sandy floor behind the wall.

"What did the text say exactly?" Bishop asked.

"Follow the line to the truth that's hidden in the sand behind the Luchot HaBrit," Monroe answered, raising an eyebrow.

Bishop examined every inch of sand on the floor, but there was nothing. No lines, threads or any other clues.

"What now?" Monroe asked.

Bishop thought for a second. "Only one thing we can do. We dig."

Placing the flashlight on the side, lighting most of the alcove, Bishop reached into his backpack for his hand sanitizer and put it where he could easily reach it.

Monroe knew about Bishop's quirks and didn't react.

Bishop then put on a pair of latex gloves and started digging with his hands.

"You don't keep a shovel in that backpack of yours?" Monroe asked.

Bishop shook his head. "Can you at least spare me a pair of gloves?"

Bishop nodded to the backpack and after Monroe found some gloves he also started digging. Carefully, they shoved sand from the middle of the room to the sides of the alcove like archeologists recovering a fossilized dinosaur. For more than ten minutes they dug at the floor creating two large mounds of sand on the left and right until both men were on their knees, deep in the pit they had created.

"We should have started at the back," Monroe complained.

"Smartass," Bishop replied smiling. "I don't hear anything anymore. I guess the place must be empty by now."

Monroe took another handful of sand and swept it to the side of the pit only to find himself snagged by something. Bishop noticed and stared at Monroe who shrugged before using two hands to dig deeper around the obstruction. From the hole, he lifted a length of leather strap a few inches above the sand before it got stuck.

"You pull. I'll dig," Bishop said, and Monroe lifted the rope as high as he could.

With two hands Bishop dug as fast as he could to the right of the rope until he reached the wall of the alcove where the rope was tied to a heavy brick.

"Shoot," Bishop said and moved to the other end of the rope which Monroe was already pulling at. As they worked together, digging and pulling, the rope snaked through the pit until it disappeared under the back wall. He grabbed hold of a piece of rock protruding from the brickwork and pulled, only to be covered in sand from the wall. Taking a glove off he shook the sand out of it.

"Here." Monroe handed Bishop the rope. "Let me."

Using two hands, Monroe took hold of the rock and pulled, but it wouldn't budge. He sat down in the sand, placed his feet against the back wall and pulled again. Giving it all he had he grunted loudly as a large piece of wall broke away and he tumbled backward.

Bishop laughed out loud. "Are you okay?"

Monroe nodded. He pulled the rope taut and felt something behind the wall give way. Quickly getting to his feet, he worked to free the next part of the rope when suddenly the rope in Bishop's hands began to move.

"Wait a minute. I feel something," Monroe said with his hands deep in the sand behind the wall. As he removed more sand he touched something hard. "This must be it," he said as he searched for the edge of the object. He pulled again and a small round metal box, about the size of a cookie jar, materialized from the sand. Monroe dusted the sand away before handing it to Bishop. "You do the honors."

"Thanks," Bishop said. As he took the box from Monroe he pinched at the lid with his finger. "Damn, the metal is disintegrating beneath my fingers."

"Open it," Monroe urged, and Bishop felt along the edge of the lid, which was surprisingly sturdy. He put a finger into the hole he had created in the center and pulled. The rusty metal lid easily gave way and the hole grew bigger. He carefully pulled back the top like peeling an orange.

Monroe took the flashlight and directed it at the contents of the box. "Sand again."

Bishop carefully removed the sand. "There's something else," he said as he pulled a small brown tubular ceramic jar from the box. Taking a brush from his backpack, he dusted the flask. There were no markings on it, no inscriptions or pictographs. On top of the jar, a round opening about one inch in diameter was sealed with what looked like some kind of wax. Bishop peeled the wax at the side. It broke off easily. Then he looked at Monroe.

"You want to do it here or take it with you?" Monroe asked.

Bishop took a deep breath. "Why wait?" Seconds later he had removed the wax completely. Monroe pointed the flashlight into the jar revealing a rolled-up piece of paper. Bishop turned the jar upside down and shook it gently. With his other hand, he caught the scroll as it fell. After blowing off dust, he carefully unrolled the paper.

"That looks familiar," Monroe said, recognizing the style of the document from the one uncovered in Safed. "Text, pictures of plants and prescription tables. Only this time the text seems shorter." He pointed at a single line of text at the top of the scroll, written in what looked like Enochian.

"Indeed," Bishop said before handing the scroll to Monroe and taking out his cellphone. "Can you please hold it open for me? It can't hurt to have a copy."

Bishop took a few photos before taking the scroll from Monroe and placing it back in the jar, which he put in his backpack.

"Let's get out of here," Monroe said.

Moving the sand back to cover their tracks, they returned the parokhet to its normal position. "Just a second." Bishop took off his gloves and cleaned his hands with the sanitizer. "Now we're good to go."

They re-entered the main room, which was dark and slightly creepy. Within seconds they made it back to the exit, hearing the loud festivities taking place outside of the tomb. The two men then stopped, seeing the Meleke stone in the courtyard glowing orange from the large bonfire now blocking their escape through the archway.

"That's not good," Monroe said, his eyes reflecting the flames from the fire. "They must have sealed off all the entrances, just as Yochai did back in the day."

Bishop shook his head and looked around the square. The walls were smooth, about ten feet high and topped by barbed wire. He nodded toward the fire blocking their path. "That's our only way out."

"Matthew," Monroe said fiercely. "I hate fire."

As he neared the flames, Bishop noticed a narrow opening, no more than three feet wide to the right of the arch. The sound of the crackling fire and people cheering and singing from the other side of the wall was almost deafening. And as he approached the bonfire, the heat was close to unbearable, singeing through his clothes.

"We have to try," Bishop called out.

"Why?" Monroe asked. "We can wait it out."

"We don't know how long that will take and they won't let us go without an explanation once security is back in place."

Monroe knew Bishop was right. With all the festivities going on no one was taking any notice of what was happening at the entrance. Once the festivities were over, the guards would return to duty and they would be unlikely to allow two tourists, who spent the night in the tomb, to leave without questioning. They might even inspect the tomb before letting them go. He shook his head. Damn.

Behind the opening Bishop saw Jennifer walking to the fire. "Professor! I texted you when they lit the fire."

Bishop took out his phone and saw the missed message.

"We need to get out, now!" he shouted while turning to his side, pushing his back against the wall to squeeze through. As the heat became more intense, Monroe pulled him back.

"Your backpack," he said. When Bishop didn't seem to understand Monroe tapped him on the back. "You need to take it off."

Bishop nodded, realizing his mistake. Quickly taking it off, he swung it by the straps though the gap toward Jennifer, who caught it. He then pushed himself against the wall again and inched his way past the flames, until the heat became unbearable and he had to speed up. As he almost cleared the fire, a burning log fell away, narrowly missing his head only to land on his leg. Bishop pulled to free himself, but the log wouldn't budge. Monroe reached for the end of the log, but the fire was too intense. Meanwhile, Jennifer grabbed Bishop's hand and pulled.

"Here, let me," a man said.

Looking to her side, she saw a young bald man in his late twenties. It took a second before she recognized him from the hotel hallway the day before. "Please," he said, taking hold of Bishop's arm.

Jennifer stepped aside, and with one big pull, Malkuth brought Bishop sprawling onto the street where he fell on the ground, his pants around the left ankle on fire. Malkuth took off his coat and smothered the flames. Bishop jumped up, turned toward the fire and gestured Monroe to come through.

Monroe hesitated. As a child he had set fire to a waste paper basket and his father had pushed his head close to the flames as a punishment. The memory of this hadn't waned over the years and he was terrified of getting too close to the flames. Inching closer to the heat, feeling the flames burning his face, he finally felt able to squeeze himself into the gap and reached for Bishop who grabbed his arm and pulled him to safety.

"Let's not do that again," Monroe said after catching his breath.

"I'm with you there," Bishop agreed, unwrapping the jacket from his ankle. He looked for the man who had helped him. "Where did he go?"

Jennifer looked around and shook her head.

"Who?" Monroe asked.

"The man who helped me. The man whose jacket this belongs to."

Bishop showed him the black tracksuit top and they all scoured the crowd in search of the bald stranger but found only traditionally-dressed Jews. The bald man wasn't among them.

"That's curious," Bishop said.

"I recognized that man," Jennifer said. Bishop and Monroe turned to look at her. "I met him in the hotel yesterday. He gave me a scare when I was getting ice. Here, give me the jacket. Maybe I can return it to him at the hotel." Bishop handed her the jacket. "Are you okay?"

Bishop rolled up his pant leg and saw nothing. "Looks like the fire didn't get through. I should be fine thanks to my secret savior."

"Weird," Monroe muttered.

"Did you find anything?" Jennifer asked.

"We did," Monroe replied. "Where's the backpack?"

Jennifer looked around, panicking. "I think I put it down somewhere around here. I'm not sure."

"You're not sure?" Monroe asked.

"No, I'm not!" Jennifer snapped. "If you recall your friend was on fire only five minutes ago."

"It's okay. Let's look around," Bishop said and all three of them searched the area, but there was no backpack in sight.

"What do we do now?" Jennifer asked.

"Could the man who helped you have taken it?" Monroe asked.

Jennifer shrugged and raised her arms. "Was whatever you found in the backpack?"

Bishop and Monroe looked at each other.

"We need to get back to the hotel," Bishop said. "We need to get hold of that man."

"What's going on?" Jennifer asked, but Bishop was already heading for the car. Catching up to him, she repeated her question.

"Let's get to the car first and we'll update you on the way back," Monroe replied.

Before the gate was even fully open, Bishop drove the Fiat 500 out of the driveway at full throttle.

"Will someone please tell me what's going on?" Jennifer demanded.

"Check the coat," Bishop said.

Monroe reached for it and inspected the pockets. "Chewing gum," he said, taking out a packet of Wrigley's. "A pen, some Israeli change and that's about it. Oh, wait." He took out a piece of tightly folded paper. Unwrapping it, he held his breath.

"What is it?" Bishop asked.

Monroe handed the paper to Jennifer. "See for yourself."

Jennifer looked at it, immediately recognizing the text. She held the paper up in front of Bishop's face. He took it from her hands.

> *'The secret wisdom eternal reveals itself in the graves three all-powerful men...'*

Bishop gave a deep sigh and glanced at Monroe. "You were right." When Jennifer coughed for an explanation, Bishop apologized. "Sorry, but it seems we're not the only ones chasing this mystery."

"What do you mean?" Jennifer asked.

"The death of Father Matula in Poland wasn't an accident. It was murder."

"Okay...." Jennifer said, expecting more.

Bishop then waved the piece of paper retrieved from the man's coat in front of her. "This is your part of the paper we divided between us in the library. Where did you put it?"

The blood immediately drained from Jennifer's face. "My home," she replied, bringing a hand to her mouth. "Someone must have broken into my home and taken it. Oh my God." Her eyes widened. "Do you think that the person who broke into my house is the same person who murdered Father Matula? The same person who saved you from the fire and took your backpack?"

"You know just as much as we do," Bishop replied.

Jennifer looked at Monroe to see if he had anything more to add.

Monroe sat back in his seat, nodding in agreement with Bishop.

"But who?" Jennifer asked.

"We have no idea," Monroe replied, waving his arms.

"The only thing we know is that it changes everything," Bishop said.

"What do you mean?" Jennifer asked.

"If the ones who also search for this secret are here, this quest has just become a lot more dangerous."

Jennifer frowned. "So, what do we do?"

Bishop pushed the pedal to the floor and gripped the steering wheel firmly. "For now, we go to the hotel and see if we can find or at least identify our bald friend."

CHAPTER 22

The Garden of Eden

"Excuse me, can I ask you something?" Bishop asked the man behind the counter in the hotel lobby.

"Of course, sir," the man answered politely.

"Do you have a young, bald man staying here? English accent, blue eyes, about six-foot-two?"

"I'm sorry, but I can't give you that information, sir. Privacy, you know."

"I understand," Bishop replied. "But we met at the Lag B'Omer festivities and he left his coat." Bishop held up Malkuth's coat.

"Ah, I understand, sir." The man behind the counter thought for a moment. "Not a problem. Indeed, I believe we had such a young gentleman staying with us, but he checked out before you arrived. You must have just missed him."

"Do you have a name or address so we can return his coat?" Jennifer asked. The man paused again, thinking while looking at the three of them, one by one, deep in the eyes. Then he punched some keys on his computer keyboard and looked at the screen.

"I'm sorry. There's no home address registered," he said.

"A name?" Bishop asked.

"Uh...." the man searched the screen pointing at it. "Ah, here it is. Yes, Michael Robarts."

"Thank you," Bishop said and the man nodded.

"So, what do we do now?" Jennifer asked as they stepped away from the counter.

"We can try to find this Michael Robarts," Bishop said, "but we also need to take a look at the new message from the grave."

Jennifer shook her head in confusion.

"The original text was in the backpack, but we took pictures of it when we were inside the tomb." Bishop took his phone from his pocket to show Jennifer.

"That's great news," Jennifer said.

"There's a 'but.'" Bishop paused for a second.

"What is it?" Monroe asked.

"Well," Bishop continued. "Like I said, the search has gotten a lot more dangerous now that they have the document."

"Why is that exactly?" Jennifer asked.

"Simple. Up until now they were always one step behind us, dependent on our findings, relying on our intel and following our steps. From now on, we must assume that they're doing their own research on the document. Maybe drawing the same conclusions we do. Maybe even *before* we do. So, they might be dependent on us no longer and that means they could decide that we are in their way."

Bishop gave a grim smile and Jennifer and Monroe sighed.

"That's not good news," Monroe said.

"No, it isn't," Bishop replied. "And if—and it's a big if—we decide to go on, we've just added a ticking clock to our search. From now on, we need to assume that whoever they are will try to beat us to the punch. Our search just became a race."

For a long moment, the three of them stared at each other in silence.

"So, what do we do now?" Jennifer asked, breaking the silence.

"Well," Bishop answered, "I guess before we decide if we go on we can try to translate the new message and see if we can find out who this, uh...."

"Michael Robarts," Jennifer reminded him.

"Indeed. Who this Robarts guy is," Bishop said.

"I can see what I can find out on social media," Jennifer suggested.

"That's good," Bishop answered, "and I can help you search any educational databases. If there was ever a Michael Robarts registered in some school I should be able to find him."

Bishop looked at Monroe.

"I know my job," Monroe smiled and he gestured that they should make their way upstairs to the room.

"By the way, what else was in your backpack?" Jennifer asked.

"Nothing that can't be replaced easily. I can always pick up some new things in the city or at the airport."

As the three walked toward the stairs, Monroe suddenly stopped, his forehead creased with thought. He turned to the counter and called out. "Excuse me, sir!"

The man at the desk looked up.

"Can you please spell Mister Robarts' last name for me?"

The man looked briefly at his screen. "R-O-B-A-R-T-E-S."

"Thank you." Monroe nodded and breathed in deeply.

"What is it?" Bishop asked.

"I was wondering where I'd heard that name before. Michael Robartés," Monroe said emphasizing the accent on the name. "Robartés was a fictional character created by William Butler Yeats. He figured in a few of his poems before becoming the lead in Yeats's "Rosa Alchemica." The Rosa was a short story about a spiritual and cultural movement called the Rosicrucianism as well as God, alchemy and the occult. Many know Yeats only through his love poems, but all except one of his short stories are about the occult and magic. The man was obsessed with it. He even joined some mystical cults during his lifetime."

"So, probably not his real name," Jennifer said. "Robartés, I mean."

"We should check it out anyway," Bishop replied and started walking again. "Let's get to work."

Malkuth stopped the black sedan in a parking spot along the deserted road. He took Bishop's backpack from the passenger seat, turned it upside down and shook out the contents. He sorted the items, one by one, picking them up, inspecting them and tossing them onto the floor of the passenger seat. A pair of reading glasses, a Zippo lighter bearing a symbol he didn't recognize, a bottle of hand sanitizer, a flashlight, a leather etui. He unzipped it. Lockpicking tools. *This man came prepared,* he thought. His eyes were then drawn to the brown tubular ceramic jar. Thinking it looked old, he inspected the outside. Turning the lid to the light he took a look inside. At first, the jar appeared empty, but then he saw what looked like a rolled-up piece of paper hugging the sides. He shook out the scroll and opened it on his lap. He saw there was some kind of text, but he couldn't read it. The only thing on the paper that made sense were the pictures of plants. But he knew this was what Bishop and his friends must have been looking for. He smiled. Father would be proud. He quickly took out his cellphone and took a few pictures, making sure to get every angle before sending them to Kether.

"Did you find anything?" Bishop asked Jennifer, who was browsing on her phone.

"Nothing," she replied. "I checked all social media and any other Internet sites I could think of for Michael Robartés, with and without the accented e, but nothing stands out."

Bishop held his phone in the air. "Nothing here either. Enough people with the same name, but if he's among them I haven't found him. There are none fitting his age with any visible connection to religious occupations or John Dee, Olbracht Łaski or anything else we have so far come across. How are you coming along?" he asked, looking at his watch and then at Monroe, who was sitting at the table staring at his laptop. "You've had almost two hours."

"I'm done," Monroe answered. "While you two were discussing your findings, I was able to do a rough translation of the text."

Bishop and Jennifer joined him to read the text on screen.

On the time of creation of our universe, where our founding father buried his wife, Aleph, Beth, Gimel, Daleth will find each other where the water parts into four new waters.

"Do you already know what it means?" Jennifer asked.

"Well, I have some ideas," Monroe answered. "A few parts of the puzzle. The founding father burying his wife could be Abraham burying Sarah, which is an important part of Jewish history and the book of Genesis. And"—Monroe paused for a second—"Aleph, Beth, Gimel, Daleth are the first four letters of the Hebrew alphabet. A, B, G and D."

"That's it?" Jennifer frowned.

"That's where you two come in, I guess. You did do this for a while without me. Remember?"

"And we could do it without you again if we needed to," Bishop joked.

Jennifer ran her fingers across the four letters on the computer screen.

Monroe looked annoyed at the grease mark her finger left behind.

"It looks like the four letters are named as figures here, persons."

"So?" Jennifer asked.

"So," Bishop said. "I have an idea about the four waters."

"What about it?" Jennifer asked.

"Do you have the Old Testament?"

"Sure, I always keep one in the back pocket of my pants. Let me see."

Bishop looked at her, glanced at the screen and back at her again. "Uh, sorry. I mean, can you look one up on your phone for me?"

"Ah, you should have said that."

Jennifer picked up her phone, unlocked it and searched for a few seconds before she handed it to Bishop who began to scroll down the text.

"Here it is."

Jennifer and Monroe moved closer, straining to see the screen.

"Let me read it to you," Bishop said. "Genesis 2:10. 'And a river went out of Eden to water the garden; and from thence it was parted and became into four heads.'" He paused for a moment. "One river splits into four rivers."

"Oh, this is getting good," Jennifer said. "We're now searching for the Garden of Eden?" She raised an eyebrow at Monroe. "Anything relating to the Garden of Eden in the... what's it called, the Kabbalah Bible? If you know what I mean?"

"The Zohar?"

Jennifer nodded.

"Well, the Zohar is basically a novel describing a few rabbis' journeys to the promised land. As they travel, they run into weird situations and talk philosophy with people they meet along the way. Now they're called teachings. Regarding the Garden of Eden, the Zohar teaches that man can direct God instead of—as normally believed—the other way around. So, the question in the Zohar is who kicked whom out of the garden. It has been suggested that Adam expelled God, in which case we would still live in the garden, but just not know it. Anyway, that's supposedly how we lost contact with God. And—"

Bishop coughed to stop Monroe. "Though I'm usually the first to enjoy a good Zohar lesson, I was rather hoping you might have a concrete location."

"Well, uh, no. One of the four rivers is generally considered to be the Euphrates, but that's not specified in the Zohar. It's a general interpretation."

"But we do know where Abraham buried his wife?" Bishop asked pointing in the air before apologizing as he saw Monroe and Jennifer staring at his finger. "All right," he scrolled down Jennifer's phone again and read. "'And after this, Abraham buried Sarah his wife in the cave of the field of Machpelah before Mamre.'"

"Of course," Monroe said. "Machpelah."

Bishop took a deep breath. "The Cave of the Patriarchs."

"I know it's in the Bible," Jennifer said, "but that's all I know about it."

"Nobody knows for sure, but it's thought that Machpelah means the double. One explanation for the word is that three prominent couples are buried over there: Abraham and Sarah, Isaac and Rebecca, and Jacob and Leah. They were buried in what's now called the Cave of the Patriarchs."

"Of course," Monroe interrupted in a high-pitched tone, "the Zohar states that the Cave of Machpelah isn't special because of those who are buried there, but rather because it is the gateway to the Garden of Eden. Another interpretation of the Zohar is that God created a burial place in front of the entrance to Eden. When Eve died, God sent down a ray of light showing Adam where to dig. When he dug deeper it's said the scent of the Garden of Eden grew stronger. Adam kept digging and digging following the scent until he dug out a huge cave. When Adam wanted to dig deeper, to get back to the garden he'd been kicked out of, God commanded him to stop and lay Eve to rest, there in the cave."

"So, one interpretation is that we're actually living in the Garden of Eden?" Jennifer asked. "I believe a lot of people would disagree with you. Even in these neighborhoods."

Monroe shrugged. "I think everyone should decide for themselves. Anyway, the legend continues that when Abraham's wife died she did so near the cave and when Abraham found her near Adam's body he knew that was where he had to bury her. Kabbalists say that Sarah was the reincarnation of Eve. One theory is that God guided Sarah to the grave of her previous body. So, when Abraham found the body of his wife, he knew he had to own the land to be used as a burial site for his family and for four hundred shekel he purchased the cave from a Hittite named Ephron. That's the story of the cave."

"A graveyard with a direct entrance to the Garden of Eden. That would be a priceless piece of real estate," Bishop joked.

"And that would be one impressive grave to find," Jennifer added.

"Anyway," Monroe continued, "more to the point, they built a Christian church on top of the cave. The Roman emperor Justinian later converted the church into a Mohammedan mosque. Nowadays half of the structure, the Isaac Hall, serves as an Ibrahimi mosque, while the other half, the Abraham and Jacob Hall, is a synagogue. The huge structure is enclosed by el-Haram, an immense sacred enclosure about two hundred feet long, fifty feet wide and about fifty feet high. The holy place now marks the origins of all three Abrahamic religions: the Jews,

Christians and Muslims. It is a place where they worship the Torah, the Bible and the Quran. They all come to visit and pray. The cave with the graves should be below the structure, but it's not accessible to the public and no one is sure what's really below."

"True," Bishop confirmed. "I visited the place once, seven years ago, with a group of students. Quite impressive. But I don't think there's a way to visit the caves."

"Well, you wanted a specific location." Monroe smiled.

"Where is it? And are we sure that's the place we need to go next?" Jennifer asked.

"It's not too far, about a three-hour drive south," Bishop said. "And Mamre is the name of the place in the Bible, but now it's called Hebron."

"I agree with Jennifer," Monroe said. "How can we be sure it's the right place? We need to solve the other clue."

The three of them fell silent for a moment.

"What was the line at the beginning?" Bishop asked.

Monroe turned back to his laptop. "On the time of creation of our universe," he mumbled.

Jennifer cocked her head. "What was the Old Testament verse you quoted?" she asked Bishop.

The professor thought for a moment. "A river came out of Eden to water the garden; and was split into four. That one?"

"The number," Jennifer said, slightly frantically. "The number of the verse." She grabbed her phone out of Bishop's hands and began to scroll. "Two-ten!" she cried before walking to the safe to take out the Aldaraia and the crystal and bring them to the table. "Page two, ten o' clock."

"You think?" Bishop asked, opening the Aldaraia.

"I bet you a month's salary," she replied.

"I bet you do," Bishop replied. "You don't have a salary."

Monroe laughed out loud. Bishop took the flashlight and positioned it carefully at ten o'clock. The five beams of green light appeared on the page.

Q.E.Z.G.O.

"Qezgo," Bishop said.

"Qezgo," echoed the others.

"Could it be an anagram?" Monroe asked.

"The other messages read from left to right and top to bottom, but can you solve an anagram of it that makes sense?"

In silence, they all ran the letters through their heads trying to create a word from it.

"I've got nothing," Monroe admitted after a short moment and Jennifer shook her head. The room fell silent again.

"What was the other one?" Jennifer asked, breaking the silence. "The one about the founding father?"

Bishop thought for a second. "About Abraham burying Sarah in the cave of Machpelah?"

"Also Genesis, if I'm not mistaken." Jennifer began scrolling through the screen on her phone, reading aloud and fast as she went. "And after this, Abraham buried Sarah his wife in the cave of the field of Machpelah before Mamre. Genesis 23:19. Try page twenty-three, seven o' clock."

Bishop quickly leafed to page twenty-three, put the crystal on top and turned to seven. The three followed the five beams of light to the letters. Reading the highlighted letters, they all exhaled.

S.A.R.A.H.

Jennifer held her hand up to Bishop. "High five!"

Bishop hesitated before clumsily slapping his hand against Jennifer's. He then looked around for his hand sanitizer as Jennifer repeated the move with Monroe who almost missed her completely. *College professors*, she thought.

"Thanks, great work," Bishop said and Monroe nodded.

"The Cave of Machpelah," Monroe sighed. "That's something else completely. So, what do you think?"

"As I said, I once visited the place, but I didn't see a way to visit the caves. In the late fifteenth century they were closed for good and it has been said that no one has ever gone into the cave itself and returned."

"Except...." Monroe added, grabbing Jennifer's attention.

Bishop smiled.

"Legend says that one man did survive, a Jew named Rabbi Abraham Azulai."

"I know him," Monroe replied. "As a Kabbalist he was known as the 'Chesedl Avraham.'"

"Ah," Jennifer said, nodding to Monroe at the Kabbalah link.

"It has been said that some three hundred years ago the Turkish sultan dropped his sword into the cave. The sultan sent soldiers into the cave to retrieve it, but no one came back. After a number of tries the sultan asked the Jewish community to volunteer someone to retrieve the sword. The elderly Rabbi Azulai volunteered, knowing his people would be killed if no one stepped forward. He retrieved the sword and after a huge celebration, he spent the next seven days teaching his Kabbalistic students the secrets of the cave before dying."

"What was the secret?" Jennifer asked.

Bishop shrugged. "No one knows. If there ever was a secret, it didn't survive time."

"'O ye of little faith," Monroe joked. "The road to success is paved with failure."

"I can contact the local rabbi who guided us on my first visit, Rabbi Naphtali Cohen. We've kept in contact and he visited me once in the States and gave a guest lecture on interreligious dialogue. Maybe he can help us," Bishop suggested.

"We first need to decide what we do," Monroe replied.

Jennifer thought again of the bald man also looking for answers. "I think contacting Rabbi Cohen is our best option. We can decide after that."

Monroe nodded and he and Jennifer gazed at Bishop.

After a moment Bishop took out his cellphone. "I guess I can give him a call."

The Santa Monica airport was a 3,500-foot, single strip of asphalt in the middle of urban Los Angeles. A few miles from Malibu, Beverly Hills and downtown Los Angeles, it served the most elite neighborhoods in L.A. Shining under the bright sun, a speckled white Gulfstream G150 plane started with a searing high-pitched whir. On the staircase to the plane, a man dressed in jeans, white T-shirt, sports jacket and wearing a pair of Oakley sunglasses below a red Dodgers baseball cap stopped. He felt his cellphone vibrating in his pocket. Below the baseball cap, the slender-bodied, graying, middle-aged man hid his scarred face. He took off his glasses revealing piercing blue eyes and looked at the phone's screen.

"I'm about to board a plane that will take off in seconds so we need to keep it short." His voice fought to be heard over the wind and the noise of the engines. "Just a moment," he said as he stepped inside the plane to collapse on a large white leather sofa. The rest of the aircraft was empty. "That's better. Now, what can I do for you?"

"Thank you for taking my call," Kether said. "I just wanted to know if you received the package in good order?"

It had only been a few hours since he'd sent the pictures taken by Malkuth, but he was curious to know what his employer thought and having heard nothing, he had grown concerned. Usually, the boss was much quicker to respond and always with a thousand questions asked in that gravelly voice that gave him the chills. He'd never met the man, but he hated the sound of his voice.

"I got everything."

"And what do you think?"

"I meant to call you, but my attention was needed elsewhere. The information you sent is good."

"So, what do we do now?" Kether asked.

"For now, I need you to lie low." The man glanced at the stewardess approaching him to hand over a glass of wine before advising him to buckle up his seatbelt.

"What do you mean?"

"Well...." There was a short pause. "For now, we've translated all the information we need so we don't need your services. We'll pick it up from here. I understand your man has been seen, but as we have all the information we need to proceed, there's no need for your man to continue for now. He can only jeopardize the mission."

Kether thought for a moment, hearing the engines of the plane whirring at an ever-higher pitch in the background. "Do you have someone on the ground over there?"

"Not yet, but we can be there in twenty-four hours."

"Twenty-four hours?" Kether said somewhat desperately. "If you think you have a head start now, you'll have lost it by the time you hit the ground in Israel. We need to act now. If we discover the next lead before they do it will all be over for them. They'll have no other option but to quit."

The line went silent for a long moment and Kether could almost hear his employer thinking on the other end.

"I'll send you instructions in a few minutes."

"Thank you, sir. We won't disappoint you. If you can—"

The line went dead.

CHAPTER 23

Machpelah

The Yitzhak Rabin Trans-Israel Highway ran all the way from Nazareth in the north to Beër Sjeva in the south. Without any tollbooths, the highway was the first privately-funded and operated toll road in the country to use a system of cameras and transponders to toll vehicles automatically. For the most part, the 115-mile-long road snaked south about a mile from the Mediterranean seaboard often creating a green, fertile and populated sight to the east and a desolated desert to the west.

"Follow the highway for fifty miles," commanded the Fiat 500's GPS.

Jennifer lifted her head from her chest, waking from sleep. The car passed a huge sign that read *Jerusalem.* Jennifer stared into the distance, seeing only sand and trees.

"Good morning, sleepy head. You won't be able to see it," Bishop said as he drove. "It's another ten miles or so through the mountains and forests."

For the first hour on the road Jennifer had played with her cellphone until the battery died. She had then grown bored, closed her eyes and drifted away. Looking behind her, she saw she wasn't the only one. Monroe had also fallen asleep, curled up on the back seat.

"What time is it? How long did I sleep?"

Bishop looked at his watch. "It's almost nine. So, about an hour, I guess. We're about halfway there."

"So, this friend of yours we're about to meet. What's his story?"

Bishop cocked his head. "There's not much of a story to tell. He's a young rabbi with very good connections in the community. He's a big advocate of religious tolerance."

"And you think he'll help us?"

"Well, he was very pleased to hear from me. I explained the situation and I think he'll do what he can, but I doubt he can get us into the caves. But he promised to help us get protection. Police, I guess."

"Did you tell him what it is we're looking for?"

"I told him we were on an archeological search based on the findings of some old documents and that there's another party also interested and they don't seem to be shy of violence." As Bishop explained he realized he was actually telling the truth. "We'll meet him at his home in Hebron in about an hour."

From the back of the car came grunting noises. In the mirror, Bishop saw Monroe heave himself up with more grunts.

"It's alive," Bishop said, smiling.

Monroe rubbed his eyes and tried to stretch his back only to be obstructed by the low roof. "You call this alive?"

"Don't be such a baby," Bishop joked.

"Where are we?"

"About an hour out," Jennifer replied, smiling, as she looked at the big man struggling to make himself comfortable in the back seat.

Monroe nodded. "Good, I can't wait to get out of this, uh... never mind." In the pockets of his pants he felt his cellphone vibrate. He took it out to see a new text message had arrived. He opened the message and read.

It's done as requested. Be careful.

He cleared his throat and stared at the screen for a second.

"What is it?" Bishop said looking in the rearview mirror.

"Oh, uh, nothing." Monroe tucked the phone away. "Tiny problem in the family."

Monroe positioned himself in the middle of the back seat, his knees digging into the seats in front. Bishop looked at his friend in the rearview mirror. There was nothing alarming about what he had said. It was a casual, off-hand remark, but there was something in the way he said it. Before Bishop could inquire, Monroe spoke.

"Did I tell you about the time I was in Jerusalem, when I visited the National Library of Israel for a week's research on Palestinian books?"

Kether's black rental stood in a small parking lot at the foot of a huge Meleke stone staircase. The stairs ran some 150 feet up to seamlessly merge with a huge square structure overlooked by towering minarets. Kether had expected the place to be crowded, but only a handful of people walked up the stairs and the parking lot was mostly empty. Both sides of the stairs were decorated with large flower pots filled with geraniums giving the place some color. The grass next to the stairs was barely green and almost covered by the desert sand. Kether checked his GPS. *This must be it,* he thought, and took his cellphone and started texting.

Am at the location.
Will scout the terrain looking for openings.

He put on a pair of dark, cheap-looking sunglasses, left his car and walked up the stairs.

"We're here," Bishop announced as he stopped the car in front of what looked like a small, two-story shopping center. In several languages on the façade, it said:

Gutnick Center Hebron
Machpelah Visitors Center
Cafeteria - Jewelry

"Will you get out, please?" Monroe asked Jennifer politely, but with some urgency in his voice. Jennifer got out, and Monroe clambered out after her.

"This has got to stop," he complained, struggling to straighten himself, and Bishop and Jennifer laughed.

"This is where we meet your rabbi friend?" Jennifer asked. As she looked at the stores and terraces, Bishop nodded and Jennifer looked puzzled. "Are the caves inside?"

Bishop laid a hand on Jennifer's shoulder and directed her to the other side of the street. Monroe followed.

"Look," he said, pointing to the Gutnick Center. Jennifer gazed at the huge yellow stone structure, lit by the bright sun, towering over the shopping mall in the back.

"I see," she said. "That's impressive."

"Matthew? Matthew Bishop?" A handsome tanned man in his late thirties emerged from one of the stores. As he crossed the street he raised both arms to hug Bishop and then kissed him on both cheeks. "It's so good to see you. It has been too long, my friend."

Jennifer stared at the man. He had short hair, a trimmed black beard and he was dressed in modern dark blue jeans and a matching light blue shirt. Only his tallit, the traditional Hebrew shawl he wore, gave away his religious background while his thin-rimmed glasses suggested a certain intelligence.

"Rabbi Naphtali Cohen." Bishop introduced the man to Jennifer and Monroe and they all shook hands.

"Please, call me Naphtali," the rabbi said.

Unable to stop herself, Jennifer stared at the rabbi until she realized what she was doing and apologized.

"Were you expecting something else?" asked Cohen. "An old, gray-haired, long-bearded man, perhaps?"

Jennifer blushed and they all laughed.

"It's no problem. We're not all old, scruffy-looking dudes. Come."

Cohen pointed to a terrace. A few minutes later they were seated on it and drinking Limonana.

"So, you want to visit Machpelah?" Cohen asked.

"Well," said Bishop, "as I told you over the phone, it's not so much the building we are interested in. We're more interested in the caves."

"Yes, you explained. And you were afraid someone was following you?" All three of them nodded. "You know I can't take you into the caves."

"We know," Jennifer said. "Is it true no one has visited the caves in the past millennium or so?"

"It is," Bishop said before Cohen could respond.

The rabbi frowned and paused for a long moment.

"Or is it?"

"It is true that the last officially-reported visit to the caves was in 1119," Cohen said. "They discovered the entrance by chance after cutting through the Herodian paving during construction work and found a passage leading to them. It has been said the bones of the patriarchs were found inside the cave and brought to the upper court where they were placed in labeled reliquaries before being returned to their place of rest. Although some bone parts were sold to pilgrims and found their way to the west as prized relics." Cohen paused and shifted uncomfortably on his seat.

"But that's not the whole story," Monroe said, shaking his head.

"Officially, it is." Cohen sighed. "Unofficially, there were two more known events."

Bishop cocked his head. "Do tell."

"Well, in '67, Moshe Dayan, the then Secretary of Defense was an amateur archaeologist and he wanted to know what was inside. The entrance only had a small opening where believers dropped coins and messages. Dayan was a big man and couldn't get in so he lowered a young girl named Michal through the round hole. When she came back, she described a corridor with a room leading to another room and a staircase that was blocked by large stones." Cohen took out his cellphone. "Here, I have something of a floorplan as she described it."

He held his hand over his cellphone protecting the screen from the sunlight.

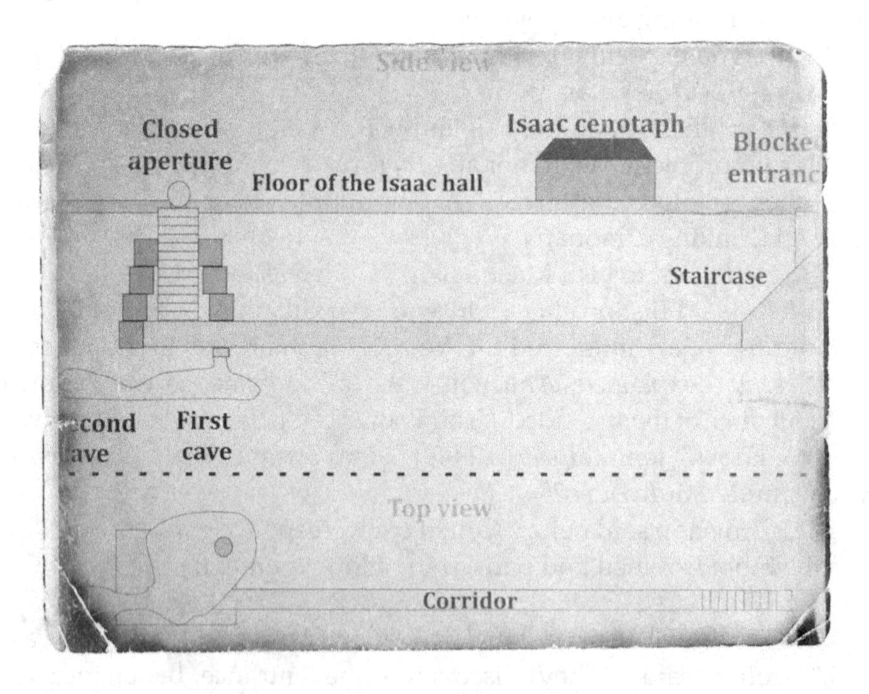

The phone was passed around the table.

"Did she bring up anything?" Bishop asked.

"Not that we know of," Cohen replied. "As the story goes the rooms were completely empty."

"And the other one?" Monroe asked as he passed the phone to Jennifer who seemed to be in some kind of trance-like state, staring at the rabbi. "Jennifer?"

At the sound of her name, Jennifer snapped out of it and took the phone.

"The other visit," Cohen continued, "the last one, was reported to have happened in '81. A small group of men, by their own account, entered the caves from the other side, from the hall of Isaac. Based on the girl's description, they cut through the bedrock and found the blocked staircase leading down to the corridor. They cleared it and searched the cave. The men claimed to have found bones and shards of pottery that they brought back. The shards were later dated by the IAA, the Israel Antiquities Authority, to be from the Bronze Age, the same period of the age of the Patriarchs and the First Temple. But the whole thing is highly disputed."

Bishop took out his cellphone and showed an image to Cohen. "Does this mean anything to you?"

Aleph, Beth, Gimel, Daleth will find each other where the water parts into four new waters.

Cohen looked at the screen for a second. "Nothing more than, I guess, you already know. The four waters describing Eden and the four first letters of the alphabet. But as for a connection between the two...." Cohen spread his arms wide. "So, you told me you're looking for something, but you don't know what it is and someone is after you or after whatever you are looking for."

Cohen glanced around the table.

"Hey, don't look at me," Monroe said, stroking his bald head. "I'm just here for the ride and to enjoy this foolish quest. Who knows what they'll come up with."

"Who's more foolish, the fool or the fool who follows him?" Bishop asked.

Monroe's eyes sparkled good-naturedly. "I must admit I'm having great fun, most of the time."

"Can you help us?" Jennifer suddenly asked.

Without saying a word, the rabbi looked at Bishop as if for confirmation.

"Sure, I can show you around, but again, I can't take you into the caves. I have, however arranged for you to visit the building after closing, which is nine o'clock tonight. I took the liberty of arranging a room in the back of the store behind us so you can rest and freshen up a little afterward."

"I can come?" Jennifer asked.

"Sure, you can," Cohen replied, smiling.

Jennifer clapped her hands together. "Great."

"And the other thing?" Bishop asked.

Cohen nodded his head toward the table on the terrace behind them. At the table sat four big men wearing plain clothes and dark sunglasses.

"Police?" Bishop asked.

"Something like that." Cohen gave a wry smile. "But I think you're safe with them," He said as he leaned back in his chair.

Trying not to be conspicuous, they glanced at the table behind them. On one of the men's wrists, Jennifer noticed a red ribbon. Just as she was about to ask Cohen about it, he spoke.

"Now, are you ready to tell me what this is really all about?"

Jennifer and Monroe both turned to Bishop.

"Sure, why not," Bishop said. "Let me see, where to start?"

CHAPTER 24

Water

In the dark sky thousands of stars cast their light on the stairway leading to the Cave of the Patriarchs. The walls were lit by orange floodlights giving it a beautiful and mysterious look. Bishop looked at the crenellation on top of the walls as he walked up the stairs.

"I never noticed before, but the battlements make the place look more medieval than Bronze Age," he said.

"I guess, even in those days, they knew how to defend themselves," Monroe replied, breathing heavily though they were only two-thirds of the way up.

"Do you work out?" Jennifer asked.

"I'm British. We don't work out."

"I bet *they* work out," Bishop said as he looked back at the four silhouettes following them up the stairs.

"You have nothing to worry about," Cohen told them. "They won't leave our side."

"I feel safe already," Jennifer said with a chuckle and Cohen smiled at her.

"The walls are about a century younger than the caves," Cohen revealed. "They protect the caves and the crenellation was the work of Herod the Great who was known for his colossal building projects like the construction of the ports at Caesarea Maritima, the fortresses of Herodium and Masada, and the Second Temple in Jerusalem, Herod's Temple. The walls are six feet thick and they can withstand anything. It was built to last and that's probably why it is now the oldest building in constant use that's still used for its original purpose. Anyway, we're here. This is the western entrance."

Once past the 150-foot-long wall, they turned a corner and stopped in front of a smaller, more modern building. Standing next to the doorway a man in military uniform greeted Cohen and gave him a small nod as they walked through the arched doorway and headed for several smaller, connected buildings, all of them well-lit. The absence of people gave the place an eerie feeling. As they walked, Cohen explained that the one-room buildings were each dedicated to Abraham, Sarah, Jacob and Leah, providing extra space to worship. In each room a green, wrought iron fence protected one wall bearing black velvet robes and Hebrew texts. Cohen explained that behind each fence was a smaller room filled with ancient relics relating to the person the room was dedicated to. He stopped in front of two large green doors with brass hinges.

"Are you ready?" he asked.

Bishop grunted, Monroe nodded and Jennifer said "Yes."

Cohen dramatically swung open both doors.

"The Abraham and Jacob room," he said.

Bishop took a small step forward and Jennifer and Monroe carefully looked around the door to find an enormous octagonal room in front of them. Large white pillars supported glorious archways and the floor was covered by a red carpet and prayer mats.

"Wow." Jennifer's voice echoed through the room.

"Enter. Enter, please," Cohen said as he walked toward a row of columns before stopping to point at a copper fence at the side of the hall. "The cenotaphs. Behind every fence there's an octagonal structure encasing a monument to the spirit of one of the Patriarchs or Matriarchs."

Jennifer and Monroe placed their hands against the glass between the copper bars and saw what looked like a huge stone sarcophagus upholstered with green fabric decorated with golden symbols.

"There are six of these monuments," Cohen continued. "They're all dedicated to those buried below, in the caves. Four of them are inside this room, Jacob and Leah in the northwest and Abraham and Sarah in the southeast. The cenotaphs of Abraham and Sarah were built in eighth century and the rest of them were all in place by the tenth century. The Mamluks designed their current look a few centuries later. Please, follow me."

The three of them fell in behind Cohen as he walked southeast through an open archway and into another hall, smaller than the one before. Between four large columns were another two cenotaphs.

"The Jacob hall," said Cohen before pointing to two golden gates. "And there are Isaac and Rebecca. Behind the gates are the cenotaphs erected for them."

Walking up to the gate, they saw what looked like a sarcophagus—fifteen feet wide and ten feet high—covered by a green velvet blanket embroidered in gold.

"Come," Cohen urged them as he headed toward a small, domed structure topped by a crescent moon. "Now, this might be of the most interest to you."

Cohen looked at the cracked marble flooring between two large marble columns, designed with a large flower, in the center of which was a two-foot circular hatch filled with holes complete with a brass ring that was used to lock the hatch with a stainless steel padlock.

"The entrance?" Monroe asked.

Cohen nodded. "The only visible one. The other one is sealed off and should be over there, somewhere behind that eastern wall."

"What are those holes?" Jennifer asked pointing to the hatch.

"That's where worshippers throw their prayers, written on small scrolls of paper," Cohen replied.

"So, what do we do now?" Monroe asked.

Bishop kneeled down and took a look at the padlock, thinking it didn't look too difficult. He looked at Cohen who gave a deep sigh.

"Look," the rabbi said, shaking his head and crossing his arms over his chest. "I can't stand here and watch you desecrate one of the world's holiest places."

"What do you mean 'desecrate?'" Bishop asked. "We only want to take a quick look inside, touch nothing, wear gloves and protective clothing. And you don't have to stand here. You can wait somewhere else. Besides, I told you we are not alone in this search so someone else will come, I guarantee you that. And from what we've seen they might not have the manners we do."

"We could set up extra guards to intercept whoever is coming," Cohen replied.

"Sure, but how long can you keep that up?" Monroe responded. "You don't know what you're dealing with."

"But more importantly," Bishop said, "don't you want to know what's down there yourself?"

Cohen gave the question serious thought before telling him, "It doesn't matter what I'm curious about; you are never going to fit through that hole."

The four of them stared at the hole. Bishop kneeled down again and put his hands on the edges of the hatch. "I might not fit and you certainly won't," he said looking at Monroe. "But you might," Bishop said, turning to Jennifer.

Jennifer took a small step backward. "You want me to go down there? All by myself? Not knowing what I might run into and what to look for?"

"Look," Bishop said, standing to place his hands on her shoulders. "It makes sense. You're the only one who probably fits and this is an opportunity of a lifetime. You can do this." He shifted his attention to Cohen. "Do your security guards have communications systems?"

Cohen hesitated before reluctantly admitting they did.

Bishop returned his attention to Jennifer. "See, we can use the system to keep in contact with you. You can be our eyes and ears down there and we'll guide you every step of the way. So, what do you say?"

Jennifer took another step back before running her hands through her hair. "I must be crazy to even consider this," she mumbled.

The rabbi grunted his agreement.

As their every breath echoed around the room, the rabbi eventually turned to one of the guards and nodded. He, in turn, nodded to his colleagues and they all took out their earpieces and handed them over.

"Here," Cohen said, handing them each an earpiece while keeping one for himself and pointing to a door a few yards away. "I'll be over there. Please don't make me regret this."

"We won't," Bishop said. He then handed Jennifer a small plastic package containing overalls. "Put them on," he instructed. "I'll open the lock."

As Bishop started fiddling with the lock, Jennifer shook her head, not quite believing what she was about to do and wondering whether this was the kind of thing her father had gotten up to when he was away. As she imagined his Indiana Jones exploits she realized she was not only afraid but also excited, and a single tear fell from her eyes. *Just do it,* she told herself. Minutes later, she was dressed in paperwhite overalls, overshoes and felt gloves with her long blonde hair hidden under a white cap.

"With a carrot and two pieces of coal you'd look just like—"

Jennifer interrupted Monroe before he could finish. "Yeah, yeah, I know."

A small click echoed around the hall as the padlock sprung open. "Okay. Let's check our comms systems," Bishop said. "Do you hear me clearly?"

Once everyone had replied in the affirmative, Bishop took a small backpack and gave it to Jennifer.

"All right, let's do this," he said, handing over a flashlight.

"But what do I look for?" Jennifer asked.

"Just tell us what you see. Every little detail can be important and we'll take it from there. One step at the time. Are you claustrophobic?"

"Now he asks," Jennifer replied.

"You do the honors," Monroe said and Bishop grabbed the brass clasp with both hands.

Having anticipated some resistance, he pulled hard, but it fell easily open with a loud bang on the marble floor. "Sorry."

All three of them moved forward to shine their lights into the hole, finding a narrow staircase covered with paper scrolls.

"Looks narrower than I thought," Jennifer said.

"You can do this," Bishop assured her as she sat on the edge of the opening and carefully lowered her feet into it.

"There we go," she said as she touched the first step holding on to Bishop and Monroe. She carefully descended, step by step, until she slipped on scrolls of paper and fell down the rest.

"Ouch," she muttered as she hit the bottom.

"Are you okay?" Bishop asked, shining his flashlight on Jennifer on the floor.

"About sixteen steps," she said. "You said every detail is important and I counted sixteen steps with my butt."

"That's perfect," Bishop said as he laughed. "What do you see?"

Jennifer stood up, put on the backpack and looked around with her flashlight. "I'm in a small room with no markings, knee deep in paper. There's a hole, about five yards to my right. Looks like a tunnel, about four feet wide and three feet high. I can't see where it leads."

"Can you reach it and climb into it?" Bishop asked.

"I think so. Wait a minute." Jennifer waded through the paper scrolls, which was harder work than it looked. She stuck her head into the opening of the tunnel and shone her flashlight inside. "Looks solid," she said, tapping the carved stone wall. "The tunnel runs for about sixty feet or so and if I'm not mistaken I see a staircase at the end."

"That must be the other entrance," Monroe said.

"Good," Bishop said. "Is there anything else in the corridor? An entrance to any other tunnels or rooms?"

Jennifer looked carefully. "I don't see any, but I can't say for sure. My light is bouncing off the light-colored bedrock. I need to get in to check it out."

"Are you sure?" Bishop asked.

"Here you go again with your ill-timed questions," she joked. "Sure I'm sure. Not a good moment to back down now."

"Spunky girl," Monroe said.

Bishop turned to him. "I hope you realize something better not go wrong," he replied quietly. "We have no way of getting down there to help her."

As the two men exchanged a glance, Bishop told Jennifer to proceed with care.

"I will," she said before putting the flashlight in her mouth and crawling on her hands into the tunnel. After a few yards, she stopped with a grunt.

"Are you all right?" Bishop asked, and for a moment there was silence.

"I'm okay," Jennifer eventually replied and Bishop and Monroe both sighed with relief. "I didn't see it from the entrance, but there's a large opening on the left. I'll look into it."

Poking her head down the hole, she shone the light and found the floor of a hall. "That's strange," she said, "there's another level some ten feet below."

"Can you get down to it?" Bishop asked.

"That's the strange part. There's a ladder down to the floor—a brand new aluminum ladder, if I'm not mistaken."

Bishop and Monroe looked at each other.

"Okay, I think you better come back now," Bishop said.

"I think so, too," Monroe added. "This is clearly not what we expected."

"I'm already on the ladder, halfway down," Jennifer told them. "Going on. It's very wide down here and sturdy as a rock. Don't worry."

Bishop rubbed his hands over his eyes. "I heard her father was just as stubborn."

Jennifer stepped from the ladder. The stones felt sturdy below her feet. Able to stand upright, she touched the ceiling a foot above her head. The rock was hard and solid. The air smelled a little stale, but there seemed to be enough oxygen to breath. There was surprisingly little dust. "I'm in a room carved out in the bedrock, somewhat circular, about thirteen feet in diameter and seven feet high." She rested her back against the ladder. "There doesn't seem to be any markings on the walls. Wait a minute." She stepped a few feet from the ladder, kneeled and picked up something from the floor. "There are shards of pottery on the floor. Looks old, but nothing special."

"Leave it," Bishop said. "What we're looking for won't be in that room. You're in the first cave. Do you see another tunnel or a doorway?"

Jennifer moved her flashlight around the cave and stopped some five feet to her left. "There's a gap in the bedrock to the left of me. It's not that wide, but it could be a passageway. I'll check it out."

"Be careful," Bishop said, but Jennifer was already moving her body sideways through the gap holding the backpack in her hands. It was a tight squeeze, but after only a few feet she came to another opening.

"I'm through," she said. "I'm in another cave." The beam of her flashlight moved along the walls. "Looks like a copy of the first room, but about four times as big. Again, some shards on the floor, but otherwise empty."

Jennifer pointed the flashlight at the floor to see where she was going.

"Nothing?" Monroe asked.

"Please look for any irregularities in the floor, the walls, the ceiling," Bishop told her.

"I checked the floor," Jennifer replied, "but there's nothing there. I'll check the walls. Oh, hang on. The wall here is different from the first cave. Looks like it's plastered, though most of it has come off." She ran her fingers up and down, left to right, along every inch of the wall. "Almost halfway...." she muttered before suddenly stopping as she came across a slight bump.

"What is it?" Monroe asked anxiously.

"Hold on," Jennifer replied. "Feels like there's something in the plaster here. Some kind of form or shape beneath it." Jennifer rubbed her fingers over the plaster, but only a small part came away. "I can't free it. I'm afraid to damage it."

"Jennifer, listen," Bishop said. "In your backpack there's a small canteen with water. Sprinkle some on the wall and try again. If I'm correct the water will dissolve what little of the solvent they used. Then you can use the brush to reveal the stone wall behind it."

Jennifer took the canteen and splashed water on the wall before taking the brush to tackle the irregularity in the wall. "There's definitely something here," she said as she worked. "It looks like they filled it with sand or something and then plastered over it."

As Jennifer continued to brush, muddy water trickled to the floor. Taking a small step backward, she tilted her head to try to make sense of the lines carved into the wall. As she stared, a figure began to emerge before her eyes, and she gasped in wonder.

CHAPTER 25

Aleph, Beth, Gimel, Daleth

"Jennifer?" Bishop called, but the young woman was too transfixed by the sign on the wall to answer.

"Jennifer Porter?" Monroe called urgently.

Bishop looked at him, wondering how many Jennifers he thought were down there.

"I'm here," she finally said. "I uncovered a sign on the wall. Looks like C, but in reverse, rounded at the top and square at the lower corner."

"Beth," Monroe said. "There's our first letter."

"Or person," Bishop added. "Jennifer, please continue along the wall to your right, about the same height as you were, and look for another letter."

"Already doing it," she said as she moved her fingers over the wall, a little more carefully than before so she wouldn't miss anything. Some two feet along she stopped again. "Might've found something." Jennifer grabbed her brush and water canister and got to work. "It looks like an X. Perhaps 'X' marks the spot?"

"That's Aleph, the first letter of the Hebrew alphabet," Bishop replied. "Good work. Two to go. If they're in sequence you need to go back to the left and look for Gimel. It should look a little like Beth, the inverted C, only narrower. Probably at the same distance away as the other two are."

"In sequence?" Jennifer asked.

"You remember?" Bishop asked. "You need to read it from right to left."

Jennifer moved to the left.

"You know why people read from right to left?" Bishop asked, and without waiting for an answer he started to explain. "The popular theory is that in ancient times Hebrews chiseled out text on a stone tablet using a hammer. The engraver would hold the hammer in his stronger right hand and the chisel with his left. That way it was far easier to write from right to left."

"What do you think the signs mean?" Monroe asked Bishop.

"Not sure, but this can't be a coincidence. We need to see the whole picture."

"Found something," Jennifer told them, and reached for her tool kit. "This one looks a little like a J."

"Yes, that's good." Bishop shook his fist excitedly. "One to go, also to your left."

"I'm on my way." Seconds later Jennifer discovered the final letter. "Done."

"What do you see?" Bishop asked. "Describe every detail."

Jennifer took a few steps back and lit the wall with her flashlight.

"I see four signs within squares, about five by five inches, locked into the bedrock."

"What now?" Monroe asked.

"Are they carved or slotted into the wall?" Bishop asked. "Can you move them or push them?"

Jennifer put the flashlight in her mouth and with both hands grasped the edge of the first sign, the *Daleth,* but no matter how much she pulled or pushed it wouldn't budge. She moved on to the next sign with no more luck. The third and fourth letters also refused to move.

"Nothing," she said.

"There has to be something else down there," Monroe said.

Jennifer shone her light along the walls to see.

"Aleph, Beth, Gimel and Daleth," Bishop mumbled. "Adam, Eve, Abraham and Sarah. What does it mean? What are we missing? If you had a cave and you had four signs in the wall and needed to hide something where would you hide it?"

"Behind door number three?" Monroe joked.

"What did you say?" Bishop asked, putting a hand on Monroe's shoulder.

"Just now?" Monroe asked and Bishop nodded. "Behind door number three?"

Bishop pinched Monroe's shoulder and the big man yelped.

"Sorry," Bishop apologized, "but you might've just solved the puzzle."

"What's that?" Jennifer asked.

"Aleph, Beth, Gimel and Daleth. What are they?" Bishop asked.

"The first letters of the Hebrew alphabet?" Jennifer answered.

"Correct. And what else are they?"

"People?" Monroe asked.

"No, not people," Bishop replied. "That's what we thought."

"Numbers!" Jennifer shouted.

"That too," Bishop said. "But again, that's not what I mean." Bishop paused for a second. "Nothing?" he asked, before giving his colleagues a little more time until his patience ran out. "Nouns," he finally said. "Every letter of the Hebrew alphabet stands for a noun."

"And that helps us how?" Monroe asked.

Bishop smiled. "The Hebrew alphabet, being among the oldest in the world, was derived from the original Phoenician alphabet. The word 'alphabet' even comes from the first two Hebrew letters: Aleph and Beth. Before the alphabet, words and sometimes entire phrases were presented as a single picture. When they started to expand their vocabulary around 19 BC they probably ran out of ideas, constructing signs for words. Then the alphabet was born and pictures used for words started to die out. Nowadays, all that's left are the twenty-two nouns that were once depicted by the signs that now form the modern Hebrew alphabet, probably the greatest invention ever after the discovery of the wheel. Anyway, Aleph, the first letter of the alphabet once stood for ox, Beth meant house, Gimel was camel, and Daleth...." Bishop paused again. "Daleth stood for door."

Monroe tilted his head as Bishop asked Jennifer to have another look at the Daleth figure.

"I'm in front of it," she said. "I'm looking, but I see nothing special."

"Please look carefully. There must be something besides that figure. The Daleth must signify a doorway of some kind."

Jennifer pushed and pulled to no avail until finally she scratched the surface carefully with the back of her flashlight. A few specks of marble fell to the floor. She then went to the next sign and tested it by scratching at it, but nothing came away.

"The Daleth sign appears softer than the others. They look the same, but I scratched the bedrock on two signs and the Daleth sign crumbles while the other is marble hard."

"Scratch it some more," Bishop urged.

Monroe looked at him, frowning.

"Are you sure?" Jennifer asked.

"I'm positive. Just do it."

"This is a 3,000-year-old religious monument you're desecrating," Monroe hissed.

"I don't think so," Bishop replied before turning at the sound of footsteps nearing. Seeing Rabbi Cohen approach, he spoke hastily. "Jennifer, trust me. Scratch it again and use all the force you can muster."

Jennifer took a deep breath. "All right, you're the boss," she said and scratched away at the sign with greater vigor until a small dent became apparent. "The top is coming off. Still scratching. Aw, what the hell." Jennifer suddenly flipped the flashlight and bashed at the wall with the base of it. Bigger chunks of soft rock fell away until, after four more hits, she found what she was looking for. "There's something here. I see a small opening. I'll try to widen it." Giving the stone a few extra punches, the hole widened considerably. "There's a square opening!"

"Door number four." Bishop smiled. "What do you see?"

Jennifer pointed the flashlight into the hole. "I see something about two feet in."

"Be careful," Monroe said, but by then Jennifer's arm was inside the hole.

"I feel it. Pulling it out now." From the hole in the wall, Jennifer retrieved a bag made of cloth with lace on top. "I've got something. A cloth bag of some kind and it feels like there's some kind of cylinder in it."

"That's it! Put it in your backpack and get out of there." As Bishop spoke he felt the rabbi's hand on his shoulder. He looked behind him to find Cohen shaking his head. Bishop tried to assure him that nothing untoward had taken place. "You see, it wasn't an ancient carving. Łaski must have somehow entered the cave in the sixteenth century and put it in and then replaced the Daleth sign with one he cut out of soft stone, soapstone I guess."

Cohen didn't speak. He just sighed.

As she made her return Jennifer took as many pictures of the rooms and corridors as she could on her cellphone. "I'm at the stairs to the corridor, coming up," she told them.

"That's still a mystery," Monroe said.

"What is?" Bishop asked before remembering the aluminum ladder and shrugging.

Jennifer climbed, panting a little. As she got to the top of the ladder, above the corridor, she felt a hand on her shoulder and cried out in alarm, almost falling until the hand grabbed the strap of her backpack and held her steady. She was then pulled up and out of the hole. Aware her flashlight was lighting only the floor she steeled herself and pointed it up, straight into the face of Malkuth. Jennifer froze.

"You?"

"Jennifer?" Bishop called out. "Jennifer, are you all right?"

Jennifer opened her mouth to speak, but before she could say anything Malkuth put his finger to his lips.

"Sh," he said softly. He took her backpack and placed it on his shoulder before waving at her to follow him to the other end of the long, dark corridor.

"But the entrance is...."

Malkuth put one hand on her mouth. With the other, he gestured for her to remain silent. For a second, they locked eyes and Jennifer found herself nodding. With his hand on her shoulder, Malkuth pushed her in front of him.

"It sounded like there was someone else down there," Monroe said. "Jennifer, are you there? Please say something."

"Impossible," Cohen said. "There hasn't been anyone down there in ages."

"What about the aluminum ladder?" Monroe asked smugly and Cohen stayed silent.

"Where was the other entrance, precisely?" Bishop asked.

"There, on the other side of the Isaac hall." Cohen said, pointing near a door in the far corner of the hall.

"Can we take a look over there and see what's going on?"

Cohen nodded and waved to his security guards to join them.

"I'll stay here in case she comes out," Monroe said.

As the guards' footsteps echoed around the hall, Bishop put his finger to his mouth and they halted before tiptoeing to the heavy, green wooden door. Cohen nodded to one of the guards who stepped forward to take hold of the brass handle. After another nod from the rabbi, he slowly opened the door, which barely made a sound despite its age. The guard looked left and right before stepping inside, gesturing to his team to follow.

"Isaac and Rebekah," Cohen whispered, pointing at what looked like two small houses set behind large columns supporting the roof. The cenotaphs were made of red and beige striped marble with slanted green rooftops. Though the room looked empty, Cohen sent two guards ahead of them to check it out. A few seconds later, one of them waved them over to the Isaac memorial. As quietly as possible, they joined the guard who pointed a few feet in front of him. On the floor was a large tripod with a large square concrete tile hanging from it. Below it a piece of the carpet had been removed and a hole in the floor revealed what looked like a stairwell.

"The second entrance," Bishop whispered as they heard sounds coming from beneath them. The security guards took their guns from their shoulder holsters and pointed them at the hole in the floor.

"Quickly," Cohen hissed as he moved behind the cenotaph, out of sight of the hole and Bishop joined him. The guards took a few steps back and waited. The sound of shuffling footsteps moved up the stairs. Jennifer's raised arms emerged from the hole. As she pushed herself up she saw one of the armed guards, she gasped as he put a finger to his lips. The guard gestured for her to get up before lifting her out of the way as Malkuth's hands appeared, quickly followed by his head. The guards grabbed his shoulders and forced him out.

"Get down! On the floor!" the guards shouted in both English and Hebrew, and Malkuth hit the floor to find his hands immediately bound with zip ties. Jennifer ran into Bishop's arms.

"You're okay?" Bishop asked.

It took Jennifer a moment to answer. "Yeah, I'm fine. Nothing happened."

Bishop looked her in the eye.

"Thank God you're safe," Monroe said, arriving from the other room to pat her on the shoulder.

From the other side of the building, they heard voices in the distance. Bishop and Monroe looked at Cohen.

"Who's that?" Bishop asked.

"I'm sorry," Cohen said. "There was nothing I could do."

Bishop and Monroe frowned.

"You informed the authorities?"

"No," Cohen said. "I did no such thing. We must have triggered some alarm. One of the guards at the entrance just informed me." He touched his earpiece. "I have nothing to do with this. But I can help." He gestured for the backpack next to Malkuth and one of the guards handed it over. Cohen then passed it to Bishop and pointed to a door in the north of the hall. "Go through that door, turn right and follow the corridor right again until you reach a gate with stairs behind it leading down. The gate will be unlocked and your car will be there to the left."

For a second, Bishop, Monroe and Jennifer hesitated.

"If you don't want to be arrested, you need to go now!"

"Thank you," Bishop said while the others nodded. "I'll contact you later."

"Hurry and be silent," Cohen said as the three made their way to the door. As they disappeared from the room they heard loud voices shouting in Hebrew behind them.

They followed the path as quickly and quietly as they could until they reached the gate. Monroe carefully swung it open, but couldn't prevent a screech of protest from the old iron hinges. He stopped and looked back into the corridor.

"Just go," Bishop whispered. "We'll fit through."

One by one they wiggled through the opening, ran down the stairs and turned left to see their car some hundred feet in the distance. As Bishop took a step forward, Monroe tapped him on the shoulder and pointed to the other side of the parking lot. Two police cars waited in the dark and two uniformed men guarded the entrance.

"Give me the keys," Monroe said. Seeing the doubt on Bishop's face, he urged him to hand them over and Bishop reluctantly did. "Stay here and be ready."

Crouched low, Monroe sneaked around the back of the parking lot to get to the car without being seen. With a soft click he opened the door and got in. Then, taking a deep breath, he pulled the passenger's seat forward, knowing he'd need to be fast once he started the car.

With a click he turned the ignition and the two cylinders of the Fiat 500 gave their distinctive roar. He shifted into gear and put the pedal to the floor, spinning the wheels and spraying sand. At full speed, he drove toward Bishop and Jennifer. A quick glance in his mirror revealed the policemen were nervously walking around their cars. With a screech of tires, he stopped next to the stairs and swung open the passenger door. Jennifer threw herself into the backseat, reclining the front one as she got in and Bishop jumped in, next to Monroe. Not waiting for the door to close, Monroe took off at high speed and onto the main road. With a sharp turn he drove up the road, looking in his rearview mirror to find no one following. The streets were empty.

"Hey, will you look out?" Bishop said as Monroe shifted the Fiat to the left side of the road. "We're in Israel."

"Sorry. Old habits die hard when stressed," Monroe shouted.

Bishop and Jennifer kept their eyes on the road behind them, but it remained clear. Monroe put the pedal further to the floor, turned another corner and automatically returned to driving on the left, heading for another car's headlights. As the other car honked, Monroe realized his mistake and swerved with less than a second to spare. But even as he corrected himself he moved to his default position and into more oncoming traffic.

"Monroe!" Bishop screamed and again, at the last minute, he spun the wheel to the right, heading straight for a lamppost, then a house, then a fence, and then there was nothing—nothing but blackness.

CHAPTER 26

St. Mary the Virgin

2009

Porter looked at his watch. It was four in the morning and he realized that for the past four hours he'd been scrutinizing every inch of the sketch of the church. Just to be sure, he zoomed in again on the headstone. His finger moved along the screen, tracing the lines he had found. Unmistakably, they formed the initials 'JD.'

"John Dee," he whispered, not for the first time, kicking himself for not having noticed before. The answer had been evident the whole time. It shouldn't have been such a mystery. The entire contents of the box revolved around John Dee, so how he had not immediately jumped to the conclusion he had now reached was beyond him.

After rubbing his eyes, Porter turned to his laptop and typed 'John Dee grave' into thesearch engine. It yielded 2,990,000 results, but he figured he only needed to look at the top one. 'Dr. John Dee (1527-1609) - Find A Grave Memorial.' He clicked on the link and a portrait of John Dee appeared. It was the same picture found on just about every webpage or article written about the famous alchemist. To the left of it, he found the information he was looking for.

Dr. John Dee
BIRTH 13 Jul 1527
Greater London, England
DEATH 26 Mar 1609 (aged 81)
Greater London, England

BURIAL
St Mary the Virgin Churchyard
Mortlake, London Borough of Richmond upon Thames
Greater London, England

He clicked on the link to 'St. Mary the Virgin Churchyard' and was directed to findagrave.com. There he found general information about the place such as the address as well as a small photo of a sign giving the days and times of services. Then, as Porter scrolled down the page, he saw a small picture of the church. Clicking to enlarge it, Porter reached for the sketch he had spent all night scrutinizing and compared the two images. *This is it,* he thought. He took a deep breath and then exhaled slowly. Although the two images were taken from completely different angles, the resemblance was clear. John Dee had described his own resting place. Then the small smile on his face faded as he realized that even though he knew where to find the church he was no clearer on the other details. He had no idea what the words *Sanctum lavacrum loco nativitatis* implied beyond their literal translation of 'holy place of birth and rebirth.' And why 'rebirth' instead of the more common ecclesiastical term 'resurrection?' What was behind the image of the Monas in the picture?

Porter closed his eyes for a second. He could no longer think straight and knew he should quit while he was ahead. He needed to sleep, if only for a few hours.

As Porter rose from his desk, he gave the screen on the laptop one more look and smiled. At least he had found his church.

Despite his tiredness, Porter spent what was left of the night tossing and turning in bed. After finally falling asleep, he awoke just a few hours later. His body ached and his eyelids felt heavy. Dragging himself to the kitchen he turned on the brand new Dolce Gusto coffee maker he had bought because it made a decent cappuccino in seconds without any hassle. That morning, however, he needed something stronger, so he made himself a double espresso. When he took his first sip, he sighed with relief. He then returned to his study, sat down at his desk and powered up his laptop.

The screen showed the image of St. Mary the Virgin Churchyard in London. He wasn't sure what he was looking for. John Dee's grave, perhaps. But nobody knew where it was. Searching the Internet, he found there was speculation that he was buried at the church in Mortlake, London, but there was no grave, not even a memorial to him. Some claimed he was buried under the chancel, but there was no evidence to support this. Porter shook his head. Up until a few months ago, he'd always thought of Dee as a medieval quack who had somehow found popularity in high society. Rather like Nostradamus, the pharmacist who became the royal court's fortune teller in France or

Russia's Rasputin, the self-proclaimed holy man who became the tsar's favorite faith healer. Even so, Porter couldn't shake the feeling he was missing something, though he wasn't sure whether this was due to Łaski's box and the documents within it or the third-party interest in it.

Porter shook his head again and opened his copy of the Monas Hieroglyphica on the laptop because, according to Dee, that held all the secrets waiting to be uncovered. He zoomed in on the text below the Monas hieroglyph engraved in the pedestal.

Arcanum est quod latet in loco sancto prope domum meam, ubi vita incipit

He mumbled while writing on a piece of paper in front of him. "The Monas hides a secret which lies concealed in the holy place, adjoining to my house, where life has its beginning."

It was a text many had read but no one had been able to explain. He looked again at the picture of St. Mary's that he had found in the metal box. On top of the page was written *Sanctum lavacrum loco nativitatis*, a holy place of birth and rebirth. What was hidden and where? He had read that Dee spent a large part of his life in London living opposite the church. So, if he had hidden something somewhere, the church would be the logical place to look.

"Good morning, Dad." Jennifer walked up to her father holding a large ceramic mug bearing the accolade *Best Dad Ever* in red and black letters. "Cappuccino?"

"Good morning." Porter took the mug and sighed with satisfaction as he smelled the coffee. "That's fantastic, dear."

"What are you doing?" Jennifer looked at the laptop screen.

Porter smiled. He liked it when his daughter showed interest in his work even though he found it hard to explain. Hell, from time to time, he didn't understand it himself.

"I'm looking for something hidden in this church." He pointed at the picture on the screen. "And the only hint I have is this." He showed Jennifer the paper on which was written 'The Monas hides a secret which lies concealed in the holy place, adjoining to my house, where life has its beginning.'

"What's a Monas?" she asked and Porter showed her a picture of it on his laptop. "It looks a bit like a bull, don't you think?"

"I guess you're right." Porter looked at the screen again. "Actually, wait a second."

Porter opened his copy of the Monas Hieroglyphica and turning to page 45, he pointed at the image there.

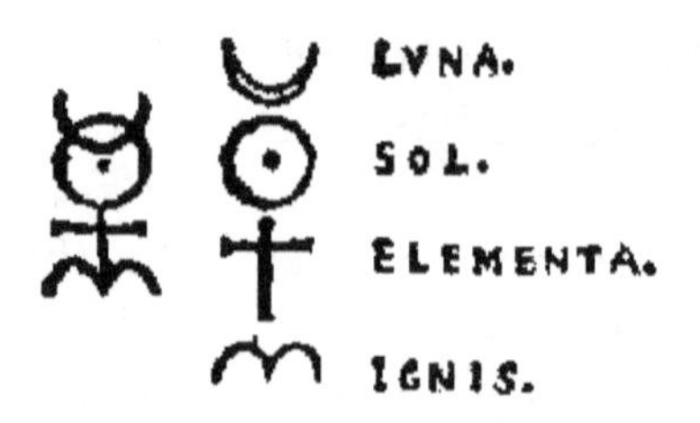

"The moon, the sun, the elements and fire," Jennifer said.

"Very good," her father replied before drawing her attention to the text below the image. "And here it says, 'The Sun and the Moon of this Monas desire that the Elements in which the tenth proportion will flower, shall be separated, and this is done by the application of Fire.'"

"Which means?"

"I have no idea, but neither does anyone else. It's just another mystery."

"And is that symbol anywhere to be found in that church?"

"I don't know. There's not much information about the church online. I may need to go there and take a look for myself."

"Where's there?"

"Mortlake in London."

Jennifer raised her eyebrows. "Can I come?"

Porter laughed out loud. "I'm not even sure if I'm going. Trust me, these trips aren't much fun for a young woman and, besides that, you've got school. I promise you that one day we'll take a research trip together. Finish your school and we'll talk again."

"Figures," Jennifer said, shaking her head. Stamping her way to the door, she turned to find her father once again glued to his laptop. "I guess I won't tell you then that I'd look for that symbol at the baptistry."

Porter slowly lifted his eyes from the screen. "What do you mean?"

"The Monas hides a secret which lies concealed, where life has its beginning?" She paused to allow her father to catch up, but he merely cocked his head in puzzlement. "No? Okay, what's the most important happening in church after birth?"

He thought for a short moment. "The baptism," he replied. "Of course. That's actually quite helpful."

Jennifer gave a small bow.

"And no, you still can't come."

Once Jennifer had walked away, sulking, Porter returned to the search engine to see if there were any pictures of the church's baptistry online. On typing 'St. Mary's Mortlake baptistry' into the search box some 453,000 results came back. However, only the first three somewhat blurry pictures were from the London church and they were either blurred or taken at an obscure angle. Useless. Porter checked the video results finding one titled 'Baptism at St. Mary the Virgin Mortlake.' He play the video.

On the screen, a priest explained that the font was positioned next to the entrance because baptism marks a Christian's entrance into the family of faith. *So far, so good,* thought Porter. A few minutes later, the priest took a large silver jug and poured water into the font. Porter paused and zoomed to scrutinize the hexagon-shaped marble basin that sat on a pedestal, some four feet high and three feet wide. On the two visible sides were symbols carved into the stone. One clearly depicted a cross, another looked like a five-petaled rose. Porter was reminded of the Christian expression 'under the rose.' It was a phrase that indicated something was to be considered confidential or secret. Usually the symbol was found on confession stands so that it looked out of place on the font.

Porter tried to make out some of the other symbols, but nowhere on the video were the other six sides shown. He switched to the church's website and clicked on a contact form, just as his wife walked in.

"Sylvia!" he said, somewhat startled. "Good morning. Did you sleep well?"

She nodded and put her hands on her sides. "What are you up to now?"

"What would I be up to, dear?" Porter grinned, closed the laptop and walked up to her. "Coffee?"

A tall man dressed in a classic Boglioli suit stared through the floor-to-ceiling window overlooking California's Marina del Rey. In the dusk, the lights of dozens of yachts danced on the soft ripples rolling in from the ocean, like moths over a campfire. Behind him, the door opened.

"He's here, sir."

"Send him in," he said without turning around and almost immediately a clean-cut man entered the room. "Please sit down," he said and turned to find the man lowering himself into a chair. "What did you find out?"

The visitor threw a paper folder onto the desk between them. *Culver BioPharma* was written below the company logo.

"Tell me," the man demanded, ignoring the folder. Dave Matthews bit his lip, trying to keep calm. The man opposite him might be rude but he paid him a lot of money to have him look into the documents. "All right," he said. "We researched the texts and although our experts have more questions than answers they're convinced there's a link to our own research in the field."

"So? A medieval quack, an alchemist, did some research six hundred years ago. How is that of benefit to me?"

"That's not all. Along with some vague references on one of the papers, my men found an unmistakable reference to a specific location. If you look in the folder...." The visitor paused and the man reached for the folder. "The first page has a summary," he explained.

The man took a few minutes to leaf through the dossier before fully reading the summary. He then closed the folder and threw it back on the table.

"Okay, so what do you need?"

"We've set up a foundation with a small trust fund focusing on restoring medieval religious structures in old Britannia. The archbishop's office has already agreed to an architectural inspection next week, closing the building down so we have it all to ourselves."

"And Porter? Any action from his side?"

"We have him under constant surveillance, but there's no indication he's about to do anything."

"Take...." The man paused to clear his throat. "Take the two days. Turn the place upside down and put it back together again and report back to me, and only me. And keep it legal. I want no loose ends leading to Culver."

Matthews nodded. "Will do, sir."

CHAPTER 27

Lockup

The Present

As the first rays of the sun lit up the room, Jennifer woke to see a nurse changing a drip attached to her. She turned her head slowly, taking in her surroundings. She was in a simple, sparse hospital room with bare walls and no furniture save for the bed she was in, a bedside table and a single chair in the corner, on which sat a uniformed police officer. The light and movement made her head spin and she felt nauseous, nearly throwing up. The nurse turned and noticed Jennifer was awake.

"Doctor!" she called before speaking to Jennifer in Hebrew.

Jennifer squinted as a man in a white coat joined them.

"Miss Porter, how are you feeling?"

Jennifer's eyes surveyed the room, coming to stop on the young man's face. She tried to speak, but the words couldn't pass her lips. She cleared her throat.

"Here." The man handed her a glass of water from the small table next to the bed. Carefully, she took the glass and sat up before sipping. She was grateful to feel her limbs still functioning.

"Where am I?" she asked in a hoarse whisper.

"You're at the Al-Ahli Hospital in Hebron. I'm Dr. David Elder. I'm an intern here."

"You're American," Jennifer noted. "What am I doing here? Wait, there was a car accident."

As a rush of images coursed through her head, the doctor spoke to her softly to calm her down. "Take it easy. You were in an accident, but besides having a concussion, you seem to be fine. You'll have to be careful for a few days, but otherwise I don't see a problem."

"And my friends? What about my friends?"

"I don't know," replied the doctor. "You were the only one brought in. That was almost two days ago."

Jennifer shook her head, feeling another rush of nausea come over her. "Two days?"

"Easy," the young doctor soothed. "They brought you in with a police escort, but without explanation." Taking a small side step, he revealed the officer sitting by the door. The officer spoke in Hebrew into a microphone attached to his shoulder. "You see?" continued the doctor. "You must be of importance to the law somehow."

"Excuse me!" Jennifer called out to the policeman. "Excuse me, do you speak English?" Her throat ached.

The officer rose from his chair and approached the bed. "Yes, I do speak English, miss."

"Do you know where my friends are?"

He shook his head. "I don't know, miss. I'm only here to watch you and call in when you wake up, and I just did that. I expect someone to be here soon to talk to you."

A few miles from the hospital a policeman rattled a ring with keys against the metal bars of the lockup.

"You have a visitor," he called out to the two figures in the back, who woke with a grunt from wooden benches covered with a thin mattress.

"My back is killing me," Monroe said.

"Trust me, that has more to do with your driving skills than these beds," replied Bishop, rubbing his eyes before standing to take a look at a man dressed in a cheap suit waiting for them on the other side of the bars.

"Matthew," the man greeted Bishop.

"Victor," Bishop replied. "It took you two days?"

Monroe joined the two men. "This is him?"

Bishop nodded. "Walker Monroe meet Victor Conway, attaché at the U.S. embassy, at the Public Diplomacy Office."

Victor Conway looked to be in his early forties, almost bald and sporting a three-day beard. Bishop and Conway went back a long way—more than ten years. It was Conway who helped him gain access to Tel Aviv University to research the use of mathematically-perfect spherical jugs to measure trade volumes used some 3,000 years ago. Since then they'd considered each other a friend, kept in touch and visited occasionally whenever they were in the same country at the same time.

"Pleased to meet you." Monroe shook Conway's hand through the bars.

"I was out of the country," Conway replied. "Anyway, a few nights behind bars might not be such a bad thing for you right now. Desecrating and destroying historic property, really? Not your usual style."

"I have an explanation," Bishop said.

"I'm sure you do. I spoke to Rabbi Cohen on my way here. Still, you should have come to me before you started your little adventure in Israel."

"I know, but this entire venture wasn't really planned and one thing kind of led to another...."

"And yet, here you are." Conway smiled.

Monroe noticed that he hadn't stopped smiling since he arrived.

"Do you know anything about Jennifer Porter, the young woman who was traveling with us? They told us she was in hospital and going to be okay."

"Yes, she's fine. As a matter of fact, you'll be joining her soon. You're free to go. There will be no further inquiry—on the condition that you leave the country immediately upon your release."

Bishop looked at Monroe.

"You too," Conway confirmed and reached into his inside jacket pocket to show them three plane tickets. "You'll all fly out of here to New York in three hours. Right now, you are entrusted into my care and I have had to personally vouch for your departure."

"That's generous of you. Thank you," Bishop acknowledged.

Conway nodded to the guard who opened the gate.

"All your stuff is in my car. I'll take you to the hospital to pick up your companion. It's a fifteen-minute drive. From there you'll be taken to Ben-Gurion Airport, which is about sixty miles away."

"What happened to the man who ambushed us at Machpelah?" Monroe asked as they walked through the police station.

"Michael Robartés?" Conway asked.

"Yeah, not his real name," Bishop said.

"It isn't. They found a fake passport he was using. He's in Israeli custody at an undisclosed location. They promised to take me to him later this afternoon."

"There's more to him than being a simple thief," Bishop warned. "We think he might be connected to our search and the murder of a Polish priest."

"Cohen told me a bit about your search, without specifics. And while I'm dying to hear all the details, for now, we need to get you out of here as quickly as possible. The Israelis owe us a favor, but the situation is far from stable so, if you please, before they change their minds."

Conway picked up the pace, smiled and gave a friendly wave to the police officer sitting behind a desk. Moments later they were in the car and driving away from the police station.

Fifteen minutes later, as Bishop finished filling him in on the details, Conway drove through the barrier at the Al-Ahli hospital parking lot.

"That's quite a story," he said as he stopped the car.

"And all true," Bishop replied. "You need to talk to Robartés."

"I'll talk to him, but you have to remember that to the Israelis, Robartés is just a grave robber and to the U.S. that's a domestic problem. From what you have told me there have been no reports of wrongdoing on U.S. soil, just suspicion of a crime in Poland. We can relay that to our Polish friends, but that's about it."

Bishop sighed. "Well, if you learn anything, please let me know."

"Will do."

"There she is!" Monroe shouted as he pointed to the hospital exit where Jennifer emerged in a wheelchair. "I'll get her."

Monroe left the car and to greet Jennifer who immediately stood up and wrapped her arms around his neck.

"So good to see you again," she said.

"You have no idea," Monroe answered. "I'm so very, very sorry. It's all my fault. How are you?"

"I'm okay. Just a bit of a headache, but they told me it will pass soon if I take it easy and take two aspirins every three hours. How are you?"

"Come. Bishop's waiting." Monroe turned and walked back to the car. "We're fine. They kept us in lockup for two days, but we're healthy. We need to get on our way to the airport. They want us to leave the country."

"I heard. And I must confess that I'm not disappointed. It will be good to be home again for a while."

As they reached the car, Bishop and Conway were already collecting their things from the trunk. Conway gave Jennifer a quick handshake and introduced himself.

"There's your drive." Conway waved to a nearby old Land Rover Defender. An older man with a gray beard, completely dressed in black, stepped out of the car, threw his burning cigarette away and approached them. "This is Youssef," Conway said. "Youssef doesn't speak or understand any English. I've found that very useful from time to time."

Youssef nodded at everyone and took the rest of the luggage from the trunk back to his car.

"He'll take you to the airport," Conway said as he handed Bishop the tickets. "I hope next time we meet we have more time to socialize."

"I hope so too," Bishop replied as he shook his friend's hand. Jennifer and Monroe followed suit before gathering their things and moving to the Defender where Youssef had already opened the back doors revealing two bench seats, opposite each other, screwed to a dusty floor.

"How old do you think this car is?" Monroe asked pointing to the rust on the door.

"I think it's from the nineties," Bishop answered. "I thought you, of all people, would appreciate one of the last surviving British car models."

"Now owned by the Indian Tata Steel company," Jennifer added while climbing in.

Both men raised their eyebrows before following her.

The instant Monroe closed the door, Youssef set off. A minute later they were on the highway and the view quickly turned to desert.

"Can you hand me the backpack?" Bishop asked Monroe, who gave it to him. Bishop opened it and searched inside before emptying the contents on the floor in front of him. "Gone."

"Figures," Monroe said. "They wouldn't let us leave with it. The only reason they let us go is that they don't want the public to know the cave was entered, let alone that something was taken from it. It would ruin the myth. No one will ever know we were there."

"But they can't prevent us from talking about it and making it public," Jennifer responded.

"Who would believe us without evidence?" Bishop asked.

With a start, Jennifer checked her jacket pockets. "My bag," she demanded, pointing to her green travel bag in the front of the car.

"Yes, ma'am," Monroe said as he unclipped his seatbelt and reached for the bag, just as his phone pinged in his jacket pocket. He passed Jennifer the bag, took out his phone and read the message. Without saying anything, he returned it to his jacket pocket. Bishop glanced at him and Monroe hesitated for a moment.

"Oh, it's work," Monroe said.

"Nothing," Jennifer said as she swiped her fingers over her phone. "All the pictures I took in the caves. Everything wiped."

"Check your trash bin," Monroe suggested.

"There's no trash bin on an iPhone and I already checked my recently deleted pictures. Everything is gone."

An hour and a half passed in near silence. For much of the journey the landscape barely changed, but then, like a Fata Morgana, the scenery turned green before slipping into the urban gray of the city.

"What now?" Jennifer asked, finally breaking the silence.

Her question was met with deep sighs. Monroe shrugged while Bishop wiped his hands with sanitizer for the third time.

"This is it? All this work for...." Jennifer waved her hands in despair as the car drove onto the airfield parking lot.

"What would you have me do?" Bishop asked. "We have no clue to study, no idea about a next location, and the only man who could possibly tell us more is held in an Israeli jail. For now, I think we've run out of luck."

Jennifer said nothing as the car stopped and Youssef jumped out with surprising agility to open the back door. As they all piled out and collected their bags he pointed to a nearby dirty beige building before jumping back in the car and driving off.

"So much for goodbyes," Monroe joked.

Bishop checked his watch. "We only have half an hour to check in so I guess we should hurry."

As he bent to grab his suitcase he felt his cellphone vibrate in the pocket of his pants. For a second he hesitated before letting go of the case. He took out his phone and read the message on the screen.

You have 1 new image(s).

Bishop pushed his thumb on the fingerprint scanner and the screen changed. For a long moment, he stared in silence at the screen before a small smile lit up his face. "We might've just run into some new luck. Let's hurry and board the plane. I'll explain later."

CHAPTER 28

Calling Uriël

As the Boeing 787 Dreamliner hit 180 miles per hour, the wheels left the runway and they were airborne. Strapped into her seat, Jennifer looked out of the window to watch the ground drop away below her.

"At least they bought us some decent plane tickets," Monroe said.

"That's true," Jennifer replied. She pushed a button to dim the LCD's window opacity.

Monroe turned to Bishop. "So, are you ready to reveal our newfound luck?"

Bishop took out his cellphone, worked the screen and handed it to Monroe who held it halfway between himself and Jennifer. They both immediately broke into smiles as they looked at an image of an old document.

"Is that...?" Jennifer asked.

Bishop nodded. "What else could it be other than the document from the canister that you found in the cave? You see, it has the same structure, text, pictures of plants and the prescription tables at the bottom."

"Who sent you it?" Monroe asked.

"It's an undisclosed number, but if I were to guess...."

"Rabbi Naphtali Cohen," Jennifer said.

Bishop tipped his head in her direction.

"A good friend," Monroe noted as he handed back the phone. "Can you send me the picture so I can load it onto my laptop? Maybe I can make it a rewarding flight."

"And while you boys play, I'll watch a movie or two," Jennifer said, reaching out to touch the screen in front of her that displayed a menu of new movies and golden oldies.

"You've got mail," Bishop said, "and about twelve hours to knock yourself out."

Between them, Monroe took his laptop from beneath his seat and got to work.

In contrast, Bishop took a pillow and a blanket from the overhead bin and tucked himself in.

"Wake me up when you get something," he said, but no one seemed to be listening. He gave a small smile and leaned back.

> *"Look at this. It's worthless. Ten dollars from a vendor in the street. But I take it, I bury it in the sand for a thousand years, it becomes priceless,"* a voice sounded from the movie playing on the seat-back on-demand system.

Jennifer jumped as a hand landed on her arm, distracting her from the movie. She looked to her side only to see Monroe now waking Bishop.

"What is it?" she asked as she paused the movie and took off her headphones.

"What time is it?" Bishop asked.

Monroe looked at his watch. "It's half past three. You slept for over three hours."

"You got something?" Bishop asked, rubbing at his eyes.

Monroe positioned his laptop on the tray table. "Yes and no. You see this part?" He pointed to the first piece of text. "It's plain it's Enochian. We've seen it before. Except for the tables that are written in Latin, everything else is also in Enochian and I've just finished the translation."

"That's fast work," Jennifer said.

"I'm getting the hang of translating Enochian into English," Monroe replied with a smile. He pressed a key and the screen showed English text. "And this is what it translates to."

Jennifer and Bishop started mumbling the words on the screen.

> *Perspective is an art mathematical which demonstrates the manner and properties of all radiations direct, broken and reflected.*
>
> *And he made a laver of brass, and the foot of it of brass, of the looking glasses of the women assembling.*
>
> *With the blood of the women the brazen glass speaks the concluding place to the undying truth.*

"More riddles," Jennifer concluded, sounding somewhat disappointed.

"You didn't expect a clear message, I hope?" Bishop replied.

"I guess not," Jennifer told him.

"So, what didn't you get?" Bishop asked Monroe.

"What I didn't get...." Monroe turned to the screen. "Well, the earlier texts all somehow translated into numbers corresponding to a page of the Aldaraia and a time for the crystal to set to. But I've been staring at this text for over an hour now and I don't see it."

Bishop reread the translation. "All radiations. What could it mean? The amount of radiations reflecting from the alloys, or the amount of alloys? Brass is made of copper and zinc, so that's two."

"But it can also contain elements like arsenic, lead, phosphorus, manganese and more," Monroe added.

"So, two is unlikely," Jennifer concluded. "Anything else?"

Monroe nodded. "I found one other reference. 'He made the laver of brass, and the foot of it of brass, of the brazen glasses of the women assembling.' That's from the Old Testament, Exodus 38:8, where Bezalel, Moses's chief artisan, took the brass mirrors taken by the women from Egypt and melted them into a sacred wash bowl for the priests."

"38:8," Bishop repeated.

"Page thirty-eight, eight o'clock?" Jennifer asked.

"Been there, done that," Monroe replied.

"But there are only thirty-six pages with tables in the Aldaraia," Bishop said.

Monroe nodded again. "So, I tried page eleven—three plus eight—nothing. Thirty-eight minus twenty-four hours leaves fourteen, two o'clock. Again, nothing. Just jumbled up consonants with an occasional vowel. I tried every possible combination that I or, rather, my laptop, could possibly think of."

"If the second sentence is from the Bible, where are the other two from?" Jennifer asked.

"The first one is simple," Monroe replied. "Perspective is an art mathematical. This was written by John Dee in one of his works in which he defines dozens of conceptions like astronomy, music, astrology, navigation and perspective. I looked it up but discovered nothing that might lead to any numbers."

"And the last one?" Bishop asked.

"Nothing," Monroe answered. "I've searched everywhere on the Internet and every college database available, but I can find nothing that relates to the blood of women speaking to an undying truth."

"So, that's it?" Jennifer said. "No hints as to what it is we are looking for or even a new location?"

Monroe shrugged and the three fell into silence as they stared at the image on the screen.

"What's a brazen glass?" Jennifer asked after a few minutes, turning to look at the two professors.

"Brazen in Middle English meant made of brass," Bishop answered.

"So, a brazen glass is...?"

"A mirror," Monroe told her. "A metal mirror. Before glass mirrors were invented the Egyptians polished brass dishes until they could be used as mirrors."

"What's that?" Jennifer cried out as the plane began to shake and rumble.

"Nothing," Monroe said. "Just a bit of turbulence. Nothing to worry about."

Above them, the 'Fasten Seat Belts' sign lit up and Bishop quickly strapped himself in and grabbed on to the armrests.

Jennifer turned to look again at the screen of Monroe's laptop. Her eyes then widened. "What if we are looking for the wrong clue?"

"What do you mean?" Bishop asked.

"Well, we're searching for numbers to lead us to another page of the Aldaraia, but what if the numbers aren't the clue? What if the clue was hidden directly in the text?"

"What do you see?" Monroe asked.

"Maybe it's nothing, but the sentences seem randomly chosen: a quote from a Dee book, a Bible verse and a mystery sentence. But what if they're not randomly chosen? What are the similarities between them?" Jennifer raised her eyebrows and grinned.

"But why would he change his method halfway through?" Monroe asked.

Jennifer shrugged. "I have no idea. Maybe to test our creativity or maybe because he wants to steer us in another direction."

"Sounds a bit farfetched," Monroe replied. "I don't think—"

"Of course," Bishop interrupted. "The mirror. They all talk about a mirror, in different ways and words, but unmistakably, a mirror."

Bishop raised a hand to Jennifer who high-fived him.

"I take it a mirror means something to you?" Jennifer said.

"Of course," Monroe said as he typed on the keyboard.

"Don't you remember?" Bishop asked Jennifer. "I told you about it when we met in my office."

Jennifer shook her head before it dawned on her. "Yes, I remember now. You said something about Dee and his aid, uh, Kelley, talking to God through rubbing a mirror?"

"Almost," Bishop said. "They used it as a shewstone, an object like a crystal ball or special amulet. The two talked to Archangel Uriël using a special mirror. Dee asked the questions and Kelley was the medium who answered for Uriël. The same method they used in Poznań."

"Here." Monroe nudged them both before enlarging a picture on the computer screen.

"What's that?" Jennifer asked.

"Dee's Tezcatlipoca mirror," Monroe answered.

"It's black?"

"Jet black, they call it," Bishop told her. "It's forged from obsidian, which is basically black volcanic glass created from the felsic lava that flows from a volcano and rapidly cools down. The rapid cooling prevents crystal growth and creates a super dark surface that can then be polished into a highly glossy surface."

"How big is it?" Jennifer asked.

"Not much bigger than any standard hand mirror." Monroe estimated the size with his hands. "As you can see, it's circular and made out of one piece of obsidian with a short handle at the top."

"The Aztecs used them to make prophecies and worship their god of sorcery and magic, Tezcatlipoca," Bishop continued. "His name literally translates as 'smoking mirror' and when depicted he was usually shown with an obsidian mirror in the place of his right foot. After Hernando Cortés's conquest of the region in the sixteenth century, he brought shiploads of these trinkets to the west. Spain's plundering of Aztec gold and obsidian helped it become the world's first global empire."

"Obliterating a complete civilization, spreading disease, raging global war and inventing slavery in the process," Monroe added.

"Okay," Bishop admitted. "It's perhaps not their finest moment, but according to legend, the mirror was given to Dee by Uriël around 1580 as a means to stay in touch with him. For almost ten years Dee and Kelley used the mirror to talk to Uriël, receiving messages and writing them down. In the beginning, both believed the messages came from Uriël, but later on Kelley believed the messages came from evil demons. He urged Dee to stop their rituals, but Dee wouldn't budge. Eventually, it drove the two apart. They say Kelley went mad, traveled to Austria and promised Rudolf I of Bohemia he would make gold for him. When he didn't deliver on this, he was imprisoned and supposedly died falling from a window while trying to escape. He died at forty-two, almost half of Dee's age at the time."

"What happened to the mirror?" Jennifer asked.

"We only know that the mirror in the eighteenth century was owned by Horace Walpole, an art historian, gothic novel writer and son of the first British prime minister, Sir Robert Walpole," Monroe said. "He wrote some interesting political and social letters. We have the complete collection of them at Yale, all forty-eight of them. Walpole labeled the mirror on the back 'The Black Stone into which Dr. Dee used to call his spirits.' There's also a wooden case covered in tooled leather with the mirror. It's not known whether the case was used by Dee or added by Walpole later, but on the case there's another handwritten text, a part of a poem named Hudibras written by the nineteenth-century novelist Samuel Butler."

Monroe cleared his throat and recited part of the poem.

"'Kelley did all his feats upon the Devil's Looking Glass, a stone, where playing with him at Bo-peep, he solv'd all problems ne'er so deep.' That's it, only Kelley is spelled without a second e."

"Who put it there and what does it mean?" Jennifer asked.

"No one really knows," Bishop replied. "Walpole couldn't have written it since Butler was born about fifty years after Walpole's death. The text seems to relate to Kelley, though his name was misspelled, and to Dee but why Butler wrote it no one knows."

"So, we need to find out where the mirror is now," Jennifer said. "It's our best lead at the moment, isn't it?"

Bishop and Monroe smiled at each other.

Jennifer sighed. "What?" she asked.

"Finding the mirror isn't the problem," Monroe said. "The mirror is on permanent display as a minor asset in the British Museum. It's tucked away in the back, far from the Rosetta Stone and Elgin Marbles. And far away from tourists taking selfies."

"So, we need to go there," Jennifer said, shifting to the edge of her seat.

Bishop took a deep breath. "Maybe, but I suggest we go home first, take some well-deserved rest and evaluate our journey."

"But what if whoever is following us gets there first?" she asked.

"I don't see how that's possible," Monroe answered. "We are the only ones who know about the mirror. I don't suspect Rabbi Cohen will share the scroll with anyone else. Why should he?"

"Makes sense," Bishop said. "We're in no rush." He checked his watch. "When we get home in four hours, I'll contact my pal at the Israeli embassy and try to find out if they learned anything from our bald friend and we'll take it from there."

Jennifer settled back into her seat. "That's also a plan, I guess."

CHAPTER 29

Ein Sof

It was dusk and Yale's Beinecke library shone bright, lit up by the aureate-colored marble panels of the walls. The library was empty save for three people sitting at an antique oak English table positioned next to the Guttenberg Bible illuminated in a glass display case.

"Did you get some rest?" Bishop asked as he played with his cellphone.

"I slept like a baby the entire day," Monroe replied.

"You're a lucky man," Jennifer told him. "I barely slept at all. My home is brightly lit during the day, and being excited about something clearly feeds my insomnia."

As she spoke, Jennifer was reminded of the times when her father would leave on his travels when she was a child. For the first night or two, she would spend the night tossing and turning without understanding why. It took her until puberty to find the connection between her father leaving and the sleepless nights.

Jennifer shook the memory from her head. "Thankfully, being half your age, I should be able to withstand some sleep deprivation," she teased.

"How old do you think we are?" Monroe asked.

Jennifer chose not to answer, instead asking, "Have you contacted Conway yet?"

"No, not yet," Bishop replied. "I wanted us to do it together. It's now midnight over there, but he's expecting our call, so...."

"Then what are you waiting for?" Jennifer giggled as she pressed Conway's name on Bishop's cellphone.

As he snatched back the phone, he heard the line connect.

"Only you would call at such an indecent hour," Conway said in greeting.

"Let me put you on speaker," Bishop replied. He put the phone on the table in front of him. "Here you go."

"I said to my wife, 'There's only one man who would dare call me at such an ungodly time,'" Conway complained again, and Jennifer and Monroe laughed.

"And this time it's worse," Bishop said. "I have Jennifer Porter and Walker Monroe here with me."

"It's good to hear from you. I take it you're okay and everything went fine on your trip home?" Conway asked.

"We're peachy," Bishop said. "And thank you again for your help in Israel. Did you talk to Robartés?"

"After a two-hour wait, they finally let me talk to him, and let me tell you this, he didn't look pretty."

"Again, thank you for getting us out of there," Monroe said. "Did he speak?"

"Not much. He admitted to the robbery and kidnapping of the young woman...."

"Jennifer Porter," Jennifer called out.

"Sorry, Jennifer. Anyway, after some pressure he identified himself as Malkuth, just Malkuth. Not sure if it's his first or last name. He also stated he worked alone. He said he had no money and noticed you entering Machpelah and took his chance to follow you in the hope he might be able to steal something of value in the building."

"And he convinced you?" Monroe asked leaning into the telephone.

"No, of course not. The man had a very expensive high-tech Sirin Solarin, 256-bit AES encrypted cellphone on him. That's a fifteen-thousand-dollar device. Even so, the Israelis weren't interested so they decided to let him go. They even provided him with traveling papers and put him on a plane to a destination of his choice."

"Did you get a look at his cellphone?" Jennifer asked, surprising Bishop and Monroe. She shrugged in response. "What?"

"We did, but we didn't get very far due to the encryption. The only thing we could see when the screen opened was a header from a message addressed to someone called Imperator. As soon as we touched the phone it froze."

"That's a pity," Bishop said. "Where did he go?"

"London, England. He has already arrived and he immediately headed for a London suburb. He's still there."

Bishop and Monroe looked at each other, frowning.

"How do you know?" Bishop asked.

"I'll give you a second to figure it out," Conway joked. "Our Israeli friends at the IEF have helped out."

"IEF?" Monroe asked.

"The Israeli Elite Force. A group of world-renowned Israeli hackers who, from their early anarchic hacking days, now tend to cooperate with the government most of the time. They weren't able to hack the software of the phone and read messages, but they did hack the hardware cloning the GPS transceiver to a remote server."

"And now you can follow him wherever he goes," Monroe concluded.

"As long as he keeps his phone on him, yes. Even if it's switched off."

"That's impressive," Bishop said.

"I knew you would be pleased," Conway replied. "I'll text you the IP address and credentials to log on to the server. You can watch it live yourselves."

"Now I'm even more impressed," Bishop said.

"Enough impressed to let me go to sleep?"

"More than that," Bishop replied. "Next time you're in the neighborhood I'll take you on that fishing trip in Canada you've always talked about. What's it called again, Tampa Bay, Botany Bay, Nemo Bay?"

"Nimmo Bay, and it's heli-fishing in British Columbia," Conway told him. "And you better start saving big if you want to take me there on a professor's salary."

"I'll start saving," Bishop replied, smiling. "Thanks again. We'll talk soon."

"You're welcome, and please let me know what you find out. Oh, and be careful. The phone convinced me there's a lot of money behind this and you can imagine what that could mean."

"Will do. Sleep tight." Bishop hung up the phone and looked at his messages. "May I?" he asked, pointing to Monroe's laptop on the table.

"Sure," Monroe said and Bishop read from his phone before typing on the laptop. Almost immediately, Google maps appeared, in 3D satellite view, and showed a red dot blinking on a street corner.

Monroe moved closer to the screen. "Kensington, the corner of Blythe and Hazlitt."

"You know it?" Jennifer asked.

"I know of it. It's where the science museum is. It's an old-fashioned street gone yuppie over the years."

Jennifer leaned back into her chair. "I didn't picture—what did he call himself, Malkuth?—as a yuppie."

"Maybe he likes Indian cuisine?" Bishop said pointing to the knife and fork icon next to the blinking dot showing the Karma Indian restaurant.

"Well, I don't believe he's a yuppie," Monroe said. "Malkuth, Malchus or Malchut is ten on the Sephirot, the Kabbalistic Tree of Life. Here, let me show you."

Bishop and Jennifer looked in wonder as Monroe took the laptop and opened a drawing on the screen.

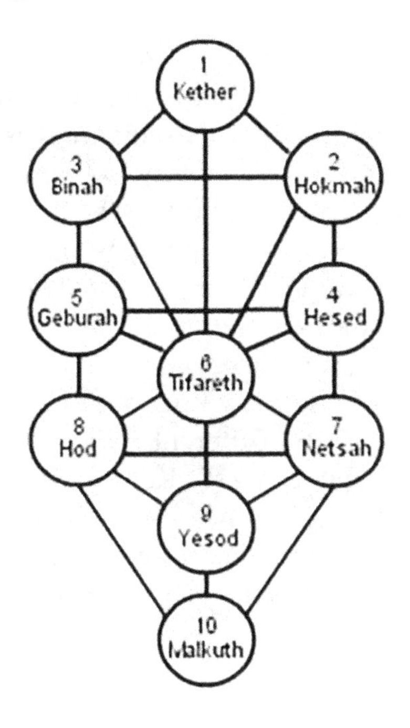

"The Sephirot, also known as The Tree of Life," Monroe said, showing the others the screen. "Sephirot translates as 'emanation' and holds ten attributes or 'emanations' in Kabbalah tradition. The original reference to the Sephirot is found in the Sefer Yetzirah, the Book of Formation, an ancient Kabbalistic text said to have been written by Abraham himself. Basically, the ten stages of the Sephirot are considered to be stages of awareness or consciousness from Malkuth at the bottom and at the start of awareness to Kether at the top, the fully aware or Ein Sof."

"Ein Sof?" Jennifer asked.

"How do I explain this simply?" Monroe said.

"Just try us," Bishop replied. "I think we're pretty smart people."

"It's not that. There are many different theories and variations about it all. The best way I can describe it is that the truth behind every stage of the Sephirot will be revealed to you once you get there and there's not just one truth to be written down and there are no exams that get you to the next level."

"So how do you know at what level of awareness you are, and who decides?" Jennifer asked.

Monroe shrugged and grinned. "Hard to say. No one decides. I guess you just know, the same way you know when you're ready to swim or not swim."

"But the test in that is whether you drown or not," Bishop said.

"Not very different here," Monroe replied. "If you don't have the knowledge you won't be able to use its advantages. Anyway, Ein Sof, in itself, translates to 'unending' or 'infinity.' When you start the teachings of the Kabbalah you start with Malkuth at the bottom. This is where you start to become aware of your surroundings and your role in it. The ten Sephirot are generally divided into two categories: the intellectual, Sechel, and the emotional, known as Middot. Both categories contain levels, not exactly on a gradual scale, but from Malkuth to the top you learn everything there is to know within both domains, finally ending at Ein Sof. Now, Ein Sof is a bit different. Whereas the other nine stages are about awareness, the highest, Kether, is often described as a superconscious state beyond conscious intelligence. God, prior to his self-manifestation in the production of any spiritual realm, they call it."

"You become God?" Jennifer raised her eyebrows.

"Not quite, but you could say you become God as He was before He became God."

Jennifer and Bishop shook their heads.

"Hey, you asked," Monroe told them.

"Sorry, please go on with your simple explanation," Bishop teased.

"The Zohar talks about Ein Sof, saying that before He gave form to the world and created shapes, what we now know as God was alone, without form and not resembling anything."

"But God created man in his own image," Bishop said.

"True, but what if God was something else before he was God. What if he was 'man?' You said it yourself, in His own image."

"You lost me," Jennifer admitted.

"Okay," Monroe said. "Picture God as a man, then somehow He got elevated to another higher spiritual level and from there He became God?"

"And the other higher spiritual level...."

"Is Kether," Monroe said, finishing for Jennifer.

As they tried to let the information sink in, silence fell in the room.

"All right," Jennifer finally said. "I think I've got it... a bit. The Kabbalah believes that if you eventually climb high enough up the Sephirot you can become God, almost."

"Ein Sof," Monroe corrected.

"Check," Jennifer replied. "But what does that give us except clearly another connection to the Kabbalah?"

"Maybe the question shouldn't be what it gives us, but who uses these stages of awareness as names for themselves."

"That's it," Bishop said, raising a finger in the air.

Jennifer and Monroe looked at each other, tilted their heads and waited. A minute or so later, Bishop snapped out of his own thoughts and took a deep breath.

"What was the name on the message they found on Malkuth's phone?"

"Imperator," Monroe and Jennifer said in chorus.

"Imperator," Bishop repeated. "I think I've got it."

"You said that before," Monroe said agitated. "What have you got, man?"

Bishop looked at Jennifer. "You remember I told you that John Dee made Kabbalah popular in England with the promise of ultimate knowledge, thereby giving it a romantic appeal?"

"Vaguely."

"Well, they called that the Hermetic Kabbalah, a combination of Jewish Kabbalah, western astrology, alchemy and the teachings of Neoplatonism, the Rosicrucians and the Freemasons and"—Bishop opened his arms—"the Hermetic Order of the Golden Dawn."

"The Golden Dawn?" Monroe asked. "How did you get there?"

"A few years ago, I taught an undergraduate course titled 'Social structures versus morality and justice.' For a large part I built it around the Golden Dawn, especially concerning its appeal to the masses and how successful it might be today, should it exist, in our era of communication and social media."

"What is the Hermetic Order of the Golden Dawn?" Jennifer asked.

"The Golden Dawn was a late nineteenth, early twentieth century English occult order, a cult if you will. It was started by three Freemasons and members of the *Societas Rosicruciana in Anglia,* the SRIA, the oldest independent society of Rosicrucian Freemasons in the world. Apparently, they were displeased with their own order, so they created the Golden Dawn. During their ceremonies, the members of this so-called magical order dressed up in the clothes of ancient Egypt and performed magic rituals."

"And what has this got to do with the Imperator from Malkuth's phone?" Monroe asked.

"I'm getting to it. A little patience, please," Bishop said, employing his lecturer's tone. "The Golden Dawn had a hierarchical system that was based on that of the SRIA. At the bottom of the scale there was—you guessed it—Malkuth, and at the top, Kether. And another name for Kether was Imperator."

"So, The Golden Dawn is behind this?" Jennifer asked.

"Sounds like a bit of stretch, doesn't it?" Monroe replied. "I'm sure if I Google 'Imperator' I'll get thousands of other options."

"Yes, 20,700,000 results," Jennifer said, reading from her cellphone screen.

"Besides," Monroe continued, "if I recall correctly, this group dissolved after fifteen years or so, at the turn of the twentieth century."

"You're still being impatient," Bishop admonished.

Jennifer moved a finger along her lips, zipping them.

"But you're correct," Bishop added. "Though no one really knows how or why, The Golden Dawn I'm talking about disappeared from existence about a hundred years ago. All that remains are a few groups of amateurs here and there in the world who use their free time to dress up in the clothes of ancient Egypt and perform rituals in a converted basement once a week."

"So why the leap to the Imperator of the Golden Dawn?"

"And there it is," Bishop said. "I don't think the Golden Dawn as I described it is behind this, but there are a few other major coincidences in place. Remember Malkuth's fake name?"

"Robartés," Monroe said.

"Correct. And if I'm not mistaken, you explained that the name was probably based on a fictional character created by William Butler Yeats?"

A bright smile appeared on Monroe's face. "Of course! Robartés was created by Yeats and Yeats himself was a member of the Golden Dawn."

"You said it yourself," Bishop said. "The man was obsessed with the occult and magic. In its prime, The Golden Dawn had great appeal and in its short lifespan attracted some big names like Yeats, Aleister Crowley and Bram Stoker."

Jennifer slowly shook her head. "Look who became a believer all of a sudden."

Bishop smiled. "I have one other coincidence for you."

He turned the laptop's screen with Malkuth's red dot still blinking on the map to Jennifer and Monroe. With two fingers he enlarged the street with the blinking dot on it and pointed to the street name.

Monroe and Jennifer tilted their heads to read the street name.

"Blythe Road?" Jennifer read. "We know. You pointed it out earlier.

"With the Indian restaurant," Monroe added. "By the way, doesn't anyone else get hungry?"

"Now, over here...." Bishop moved his finger further up the street stopping at another knife and fork icon.

"George's Café?" Jennifer read aloud.

"Thirty-six Blythe Road," Bishop said, in a way that suggested it held some meaning.

"Damn, that's one hell of a coincidence," Monroe replied, leaving only Jennifer bewildered. "Thirty-six Blythe Road was the official address of the first temple of the Hermetic Order of The Golden Dawn."

Bishop nodded and smiled.

"Talk about coincidences," Jennifer agreed.

"That means Malkuth is already a big step ahead of us," Monroe said.

"But he doesn't know that," Jennifer said, smiling.

"We need to go to London before he finds out somehow," Bishop said. "We need to find the mirror and, while we're there, stop on Blythe and have a drink at George's Café. Anyone in for another road trip?"

CHAPTER 30

The Font

2009

Two weeks after Jennifer pointed her father in the direction of the font at St. Mary the Virgin's Church in London, he was in a taxi coming off the B351 onto Mortlake High Street. Robert Porter glanced out the window to see a group of rowers in their skiffs on the Thames. For a moment he pictured himself as a child again, rowing his own skiff with his father when he had leave from the Navy. It felt like a lifetime ago and for a second he doubted his own credentials as a father given he was away from home so often, and away from his daughter Jennifer.

"Dad, are you still there?" shouted over the line.

Porter snapped out of his thoughts.

"Oh, yeah, sorry. I got distracted for a second. You were saying?"

"I was saying I won't help you again if you don't take me with you next time."

"Point taken, dear. But I promise you that next time you won't want to come with me anymore. You'll be living on your own, as far away as you can possibly get from your parents."

"Sure, Dad. Never make a promise you're not sure you can keep."

Jennifer had heard the line so many times during her childhood she even heard it in her dreams.

The cab slowed and came to a stop in front of a sign reading 'St. Mary's.'

"That'll be nine-ten," the taxi driver said.

Robert clamped the cellphone between his shoulder and his cheek and handed the driver a ten-pound note.

"Keep the change," he mouthed and got out of the car. "Anyway, darling, I need to go. I'm at my destination. I love you, dear. Say hi to your mother. I'll be back home again before you know it."

"Will do, Dad. Please be careful."

Porter ended the call and looked across the street. For a second, he gazed at the building behind the trees while searching in his pockets. At his third attempt, he took a piece of paper from his jacket pocket and unfolded it. Holding it in front of him, he looked at the paper and then the building before him. Now he was certain. He had been more or less convinced by the pictures he had found on the Internet, but now he knew for sure. The small windows, the short bell tower, even the flagpole was there. This was no mistake. It was the same building he had found on the sketch contained in the Łaski documents. He looked at the paper and mouthed John Dee's words, '*Sanctum lavacrum loco nativitatis,*' a holy place of birth and rebirth. As a chill ran up his spine, he grinned, recognizing the feeling. The sketch looked as though it could have been drawn yesterday, that time had stood still for hundreds of years. Porter looked left and right, sizing up the other buildings on the street. Sure, some of them looked old and were not in the best condition, but none of them could have been much older than fifty years or so. It was a strange realization that everything around this single building had been built up and broken down a multitude of times, while this church, this not-too-fancy building, had survived and witnessed it all.

Porter walked up to the closed cast-iron gate and pressed the handle, but it wouldn't budge. He looked around and noticed a small sign with the church's opening hours on it. Over part of the text was a piece of paper taped to the sign.

Due to architectural research, the church will be closed to the public from Monday to Wednesday. We would love to see you back Thursday.

As it was Monday and Porter had booked his return ticket for early Wednesday morning, he looked at the closed gate and considered his options. It couldn't be more than five feet high. He could easily jump it. From the church entrance, some thirty feet away, he heard the sound of voices. He looked up to see two men dressed in jeans and matching khaki shirts leaving the church carrying a large construction post. One of the men, a broad-shouldered, brush-cut guy, noticed Porter watching and approached.

"Can I help you, sir?"

"Yes, maybe you can," Porter answered, noticing the man's American accent, and extended his hand through the fence. "My name is Robert Porter and I've traveled all the way from the United States to visit this church. I fly back tomorrow, which means I've come a long way for nothing. Would it be possible to let me take a look?"

"I'm Bob Walton." The man shook Porter's hand. "Are you part of the survey team?"

"Survey? No. What survey?"

"They're surveying the church."

"Okay. No, I'm not part of any survey, but I'm sure they wouldn't mind if I went in briefly."

The man took a deep breath and Porter took the chance to heap on the pressure, seeing as his previous white lie that he was leaving the following day didn't have the desired effect. "Look, it's only for a few minutes."

"I'm sorry, sir, but me and my men only do the heavy lifting and the survey team seem pretty serious about what they do. Every area they work on gets wrapped in white plastic sheet and even we aren't allowed inside. They even have security."

Porter raised an eyebrow, surprised at the level of secrecy. He took a few steps back to look at the church. Nothing stood out from the outside. "Could you please ask?"

"I don't think so, sir. I'm really sorry, but that won't work. I think you better leave now."

"All right." Porter stepped further away from the gate. "Thank you for the information."

He looked at his watch. It was almost five, which meant it probably wouldn't be long until the workmen called it a day. He decided to take a look at the rear of the church. Turning right, he followed the boundary wall until he came to a small path that lead to the back. He noted the brick wall was also no higher than five feet, nothing to cause him too much of a problem. Stopping where the path crossed Worple Street, the view reminded him of a scene from a 1960s British TV drama series. He could also see clearly over the churchyard. Noticing movement behind the church's windows, Porter managed to restrain his urge to jump the wall. He then remembered passing a convenience store on Mortlake High Street and decided to go and get a quick bite to eat.

Two hours later, Porter returned to the rear of the church. The sun had almost set as he walked alongside the brick wall, peeringd over cautiously to see if there was any light or movement in the church. Nothing. Porter looked left and right before athletically jumping the wall. On the other side, he kneeled down for a moment, waiting to see if he had been spotted, but the place seemed empty. Crouching low, he approached the church, passing by ancient gravestones. He glanced at them, but in most cases the text had faded and was unreadable.

Stumbling over some loose stones, Porter briefly lost his footing.

Getting back to his feet, he shone his flashlight briefly over the terrain, noticing the labyrinth he was in. He had read about this typically English phenomenon: churchyard labyrinths originated in the late nineteenth century and were essentially patterns made from grass, stones and any other natural material that encouraged the faithful to take a specific route, rather like following a sacred path or embarking on a pilgrimage to a place of prayer and meditation. St. Mary's labyrinth was fairly new, made this century, and was a simple copy of an ancient design at Temple Cowley, near Oxford. As meditation was the last thing on Porter's mind he doggedly made his way toward the church.

After passing the last of the shrubbery, Porter squatted in front of the church wall, below one of the windows. After raising his head for a peek, he saw only the silhouette of rows of empty benches. Luckily for him, the church seemed deserted. Now all he had to do was find a way in. Not without experience, Porter knew these old buildings weren't designed to keep people out, but rather to get as many as they could in, and his best bet would be the small tower. He looked around for a way to get onto the roof and decided the porch would be the easiest ascent thanks to the step-like design of the side walls. With one leap Porter was halfway up the porch. Another small jump and he landed on a slanted roof. With the aid of a drainpipe he was able to scale another small wall to reach the base of the old bell tower. A metal screen was the only obstacle left and though it was heavy, Porter was able to lift it from its hinges. He then stepped carefully inside.

Inside the tower, he was greeted by a spiral staircase that he quickly descended. He arrived at a door, thankfully unlocked. The door lead directly to the nave. Porter shone his flashlight looking for the font, which was traditionally located near the entrance to remind worshippers of their own baptism and association with the church. Hearing a sound at the front of the church, he shone his light in that direction discovering large sheets of white plastic rustling in a draft. The entire altar was hidden behind the plastic sheeting and Porter wondered what on earth they were up to. He shone his flashlight around him seeing large floodlights on stands. Then, some fifteen feet to the left of him, he found the gray font.

The design was simplicity itself: a fairly straight pedestal with squares carved out of what looked like marble. The font was hexagonal with a round basin interior and symbols carved on the sides. Porter walked up to the font and caressed the first symbol. It was the same five-petalled rose he had seen on the video. Slowly, he walked around the font touching each symbol as he passed. One looked like a smile, the next was simply a circle with a dot inside, a cross, a lowercase "m" and what looked like a horizontal eight.

He took a few steps back and walked around the font a second time. Except for the rose and the cross the other symbols were largely unfamiliar to him. Symbols had never been his forte. He had once met a professor at Harvard who specialized in symbols, not that he could help him now. He was on his own.

Porter looked again at the horizontal eight, assuming it was an infinity symbol, something which puzzled him as it didn't have any Christian significance before the late nineteenth century. Before that, in the late seventeenth century, it was a mathematical symbol used by a man named John Wallis. Another piece of random information he had collected on his travels.

On his fourth time around the font, Porter recalled his chat with Jennifer in which she had mentioned '*Luna, Sol, Elementa, Ignis*'—the moon, the sun, the elements and fire. And there they were, right in front of him. The four symbols John Dee had used to create his Monas. They were not in sequence, but the symbols were definitely there. In his mind, he pictured the symbols superimposed on each other.

And there it was, Dee's Monas—and it somehow felt like the figurine was smiling at him as his imagination put the parts together.

Porter, now smiling to himself, touched the symbols, unsure where to go next. The symbols might have their own individual functions or they might merely be a sign that he was in the right place.

Porter self-consciously pushed each symbol in the correct sequence of the moon, the sun, the elements and fire. Nothing. He took a look at the bowl that was finished with some kind of gold foil. The bowl was dry and Porter tapped it everywhere with his fingers. Everything felt rock solid. He took his flashlight and with the heel of it he tapped every part of the font. Again, it sounded completely solid. Kneeling down, he continued to tap at the pedestal. On his knees, he circled the font, moving and tapping the squares, from top to bottom. When he almost came full circle, having reached halfway down the pedestal he heard something, a tiny change in the sound. He tapped upward, left and then right, before moving back down again. And there it was, a small, but distinguishably different sound at the upper side of the pedestal suggesting something sat behind it. It could have been a flaw in the brick, but it clearly needed greater investigation so he inspected the top of the pedestal and the base of the font and then he saw it.

It was small, no longer than an inch wide, but it was definitely the same infinity symbol from the side of the font. Porter stood up, stepped back and thought for a moment. He then smiled. *Could it really be?*

Porter stepped forward and put his flashlight in the bowl. With both arms he embraced the font and started pulling, trying to turn it on the pedestal. First to the left, then to the right. Porter grunted with effort, but it wouldn't budge. He stepped back and took another look. *It must be,* he thought. He could think of no other explanation. Stepping forward again, he gave one final turn using every ounce of strength he had, and with a grinding sound, the font loosened. Marble dust coated the floor as Porter continued to turn. A minute or so later, he let go and punched his fist in the air.

"Yes!"

Realizing his victory cry might have been a little too loud, he quickly looked around, but there was no sign that anyone had heard him. He turned back to the basin and stood in front of the infinity sign. Grabbing hold of the sides he began turning clockwise. This time, the font moved much more easily though it screeched with every movement. Once the infinity sign on the basin was aligned with the one on the base, he stopped. *The moon, the sun, the elements and fire,* he thought. He then started turning counterclockwise.

Porter stopped again when the moon aligned with the same symbol on the base of the font. He then repeated the process, aligning the sun and the elements. Pausing to catch his breath and give his weary arms a rest, Porter finally aligned the two fire symbols, and that's when he heard and felt something click into place.

Porter stepped back and looked down. One of the squares on the pedestal had slid open, revealing itself to be a safe of some kind. With a smile, he pulled the loose square from the font and it dropped to the ground. He then shone his flashlight into the hole, spying something in the back. He reached inside, feeling something soft, but just out of reach. He squeezed his hand into the hole as far as he could and then used two fingers, like tweezers, to grab hold of the object. Once he recovered it from the hole he saw it was a small, rolled leather pouch tied with lace. With the flashlight in his mouth, Porter unstrapped the pouch and unrolled it on the ground. Inside, he found a piece of parchment paper with text and pictures on it. Porter's heart now pounded in his chest as adrenalin rushed through his body. He took a closer look, but couldn't read the text. And then, perhaps because his nerves were shot, he thought he heard something. He glanced around, but saw nothing but the plastic sheeting flapping. Even so, he felt a sudden urge to get out of there.

Porter quickly rolled the scroll back up again and tied the lace. He then unrolled it again. From his inside pocket, he took his Leica camera and quickly snapped a few shots of the document. He tucked away the camera and then took a black pouch from the pocket of his pants and put it inside the hole before closing it with the square he had taken off. Then, just as he was rolling up the scroll again, all the floodlights in the room came on.

As Porter adjusted his eyes to the bright lights, he heard footsteps and voices approaching. When he could finally see, he found himself confronted by two men in uniform. Behind them was the man he had met at the gate earlier that afternoon.

"Can we help you?" one of the men asked.

Porter was dumbfounded as he realized the men were from a private security firm. "Uh, no? This is a public church, isn't it?"

"What are you doing in here?" the man asked. "This might be a public church, but it's temporarily in the custody of a private company. And even if it weren't, even a church has closing times. So, what are you doing here?"

The other man glanced at the leather roll in Porter's hand and whispered something into his colleague's ear.

"Can I see that?" he asked.

Porter hesitated for a second before handing over the roll. The guard looked at it, but didn't open it.

"I take it you weren't planning on taking anything from here," he said sarcastically, "and you still haven't told me what you're doing here?"

"Listen, this is the God's honest truth," Porter replied, looking around him and mouthing 'sorry.' "I came here earlier today and they told me the church was closed. Now, I flew a long way to visit this church and my return flight is before the church reopens to the public. I'm an amateur researcher of ancient baptismal fonts and this here is a unique specimen carved by the twelfth-century Romanesque stone sculptor Sigraf. They only discovered its origin recently and I had to see it for myself."

Although Porter had no real knowledge of Sigraf, an early medieval Danish stone sculptor, he figured the security man wouldn't have even heard of him.

"I think it's time to go, sir," the man replied, playing with the leather roll in his hand while pointing to the exit.

"My uh...." Porter pointed at the roll.

The man shook his head, smiling, and directed Porter to the door again. "Please...."

Porter picked up his flashlight from the floor and tried one more time. "Could I have my...."

"Please," the man repeated with a little more urgency.

"All right, all right, I'm going."

Porter walked toward the door. Once he stepped outside he turned to look back only to see the door closing shut. He walked through the open gate wondering about the security guards and whether they had purposely waited for him to find something before confronting him. He shook his head and looked around him, suddenly aware of a more pressing problem—chiefly how he was meant to find a cab in this neighborhood at this time of night.

CHAPTER 31

Isis Urania

The Present

Blythe Road was flooded with people attending the Fine Food Fair at the Olympia exhibition center, and that evening most of the local restaurants, from the Betty Blythe vintage tea room and The Popeseye Steak House all the way up to Karma, an Indian restaurant, were packed. On the sidewalks, small groups of men and women made their own parties, eating takeout while listening to music and dancing. And in the midst of the mayhem, Malkuth weaved his way through the crowd heading toward George's Café. Sidestepping a barbecue, he walked up to the door next to the café and pounded his fist on the wood until a small shutter opened and he saw two eyes staring at him. The shutter closed and a moment later the door opened.

"You know the way," said the man behind the door, pointing to the staircase behind him. Malkuth nodded and climbed the steep stairs. At the landing, he turned right into the narrow passageway and his breath caught in surprise. Facing him—dressed in a kilt, armed with a ceremonial dagger and wearing a black Osiris mask—was Kether.

"What are you doing here?" Kether asked as he took off his mask and placed it under an arm. "I told you not to visit me until I called for you."

"We need to talk, master."

"Yes, sure, but not now. You know we perform a ceremony every week at this time." Kether looked around the empty hallway as soft chanting started in the background. He placed a hand on Malkuth's shoulder. "Listen, I want to know everything that happened to you in Israel, but it will have to wait."

"But we need to discuss my failure and how to correct it," Malkuth told him.

"And we will, but for now, take some rest. Can you meet me tomorrow morning in the café downstairs? Let's say, around nine? We can have some breakfast."

Malkuth paused before taking a step backward and giving a nod.

"I'll see you tomorrow," Kether said. He put on his mask and disappeared into the dark hallway in the direction of the chanting.

"It's good to be home again," Monroe said as the taxi passed Jubilee Park and the London Eye.

"You think we can take a ride later on?" Jennifer asked, gazing at the huge Ferris wheel that was once the highest vantage point in the city until The Shard skyscraper was built.

"Maybe later," Bishop replied from the front seat. We have a breakfast meeting in half an hour."

Monroe and Jennifer frowned.

"Trust me," Bishop said with a smile and the two stayed silent as the taxi continued its tour of the sites of London.

Passing Buckingham Palace, the Wellington Arch and the Albert Memorial, Jennifer's eyes feasted on the abundance of history. London was a modern European city, but its architecture spoke of centuries past.

"So, why did this Hermetic Order of the Golden Dawn dissolve?" she asked.

"No one really knows, but only a few years after building the first temple here at Blythe Road, the cracks in the order appeared," Bishop said. "There was speculation that Samuel Liddell Mathers, one of the founding fathers leading the society at the time, fell out of grace with other prominent members. Remarkably, within ten years, the order had constructed temples like Isis Urania in London, all over the world, and despite progressive acts, like admitting females, most of the members weren't allowed to see or come into contact with the magical secrets the order held. The order constructed an elaborate hierarchical system and only the most privileged were allowed access to the secrets. At the turn of the twentieth century, a large group of members following Aleister Crowley was said to have become dissatisfied with Mathers' leadership, as well as his growing friendship with Crowley, who was a writer, magician, occultist, poet and mountaineer whose ideas on bisexuality—and his exuberant lifestyle—made him an unpopular member. This saw him involved in several feuds with other important members like Yeats, which effectively stopped his rise within the order's rankings. When he sought support from Mathers it got him into trouble with men like Yeats. In 1901, Yeats wrote a pamphlet titled 'Is the Order to Remain a Magical Order?' It was published privately but clearly started the order's demise. Within a few years, Isis Urania split from the Hermetic Order of the Golden Dawn and there was nothing left. Aleister Crowley, on a trip to Egypt, claimed to have been visited by a spiritual being called Aiwass who gave him the rules to start his own religion, the Thelema. This Thelema basically preached that you could do anything and everything as long as it was within the law. 'Do what thou wilt.' They even have their own holidays."

"I see an opportunity rising," Monroe commented.

"Then you're in luck," Bishop replied. "There are still orders all over the world that practice the Thelema."

"You should join," Jennifer said, tapping Monroe on the shoulder and everyone laughed.

Monroe felt his cellphone vibrating. Checking the screen, he quickly typed a reply.

"Something important?" Bishop asked.

"No, not really. The library is bug-free and fully open again."

"That's good news," Bishop said.

Monroe nodded and then pointed to a grand Victorian building to the right of them. "Look! Blythe tea room, once Britain's biggest postal distribution center. It's now used as an archive for England's biggest museums. The British Museum alone has stored over 170,000 items here."

"And those items never see the light of day?" Jennifer asked. "You can't visit?"

"Nope. But the items are shown in special exhibitions every now and then. Actually, you might recognize the building. It has been used frequently in TV shows and movies over the years. Did you know it was the headquarters for the New Avengers series?"

"The Avengers have their headquarters in London?" Jennifer asked.

Bishop and Monroe looked at each other and sighed.

"What?" Jennifer asked, raising her arms, but the cab came to an abrupt halt before anyone replied.

"We're here," Bishop said.

Moments later, the three stood on the curb.

"So, what are we doing here exactly?" Monroe asked.

"We're having breakfast," Bishop replied.

"At George's Café?" Monroe pointed across the street to a narrow four-story building. Nestled between a launderette and a restaurant, the café's name was printed in white on the green awning.

"Not George's," Bishop replied. "At the special invitation of our host, today we eat next door."

"Our host?" Jennifer asked, but Bishop and Monroe were already dodging the heavy traffic to cross the road.

Passing George's Café, Jennifer gave a quick look inside before the three walked into the restaurant next door.

"What is it?" Kether asked as Malkuth tipped forward in his seat.

"Uh, nothing, I just... well, never mind," stammered Malkuth, unsure whether to believe his eyes as he watched the young woman cross the road in front of him and glance through the window. He shook his head and leaned back in his chair. "You were saying?"

"I told you to eat your breakfast and let me do the talking for a while," Kether said sternly though he was smiling. "I know you're upset about what happened, but from what you've told me there was nothing you could have done. You really must learn to let go, my son."

On the table, Kether's cellphone screen lit up. He read the message.

It's a go.

"What's done is done," he said. "But you can help me now."

"Of course," Malkuth promptly replied. "You name it."

Kether shifted in his seat and leaned forward to whisper in Malkuth's ear. "Earlier today I received a message saying that the ones you met in Israel were probably on their way to the UK. There were preliminary orders to clear every sign of our temple and vault upstairs. This was the confirmation."

Malkuth thought for a moment. It was the first time he had considered his boss might also have a boss. "Orders?"

"I understand your confusion," Kether said while texting a message on his cellphone. "Sure, I have a boss, or rather a business partner. We do research for him from time to time and he sponsors our temple, our food and drink and travels."

Malkuth stared. "Research?"

"Things like you've been doing over the past few days. But that's not important right now." Kether leaned forward until his head was only inches away from Malkuth's ear. "Will you help me? This is urgent."

Malkuth nodded.

"Now, as I said, we need to clear upstairs. I've ordered the van I had on standby to come. Some of our members will also be here in a few minutes to help you clear as many of the floors as possible or as much as we can fit into the van."

"To help me?"

"Yes, help you. I want you to coordinate the operation. I'll text you the address that I want you to drive the van to. Leave it on the sidewalk and take the keys with you. Take as many of the relics as you can find and, whatever happens, clear the desks on the third floor. Take all the papers with you."

Malkuth gave a thin smile. "Thank you for the trust. But do we think someone is on their way here? Who can possibly know of this place?"

"That question I can't answer, but one thing is sure. If my contact says they're on their way here, you can count on it."

"I'll get right on it, master, and again, thank you for the opportunity."

Malkuth rose from his chair, but Kether pulled him down again. "Finish your breakfast first. The van will be here soon, but you have a few minutes. Take it easy."

As they walked into the restaurant known as Chez Jacque, a voice greeted them. "Matthew!"

Victor Conway greeted them from a table at the window, his hand outstretched. Monroe and Jennifer looked at each other in confusion. "You didn't tell them?"

"You didn't leave me much time," Bishop replied as they all shook hands and headed for their table. "Anyway, it's more fun to see the surprise on their faces."

"After all these years I'm still trying to understand what makes you tick," Conway replied. "I took the liberty of ordering breakfast. A little of everything."

On the table were boiled, scrambled and poached eggs, back bacon, sausages, fried mushrooms, tomatoes and baked beans. There was even black pudding, round slices of pork blood mixed with fat and cereal.

"Spared no expense," Bishop said looking at the food glistening with artery-clogging fat. *The British and their bre*akfast, he thought.

"What are we doing here?" Monroe asked Bishop.

"That I don't know. I received Victor's message late yesterday evening telling me to meet him here," Bishop said, then turned to Conway. "I guess the floor is yours."

"All right," he replied. "Please, eat some breakfast, drink some coffee or tea."

Conway gestured to the waiting pots on the table and everyone poured their drink of choice. Once everyone's cup was full, he continued.

"After we last spoke, we kept tabs on Malkuth, monitoring his whereabouts, and came to the conclusion that he must live at the end of Blythe Street, just over there." Conway pointed through the window. "He also frequently visits another address on the street, the one next door to us, in fact. We checked out the owner, a Donald Reginald Simpson. He's an American entrepreneur in imports and exports, known to be living in the UK, but with no current address."

"That can't be what piqued your interest," Monroe interrupted. "And by the way, you should try the sausages."

Monroe dangled a greasy sausage in front of Jennifer and Bishop.

"Please go on," Jennifer urged Conway.

"No, that wasn't what piqued our interest," he said, looking at Monroe. "Mr. Simpson's name also came up as a 'person of interest' in both American, French, Dutch and British databases as head of another corporation which deals in the worldwide trade of antiquities and knockoffs—legally, of course, but under heavy suspicion of large-scale illegal trading. That corporation is owned by an offshore company, where Mr. Simpson sits on the board. Through this company, Simpson owns the building next door to us and they lease the ground floor to the café. The other floors have no registered purpose other than office space. Then I ran a general Google search on the address thirty-six Blythe Road, and guess what? There it was, on the second page, a story about Aleister Crowley, William Butler Yeats and the magical battle of the Isis-Urania Golden Dawn Temple of Kensington. All in all, very interesting, but as you can imagine, nothing the authorities are specifically interested in. Even so, my embassy contacted your embassy and here we are."

Conway stopped and smiled broadly.

"What do you mean when you say 'here we are?'" Though Jennifer realized Conway was Bishop's friend, there was something about the man that ticked her off. She wasn't sure if it was the small, insincere smile, the cheap polyester three-piece suit or the smug tone of his voice that irritated her most.

Conway looked at his watch and put his cellphone on the breakfast table. "Look, we've been trying to get close to Mr. Simpson for years. And now a man fitting his description has been spotted at this place. The British police have been following him and we believe Simpson to be there now. In fifteen minutes, a Europol taskforce will raid the place to see what, and who, they find inside."

"Are you serious?" Monroe asked looking from Conway to Bishop.

Bishop shrugged.

"Why else would I invite you here for breakfast?" Conway asked. "I thought you'd be pleased. If this works out, any attention your little project might've aroused will be a thing of the past."

"Maybe so, but a little heads-up beforehand would have been nice since we could soon be in a war zone," Monroe replied. "And before breakfast."

"That's why we have front row seats at the neighbor's and that's why I got you breakfast," Conway quipped. "Look, relax. They're not the kind of criminals involved in weapons or violent crime."

"Except for our Polish priest," Jennifer reminded them all.

"Eat," Conway directed, grinning. "Waiting is all we can do, so eat."

Somewhat unnerved by what was about to happen, they all put food on their plates, but none of them had the appetite to eat. Then, after a few moments of silence, they watched a white Mercedes van take the last available parking space on the street. They all leaned toward the window pane to see what would happen next and saw two young men, in their twenties, dressed in casual jeans, shirts and sneakers get out of the van and walk to the rear of it. After opening the backdoors, two more men, dressed the same but a little older than the others, jumped out.

They all disappeared from view as they calmly walked toward the building housing George's Café.

"They're here," Kether said.

Malkuth rose from his chair. "Aren't you coming?"

"There's not much I can do. Besides, I haven't finished my breakfast. You go upstairs and I'll join you later. It's okay."

Malkuth turned and walked swiftly away, heading for the staircase. Kether glanced outside to see the first box disappearing into a van.

"Are those your men?" Bishop asked. "They look like movers, if you ask me."

"Smartass," Conway replied. "No, it's not Europol, but there's clearly something going on in there."

They watched the men carry out a continuous stream of boxes as well as paintings, loading them all into the back of the van.

"I think you're right and they're really moving," Conway mumbled as he looked at his watch. At that same time, an empty message screen appeared on his phone on the table. "Not that it matters now. They're here."

The words had barely left his lips when four dark-colored SUVs sped into view to double-park on the road, their slide doors opening to allow four men to jump out of each, dressed in full black combat gear and carrying semi-automatic rifles. Two of them immediately grabbed the men loading the white van. They offered no resistance and were taken away to one of the SUVs. The other officers disappeared inside the building, through an open door, allowing them to drop the battering ram they carried onto the sidewalk. On the back and front of their armored suits, 'Europol' was written in large, white letters.

"For a raid on a non-violent criminal gang they've brought a lot of firepower," Monroe commented dryly.

"Better safe than sorry," Conway replied.

"So, what do we do know?" Jennifer asked over the sound of heavy footsteps and shouts echoing through the building next door.

"Now, we wait," Conway told her as he listened to the footfall fading as the Europol team moved higher next door. "Shouldn't be long now."

Only Conway ate as they waited in silence. Then, when three men were escorted outside with their wrists zip-tied together and cotton bags over their heads, he told them not to worry. "That's just procedure."

The hooded men were loaded into the SUVs. Once the uniformed officers joined them, the doors closed and the vehicles drove off. From the passenger's seat of the one remaining SUV, a man in a British police uniform got out and walked up to the Chez Jacque restaurant. Conway excused himself from the table and went to talk to the man outside leaving Bishop, Monroe and Jennifer to imagine what they could be talking about.

Kether took his napkin from his lap, wiped his mouth and rose from his chair as he watched the three SUVs drive away. He put some money—considerably more than the breakfast cost—on the table and nodded to the head waiter before leaving through a back door.

"And?" Bishop asked as Conway returned to the table after a few minutes.

"Well, the top floor was piled high with all kinds of antiques."

"Who did you find inside?"

"They found Malkuth or, if you prefer, Mr. Robartés. They picked him up with four others, but as for Mr. Simpson, or your Kether, our first guess would be that he's not among them. Not unless he's some kind of Keyser Söze."

"Keyser Söze?" Jennifer asked.

"Movie reference," Monroe whispered in her ear. "Trust me, it means the chances of him being with them are slim to none."

"Anyway," Conway continued, "all rooms on the second floor were empty save for some stored furniture, but the first floor may be of interest to you. Would you care to join me?"

"We're allowed inside?" Jennifer asked.

"Only the first floor," Conway told her. "The rest is sealed off for now."

Conway got up and led the way outside. Before they got to the hallway leading to the first floor of the building, he handed out some purple latex gloves and blue cotton overshoes. "Please put these on and we'll have a look."

A shiver ran up Bishop's spine as he bent to put his overshoes on. He also smelled the faint aroma of incense in the stale air. Out of habit, he noticed the dust particles swirling in the hallway, lit by the sunlight coming in from the door behind him.

"Ready?" Conway asked once he saw everyone had their shoes and gloves on.

At the top of the stairs, they were greeted by a Europol officer who pointed them toward the room on the left. On entering, all eyes were drawn to the black and white tiled checkerboard floor before they soaked up the rest of the details: statues of Egyptian dogs, chairs lining the walls and the altar in the center of the room flanked either side with floor-to-ceiling pillars engraved with ancient Egyptian symbols.

Bishop kneeled to touch something on the floor and Monroe looked at him quizzically when he stood up again.

"Wax. Candle wax, I suppose," Bishop explained.

"That's a lot of candles," Jennifer said, noticing the droplets littering the floor as she made her way to the altar only to be shocked by the sight of a fifteen-inch blade. "My God, what have they been doing here?" She then noticed something on the blade and dropped it back on the table. "Is that blood?"

Bishop picked up the knife and closely inspected it before sniffing. "Probably blood, yeah," he confirmed. "But I wouldn't be too alarmed. The Golden Dawn was known for its experiments, but they mostly used chickens in their rituals. Believe me, there are more extreme cults and orders out there, even in these enlightened days."

Jennifer shook her head. "Yikes." She turned her attention to a cavity in the marble altar. She took out a large, silver cup decorated with two snakes curling around it. She ran a finger from the head of one of the snakes down to its tail at the foot of the cup.

"That's a ceremonial chalice," Bishop told her as he crouched to inspect the base of the altar adorned with the golden alpha and omega symbols.

"You know, those are probably real snakes on the side of the cup," Monroe teased.

Jennifer quickly put the chalice back in its place and clasped her hands behind her back. "I'm not touching anything else in this room."

"You probably shouldn't bring a blacklight into this room either," Conway joked and the other men laughed. "Did you find anything of use?"

Bishop shrugged. "There's nothing much left here. Can we take a look inside the white Mercedes van? See what they took out at the last minute?"

Conway looked at the officer in the doorway.

"I'm sorry, sir. The van has already gone to one of our sites for inspection. I'm afraid you'll have to wait."

"Sorry," Conway said to Bishop. "But what do you think of all this?"

"Well, this was clearly a temple. It fits the description of the old Golden Dawn temples with the checkered floor, the chalice and, of course, the alpha and omega signs. 'Alpha and Omega' was the name the former members of the Hermetic Order of the Golden Dawn gave themselves after the original order was dissolved."

"So, the Golden Dawn still exists?" Jennifer asked.

"Probably not. Not really anyway," Bishop replied. "Of course, some people will always follow ancient religions or lifestyles, but my guess is that this was nothing more than a small group of hobbyists trying to pick up where someone left off more than a hundred years ago."

"Or it was a cover for something else entirely," Conway said.

"I guess that could be true also," Bishop agreed.

"Anything else?" Conway asked the police officer in the doorway.

"There's a small room over here, sir."

He led the way to a room hiding at the back.

"What is this?" Monroe asked as he entered the room to be confronted by an array of brass plaques.

"Wow," Jennifer said. "There must be hundreds. What are they? Commemorative plaques for the deceased? They have some kind of statement on them and numbers. Wait, are those years?"

Bishop wiped the dust off a plaque using his gloved hands. "Two hundred and twenty-four."

"What?" Conway asked.

"Two hundred and twenty-four plaques," Bishop told him. "And I don't think they're tombstones. You see over here." He pointed at the top left where the plaques were darkest in color. "These are more than 120 years old. Here, the date is 1885, and over there on the right wall, there are two from this year."

Jennifer stepped up to the wall. "It stops at 1932 and starts again at 1992."

"They must have been out of order for a couple of decades." Monroe said, laughing. "No pun intended."

"But what are they?" Jennifer asked.

"Commemorative plaques," Bishop replied. "You were right, in part. You see over here? The plaque is inscribed with *Demon Est Deus Inversus, 1890.* 'The Devil is God inverted.' Do you recognize the saying?"

Everyone in the room looked at each other before shrugging.

"No one knows for sure where this sentence turned up for the first time, but what is known is that all members of the Hermetic Order of the Golden Dawn chose a motto to live by inside the order. Any guesses as to the motto William Butler Yeats chose?"

They all smiled and Conway said, "*Demon Est Deus Inversus.*"

"Probably not in that terrible accent," Monroe teased.

"Probably not," Bishop confirmed. "But you're correct."

"So, we know for sure this is a Hermetic Order temple."

"The original one," Bishop said. "The Isis Urania."

"And where does that bring us?" Jennifer asked.

"Nowhere, I guess," replied Bishop. "It's interesting, at most, but without Kether, we're no further on."

"Maybe you can wait for all the confiscated goods. Maybe there's something of interest in there," Conway said.

"Any idea how long that might be?" Monroe asked.

"Weeks, at best, but I'd count on months."

"In that case, we know what to do."

Jennifer and Monroe gazed at Bishop, clearly not knowing.

"We need to take the rest of the day off and go visit a museum." Bishop smiled.

Monroe and Jennifer joined him.

"I guess you're not telling me what this is all about?" Conway asked.

"Maybe later," Bishop said. "Maybe later."

CHAPTER 32

The British Museum

Just before noon, the taxi dropped them off in front of the northeast entrance of the British Museum. With the sun high, the Greek revival façade with its forty-four-foot high Ionic columns, created such a striking image that the London landmark could have been easily mistaken for the temple of Athena Polias in Priene, Greece.

"Impressive," Jennifer noted as they walked up the wide stairwell.

"And free admittance," Bishop replied.

"We British are generous, you know," Monroe said as they walked into a large courtyard. "Over thirteen million objects displayed on almost a million square feet of exhibit space. Once, the museum consisted of the four buildings that surround us here, creating this courtyard. In 1753 it was just the one wing that was steadily built on until the late 1950s. Now, the boundary consists of the four main roads surrounding the place. Late last century they added a glass roof over the entire square and laid white marble flooring, giving more exhibition space, if needed."

"And what's that?" Jennifer asked, pointing to a large round building in the center of the square that reached all the way to the glass roof.

"This one I know," Bishop said. "It's the reading room. These days, the museum houses mostly cultural art objects and antiquities, but the library once held one of the biggest book collections in the world. As well as collectibles, in the nineteenth century King George IV donated a copy of every book published to the library and it started to grow fast. People came from all over the world to read here and conduct research."

"But not anymore," Monroe said. "Most of the books have been moved to make way for the enormous collections of ancient Greek, Roman, Middle Eastern, Asian and Egyptian artifacts."

"And the mirror?" Jennifer asked.

Monroe pointed east. "Room Number One. Strangely enough, it's part of the Enlightenment collection."

"Why's that strange?"

"You've heard of the Enlightenment era?" Monroe asked.

Jennifer nodded.

"Well, generally, that era was set between 1680 and 1820 and known as the Age of Reason and Learning."

"And John Dee died in the early seventeenth century," Jennifer said. "So, the mirror is placed in the wrong timeframe. Why is that?"

As they crossed the grand courtyard, passing to the right of the old reading room which was now home to souvenir shops, Monroe shook his head.

"Don't look at me," Bishop said. "They're British. The only thing I can add is that the mirror itself is probably hundreds of years older than that." Noticing Monroe checking his watch for the second time since they entered the building he asked, "Do you need to be somewhere?"

"No, not at all," Monroe replied before gesturing toward a small, dark wooden door leading to the east wing. "I think we need to go this way."

Leading the way, Monroe turned left into a long hallway filled with display cases that lined the walls and cluttered the floorspace. There was no one else in there and their footsteps echoed as they walked.

"G1-fc20, or just fc20, should be the number on the display case, according to the website," Monroe told them and the three of them went in search of the display case.

"Over here," Monroe called a minute later, and Bishop and Jennifer joined him at a large glass display case. At the bottom of the glass, a sign said:

RELIGION AND RITUAL – Case 20 – MAGIC MYSTERY AND RITES

"Sounds about right," Monroe said.

On the display case were two information boards, one briefly explaining who Dr. John Dee was and the other offering a brief explanation of the goods on display. Much of it was made of brass alongside some waxy-looking disks, a crystal ball and some urns.

"The mirror," Bishop said, pointing to a black stone disk. "And that wood and leather pouch over there must be the mirror's case with part of Butler's Hudibras written on it."

"And what are all these other things?" Jennifer asked.

Bishop pointed to a ten-inch wax disk. "This is called the *Sigillum Dei,* the seal of God. A magical diagram with two circles, three heptagons and a pentagram. On it are the names of God and his angels. It's thought Dee used it as an amulet, giving him power over all beings except archangels. All the other items, like the glass marble and the gold disk, were used for scrying."

"Scrying?" Jennifer asked.

"Seeing or fortune-telling," Monroe explained. "All of which is well and good, professor, but we came here for the mirror, not a history lesson."

Bishop smiled. "You're right."

"So, how do we get a closer look at the mirror?" Monroe asked.

Jennifer stood in front of it, looking straight into the polished stone. Feeling a shiver run up her spine, she quickly stepped away again.

"What is it?" Bishop asked.

"Nothing," she said. "I guess seeing my dark self for a second gave me the creeps. Sorry. So, what now?"

Bishop inspected the edges of the display case, which was held together by an aluminum frame, and noticed there were no locks. Next to him, Monroe sighed and looked at his watch again.

"Why are you still...?" Bishop's voice tailed off as he saw a man approach them.

"I'm so sorry I'm late," he said, almost running to join them. "William Pierce-Holden."

The man held out his hand to Jennifer. He was in his fifties with curly blond hair and wore a somewhat shabby sweater, jeans and sneakers.

Jennifer looked at him warily. "Jennifer," she said in greeting.

"You had to be," Pierce-Holden replied.

"That leaves you to be Matthew Bishop." The man turned to Bishop and shook his hand. "From the look on your faces, I guess James here didn't announce my arrival?"

"James?" Jennifer said.

"Walker James Monroe," Pierce-Holden said. "I know he goes by the name of Walker these days, but I like his middle name better. Walker is such an American name, you know? No offense."

Bishop and Jennifer looked at Monroe, who smiled.

"Guys," Monroe said, "Meet William Pierce-Holden, curator and manager of the Enlightenment gallery and curator of Room Two, Collecting the World. You didn't think I'd let you vandalize a historic art collection on British soil, did you?"

Bishop shook his head. "And you didn't think to tell us?"

"Well, William was to meet us here at the entrance. When he was late I figured it would be fun to see what you were planning to do. But anyway, William and I worked together in the past on an exhibition about the Egyptian Book of the Dead, right here at this museum. So, naturally, I contacted him when I knew we were coming here and asked him to help."

"And I'm very happy to do so," Pierce-Holden said. "So, I hear you're interested in the mirror?"

"We are," Bishop confirmed and Pierce-Holden took a keychain from his pocket. Pushing the keys aside, he took a simple flat strip of metal and held it against the top left corner of the case. A soft click followed.

"Ah," Bishop said. "That's where the lock is."

Pierce-Holden smiled and slid the glass panel across.

"Here," he said, handing the three of them white cotton gloves before putting on a pair himself. "Please, take a seat at the table over there and I'll bring you the mirror."

The three of them sat down at a nearby wooden table covered with green velvet lit by a traditional copper and glass library lamp. Pierce-Holden brought them the mirror, laying it down on the velvet cloth.

"May I?" Bishop asked.

"Sure," Holden said. "Basically, it's just polished rock. It's virtually indestructible."

Bishop picked up the mirror and felt over the front and back with his cotton fingers. The mirror was polished flat and as smooth as a glass window. "Not a chip missing or a scratch on it. It's absolutely perfect. What do you know about it?"

"Well, we don't really know much about the mirror. It was made some 700 years ago in central Mexico from Vulcanic obsidian stone by the Aztecs who probably used it to worship their god, Tezcatlipoca. From there, we're actually not so sure what happened. We don't know how it got to Europe, we're not sure who owned it other than Horace Walpole, the eighteenth-century writer, but we don't know how he got hold of it or who he got it from. Nor do we know why he attributed previous ownership of the mirror to John Dee."

Bishop picked up the mirror again. It was heavier than it looked and he let his fingers slide inch by inch over the shining surface. Nothing. He put the mirror on its side and inspected the edges, which were slightly rougher than the surface. He moved the mirror closer to the light. Still nothing. Finally, he put the mirror back on the table and rubbed his eyes.

"And?" Jennifer asked.

Bishop shrugged. "If there's any message here I don't know where to find it."

"Could it be hollow?" Monroe asked Pierce-Holden.

"No," he said. "It's been tested for that. We know the specific gravity of obsidian black stone, multiplied by the volume, and it matches exactly so, not hollow. I'm sorry. You're looking for a message?"

"Possibly," Monroe said. "We followed a lead saying so."

"I could have told you that," Pierce-Holden said just as Bishop raised the mirror again, bringing it closer to the desk light's lamp. "What are you doing?"

"Don't worry, nothing will happen to it," Bishop assured him as he held the mirror against the light bulb. "It's not as high wattage as I'd like, but it'll possibly do the trick. Now... wait for it... just a second longer."

Bishop moved the mirror back from the bulb and inspected it, humming to himself as he did so.

"What is it?" Jennifer asked.

"Do any of you have a magnifying glass or something like that?" Bishop asked.

Pierce-Holden opened the drawer below the desk and took out a classic model eyeglass.

"Thanks," Bishop said. Placing the glass to his eye he nodded. "I thought so."

He handed the eyeglass to Monroe and turned the warm side of the mirror toward him. After Monroe accustomed his sight to the eyeglass, he suddenly smiled. There were small, dark lines on the surface of the mirror that hadn't been there before.

"Is that text?" he asked, handing the mirror to Jennifer who took a quick look before passing it on to Pierce-Holden.

"I'll be damned," he said. "*Alu... alutet ret... retni. Alutet retni*? Is that what it says?"

"I think it does," Bishop replied while the text slowly faded away again.

"What does that mean?" Jennifer asked.

"I don't know, but I think it's only part of the message."

"How...?" Jennifer asked.

"Simple," Bishop replied. "I heated only a fraction of the mirror with the bulb's heat. If you want to write a secret message you can use a number of organic acidic fluids such as lemon, apple or orange juice. Dilute them with water to the point where you can't see the dried ink with the naked eye. When later heated, the dried ink will oxidize, turning brown, revealing its secrets."

"So, the text is written in fruit juice?" Jennifer asked.

"I don't think so. Most fruit juices decay over time so the message would have disappeared by now. There are other fluids they could have used, but given the period this was written in, and the fact that it had to survive some time, I think it's more likely to assume they used blood—pureblood or diluted with water."

"Yikes," Jennifer said. "But wait, doesn't that mean we could possibly extract DNA from the text?"

"Possibly," Bishop agreed. "But the question is, what would you do with it? It would be nice to find out who wrote the text, but DNA can only help us when you have something to compare it to, and since we have no other DNA from that timeframe to compare it with, well...." Bishop picked up the mirror again and moved it to the lamp again before glancing at Pierce-Holden. "Do you mind?"

"Please, be my guest," he said. "This is kind of exciting, I must admit, and we don't get many exciting moments here."

Bishop held the side of the mirror to the lamp, starting at the top. He held it there for a few minutes before moving further along the side. Five minutes later he had come full circle and he held the mirror by the handle out before him. He looked at Monroe. "Quick, before it cools down again, will you do the honors? And Jennifer, can you write down what he says?"

As Jennifer nodded, Monroe picked up the magnifying glass.

"I think you need to start at the top right," Bishop said, and Monroe raised an eyebrow before following the order.

"Let me see." Monroe positioned himself behind the looking glass. "*Muluceps, tiget, aletut, retni, tecai, muterces, srap, amitlu, da, maiv*. That's it, I think."

"Okay," Jennifer said. "I've got something down, but I have no idea if the spelling is correct."

"Would you mind?" Bishop took the paper and pen from Jennifer's hand and laughed a little before scribbling and mumbling to himself.

"What are you doing?" Monroe asked, but Bishop didn't react.

"Is it some kind of ancient language?" Jennifer asked Monroe.

"I have no idea."

"It's much simpler than that," Bishop said, turning to look at them both. "*Viam ad ultima pars secretum iacet inter tutela tegit speculum.*"

"It's Latin," Pierce-Holden said.

"It is," Bishop confirmed. "I immediately recognized the word '*retni*' as the mirror image of the Latin word 'inter' which means 'among' or 'in between,' among other variations."

"It's Latin written in a mirror image?" Jennifer asked. "Isn't that a bit simple if you want to hide something?"

"I don't think the writer wanted to hide the text. The secret element is reflected in the use of blood. As for the backward writing, my guess is it was a joke of sorts because he used a mirror. Nothing more."

"But what does it mean?" Jennifer asked, before mumbling the words again. "*Viam ad ultima pars secretum iacet inter tutela tegit speculum.*"

"That's simple," Monroe said and gestured at Bishop to hand him the paper and pen. Monroe then started mumbling while writing before looking up a few minutes later. "The way, or path, or something like that, to the final, ultimate part of the quest or secret, lies between the defensive protections of the mirror. Wait, I think defensive in this case means protecting. So, it reads something like 'the path to the final part of the secret lies between the protection of the mirror.'"

Both Bishop, Pierce-Holden and Monroe turned their heads to the display case holding John Dee's artifacts.

"The mirror case," Jennifer said.

"Can we take a closer look at it?" Bishop asked Pierce-Holden, but he had already gotten up from his chair to get it.

"This one is a bit more fragile," he said as he laid the case on the table.

The leather was embossed with crossed lines creating diamond formations that each held a seven-petaled flower. The sides of the case were nailed together by five copper nails, but it was clear that another was missing.

"And there's the poem," Monroe said pointing to a piece of paper glued to the center of the case.

"You know about the poem?" Pierce-Holden asked.

They all nodded.

"Does it open?" Bishop asked and the older man carefully turned the case on the table.

The front was made of the same dark brown, embossed leather but without any text on it. Pierce-Holden opened four clips on the side of the case and took off the front. The inside was covered with dark red velvet that had weathered over the years showing small holes and tears in it.

"Did you ever X-ray it?" Bishop asked.

"Not that I know of. I only know the history of it from when it came into the museum's possession in 1966."

Bishop carefully pulled the case toward him and took a pen from his pocket. With the closed tip, he lifted one of the tears a little and tried to look underneath. He couldn't see anything other than cotton lining. He looked at another spot. Nothing.

"Please, wait for a moment," Pierce-Holden said suddenly. "I think I can help you. Give me two minutes. I'll be back. But please leave everything as it is for now."

Without waiting for an answer, Pierce-Holden walked away, quickly disappearing between the display cases as he headed toward the door leading to the grand courtyard.

"What's he doing?" Jennifer asked.

"I think he went to get security to arrest Matthew for befouling the case with a ballpoint pen," Monroe joked.

"Sure," Bishop said. "I didn't even take the pen out. Still, I suspect that whatever it is we are looking for is somewhere in between the layers of this case." Bishop moved his pen toward the case again.

"Don't," Monroe and Jennifer said in unison.

"Give him a minute," Monroe urged. "I think he's on our side and trying to help us. I know him to be a pragmatist so we'll be fine."

"Maybe he's gone to get a portable X-ray machine," Jennifer suggested, just as they heard footsteps approaching.

Pierce-Holden returned to the table a little breathless holding a roll of beige fabric. "I see you didn't destroy anything," he said with a smile." He rolled the fabric out on the table to reveal a number of tools including pliers, pincers, screwdrivers and a small hammer.

Bishop looked at him, clearly puzzled.

"I'm just as curious as you are," Pierce-Holden explained, "and if you promise to let me in on your findings I'm willing to help you."

"What did I tell you?" Monroe said to Bishop.

"So, I take it you believe there's something inside the case, between the leather and the velvet?" Pierce-Holden asked.

"Possibly," Bishop said. "Probably an old piece of paper."

"All right then. Let's see what we have here."

Pierce-Holden took the back of the case and placed it upside down on the table. He took a pair of small pliers, the tips of which were covered in some kind of protective material. With a firm twist, he turned one of the five nails and pulled. Without too much force, it came loose.

"The dry wood underneath makes it easy," he explained as he moved on to the next nail.

As he worked, Bishop, Jennifer and Monroe watched anxiously. Within minutes, all five nails lay before them on the table.

"Now, for the moment of truth," Pierce-Holden said, turning the case over with his gloved hands and gently tugging at the inside. Nothing happened. "Can you please give me some room?" he asked the others who were all leaning over the table to look.

Excusing themselves, they backed off and Pierce-Holden took a small plastic orange crowbar to the side of the case. He pushed gently at first, gradually using more pressure until the inside of the case finally gave way to release one side. Pierce-Holden slid the mini crowbar along the sides until he came full circle.

"Are you ready for the big moment?" he asked as he prepared to lift the velvet cover.

"Please, do the honors," Bishop said while the rest of them nodded.

Pierce-Holden wiggled the velvet a bit more until it became fully loose. He then set it next to the case on the table.

"Nothing?" Jennifer said, looking at a white piece of cloth on the bottom of the case.

"Wait another moment." Pierce-Holden ran two fingers along the inside and gently squeezed the fabric until that also came away to reveal a tightly folded piece of brownish paper. He smiled. "Is this what you're looking for?"

"May I?" Bishop said, and after a nod from Pierce-Holden, he took the paper from the case and carefully unfolded it.

"This is exactly what we're looking for," he confirmed, recognizing the same style of text and images they had seen three times before.

"You know I can't let you take it," Pierce-Holden told him.

"That's no problem," Bishop said, taking out his cellphone. "We just need a few pictures. That should be enough."

"Be my guest."

"William, you have no idea how grateful we are," Monroe said.

"That's okay. As long as you don't forget your promise."

"They won't," Jennifer told him. "I'll make sure of that."

"In that case, I believe you," Pierce-Holden replied. "Now take your pictures and find what you need to find out. I'll clean up here."

CHAPTER 33

The Mirror's Message

"Morning." Bishop walked up to Jennifer and Monroe who were busily talking over breakfast in the DoubleTree hotel in the West End of London, a place carefully chosen by Bishop because of its cleanliness and proximity to the British Museum. "You're up early."

"Or we didn't get much sleep," Monroe remarked, yawning.

"Don't look at me," Jennifer said. "I slept like a baby. Coffee?"

Bishop nodded and took a chair. "Have you found the answer to the secrets of the universe?"

"Almost," Monroe answered. "I translated the text. It wasn't too difficult once I saw that it was in Enochian and also written as a mirror image."

Monroe handed Bishop a print of the photo they had taken in the museum.

Bishop looked closely at the printout. "Hardly surprising it's in backward Enochian. Dee's method for speaking with angels became characteristic of a new Kabbalistic magic in the sixteenth century. Even the *Aldaraia sive Soyga vocor* contains words spelled backward. The title 'Soyga' is actually 'Agyos,' the Greek for 'Holy.' So, what does this fourth document say?"

"There's one more," Jennifer blurted out.

"One what?" Bishop asked.

"May I?" Jennifer asked Monroe.

"Be my guest."

"The document says there's one more place to visit, one more document to find."

"And then?" Bishop asked emptying his coffee cup in one go.

Jennifer shrugged and turned the laptop's screen to Bishop.

> *The place of my eternal death where life begins beneath the water is where you'll find the final piece where the Monas will lead you to sip on the promise of eternity.*

"The Monas," Bishop said. "I'm surprised we didn't run into it sooner since Dee was obsessed with it."

"The Monas is connected to John Dee?" Jennifer asked.

"He created it," Bishop replied. "It was Dee's way to explain all the secrets of alchemy in one image. He described the symbol in the Monas Hieroglyphica and was even granted an audience to explain it in person to Queen Elizabeth. The Rosicrucians later adopted the image in their manifesto."

Jennifer smiled. "The Monas hides a secret which lies concealed where life has its beginning? It must be almost ten years ago and it's something I had completely forgotten about until now."

"What are you talking about?" Monroe asked.

"It came back to me when I read the word 'Monas,'" Jennifer said. "When I was still living at my parents' house and my dad was still traveling, I tried to spend as much time as possible with him when he was home. I remember one day, not long after my sixteenth birthday and before one of his later journeys abroad—come to think of it, it might actually have been his last. Dad was at home working in his study, like he always did when he was home. I must have brought him a coffee early in the morning, knowing he could work all night sometimes, and I noticed he was working on a picture. When I asked him what it was, he said it was called The Monas. I don't remember everything, but what I do know is that I helped him with the puzzle he was working on at the time. It was something about a church and the beginning of life, or faith. That seemed to point him in the right direction: the baptism, I believe it was. When later that summer, he made travel plans to search for whatever it was he was looking for, I wanted to go with him, but he wouldn't let me, like always. I guess I remember this because I think it was the only time I helped my father with something. I was really proud of myself. So, subconsciously, I've known of this symbol for ten years or more. I just never made the connection to John Dee."

"So, any feelings about this message?" Monroe asked.

"Not really. It sounds a bit like the message my father was trying to decipher, but I was sixteen. I can't really remember. What I do remember is that it took him to a church abroad."

"The place of my eternal death," Monroe read. "What do we know about the death of John Dee?"

"Not too much," Bishop said. "When James I took over the throne from Elizabeth in 1603, he wanted nothing to do with astrology, alchemy and magic so Dee fell out of grace with the court. Five years later, he died a poor man in relative obscurity. There are no official records left of his death or burial, but it's been said he's buried at the church opposite the house where he lived all his life, here in London. But that's only a rumor. Like I said, there are no records and there's also no headstone in the graveyard. There's always been speculation that he was buried beneath the altar but renovations at the church have never come up with any evidence of that."

"What's that?" Jennifer asked pointing to the paper.

"Just another bunch of plants and minerals," Monroe said. "Very much like the ones we've seen before. Nothing exceptional there."

"But this one." Jennifer pointed to the last image in the row.

"Is that a plant?"

"Could be a flower of some kind," Monroe said.

"That's not what I mean. Take a closer look."

"I see it now too," Bishop said. "There's something in the image. Are those lines?"

"Wait a second." Monroe brought the image up on his laptop screen and enlarged it.

"They sure look like lines," Jennifer said, her face mere inches from the screen.

"Can you fade the background and trace the lines?" Bishop asked.

"Sure," Monroe said, and immediately got to work.

A moment later, Monroe and Bishop looked at each other and took a deep breath.

"So, that's what we're looking for," Bishop said.

"'The Monas will lead you to sip on the promise of eternity,'" Monroe quoted.

"Do you know this symbol?" Jennifer asked.

Monroe nodded. "Yes, but it doesn't make sense."

"Why not?" Bishop asked.

"It's generally accepted that the squared circle didn't exist before the seventeenth century. It was certainly never found on documents from before that date."

"The squared circle?" Jennifer asked. "Will someone please fill me in?"

"Sure," Bishop said. "The squared circle is an alchemical figure that, according to our friend here, first emerged in the seventeenth century. It's believed to illustrate the relationship between the four elements of matter: earth, water, air and fire."

"But that's not what makes this symbol so special." Monroe waved a finger in the air.

"Yeah, yeah," Bishop said. "I was coming to that. In mathematics, this figure represents the challenge of constructing a square within the same area as a given circle without changing the length of any of the sides. An impossible task which kept mathematicians busy until the late nineteenth century when it was mathematically proven impossible. It was that impossible nature that gave the figure its other, more current meaning, that of...." Bishop paused for a moment. "The Philosopher's Stone."

"Like in the Harry Potter book?" Jennifer asked, smiling.

"The very same one," Bishop said.

"I thought that was an invention by the author."

"Not really. The first written documentation about the stone was in 300 AD in ancient Greece. But Elias Ashmole, a seventeenth-century alchemist and writer, claimed the stone's history went as far back as Adam who received knowledge of it from God Himself. The knowledge of the stone was then handed down through the biblical patriarchs, which some think could explain why they all lived so long. Methuselah died at 969, his father at 365. Noah lived to be 950 years old and Isaac reached 180. The Old Testament is filled with people way over one hundred years old."

Jennifer leaned back in her chair. "So, the philosopher's stone is something that gives longevity?"

"Something like that," Monroe answered. "The alchemists believed that the stone could perform three tasks, or magisteriums, as they called it. The first magisterium was to create gold. This was said to be the easy one. Every decent alchemist should have been able to perform this task."

"Though it's never been proven," Bishop added.

"Of course not, but so says the myth. The second magisterium gave alchemists the means to heal physical illnesses and thus create longevity. And the third and final magisterium was believed to transform the human soul into an eternal state of unity with the divine spirit."

"A form of immortality?" Jennifer asked

"A sixteenth-century alchemist's wet dream. Pardon my French." Bishop smiled at Jennifer. "When you think of it, it does seem to add up with everything else we've come across."

"How so?" Jennifer asked.

"Well, in the original letters, John Dee spoke about knowledge that could benefit all mankind, revealing a potentially world-ending catastrophe or granting a life without suffering. Do you remember?"

Jennifer nodded.

"The second message spoke of the 'living breath of true ages.' When coupled with the text we found in Safed that said 'ending the premise that pain is the sensation of the absence of the upper light,' what do we get?"

"Immortality?" Jennifer tried.

"It does seem to suggest that," Monroe agreed. "And, personally, I do believe that immortality would probably lead to a world-ending catastrophe. Add that to the fact that John Dee was known for his obsession with two things—making gold and living forever—the conclusion seems logical."

"But I guess the input from the Kabbalah on the subject is somewhat strange," Bishop remarked.

"Why is that?" Jennifer asked.

Monroe answered. "There is, of course, physical and spiritual longevity. Where religions such as Christianity, Judaism or Islam all teach about some kind of heaven or afterlife, a Kabbalist believes in the spiritual eternal life, where the spirit gets reborn again and again. There's no real need for an afterlife or physical immortality. In other words, Kabbalists are already immortal."

"Then why...?" Jennifer started.

"The Philosopher's Stone," Bishop interrupted. "The *Aab-i-Hayat, Amrit Ras, Chashma-i-Kausa* or the elixir of life, is known all over the world and it has hundreds of different names. In ancient times the Irish called it *Uisce Beatha*, which literally means water of life. Nowadays, this is the Irish name for whiskey. But the elixir of life has a long history in cultures all over the world. In general, it's believed to give the drinker eternal life or eternal youth. Somehow, I believe many Kabbalists might prefer that over an uncertain spiritual rebirth. What do you say?" Bishop glanced at Monroe, who stayed silent. "Anyway, alchemists from Europe, China, the Middle East and India have been searching for this elixir throughout history. It's even described in the Bible, in the Gospel of John, where it says, 'Whoever drinks the water I give him will never thirst. Indeed, the water I give him will become in him a spring of water welling up to eternal life.'"

"Others consider the elixir of life to be the exact opposite of the forbidden fruit from Eden," Monroe finally said.

"Well," Bishop said looking at Jennifer. "If we're right, we now have four parts of the recipe to the elixir of life and a lead to the next piece. Who wants to live forever?"

"Old men," Jennifer joked and Bishop laughed. "Do you really believe there could be a secret to immortality?"

"From a scientific standpoint, sure," Bishop said. "Not long ago they found out the probable reason for aging. At the end of our chromosomes, there are telomeres. A telomere keeps our chromosomes fresh by dividing them constantly. The only drawback is that a telomere has a certain length that shrinks over time. When there's nothing left, our chromosomes no longer refresh, we age, we die. In theory, if we can lengthen our telomeres, we could stop aging."

"You think they'll be able to do that someday?" Jennifer asked.

"They're already doing it," Bishop replied. "They successfully increased the length of the telomeres in rodents. Unfortunately, the lengthening caused a cancerous side effect. But, theoretically, the rats were immortal, or rather, they would never die of old age."

"It's playing God," Monroe said.

"I agree," Bishop replied. "There's also a mathematical perspective that's more up my alley. A study published in the journal *Proceedings of the National Academy of Sciences* created a mathematical equation that proved it was impossible to stop aging in multicellular organisms. I haven't actually studied it, but basically it supports the research done on rodents and their lengthening telomeres. The choice is to age and die or stay young and eventually get cancer."

"And die," Jennifer added.

Bishop nodded. "On the other hand, we keep finding cures for illnesses and we are getting older. In the 1900s the average age was fifty. Now it's about eighty. In fact, scientists believe the first humans to reach 120 have probably already been born. As well as looking for cures for illnesses, a lot of research goes into wonder drugs capable of stretching our lifespan. Recently, they found out that diabetes patients who use the drug Metformine live up to eighteen percent longer than healthy people without diabetes. So, who can say where we will end?"

"So, do you think there's a chance we might find the secret to immortality?" Jennifer asked.

Bishop smiled. "To be completely honest... no. Not a chance. And to be even more honest, I'm not even one hundred percent convinced that this secret is even about immortality."

"You think my translations are incorrect?" Monroe asked.

"I'm positive my friend's translation is without flaw." Bishop patted Monroe on the shoulder. "It's our interpretation I have serious doubts about."

"Always the skeptic," Monroe said. "But you're forgetting the fact that we're not the only ones on this quest. So, whatever this is about, it has a lot of interest."

"We're only one piece of the puzzle away from knowing the truth," Jennifer said. "Not really the time to back out now. So where do we go next?"

"That's the spirit," Bishop said. "I suggest we finish our breakfast and take a look at the church John Dee was allegedly buried at. St. Mary the Virgin's Church in Mortlake."

"And look for what?" Monroe asked. "You told us there's no grave or headstone, so where will we look?"

"That's easy," Jennifer said and the two men turned to look at her. "I told you already, like I told my father ten years ago. 'The place where life begins beneath the water is where the Monas will lead you the promise of eternity.' We need to visit the church and find the Monas. Up until now we've been looking for graves, but because of my father's research I'm convinced this one is the opposite of that. This one's about birth and baptisms. We need to look at the font, below the water."

"I think you're right," Bishop said, smiling proudly.

"Where is this church?"

"It's further west. About an hour's drive by cab."

"So, let's finish our breakfast and go," Jennifer said as she took a piece of toast and smeared marmalade on it.

CHAPTER 34

The Recipe

2009

The printer hummed gently as it spat out a single sheet of paper. Robert Porter easily read the Latin as it appeared, despite it being upside down.

De Heptarchia Mystica Annexamus.

As the printer finished its work, he anxiously placed the page in front of him on the desk.

> *Blot owte suspition of us; for we are gods Creatures that haue. Raigned, do Raigne, and shall Raigne for eu.*
>
> *All our Mysteries shalbe known unto you. The fowntayne of wisdome is opened: Nature shalbe knowne. Erth with her Secrets discloased. The Elements with their powres iudged. At the endeth thee the myst'ries to f'rev'r life art anon to beest reveal'd.*

Below the text, there were five images of plants or herbs and underneath them was a table of letters and numbers. Porter immediately understood it was a prescription. The *Rx* at the top of the page he recognized from a picture on the wall of his brother's pharmacy that showed an ancient prescription. He often tried to read the Latin text while waiting for Jennifer who had a temporary job there. A tiny smile emerged on his face as he heard his wife's voice from the doorway.

"Robert?"

"Yes, dear?"

"Are you coming to bed?"

"In a short while. I'll just finish this page."

"Sure, dear."

Sylvia walked away and a few seconds later Porter heard the door to their bedroom close.

"A recipe? Complete with measurements?" he mumbled to himself. He then tried to translate the ingredients in the table to work out what the recipe might be for. '*Centella asiatica – drachmas quattuor, vaccinium cyanococcus – unciam unam, panax....*'

On his laptop, Porter searched the Latin names.

'*Centella asiatica*' was also known as *Gotu Kola*, an herbaceous, frost-tender perennial in the flowering plant family *Apiaceae*. Native to wetlands in Asia it was often used as a medicinal herb. '*Vaccinium cyanococcus*' appeared to be a species of shrub with edible fruit.

Although it took a while, Porter eventually found all five ingredients, which were either herbs, fruits or flowers. Most of them were locally available, but a couple he'd have to find through the Internet. Interestingly, three of the ingredients were considered to be superfoods. Below the ingredients were the words "*capiat cochleria duo magna quartâ quâque horâ ex paululo aqua, quinque diebus,*" which translated to "two large spoons, every fourth hour with a little water for five days." *But then what?* he wondered, and he went back to the Latin text at the start.

> *At the endeth thee the myst'ries to f'rev'r life art anon to beest reveal'd.*

"Could it be?"

Porter read the words over and over, and from every angle, even using three different Latin dictionaries. He had done the same with the other documents from the box, and as far as he was able to make out, they all talked about some kind of great mystery that would either benefit mankind or bring disaster. Even the letters between Dee, his daughter and Łaski spoke of a mystery so big he didn't trust the world with it. And though he had looked for every kind of meaning behind the Latin text, each translation brought him back to the same conclusion—he was close to finding the secret to eternal life.

Porter sighed. That was enough for today. He had more to think about tomorrow, so he turned off the desk light.

"I have Mr. Matthews for you, sir."

"Please put him through."

A soft click sounded followed by a man's voice over the speaker phone. "Matthews."

"You're still at the marina, sir?"

The man turned in his chair to look out over the Marina del Rey toward the hills on the other side. In the distance, large plumes of smoke rose from the hills. For the past three days, wildfires had forced thousands from their homes in Southern California and ten thousand more had been ordered to evacuate.

"We're still allowed to stay," he said. "The wind turned so the fire is moving north. I heard you succeeded in London?"

"We did, sir, but I didn't want to call you until we were sure what it was we had found."

"Any trouble?"

"Not really. We had some involuntary help from Mr. Porter, but we managed the situation."

"Managed the situation?"

"Nothing drastic, sir. He showed up at the church, broke in at night and found the text before we could. Security on site took care of it. They made him turn the text over to them and then sent him on his way. I checked. He arrived safely back in the U.S."

The man grunted before speaking. "I don't like these confrontations. You never know where they will lead."

"I assure you, sir, nothing happened and Porter is none the wiser."

"Okay, as you say. So, what's this about not wanting to call before you were sure? What did you find out?"

"We found a document and we think it is exactly what you thought it would be or, rather, suggested it might be. The document starts with some mumbo jumbo text in Latin, talking about us being God's creatures who shall reign the Earth and all secrets about to be revealed. At the end of the text, it speaks about the elixir of life being presented to the reader. Then there's a recipe, a prescription, if you will."

"So, the medieval quack really thought he was on to something?"

"Technically, he lived a century after the middle ages, sir."

"Thank you for that." The man's gravelly voice lowered a fraction in irritation.

"Sorry, sir, but you were correct about the one thing that matters here. Strangely enough, the ingredients in the recipe are simply a bunch of plants and herbs mixed with water. Nothing you'd consider to be special. They're all known to have some kind of homeopathic use, but they're of no pharmaceutical significance. If anything, in the dosages prescribed, they would be more destructive than healing."

"But you can recreate it?"

"We can and we are already on it. Some ingredients aren't indigenous to the U.S., but are being flown in as we speak. We expect to have them by tomorrow. From there we can create the elixir within a few hours. The recipe prescribes a dosage over five days on a human."

The line went silent for a few seconds. "Are you suggesting animal testing first?"

"Well, we can test the combined ingredients first to see if any new chemical substances are created, but I'm not sure what that will tell us if it does. Probably very little."

"And what do you expect to learn from animal testing? I mean, how will you know it works?"

"We probably won't know for sure for a long time. Although we could test it on single-cell organisms, which would give us a result in hours. We could then work our way up from there, but the more complex the organism the longer it will take for the results to be clear. It could be more than a year on a rat. We can, of course, measure cell division and DNA and RNA oxidation, but the human body loses between 50 and 70 billion cells daily due to apoptosis alone and, as you know, we're not even sure why we age and die as we do."

"I understand it's difficult, but this is why I hired you and your team. Mix your potion and start testing as soon as you can. I want a detailed report on my desk every day."

"Not a problem, sir. I'll keep you informed. Anything else I can do for you?" Matthews waited a second. "Sir?" But there was nothing. The line was dead.

Looking out of the window, at the smoke in the distance, the man's eye was caught by a large fleet of pleasure boats leaving the marina and sailing onto the open water. Below him, on the shore, people as small as ants were walking up and down the docks moving boxes and packing cars. He pushed a button on his phone. "Susan?"

"Yes, sir."

"What's going on downstairs?"

"Sir, we received another message from the fire department. They expect the wind will shift in the next hour. If it does the fire could reach us before nightfall. We've been ordered to evacuate as a precaution."

The man thought for a long moment before speaking. "Take whatever you deem to be of value and go to our Canefield office. I'll join you later."

"Are you going to be okay, sir?"

"I'll be fine. You go now. I'll see you soon."

With a soft click, Susan was gone.

That night Robert Porter didn't sleep a wink. The thought of having the cure to mortality kept spinning in his head. He was also unsure as to what he should do next. He didn't know whether to tell his wife or daughter or take his findings to a university or hospital and let them research it thoroughly. He could even take it to the government, although what they might do with it was anyone's guess. Of course, there was also the chance he might not be believed. And if they did, what was to stop them simply taking his research away. If they did believe him, that is. Hell, he wasn't even sure he believed it—a bunch of superfoods mixed together, rich in antioxidants no doubt, but mixed with water could be the difference between death and immortality? In his heart, Porter knew for sure it couldn't be true, which was why he was so anxious. The thought of being viewed as gullible was too much to contemplate. In fact, he'd rather test it on himself to avoid that embarrassment. The ingredients seemed harmless enough. It couldn't hurt to try. At least then he'd know for certain whether he had stumbled upon the elixir of life or an elaborate hoax.

After he finally fell asleep, waking up shortly after when dawn arrived, one thing was immediately clear to Porter—he had even more questions to answer than when he went to bed. After a quick shower, he walked downstairs and into the kitchen where Sylvia and Jennifer were already at the breakfast table.

"Look who has decided to join us," Sylvia said. Seeing the frown on her husband's face she added, "Rough night?"

"You have no idea." He rubbed his eyes as Sylvia poured him a cup of coffee.

"Can you give me a ride to school?" Jennifer asked.

Porter looked at his watch. "No problem. I have to run some errands anyway."

"Where are you going?" Sylvia asked.

Porter thought a second before answering. "Oh, it's nothing. I need some groceries for a little experiment I'm doing. I'll be back before lunch."

CHAPTER 35

The Coin

The Present

The cab turned off South Circular Road and onto Sheen Lane. Jennifer and Monroe had been chatting the entire way about immortality and how it would affect their lives.

"You do realize that John Dee was an alchemist, a charlatan who tried to make gold out of metal?" Bishop asked as he washed his hands with sanitizer.

"What do you mean?" Jennifer held out her hands to Bishop who pumped some sanitizer onto them.

"You too?" Monroe asked Jennifer.

"It's very refreshing. You should try it."

Monroe shrugged and turned to Bishop. "What do you mean, Dee was a charlatan who tried to make gold out of metal?"

"What I mean is that even though this has been an interesting treasure hunt, the chances of it leading to something have diminished drastically since our last find."

"How do you figure that? What made you so cynical all of a sudden?" Monroe asked.

"Like I said, if there's a way to prolong life drastically, maybe even forever, modern science is at the brink of discovering its secrets. I have serious doubts that some alchemist, a few hundred years ago, simply mixed a few herbs and discovered the secret. I mean, how would he have discovered it himself? I know we haven't found the complete recipe yet. We only have four documents so far with five ingredients on each sheet, but even so."

"Maybe he didn't discover it himself," Monroe suggested. "You said it yourself. Methuselah, Noah, Isaac and the better part of the Old Testament all lived to be in their hundreds. And some say the secret to old age is hidden in the Bible. Maybe Dee found it?"

Bishop didn't answer immediately. From experience, he knew that the bigger the secret or legend the lesser the chance there was any truth to it, and the bigger the disappointment. "What I do find interesting is how all the parties involved were connected. I mean, we found the Hermetic Order of the Golden Dawn and discovered that Mr. Simpson was also searching for the document. But is that the end of that line, or is Mr. Simpson working for someone else? And what's with the Kabbalah?"

"Coincidence?" Monroe said.

Bishop pulled his face in disbelief. "Yochai and Luria, the graves of whom gave us the first part of the secret, were men tied to the origin of the Kabbalah. John Dee popularized the Kabbalah in England. And in Poland, our murdered priest was a Kabbalist. And, finally, Malkuth is ten on the Kabbalistic Tree of Life and Kether is one."

"And I saw that at least one of the security guards that Cohen brought with him in Machpelah wore a red ribbon on his wrist," Jennifer said.

Bishop tilted his head toward Monroe. "That's a whole lot of coincidences, don't you think?"

There was no answer. "We're almost there," Monroe said as the car turned right onto Mortlake High Street.

"You've been here before?" Jennifer asked.

"Not to the church," Monroe replied. "But I know the neighborhood. I spent some time here as a kid. My grandparents lived a few blocks away."

The cab stopped opposite the church.

"Doesn't look like a church," Jennifer noted as they got out, pointing to the small part of the church that was visible through the trees and shrubs.

"What are you doing?" Monroe asked Bishop who had turned to face the buildings behind them.

"They're all relatively new," he said. "The buildings, I mean. And yet John Dee was said to have lived across the street from the church."

"The entire neighborhood was rebuilt in the second part of the last century," Monroe told him. "The only original building left is the church."

"And that's a good thing for us," Jennifer said as she started to cross the road. The men smiled at each other and followed quickly.

The gate to the church grounds was open and as they walked through, Jennifer glanced left and stopped. In the garden, next to the curb, weathered tombstones rose from perfectly cut grass.

"It's not a big place," Bishop said, "so I guess they needed the space. I figure that every inch of soil we walk on...."

Jennifer looked at the ground, her eyes widening. "Shall we go inside?"

The door to the church was open and as they walked in their footsteps echoed throughout the old building.

"It's bigger than I thought it would be," Monroe said.

"Much bigger," Bishop agreed, looking to the altar ahead of them, colorfully lit by rays of sunlight streaming through the stained-glass windows.

"You're early." A short, bald man in religious robes walked toward them from the back of the church. "Reverend Galen Dagley, Parish Curate here at St. Mary's. I wasn't expecting you yet."

"I'm sorry," Bishop said. "I think there's a misunderstanding. We're only here to visit your church."

"You're not the Hendersons?"

They all shook their heads.

"Oh, I'm really sorry. I'm expecting some people to talk about a christening. What can I do for you?"

"Well," Bishop started, "we're from the United States, Yale University, and we're researching the life and work of John Dee, particularly his final years, after the height of his career and his death."

"I thought that everything possible had been researched about that man," Dagley said frowning.

"Maybe so," Monroe admitted. "There's a lot written about his career and work, but little is known about his last years and his death. We understand he was buried here?"

"Please follow me." Dagley walked to the back of the church. "You may be right. There is little information about his final days. He'd stopped writing well before his death, shortly after he fell out of grace with the royal court and everyone lost interest in him. He died in relative anonymity."

"You're an expert on the subject?" Jennifer asked.

"Not really, but working here you pick up a few things and, to be frank, you're not the first ones who have come searching for some sign of John Dee. Every year there are crazy people searching for some kind of sign of enlightenment. Sorry, that's not to say that you, uh...."

"No problem," Bishop said. "We understand."

In front of the altar, they turned left to the outermost corner of the church where Dagley stopped in front of a black marble plaque fixed on the wall.

They all read the plaque in silence.

"Near this place?" Jennifer asked.

Dagley nodded. "And that's as close as it gets. There were rumors he was buried in the chancel of the 1543 church, between two servants of the Queen, a certain Anthony Holt and Edward Myles."

"1543 church?" Monroe asked. "This isn't the first St. Mary?"

"Well, technically it isn't. The first chapel was built in 1348 on the river side of High Street. That was replaced by this one in 1543. In the early years it was nothing more than a small chapel, but it grew over the centuries with the south aisle added in 1725 and the north aisle extended in 1816. Later, in the nineteenth century, an architect named Samuel Beachcroft carried out an extensive restoration. After that, there were some smaller changes and restorations, but nothing much has changed since the twentieth century apart from bits of research or architectural surveys here and there. But the fact is, there's very little you see here that dates back to the earliest years of the first chapel. Even the graves surrounding the church date from the late seventeenth century on."

"You say not much survived?"

"There's only one relic that survived from the first chapel." Dagley led them to the front of the church and into the baptistry, stopping at a gray marble font. "The only surviving relic," he said. "The font was given to the church by Archbishop Bourchier in 1428." Dagley lay his hand on the rim of the empty bowl and caressed it. "Beautiful, isn't it?"

"Indeed, it is," Monroe agreed. "Do you happen to know—"

"Hello?"

Dagley turned to see who was calling from the front of the church.

"Ah, that must be the Hendersons," he said before calling out to them, "I'll be right with you!"

"Do you mind if we stay a bit longer and have a look around?" Bishop asked.

"Not at all. Please feel free. And if you have any more questions please save them and maybe I can help you later on."

"Thanks, we will," Bishop said, and Dagley went on his way.

"So far, so good," Monroe mumbled as Dagley welcomed his visitors.

"What do you mean?" Jennifer asked.

"Well, we came for the font and now we know that it's the only surviving relic from Dee's days. So, now all we have to do is find the Monas."

Silently, they all stepped back from the font to better look at it. Bishop then stepped forward again and stroked the symbols carved on the sides.

"That must be it," Jennifer said, also stepping forward. She walked around the font and laid her hand on one of the symbols and pushed. "First the smile."

Bishop and Monroe watched in silence as Jennifer pushed with more force to no effect.

Moving on to the circle with the dot in the center, she again pushed it.

"The spot," she whispered before pressing and moving on to the cross. "And the last one, the two mountains," she mumbled before pushing at it with all her power. She stepped back. Nothing. Turning to Bishop and Monroe she said, "Worth a try."

"What did you try?" Bishop said.

"Well, the smile, the spot, the cross, and the mountains stand as symbols for *Luna, Sol, Elementa, Ignis*—the moon, the sun, the elements and fire. When you put them together you get the Monas, so I figured...."

"You figured the symbols are the code to...?" Monroe asked.

"To what indeed," Bishop interrupted. "But I think you're on the right track. I can't make any other sense of having these symbols on a Christian font. And we all know the infinity symbol." He pointed at the horizontal eight.

"And the five-petaled rose stands for a secret in some Christian beliefs," Monroe added.

"Infinity... secret... sound familiar?" Jennifer asked Bishop, but he didn't react because he was too busy staring at the font.

Bishop put on a pair of white gloves, and with his arms stretched wide, bent down and grabbed both sides of the font. With a grunt, he pushed with all his might. The bowl made a soft grinding sound and rotated a few inches. Bishop let go again.

"That's it," he said, sighing deeply as Jennifer and Monroe frowned. "It must be a single dial rotary combination lock."

"Sure, it is." Monroe laughed and shook his head.

"Locks. Kind of a hobby," Bishop explained. "Anyway, the entire bowl of the font functions like a lock on a safe. We rotate it clockwise and counterclockwise stopping at every symbol when we get there."

"And the combination?" Monroe asked.

"We know the combination, thanks to Jennifer. Smile, spot, cross, mountains. Now all we need...." Bishop kneeled on the floor and looked under the bowl. He circled the font before calling out. "Here it is! Look!"

Jennifer and Monroe came to kneel next to him.

"Look," he repeated, pointing at a marking on the font's pedestal. "You see? The infinity sign. That must be the reference point on which to align the symbols."

Jumping to his feet, Bishop grabbed the edges of the bowl. "A little help?"

"All right," Jennifer said, taking hold, along with Monroe.

"Tell us where to go," Monroe said.

"First, we go right," he said before stopping them with a raised finger so he might see if Dagley was anywhere near. "Okay, let's try to do this as quietly as possible. One, two, three."

As they all pulled, the bowl turned quietly on its pedestal.

"Stop," Bishop said and they all let go. He then checked they had alignment at the bottom of the bowl. "Perfect. Now the other way. If you two can manage this, I'll stay here and check the alignment."

"Sure, let us do the heavy work," Monroe said, smiling.

Bishop simply nodded as the other two resumed pulling.

"Stop. And again the other way."

Without needing any signal, Jennifer and Monroe got to work and the bowl started turning again.

"Stop. That's great. Right. Two more to go," Bishop said and Monroe and Jennifer immediately rotated the bowl again.

When Bishop uttered his final "stop" there was a click from the other side of the font. Bishop scurried over, still on his knees, and found an opening in the font.

"Quick, come here, take a look," he urged the other two and as they came to kneel beside him, he took a tiny flashlight and peered inside the small, dark hole. "There's something in the back. Something black."

"Will you do the honors?" Bishop said, handing Jennifer a pair of gloves.

"You're a real gentleman," Monroe teased.

"That too, but she also has the smallest hands," Bishop retorted.

Jennifer glanced around and seeing nobody nearby, she quickly put on the gloves, placed a hand on the edge of the hole and looked at Bishop.

"Go ahead," he said softly, and Jennifer inched her hand into the hole until she was wrist deep.

"I feel something. Feels like fabric," she told them. Managing to grab hold of whatever she had found by using two fingers like tweezers, she carefully withdrew her hand from the hole.

In silence, all three of them looked at the black pouch held between Jennifer's fingers.

"Hmm?" Bishop said. "That looks kind of new.

"That is strange," Monroe replied. "I'm no expert, but that pouch isn't hundreds of years old."

Still on her knees, Jennifer froze and her face turned pale as she looked at the black velvet pouch.

"What is it?" Bishop asked, but Jennifer seemed not to hear him. "Jennifer?"

As Bishop placed a hand on her shoulder, Jennifer looked up. "Oh, sorry. I just had a flashback."

Standing up, Jennifer tested the weight of the pouch in her hand.

"Open it," Bishop urged.

Jennifer took another close look at the pouch before handing it to Bishop. "You open it."

"What's wrong?" he asked, taking the pouch.

Jennifer didn't answer.

The top of the pouch was bound together with black cotton lace. Bishop unwound it, stretched the opening with his fingers and looked inside. He raised an eyebrow, turned the pouch upside down and shook the contents into his other hand. Within a fraction of a second, Jennifer felt the blood drain from her face. Feeling nauseous and dizzy she reached out and grabbed Monroe's hand as hard as she could before her legs gave way.

"Hey!" Monroe said, trying to keep her upright. "What's wrong with you?"

Bishop quickly pulled up a nearby chair and they sat Jennifer down. He then took a small bottle of water from his rucksack and urged her to drink.

"You okay?" he asked as Jennifer sipped and she nodded. "Take your time."

After a few more sips, Jennifer got back to her feet, helped by her friends.

"Thank you," she sputtered, grabbing hold of Bishop's closed hand. "Open it," she said, and he did.

Jennifer reached for the small, transparent acrylic disk and sighed as she examined it. *After all these years,* she thought. *How could it be? What does it mean? It could have been a coincidence, but it felt like a message. Was it for her?*

"I know what this is," she said finally. "When I was little, every so often my father and I played hide and seek. He left me cryptic clues that I'd search for...." She raised the disk and with a twist, she opened it. "Coins just like this one."

"Is that a gold Krugerrand?" Monroe asked, taking the coin from Jennifer.

"It is," she said. "But probably not a real one. The real ones are worth over a thousand dollars. My father had a stash of replicas. He always said that wherever he went he left a coin behind. That way, when his time came to leave this world he would have left his mark in the form of a golden trail around the globe. I don't know where he got them, but I remember that on my sixteenth birthday he gave me another one that I figured was fake as well. Only it wasn't. It was real."

Monroe closed the box. "Fingerprints. There could be fingerprints on the coin."

"And you think this coin is somehow related to your father?" Bishop asked.

"Do you think it could be something else?" she challenged.

"How are we doing over here?" Dagley appeared behind them, startling them all. "Are you okay, miss?"

"Oh, we're good, thanks," Monroe replied. "She's just a little under the weather."

Bishop stepped in front of the open hole in the pedestal, crouched low and quietly closed it. "You have a great church here. Especially this masterpiece."

Bishop stroked the sides of the font as he stood up.

"Thank you, I know," Dagley responded. "Now, is there anything else I can do for you?"

"No, thank you," Monroe said. "We know enough. Thank you for—"

"As a matter of fact, there is one thing," Bishop interrupted. "If you don't mind?"

"No problem," Dagley replied. "I have some time."

"Earlier, you said there weren't any restorations since the 1900s, but there was research done on the church. Do you happen to know what kind of research was done, let's say, in the past ten years?"

Dagley shook his head. "I'm not sure. I've only worked here for three years, but it shouldn't be too hard to find out."

Gesturing for them to follow, he quickly walked away toward the front of the church. At the altar, he turned left and disappeared through a dark mahogany door. "Are you coming?" he shouted and a few seconds later they followed.

"Sorry, we fell somewhat behind," Bishop said.

"No, I should apologize," Dagley said as he opened a steel filing cabinet. "I've been accused of running in my own church. Now, let me see." Dagley leafed through the folders, occasionally taking one out before shaking his head and returning it. "We're not that digital here yet. Actually, we're completely analog."

"Aren't you afraid of what might happen in the case of a fire or theft?"

"Ah, here it is. It's just the one." Dagley opened the folder and took out a small stack of papers. "Let me see, yes, I thought I'd heard of it. In 2009 there was an architectural survey. They closed the church for a few days to take all kinds of measurements, it says here."

"Can I see that?" Bishop asked.

"Here's the order form." Dagley put a sheet of paper on top of some others.

"The American Foundation on Restoring Religious Structures in old Britannia," Bishop said, reading from the paper.

"Americans," Monroe noted.

Bishop cocked his head.

"This is all there is?" he asked and Dagley nodded. "Do you mind if I take a few pictures of the documents?"

"Sure, no problem. Do you mind me asking what this is all about?"

Bishop took out his camera and started taking pictures. "Oh, nothing special. It's just that if they took all measurements in 2009 we can look them up and see if they're willing to share them with us. There...." He handed the stack back to Dagley. "We thank you for your kind cooperation and let me tell you again what a lovely church you have here."

"Thank you. I think so too."

Dagley shook everyone's hand and escorted them outside. On returning inside, his eyes were drawn to the font. He walked up to it and looked at the symbols on the side before frowning and shaking his head. "Nah," he said.

Back on the street, both men looked at Jennifer.

"Are you okay?" Monroe asked.

Jennifer shrugged. "I guess so. Left with a thousand questions, but I'm okay."

"I can imagine," Bishop replied. "It doesn't really make sense. Who put the coin in there, and if it was your father, why? And what happened to the original content of the font? Did your father have it?"

"I really have no idea." Jennifer shook her head. "Everything I know, you now know. If my father had the original content, it would have been in his safe. And it wasn't."

"No other hiding places? Maybe a diary?" Bishop asked.

"Not that I know of. But I must admit that we knew very little of what was going on in his study. Everything is still there. My mother didn't change a thing. So, if we want to take a look...."

"What about the survey?" Monroe asked Bishop." Why were you so interested?"

"Just a hunch at first, but now I think there may be something in it."

"How so?" Monroe asked.

"Well, you told us you remembered your father's last journey was to a church abroad when you were sixteen. If I'm not mistaken, you're twenty-six years old now. So that would make it 2009." Bishop waved his phone in front of them. "On the documents, it says the survey was in the summer of 2009. When did you say your father went away?"

"It must have been July or August," Jennifer replied.

"I bet you that your father's journey and the survey are somehow connected."

"So, what do we do now?" Monroe asked.

"Well," Bishop replied. "We're still missing the final document and we have two leads: Robert Porter's study and the American foundation's survey."

"Which are both back in the U.S.," Monroe said.

"We're going home again," Jennifer replied.

CHAPTER 36

Research

Even though the first day of school was two weeks away, The Yale campus was filled with hordes of new students scouring the site to check out the buildings they would spend the coming years in.

"They're early this year," Monroe remarked as he watched them pass Bishop's office at 451 College Street. "I don't recall us being so keen to get to school in our day."

Bishop grunted and cocked his head. "Did you get some sleep?" he asked Jennifer.

"Barely on the flight and even less at home," Jennifer replied, shaking her head. Ever since they found her father's coin in the font, she couldn't shake the thought that it was meant as some kind of message. Did he leave it for her? If he did, how could he have known that years later the coin would find its way to her? If there was one thing she had learned in the last few weeks it was that she needed to be prepared for anything, but how could she have prepared for this? Or was it simply one big coincidence? Could it be?

"I still don't understand it," Jennifer admitted to Bishop.

"You need to let it go for now," he advised her. "Given what we know, I don't think it will yield any new information at this point in time."

"I think you're right," Monroe said, turning away from the window. "But there is one new thing we've learned."

"And that is?" Jennifer asked.

"The Monas wasn't Dee's invention, as we always thought. The font was made long before Dee was ever born."

"Dee probably visited the church and saw the font numerous times as he lived across the street," Bishop said. "Maybe he saw the symbols and from there got the idea of combining them to make one symbol: his Monas."

"I guess that's possible," Monroe admitted with a nod. "That would also mean he went on to somehow create the safe lock mechanism using the font."

"I think so," Bishop said.

"So, what do we do first?" Jennifer asked. "If we want to visit my father's study I suggest we do it this afternoon when my mother's not at home. I don't think she's really touched Dad's study since his death."

"Well," Bishop replied. "If we have any chance of finding the original content taken from the font of St. Mary's, I think that is the place to start."

"What about the survey?" Monroe asked.

Bishop reached for his backpack and took out a small stack of papers. "I had these printed," he said as he handed the papers to Monroe.

"The American Foundation on Restoring Religious Structures in old Britannia," Monroe read. Then, pointing to Bishop's laptop, he asked, "Do you mind?"

"Be my guest." Bishop opened the laptop, logged in and turned it toward Monroe who immediately got to work.

"Walker James Google Monroe," Bishop teased, and even Jennifer managed to smile, something that was noticed by Bishop who laid a hand gently on her shoulder.

"You may joke," Monroe said, "but I've already found the foundation here on Wikipedia."

"An academic using Wikipedia," Bishop said. "I stand corrected, Walker James Wikipedia Monroe."

Monroe shook his head. "Very funny. I'd never use Wikipedia for academic purposes but to retrieve general information, well... Right, it says here 'Category: Non-profit organization based in California, The American Foundation on Restoring Religious Structures in old Britannia.'"

"What else does it say?" Jennifer asked.

"Not much, I'm afraid. Founded in May 2009. It was dissolved a few months later. I guess they didn't transfer all the old data to Wikipedia. No overview, history, no references and no external links."

"So much for the digital side of our research," Bishop said as he started leafing through the stack of papers he had printed. "You keep searching on the Internet and we'll check these out."

"Ah, a contest," Monroe said as he returned his attention to the screen.

"So, what are we looking for?" Jennifer asked.

"Anything with names of companies, their addresses or names of people."

Jennifer nodded and immediately started from the back of her stack of papers, as was her habit. "There's a small list of sub-contractors on the last page."

Bishop quickly leafed to the last page.

"There's just one," he said, somewhat disappointed. "Walrob Construction."

"Walrob Construction," Monroe echoed a few seconds later reading from the laptop screen.

"That's fast," Bishop said. "What does it say?"

"It's another dead end, I'm afraid. It says here they went out of business a few years ago."

"Any names or addresses?" Bishop asked.

"Just a former business address. But I've already checked it out. There's a law firm occupying the building now. Still, there's one other option...." Monroe tapped away on the keyboard as Bishop came to peer over his shoulder.

"United States Census Bureau, business register," Bishop said, reading aloud. "Is that a public record?"

"You really want to know?" Monroe asked him.

Bishop waved his hand. "What do they have?"

"All right," Monroe said. "Walrob Construction was a small local construction firm with five to ten employees. They were located in the California vicinity of Santa Monica, Culver City and Venice Beach. Founded in '82, the company dissolved three years ago."

"Seems like a small company to be working on something as international as this," Jennifer said.

"The smaller the company, the better to hide a secret," Monroe replied.

"Are there any names?" Bishop asked.

"There's a founder and lifetime CEO. Now, where was it...?"

Bishop looked at the screen trying to keep up with Monroe, but the constant flicking between open tabs made him nauseous. "How can you do this?"

"Easy. Okay, here it is. Robert J. Walton, born September 7, 1962, retired."

"Any last known address?"

"Yup. Grand Canal, Venice Beach, California."

"Nice," Bishop said admiringly.

"You know the area?" Monroe asked.

"I know of it. I believe that's one of the most used landmarks in American film and TV history. I also know that in the early 1900s some guy won the land with the toss of a coin and actually wanted to copy Venice, Italy there."

"Yet another detail that will have most people wondering how on Earth you know such trivia."

"So, we have another lead," Jennifer said, clenching her fists in excitement.

"Another clue, 3,000 miles away," Bishop sighed. "Let's see if we can find a phone number."

"Yes, sir." Monroe saluted and got to work on the laptop.

"Before traveling another 3,000 miles might I also suggest we take a thorough look at your father's study," Bishop said, rubbing his face.

"I've found two old numbers," Monroe interrupted. "Neither of which are working anymore."

Bishop sighed and looked at his watch. "What do you think?" he asked Jennifer who was checking out the time on her phone.

"It'll be one o' clock before we get there so I suggest we grab a sandwich in the cafeteria and then head to my parents' home."

"Sounds like a plan," Monroe agreed. "I could use some carbs."

Bishop nodded in agreement.

The Century Plaza Twin Towers, west of Los Angeles, were built in 1975. They were designed by Minoru Yamasaki, who also created New York's Twin Towers a few years later. From a distance, and at first glance, the 570-foot skyscrapers were identical to the ones that once stood in New York, only smaller. On the 44th floor of the building, from the penthouse office, Alice Hartman ran her fingers through her red hair while her boss gazed over the city. The office wasn't particularly grand for a CEO of his stature. There was no mahogany desk and the only color in the white room came from a portrait of Donald Trump that hung on one of the walls. At the back of the room stood a small, white desk, which was largely redundant because he preferred to work on one of the two white leather couches in the center of the room.

"I can't wait to get back to the office in the marina," he said in his gravelly voice. "Look at all the ants crawling through the streets, conducting their pointless daily business."

"Pointless?" Alice asked. "Without them and their pointless lives you wouldn't be able to look down on them from the 44th floor."

"That's something Matthews might've said to me."

"Matthews?"

"My previous assistant and confidante."

"Where is he now?"

"He's dead. He died three years ago of pneumonia. He wasn't a healthy man. I think—"

On the white desk, a phone rang and the man turned from the window to answer it.

"Yes, Sylvia?"

"I have Mr. Simpson for you."

Walking to the couch, he sat down and gestured to Alice, inviting her to sit opposite him.

"Mr. Simpson. How good of you to call back," he said as he placed the phone on the table between them with the speakerphone on. Unfortunately, the connection was so bad, neither of them could make out what Simpson was saying.

"I can't understand you. Can you say that again?"

"Sorry," Simpson apologized, sounding a little clearer. "I'm on the train in the Channel Tunnel, somewhere between the UK and France, on my way to my cabin in France."

"I heard about your little misfortune in London."

"Yes, that was too bad," Simpson said. "But I assure you there was nothing to be found that could tie us together."

"I'm sure there wasn't. But that's not why I called you. I wanted to know if you were still in possession of the original document?"

"The one you gave me ten years ago for safekeeping?"

"Did I send you any other original documents?" the man asked, sounding slightly agitated.

"I'm sorry, sir," Simpson apologized again. "Yes, sir. I have it. I mean, I don't have it on me, but I can get it."

"Here's what I want you to do. I want you to collect the document and bring it to me here, personally."

"In the U.S.?"

Alice looked at the man opposite and watched him close his eyes as he tried to stay calm.

"Yes, in the United States. I guess you know where that is? I'll have my secretary text you the specifics, but I want you to take the first flight possible."

For a short moment, the line was silent except for a hissing noise in the background. Eventually, Simpson replied. "I can be there the day after tomorrow."

"I'll see you when you get here." And with a simple click, the line disconnected.

"Why do you need the original document?" Alice asked. "Why not have it destroyed? You've got copies."

"First, how can I be sure that he will indeed destroy it? Second, with all that's happened, you know I've never even met the man?"

Alice tilted her head, confused as to why anyone would entrust such a big mission to a person they had never met. "Then how?"

"Let's say he came highly recommended by a friend. A long time ago I figured he might come in handy one day, so I gave him what he wanted in order to get what I wanted. With everything that has happened lately, it seems I was right. Anyway, it's about time we met face to face so I might determine what kind of risk he poses, and I need the original document intact and stored away safely, after which I can destroy all copies. I might need it at some point. Now, I have to prepare for the board meeting. Can you please prepare for Mr. Simpsons visit?"

As her boss rose from the couch, Alice followed his lead and walked with him to the door. "Will do, sir."

An hour after setting out on their journey, Bishop, Monroe and Jennifer drove up Livingston Street finding it empty save for a single parked car.

"Which number is it?" Monroe asked from behind the wheel.

"Over there." Jennifer pointed to a half-timbered house painted white, a hundred yards or so up the street.

"Nice neighborhood," Bishop remarked. "And, wow, what a great place. You grew up here?"

"I did. Apparently, I spent the first two years of my life in a small downtown apartment, but I have no recollection of that."

As they got out of the car and approached the house, Monroe stopped for a second to listen to the birdsong coming from the park opposite.

"Must have been great growing up here, with a park outside the front door. All that tranquility."

"I guess it was," Jennifer said as she opened the front door. "Of course, as a child you don't notice these things. You're just there, and I had nothing much to compare it with. Please, come in and follow me."

As Jennifer entered the house, she closed the door behind her and walked toward the stairs. On reaching the top, Jennifer stopped at the first door. For a second, she hesitated as she reached for the doorknob and Bishop put a hand on her shoulder.

"I understand. It's okay. We're here."

"Thanks," Jennifer said and, taking a deep breath, she swung the door open.

Before entering the room, she breathed in. Sunlight crept thought the slats of the shuttered window, lighting the dust particles that looked like small floating stars. "Nothing has changed," she said. "I can still see my father sitting at his desk, peering into his magnifying glass, inspecting the same stacks of papers that are still there."

As Jennifer spoke, the men hung back to allow her time to gather her thoughts and memories. After a minute or so, Monroe went to look at a glass bell holding a shrunken head. "From the Kalinga headhunters in the Northern Philippines, I believe. This place is like a museum."

"Okay, what are we looking for?" Jennifer suddenly asked.

"Well," Bishop replied, "the final document would be nice or a clue as to how your father found his way to St. Mary's in London. We can't actually be sure he found anything in the font. Where is his safe?"

Jennifer stepped behind the desk and pointed to the floor. "Over here."

Bishop bent down to find the safe open and empty. "Well, if there was ever anything there it's gone now."

"We opened the safe after my father died," Jennifer said. "There was a bag of old coins, his passport and some insurance papers."

"And in there?" Bishop pointed to a filing cabinet next to a wooden statue of what looked like a cigar-store Indian.

Jennifer shrugged. "Don't know. His research, I guess."

"May we?" Bishop asked.

"That's why we're here," Jennifer answered gesturing for him to go ahead.

"You take the cabinet. I'll take the desk," Monroe told Bishop.

"And what should I do?" Jennifer asked.

"You take the rest of the room," Bishop replied.

Jennifer looked around, wondering where to start.

Monroe started working through the hundreds of documents on the desk. Most were copies of old texts from all over the world, including the Japanese Genealogy of the Amabe Clan, the oldest family tree in existence. There were also copies of the Dead Sea Scrolls and the

Novgorod Codex, the waxed wooden tablets made by the Rus in the eleventh century.

"This place might be a museum, but it's giving up nothing we're looking for," Monroe said.

"Same here," Bishop replied as he continued to carefully open and inspect every folder in the filing cabinet. "There's a lot of original stuff in here that various researchers or museums would die to get their hands on."

"My mom spoke about donating all this stuff to a museum or university," Jennifer admitted. "Have you found nothing at all?"

"Actually, I think I might've found something." Monroe held up a charcoal sketch drawn on a single sheet of old paper. Bishop and Jennifer joined him at the table.

"'*Sanctum lavacrum loco nativitatis,*'" Monroe said, reading the latin text at the top of the paper.

"The holy place of birth and rebirth," Bishop translated.

"That's our church," Jennifer said. "St. Mary's. Look at the bell tower."

"I thought so too," Monroe said.

"May I?" Jennifer asked, and without waiting for an answer she took the document from his hands and held it below the large magnifying glass. "You see that? There, on the bottom righthand corner?"

Both men peered through the glass.

"The Monas," Bishop said before pointing out a sketch of a tombstone. "And there's something underlined in pencil here."

Monroe squinted into the magnifying glass. "I think it says 'JD.' This must have been the document that persuaded your father to visit the church."

"It must have been the document he was working on before his last trip," Jennifer said.

"Are you okay?" Bishop asked and Jennifer nodded. "All right. We need to keep looking for something relating to what he found over there. Did your father have a computer or a laptop?"

"He did, but I believe my mother had it cleaned before giving it to a nephew who was going to college. I guess she couldn't stand the thing because my dad was always glued to it."

"That's a shame," Bishop said. "Then I guess we have to keep searching."

In relative silence, the three of them continued to pick through Robert Porter's possessions. Eventually, it was Jennifer who stumbled upon her father's camera case.

"What's that?" Monroe asked.

"Dad's camera," Jennifer answered. "He was really proud of it. He was always bragging about the picture quality."

"A Leica M9," Bishop said appreciatively as he watched Jennifer take the camera out of its case. "Eighteen megapixel, I believe. Expensive. Is there any power in it?"

Jennifer turned a knob on the top of the camera and the backscreen lit up. A red lightning bolt immediately started flashing and Jennifer quickly grabbed the charger from the bag and plugged it in.

"We're good now," she said, and began to look through the last pictures taken on the camera while Bishop and Monroe peered over her shoulder. The last pictures were of birds and squirrels in a park. "My father took pictures of just about anything, but he especially loved capturing wildlife in the park."

As Jennifer scrolled further down, more animal photos were found. Getting bored, Bishop checked out the camera case and found a small box of memory cards.

"This could take a while," Monroe said, keeping his eyes on the small screen. "Wait a minute, stop! Okay, go back. What's that? Can you enlarge it?"

"Sure," Jennifer said, pressing a button to show the picture on full screen.

"Is that...?" Monroe asked. The image was fuzzy, but it was clearly some kind of document. "Can you make it even bigger?"

Jennifer enlarged the document further, but it made the text unreadable.

"Look!" Bishop said. "You can just about make out the outline of a prescription table, and I'm assuming the gray blobs are the plants we need."

"This has to be part of the secret recipe," Monroe said.

"I see it too," Jennifer told them.

"Yes, it must be the final document." Bishop smiled. "Your father found it."

Bishop reached for the camera, but Jennifer immediately turned away to stop him. "Matthew!"

"Sorry, you're right. What's the date on the picture?"

"August 24, 2009."

"That's around the time the survey was done at the church. That must be it." Monroe clapped his hands softly.

"Check if there's a better picture," Bishop demanded.

Jennifer sat against the wall and started going through the images, one by one. After a good three minutes, with Bishop and Monroe patiently waiting, Jennifer handed the camera to Bishop. "Nothing. Just some pictures of London and the exterior of St. Mary's. That's it. Just one blurry picture."

Bishop put the camera back on the table. "That's too bad. We're back to square one."

"Not entirely," Monroe told them, taking hold of the camera. "We now know Robert Porter did at one time...."

He stopped suddenly as he clicked through the pictures of the church and the blurred document.

"What is it?" Jennifer asked.

"Look." He held the camera up and jumped through the pictures. "Picture of a bird, picture of St. Mary's outside, picture of the document, another one outside and a park somewhere. Notice anything strange?"

"The numbers," Jennifer said. "There's a gap in the numbers."

"A gap of two numbers, to be precise," Monroe said. "Two pictures have been deleted from the camera."

"Aren't they in the trashcan?" Jennifer asked.

"The Leica M9 has no trashcan."

"But that doesn't mean much. Usually, cameras don't delete a picture they just mark the deleted picture space as writable. As long as you don't overwrite it, the deleted picture should be retrievable."

Willing to give it a go, Monroe pushed a few buttons and twiddled a few knobs. "I'm sorry. I'm afraid the images are gone. The memory card is completely full so the pictures have been overwritten.

"So, we've got nothing?" Jennifer asked.

"Well, we know your father at one time had the document." Monroe said.

"And we found Robert Walton in California," Bishop added.

"Thank God it's only 3,000 miles and three time zones this time." Monroe sighed. "I think I can handle that one more time."

Bishop smiled while Jennifer's eyes sparkled.

CHAPTER 37

The Foundation

The early morning sunlight painted the canals of Venice Beach gold. Separating narrow strips of land, they shone in front of houses that were so diverse in architecture, Jennifer was mesmerized.

"I love these wooden bridges," she said as they walked over a canal as a man in a canoe passed below them. "I could live here. The weather is good and you get a small boat in front of your house to take you to your car, or you can even jump in a canoe for a day out."

"Island property is about double the price of mainland property. You won't find anything here under two million dollars," Bishop said.

"I'll start saving." Jennifer giggled.

"Here it is." Monroe pointed at a mailbox marked 'R.J. Walton.' It was positioned at the foot of a pathway flanked by large green conifers leading to a relatively small garden designed with palm trees in front of a large, white Victorian-style mansion with a thatched roof.

"Not too shabby," Monroe commented before gesturing to Jennifer. "After you."

Being the first to reach the arched, oak front door, Jennifer rang the doorbell. "I hope someone's home."

"I hope they're awake," Monroe said as he looked at his watch. "It's not even nine."

"If he's here he's awake," Bishop said. "He's retired so he'll need little sleep."

"I think you're right," Jennifer said as the hallway lights switched on. Through the side windows, they saw the shape of someone coming to the door. A small hatch opened revealing a pair of eyes.

"Can I help you?"

"Mr. Walton?" Bishop asked.

"Who wants to know?"

"We're from Yale University following up a 2009 survey of old English churches. The results of that survey have brought new discoveries, and questions, and we're trying to contact anyone involved in the original survey."

In reply, the hatch closed. The sound of deadbolts unlocking soon followed and the door opened to reveal a tall, broad-shouldered man in his fifties, still dressed in a bathrobe.

"Morning," he said in greeting, before running a hand through his long gray hair. "What can I do for you?"

"Thank you for seeing us," Bishop replied. "We tried to call in advance, but couldn't find a registered number."

The man grunted.

"Anyway, like I said, we're following up on a survey conducted at an English church in 2009 that we believe you were part of."

"Maybe," the man said cautiously. "I've been a contractor all my life and did many odd jobs over the years."

"Okay," Monroe said, taking over from Bishop. "In 2009, the American Foundation on Restoring Religious Structures in old Britannia conducted a survey of a church in the UK—Mortlake, London, to be specific. We have papers that say your company was one of the sub-contractors on that survey."

The man glanced at the trees behind them before nodding slowly. "It's almost ten years ago, but I remember the job. We were there for a week, helping out a team taking measurements of a small church. What's it to you?"

"Well, to be honest, we're not sure," Monroe continued. "But we believe that the survey did more than just take measurements."

"Please, come in," Walton said, stepping aside to allow them access before pointing them in the direction of the living room. "Please take a seat."

Jennifer looked around, amazed that such a beautiful house externally could be so hideous inside thanks to an over indulgence of baroque furniture, plush fabrics, high gloss golden lamps, chandeliers, richly-colored rugs and other ornate ornaments. In truth, there was little room to move between all the kitsch furniture.

"I remember the job well," Walton said as they all chose a seat from the mishmash of colorful chairs. "I'd never been abroad and always wondered why a relatively small, American company was asked to take on such a job. But they paid well, so... Wait a minute, please." Walton rose from his chair and walked out of the room. "I'll be right back. Please have a cookie."

"You know what?" Monroe looked at the chocolate chip cookies on the table.

"Sure, why not?" Jennifer said as she followed him.

Bishop shook his head and frowned just as Walton returned.

"They're very good," he said. "Fresh. My wife bakes them. Here, I have it."

Sitting back down, Walton opened a file folder and pulled out a sheet of paper. He then read aloud from it.

"Order number 7.1060.8, the American Foundation on blah, blah, blah.... 2009, Mortlake, London. They paid in advance, and quite handsomely."

"Do you mind?" Bishop reached across the table.

Walton thought for a short moment before handing him the paper. "Why not? It's all ancient history now."

Bishop took the paper and started reading, softly mumbling to himself.

"What else can you tell us about the job?" Monroe asked.

Walton took a deep breath. "Well, it was a strange job. I remember I was with a five-man team. Basically, we moved things around the building for the survey team. Some laser equipment, scaffolding, big lights, tools and so on. They even brought something that looked like an X-ray machine."

"Can you tell us anything else about the survey team, what they actually did?" Monroe continued.

"Not much. Whenever we set up at a new location in the church we were excused until things needed to be moved again. We never really built or excavated anything. They might as well have hired a removal firm."

"Sorry," Bishop interrupted, holding the order form up. "It says here that the payment wasn't made by the foundation."

"It wasn't?" Walton asked, gesturing to Bishop to pass the paper back. Once in his hands, he raised his eyebrows in surprise before laughing. "I guess it wasn't. I don't recall it, but as long as the money came in I guess it didn't matter."

"It says the payment was made by a company called Culver BioPharma. Does that name mean anything to you?"

"Never heard of it," Walton said as Monroe reached for his phone.

"Culver BioPharma," Monroe quickly read from his phone. "Advancing affordable healthcare. They have several offices in the U.S. and their head office is right here in Los Angeles in Culver City."

"Still doesn't ring a bell," Walton replied. "But it's not uncommon for a foundation to have their bills paid directly by financiers or sponsors. That way they know for sure nothing sticks with the foundation, so to say."

"Do you mind if I make a copy?" Monroe asked.

"Be my guest," Walton replied.

"Is there anything else you can you tell us about the job?" Bishop asked. "Anything out of the ordinary that happened in those days or any specific orders? Did you hear or see anything strange?"

"I guess everything about that job was strange. They closed down the church completely. No one was allowed in or out. Everything seemed very hush-hush and every time we created a new setup, the place we created had to be covered with floor to ceiling plastic curtains—like they were working in a sterile environment. For the rest of the time we did nothing, just waited."

"They never told you about any specifics of the job?"

"All they said was that they were doing an architectural survey, and I didn't ask for more. It was good money for an easy job." Walton fell silent for a moment. "Wait a minute, come to think of it, you asked me if there was anything out of the ordinary?"

Monroe nodded.

"Well, I don't know if this counts, but one night we had a somewhat strange break-in."

Bishop and Jennifer shifted to the edge of their seats.

"Do go on," Bishop encouraged.

"Well, in itself a break-in isn't that special on a construction site. We saw it all the time. People, mostly drug addicts and gang members, trying to steal your equipment. But this was different. During the daytime a man, an American, came to the church wanting to visit. I met him at the gate myself. He said he was a tourist from the U.S., visiting churches in Europe or something, I don't remember exactly. But anyway, he had little time, he said, so he was pushing me to ask my supervisor to let him in. I didn't. Our instructions were clear, so I sent him on his way."

"What happened then?" Jennifer asked, shifting even further forward in her chair.

"That night I got a call at my hotel telling me to come as quickly as I could and open the church. When I got there, I was met in the street by two security teams. I opened the door and one team stood guard while the other went into the dark church. They were gone a fair amount of time yet the church remained dark and I got curious. I sneaked in. Just as I entered the main hall, the floodlights switched on and the security guards surprised a burglar. I recognized the man from earlier that day. He'd come back and somehow found his way into the church."

"What did they do to him?" Bishop asked.

Walton shrugged and frowned. "Nothing, as I recall. They talked some and then removed him from the premises." Walton paused for a moment. "I believe he did try to take something with him, but the guards made him give it back. Then he went. That was it."

"You didn't get a name?" Bishop asked.

Walton shook his head. "Not that I recall. As far as I know, there was never an official complaint made to the police. Now, if you don't mind. I have to tee off at eleven so I need to get ready."

"Of course," Bishop said and they all rose from their chairs and walked to the hallway where Walton opened the door and shook their hands.

"Don't know if I've been of any help, but I wish you good luck in your search."

"You've been a big help," Bishop replied. "Thank you."

"Wait a minute, please." Jennifer turned to face Walton and searched her pockets for her cellphone, asking him to humor her as she scrolled through a number of images until she found the one she wanted. After enlarging it on screen she showed it to Walton. "Do you recognize this man?"

Walton took the reading glasses hanging from a lace around his neck and looked at the screen, squinting. "That's him," he said. "That's the man I spoke to on the day of the burglary and whom I saw that night in the church. Who is he?"

Jennifer waited for a second before answering with a smile. "A very good friend."

Outside, the three of them sat down on a bench by the canal.

"What do you think?" Jennifer asked Bishop.

"I think it's peaceful," Bishop answered. "The water, the small boats. No one seems to be in a hurry." He pointed at a man in three-piece suit walking a Yorkshire terrier.

"I mean about the foundation. About my father breaking in and the pharma corp... what was it called?"

"Culver BioPharma," Monroe answered.

"Thank you. That one."

"I'm not sure what to think," Bishop told her.

"I might have one thing to add," Monroe said. "There was one thing I noticed when I looked up the company." Monroe took out his phone and showed it to Bishop and Jennifer. "Look at the logo."

"The Bowl of Hygeia," Bishop said. "The symbol of the pharmacy. What about it?"

"I know, right?" Monroe said. "Hygeia, the Greek goddess of health and hygiene, but...."

"But what?" Jennifer asked.

"Of all people present I thought that you would be the one to see it," Monroe said to her.

"The two snakes, or serpents, are from that other medical symbol, the caduceus, the one that doctors often use with two snakes around a staff. The Bowl of Hygeia, on the other hand, has only one snake winding around a bowl."

"You're right," Bishop said. "But that could—"

"I know what you're getting at," Jennifer interrupted. "I remember now. The ceremonial chalice at the Isis-Urania. The one you told me were probably real snakes. A shiver still runs up my spine when I even think of touching it."

Monroe gave a bright smile. "That one, yes."

"Good catch," Bishop said. "Symbols, not my thing. I never would have noticed. Of course, it could all be one big coincidence."

"Sure," Monroe said, "a big one, but sure."

"So, what do we do now?" Jennifer asked.

"Well, we have our tie to Culver BioPharma," Bishop said. "So, I think we should find out everything there is to know about them. But maybe we could find a place to have lunch first. I know I could use a bite to eat."

"You should have taken the cookie," Jennifer teased.

CHAPTER 38

Not Just a Club

2009

"This can't go on any longer," Sylvia Porter said, standing over her husband as he lay in bed. "You haven't gotten up for three days, you won't allow me to open the curtains and you barely eat. I called the doctor. He'll be here any moment."

It had been three weeks since Robert Porter collapsed during a guest lecture on Ancient Mesopotamian Mysticism at Columbia University. An ambulance was called and paramedics raced him to Mercy Hospital where he was diagnosed with dehydration. After a few hours on a saline drip he was declared healthy again and dismissed. He took a taxi back to his car, still parked on the grounds of the university. But ever since that moment he had been dogged by ill health.

At the sound of the doorbell, Sylvia ran downstairs, returning a minute or two later with the family physician, Dr. Pembroke. At the bedroom door she tried to prepare him for what he was about to see.

"For two weeks?" Pembroke gasped. "You should have called sooner."

"We thought he was getting better after your last visit, but a few days later he took a turn for the worse. Since then he's been up and down, some days feeling okay, other times wretched and unable to leave the house. But now he hasn't left the bedroom for three days. This isn't my husband. Of course, you know how Robert is. If I didn't force his hand you still wouldn't be here." Sylvia knocked on the bedroom door. "Honey, Doctor Pembroke is here."

As the door opened, Porter squinted at the sudden light and raised his hands to his face. "Oh honey, you shouldn't have," he moaned before lowering his hands to reveal his pale face and the dark bags under his eyes.

"Hi, Robert," Pembroke said in greeting as he sat down next to the bed. "How are you doing?"

"A bit under the weather, but I think the worst is behind me." Robert grunted as he tried to sit up straight.

"Can you give us a minute?" Pembroke asked, turning to Sylvia.

"Sure," she said. "I'll be downstairs in the kitchen."

As she left the room, she heard Robert breathing heavily and the sound of his labored breaths scared her. She had never seen her husband so frail. Come to think of it, he was hardly ever sick. Even a common cold was rare. Sylvia headed for the kitchen, feeling the need for a cup of tea to soothe her nerves, but her head was swimming with worst case scenarios. What if he had lung cancer? It runs in the family. Or what if Robert had contracted some kind of incurable disease on one of his travels? She shook her head trying to rid it of such thoughts. She then stared into her cup of hot tea until her glasses steamed up and the kitchen door swung open to reveal Jennifer.

"How's he doing?" she asked, breathless from the bike ride home from school.

The sound of Chopin's Ballade in G Minor echoed through the crowded, marble lobby of South Century Plaza Towers. Above the access port to the elevators hung a huge banner that said 'Welcome Home, Boss.'

In front of the glass façade, a Lincoln Town Car stopped and a chauffeur jumped out of the driving seat to hurriedly open the passenger door. A man stepped out of the car. Before he had even reached the door of the building, the crowd inside started clapping their hands. As he entered the premises the clapping grew louder and he found himself surrounded by his employees who quickly parted to make way for him, patting him on the back as he walked by. At the elevator he was met by Dave Matthews.

"The minions crawled out of their offices to welcome the returning freakshow."

"Let me see?" Matthews asked, and his boss reluctantly turned the right side of his face toward him, two-thirds of which was covered by heavy scar tissue.

"It's not too bad," Matthews assured him. "You're very lucky that it didn't damage your eye."

"Oh yes, I'm very lucky."

"Look, they told us you were trying to escape the wildfire in your boat when a burning tree fell on the deck, trapping you. As you were also in a coma for nearly three weeks, I'd say you're pretty lucky—things could have ended a lot worse."

Unwilling to continue the conversation, the man stepped into the elevator and changed the subject. "How are the tests coming along?"

Matthews sighed. "The tests are going okay, sir. But the results are disappointing so far."

"What do you mean?"

"Well, we started on simple organisms, but didn't see any significant change so we moved on to trials on rats. So far, the rats also show no progress or change. We think there might've been a problem with the dosages. We assumed the stated dosage was for humans and so we recalculated it based on body weight, but like I said it brought no results. We're now experimenting with different dosages."

"And Porter?"

"Porter? Well, we still have a tail on him, but for the past few weeks he hasn't left the house. We identified one visitor as a local GP so we think he might be sick."

"Anything else?"

"Maybe." Matthews wavered slightly. "On further examination of the document, experts found clues alluding to this document being only a part of the whole."

"Meaning?"

The elevator stopped and they walked in silence along the corridor until they came to a bright white-painted office. Closing the glass door behind them, Matthews continued. "Meaning, there is probably more to the recipe and we are missing it. Or at least missing one more part."

For a long moment there was silence.

"Do your job and do whatever you need to do to speed things up with the tests," the man said in his deep gravelly voice. "Now, please leave."

Matthews nodded and walked back out of the door. Once he was gone, the man took his cellphone from a pocket and began to dial.

"Simpson," said a man on the other end of the line.

"Donald, it's me. How are you doing? Listen, remember your proposition to help you with that, uh, club of yours, the one you wanted me to help fund?"

"The Hermetic Order of the Golden Dawn, sir. Not just a club, also a useful network to get things done, like retrieving sensitive competition data."

"So you told me. Can you please send me the specs again? I might be interested after all. Also, I'll send you a small package for safe keeping. Stow it away safely, but be prepared to give it back someday. I have to go now to get ready for a meeting. I'll await your details."

As he ended the call, his secretary entered the room.

"It's good to have you back, sir."

"Thank you, Susan. Did you get my tux from the dry cleaners for the initiation tonight?"

"I did, sir. It's hanging in the changeroom. Anything else I can do for you?"

"No, thank you. Just alert me when it's time to leave."

"Will do, sir."

"I don't know," Sylvia told Jennifer as she poured herself a cup of tea. "The doctor is with him right now."

Jennifer sat down next to her mother and put an arm around her. "I'm sure he's going to be okay, Mom."

"He's never been sick for even a day for as long as I can remember," Sylvia sobbed.

"I know," Jennifer whispered.

Above them they heard the bedroom door open and close again, followed by footsteps on the stairs.

"How is he?" Sylvia asked as the doctor entered the kitchen.

"To be completely honest, I'm not sure. He's roasting hot, but has no fever. He has joint pain that could suggest fibromyalgia, but that's not consistent with the rashes." He handed Sylvia a prescription. "Something for the rashes. That's all I can do. He doesn't seem to be in any real pain. You need to see a specialist. I'll refer you to a friend of mine, an internist at Yale New Haven Hospital. I suggest you see him as soon as possible." Pembroke handed her a card. "Please tell him I referred you."

"Thank you, doctor." Sylvia replied, getting up from her seat to take the card and open the back door for him. As she bid the doctor goodbye she turned around to speak to her daughter only to find her gone.

"How are you, Daddy?" Jennifer asked as she came to sit at his bedside.

Porter gave a small smile. "I'll be okay. Really. You don't think some silly bug or virus is going to keep your father under the weather for long, do you?"

"I'm afraid, Dad."

"Afraid of what?" Porter asked before turning away to cough. "Many people get sick every now and then. There's nothing to worry about."

Jennifer held her father's hand tightly between her own. "You promised me that once I finished school you would take me on one of your trips. You better not break that promise."

Porter chuckled. "I promise."

CHAPTER 39

Drugs

The Present

The terrace of Craft, the restaurant owned by celebrity chef Tom Colicchio, overlooked the gardens of the Century Plaza Twin Towers. A popular haunt in L.A. for those wishing to be seen in the right places, the restaurant was packed with the rich and powerful of Century City enjoying one hundred-dollar business lunches.

"I'm amazed you were able to get us a table," Monroe said as he looked around at all the 'suits' in the room before glancing at his dark jeans and sweater. "I feel a bit out of place."

"A big tip will get you far," Bishop replied before pointing to two towers glowing silver in the noon sun. "Did you know the Century Plaza's Twin Towers were created by Minoru Yamasaki, the same architect who designed the original twin towers in New York?"

"I see the similarities," Jennifer replied, staring at the towers across the gardens.

"And how are you holding up?" Bishop asked her.

"I'm okay, I guess. I've been thinking about my father a lot. When he was sick, the first time, he promised he'd take me on one of his trips when I finished school." Jennifer paused to laugh hollowly. "Of course, it never happened, but now, here I am, following in his footsteps and feeling like he's a little bit with me after all. When I think about what Walton said about my father being a burglar, I have to smile. In fact, when I think about everything we've done these past weeks I feel close to him again, in a way I never thought possible. But anyway, enough about me. What do we do next?"

Monroe glanced around the room and picked up his laptop. "This way we look like locals," he joked. "Right, let's see what we can find out about Culver BioPharma."

After browsing a few Internet sites, Monroe nodded to himself before reading aloud. "Apparently, they're advancing affordable healthcare, proteins, vaccines and lab services. According to this, Culver BioPharma is one of the leading companies in researching, developing and producing biopharmaceutical drugs. Biopharmaceutical, meaning they develop drugs from biological sources, unlike the usual synthesized pharmaceuticals on the market. Apparently, they specialize in drugs created from living systems such as blood, organs, antibodies and human reproductive cells."

"No plants or herbs?" Bishop asked.

"Not that I can see."

"Anything about immortality?" Jennifer asked, and the others looked at her in confusion. "What? Why couldn't they be working on your 'Elixir of Life?'"

"All right. Okay," Monroe said. "I can see nothing about the Elixir of Life or the Philosopher's Stone. However, it does say here that they produce over a quarter of all NSAIDs produced in the U.S."

"NSAIDs?" Jennifer asked.

"Non-steroidal anti-inflammatory drugs," Bishop explained, "like Ibuprofen. I read an article about it a while ago. Over seventy million prescriptions a year are written in the U.S. alone. Including over-the-counter sales, more than thirty billion doses are consumed in the country. It has been said that Americans are in more pain than any other population in the world. Did you know eighty percent of the global opioids produced worldwide are consumed in the United States?"

Monroe shrugged. "Eighty percent of thirty billion makes—"

"A whole lot of pills and dollars," Jennifer interrupted.

"Many billions," Bishop added. "But I thought they specialized in biopharmaceutical drugs. NSAIDs are synthetic."

"It says here they use the revenue from their traditional factories to pay for research on biopharmaceutical drugs," Monroe replied.

"Of course they do," Bishop said.

Jennifer looked up at Bishop. "I assume you don't care much for the industry?"

"Did you know that for every member of Congress there are currently more than two pharmaceutical lobbyists? The overuse and prescriptions of painkillers and antibiotics is slowly outgrowing the problem of illegal drugs in this country, resulting in sterility and the inability to develop our bodies' natural defense systems."

"How do you know so much about the subject?" Jennifer asked.

Bishop gave a wry smile. "As a child my loving, but overprotective, parents medicated me whenever I got the slightest cold or tiniest scratch. That resulted in a stack of allergies at a later age and, according to my doctor, low body resistance as an adult. A common cold or a small bacterial infection can send me to bed for weeks if I don't watch out."

"That explains the hand sanitizer," Monroe noted.

Bishop smiled. "What else have you found?"

"Just a moment." Monroe tapped away on his keyboard. "I've compared the board members of the Foundation on Religious Structures with the current board of directors of Culver and guess what?"

"You found a match?"

Monroe smiled broadly. "There were three board members of the original foundation. One of them is dead, another lives in an Alzheimer's clinic and the third...." Monroe paused for a short moment. "The third is a match. A big match. Thomas J. Nichols, fifty-eight, board member of the Foundation on Religious Structures and current CEO of—you guessed it—Culver BioPharma."

"But why?" Jennifer asked.

"What do you mean?" Bishop replied.

"Well, if there's any truth to Dee's claim of immortality, how would a big pharma company benefit from it?"

"I told you I wasn't convinced about this whole mortality thing. All the clues from the translated texts could just as easily point to pain relief." Bishop turned to Monroe. "You said it yourself, Culver BioPharma makes billions from painkillers. If another company got their hands on a biologically perfect working painkiller, they would stand to lose those billions. However, if they have it they can patent it and practically dominate the world of painkillers."

"That's it?" Jennifer asked. "All this just to get their hands on a great painkiller, to even kill for it?"

Monroe rubbed his face. "I guess people have gone to war and killed millions for less."

Jennifer sighed and shook her head.

"Are you ready to order?" A young woman dressed in a pink apron stood at their table holding a small handheld computer.

Bishop took hold of the menu. "Can you give us a few minutes?"

"No problem," the young woman said and walked away.

"We should order," Bishop said and everyone reached for their menus.

"You said you didn't really believe in immortality," Jennifer said to Bishop. "But you do believe in a pain-free existence?"

"Physical pain? I guess I do. Emotional pain is something completely different, but being free of physical pain isn't unheard of. In India, in the city of Jammu, there supposedly lives a man, Rattan Singh, who works in a small dental clinic. Apparently, he has a concoction that allows him to remove a tooth completely painlessly without anesthesia. The medicine is a family recipe that has been passed down over the centuries as part of some ancient medical heritage."

Monroe shook his head. "It sounds a lot like the physicians in the Philippines who claim to remove tumors by hand while splashing fake blood around and coming up with a chicken liver, or something like that."

"Well, here's something more fact-based," Bishop replied. "Congenital Analgesia, a rare condition whereby a person can't feel any pain. It's caused by a genetic disorder that increases the production of endorphins to the brain."

"I can see the appeal in that," Jennifer said.

"I bet you do, but it's worth remembering that infants born with this disorder tend not to grow very old. Most of them die young due to injuries or illnesses going unnoticed. They bite their own tongue, they don't recognize broken bones, they don't even flinch if they're on fire."

"I see your point," Jennifer conceded. "So, what do we do now?"

"You need to talk to Nichols," Monroe said. "Try to find out what he knows."

"'You?'" Bishop asked. "What do you mean?"

"Well, I'm guessing he isn't an easy man to get an appointment with, but I see on Culver's website that tomorrow he'll make a public shareholder appearance commenting on the results of the past six months. Thanks to the Internet I can probably get you in if I buy some shares and sort out an online invitation."

"There's that 'you' again," Bishop said.

"The shareholder meeting is tomorrow, but I need to return to work this evening. So, you're on your own on this one."

"Are you sure you can't stay a few days longer?" Jennifer asked.

"I'm sorry, but tomorrow I have an appointment with some very big benefactors at the library. If I don't show up, well, let's just say the library and me could be in big trouble." He smiled. "You'll do fine on your own and if you're still here in a few days I can come back for the weekend. In the meantime, you can always call if you need me."

Jennifer stood up and hugged him from behind his chair. "I'm going to miss you."

"We'll meet again in a few days. Just let me know what you find out. I'm curious as hell."

"Have you decided yet?" asked the waitress, returning to their table.

CHAPTER 40

Weaving Spiders

On the top floor of Century Plaza Tower One, Culver BioPharma's boardroom quickly filled with shareholders arriving from all over the country. For the occasion the removable walls of the top floor had been dismantled, creating a huge open space with glass on all sides giving a stunning view over Los Angeles. On one side of the room stood a small podium.

On the ground floor, a red-haired woman with a British accent greeted everyone carrying an invitation card before directing them to one of the elevators that were specifically programmed to take guests straight to the top floor.

One floor below the gathering crowds, Thomas Nichols sat on a white leather couch rehearsing his speech when the intercom beeped.

"Mr. Simpson has arrived," his secretary informed him.

Slightly irritated at the timing, Nichols smacked the folder he held down on the table in front of him and pushed the intercom. "Send him in."

"You're an hour late," Nichols bellowed as Simpson walked into the office.

Ignoring the remark, Simpson walked up to Nichols and stretched out his arm. "It's an honor to finally meet you, sir," he said while trying not to look too obviously at the man's half-burned face.

Nichols quickly shook his hand before pointing to the couch opposite. "What do I call you these days? Simpson or Kether?"

"Just Donald will do. I'm afraid the days of the Golden Dawn in London were abruptly ended, and sorry I'm late. I greatly underestimated the traffic in L.A., and I had to get through a lot of people and security in the lobby before being escorted to the elevator bringing me to you."

"There's a shareholders' meeting in half an hour so all except one of the elevators go to the top floor."

"And you don't want people wandering around the building. I understand."

"You brought it?" Nichols asked.

From his inner jacket pocket, Simpson produced a small aluminum tube and handed it to Nichols.

"Is this everything?"

"That's it. After all we've been through you'd expect something more grandiose perhaps, but this is it."

Nichols unscrewed the lid from the tube, took a quick look inside and then shook it upside down. A small roll of old, yellowed paper fell into the palm of his hand. He carefully unrolled the paper and, holding it with two hands, he took a deep breath. "Hard to believe such a small piece of paper could have such a big influence on the world."

"Well, technically it doesn't," Simpson said. "Without the other documents I guess it has about as much value as a recipe for a good tomato soup. Did you ever find the final missing document?"

Nichols sighed. "I didn't. But it doesn't matter. We're too exposed as it is and we're confident we're the only ones who have this piece to the puzzle." He rolled up the document and placed it back inside the tube. "For now, I need your word that there are no copies of this document anywhere."

"In all the time the document was in my possession there were never any copies made. The rest of the time the document was safely stowed away in a French bank vault so...."

Nichols gazed into Simpsons eyes for a long moment. "I believe you." He put the tube into his jacket pocket and got to his feet. "For now, it's enough to safely stow away the documents we have and, who knows, maybe someday... I thank you for your service, Mr. Simpson. I trust our previous association will stay between us and I hope to call on you again if I need you."

"You always can," Simpson promised, standing up to shake Nichols's hand.

"Okay. I know where to find you."

As Simpson left the room, Nichols sat down again. He took out his cellphone and made a call.

"Yes, it's me... Yes, I have it. He just left... Tonight... I'll bring it to the location and we can finally put this behind us next weekend... Great. I'll see you there at the ceremony."

"Sir?" came a familiar voice through the intercom. "The doors are closing."

"Thank you, Susan. I'll be right up."

In the lobby, the red-head was still directing shareholders toward the elevators.

"Thank you and have a good meeting," she told the men standing in front of Bishop and Jennifer before turning to greet the pair.

"Hello, my name is Alice Hartman. Welcome to our presentation. Can I see your invitation, please?"

Bishop handed her a piece of paper, noticing Jennifer freeze for a brief moment as she watched the woman.

"Thank you," Bishop said as the woman handed him the paper back and she pointed them to an elevator. Once inside, he asked, "What was that?"

"I know that woman."

Bishop frowned. "What? How?"

"I don't know. But I'm sure I've seen her before and heard that accent. And, somehow, I get the feeling that it's not in a good way." Jennifer shook her head. "It doesn't matter for now. It'll come back to me later. It always does. So, what's the plan?"

"Plan?" Bishop grinned. "We may need to make one up as we go. Monroe has got us close to Nichols so I figure we need to look for an opportunity to ask him some questions."

"Sounds like a plan to me," Jennifer said with a smile before the elevator opened on the 44th floor.

In the boardroom, all the chairs were filled and every inch of the glass wall was covered by those standing, three deep. At the elevator, a young woman handed them a folder, on the front of which was a large image of the two-snaked Bowl of Hygeia.

"Wow," Jennifer said. "I never expected shareholder meetings to be like this."

"I must admit that this is my first meeting too. I always imagined they would be attended by a small group of hobbyists with the majority of shareholders watching the news at home on TV or the Internet."

Bishop pointed to a spot in front of two rows of men and women, just as a small door opened and four VPs—all men—took their places behind a table placed on the podium. A fifth man quickly followed and sat on the center chair. As Alice Hartman took her place next to the podium, Jennifer kept wondering where she knew the woman from.

"Good afternoon," the man in the center started, his gravelly voice silencing the room as he adjusted the microphone in front of him. "My name is Thomas Nichols. I'm the CEO of Culver BioPharma and I welcome you to a presentation of our first six-month results of the year. I'm very proud of them, that much I can tell you."

Behind Nichols a projection screen lowered, lit up with the company logo.

"What happened to him? It looks as though his face was burned," Jennifer whispered to Bishop.

"When I looked him up on the Internet last night I read that he had been caught in a wildfire ten years ago."

"Must have hurt like hell."

For thirty minutes or so, Nichols and his VPs took turns presenting figures, charted by graphs, revealing the company's results. Jennifer fidgeted as the weight of her body started to tire her legs.

"Won't be long now," Bishop said, as Nichols began to wrap up the proceedings.

"So that's it for our promotional speech." Nichols's smile was met by laughter from the audience. "But, seriously, I think we can all agree that Culver BioPharma is a healthy company with good results and a clear view of the future where growth is not only a prediction but a fact. You can find all the details and figures in the folder given to you on arrival. We now have some time left for questions."

"I have a question!" Bishop raised his hand, startling Jennifer.

"The gentleman at the back," Nichols said, and a man rushed to Bishop and pointed a microphone in his face.

"Thank you," Bishop said, hearing his own voice come back to him through the speakers at the front. "I have a question about your research. There's a rumor circulating that Culver BioPharma is developing a new kind of pain relief based on ancient methods."

For a short moment, Nichols stayed silent. "And you are?"

"Oh, excuse me. My name is Matthew Bishop, professor at Yale University."

"Well, Professor Bishop, as you're probably aware, the process of killing pain involves stopping electric signals to the brain and reducing the production of prostaglandins by blocking Cox-1 and Cox-2 enzymes. This is a very complex and high-tech process and I'm not sure the answer lies in some ancient method or other such hocus pocus."

"Is that a no?" Bishop smiled, though he was slightly irritated by the smug grin on Nichols' face.

"That's a definite no. It took us hundreds of years to get to where we are today in the development of modern pain medication. I'm positive all the past contributions made to medicine are well known and they've been extensively tested and used where possible. Thank you for your interest. Any other questions?"

As Nichols addressed the crowd he gave a brief wave to a man who immediately approached him as another shareholder took hold of the mic.

"How much time does Culver expect will be needed before the NX-1 program is ready for FDA approval?"

"This question is best answered by my colleague next to me," Nichols replied. Then, with a hand covering the microphone he spoke into the ear of the man he had summoned. The man walked back into the crowd and straight to Bishop.

"I guess this is it," Bishop said to Jennifer. "Hook, line...."

The man stopped next to Bishop and spoke briefly into his ear before disappearing again.

"...and sinker." Bishop turned to Jennifer. "We are invited up to Nichols's office after the meeting."

"That was easy," Jennifer replied.

Bishop tilted his head toward the elevator. "Shall we?"

"Are you sure you don't want another coffee?" Nichols' secretary asked after they had been waiting on a couch in her office for more than fifteen minutes. "I've just heard the presentation is over, so I expect Mr. Nichols any minute now."

"No, thank you," Bishop replied just as a loud ping came from the elevator. When the doors opened, Nichols walked out.

"Thank you, Susan." Nichols sounded agitated before turning to Bishop and noticing Jennifer. "She's with you?"

"She's my research partner."

"Jennifer Porter."

As Jennifer introduced herself, Nichols's eyes widened as he recognized the last name.

"Welcome," he said and opened the door to his office. "Please, take a seat. I'll be right with you."

As Nichols left the room, both Bishop and Jennifer made themselves comfy on the white leather couch.

"Nice office," Jennifer remarked.

"Nice and clean," Bishop replied with a smile. He then inspected the logo stamped on a business card holder on the otherwise empty table before them.

"'Weaving spiders come not here,'" he read. "I know that phrase from somewhere."

"All right," Nichols said as he walked back in. "I'm a little pressed for time so excuse me if I come straight to the point. I'm sorry if I had to cut you off earlier, but I didn't think that particular discussion belonged at a shareholders' meeting."

"I agree. This is a better setting," Bishop replied amiably.

"Well, I called you here not because there's any truth to these rumors but rather because it isn't the first time I've heard the rumors and I'm curious as to where you came by them, and why you're interested."

"Miss Porter here is researching the effect of ancient medical practices and their influence in modern medicine."

Jennifer shifted uncomfortably in her seat.

"And what did you find out?" Nichols asked her before she had even had time to adjust to her new role.

"Well," she replied after a short pause. "My father... maybe you've heard of him? Robert Porter?"

Nichols took a moment and then shook his head. "Can't say I have."

"Anyway, he researched the matter before me and I'm taking over his work as part of my study. He never finished his work, but in his notes he left a message that named your company."

"That's strange," Nichols replied. "Just our name?"

Jennifer nodded.

Nichols leaned back, into the couch, and cleared his throat. "I'm afraid I can't help you and from what I hear, I don't believe you can help me either."

"Why is it so important to you to find out where the rumors have come from?" Bishop asked.

"Well, you must know that any kind of rumor in our business can seriously influence stock value. But if you don't mind, as I said, I'm pressed for time so...." Nichols rose from his chair and stretched out his hand. "Thank you for your interest. I wish you luck on your search."

"Thank you," Jennifer said, shaking the sweaty hand offered her. Bishop simply nodded goodbye before leaving the office.

"What do you think?" Jennifer asked once they were in the elevator.

"Did he seem nervous to you?"

Jennifer tilted her head. "A little. He had sweaty hands and his story about influencing stock value didn't sound very convincing."

"Well, I'm convinced," Bishop replied. "I'm convinced he's hiding something."

"But what?" Jennifer asked. "You think he has the fifth document?"

"I hope so." Bishop smiled. "If not, we've come to the end of our journey."

CHAPTER 41

To the Grove

Nichols tried to squint as the early morning sun hit the windows of his penthouse office, but the scars on his face made it impossible. *Dammit,* he thought, putting on his shades. Ever since the fire burned away part of his eyelid, he hadn't been able to blink or squint, he had to wear sunglasses most of the time, a blindfold at night, and he needed to spray his eyes throughout the day to keep them lubricated. On top of all that, he had been feeling uptight and nervous since Bishop and Jennifer visited. He wasn't sure what had triggered his nerves or what he had to be nervous about, but he was. That in itself bothered him because he wasn't the nervous type, but he wondered whether the coming evening might be to blame.

Reaching for his cellphone he punched in numbers and waited. The phone rang for such a long time he almost hung up.

"I thought we agreed you wouldn't contact me?" a calm voice said in greeting. "Not until tonight."

"I know and I'm sorry, Mr. Chairman, but I need you to know something. Yesterday I had a visit from Matthew Bishop and Porter's daughter. They were asking indirect questions about rumors involving Culver working on some kind of wonder drug."

"You sound anxious. How did they get to you?"

"I have no idea, but it's clear they knew more. There are too many loose ends that I can't tie up. We need to put an end to this as quickly as we can."

"It doesn't matter. After tonight everything will be solved and all complications will be gone. I really don't see the problem. If you feel the need to, you can come earlier today. We are in place, working on preparations."

Nichols breathed slowly to calm himself. "Maybe I'll do just that. The sooner we put an end to this, the better. I'm planning to have myself driven there so I'll probably arrive late in the afternoon."

"You're looking at a six-hour drive. Are you sure?"

"It'll give me plenty of time to do some work. Plus, I love the scenery on the way."

"All right, and trust me, once you're here, you're safe. No one can get to you. Just get in your car and come."

"Thank you. I'll do that. I'll see you later today."

"And don't forget to bring the document."

Nichols smiled and sniffed. "Will do, thanks."

On ending the call, he pushed the intercom on his desk.

"Yes, sir?"

"Susan, is my suitcase packed for the weekend?"

"The dry cleaner should deliver the final pieces within the hour, sir."

"Thank you. I'll be leaving around eleven. Can you please ask Miss Hartman to be ready to drive me?"

"Will do, sir."

Opposite Culver BioPharma's headquarters in Century Towers, the Greenleaf Gourmet Chopshop's terrace was empty save for a few office workers eating a quick breakfast.

"Are you sure?" Jennifer asked as she put down the menu.

"Yes," Bishop replied. "I'll have the eggs benedict on pretzel bread and I'm sure you'll enjoy it too."

Jennifer smiled. "You know what I mean."

"Look, my gut tells me the final document is in there with Nichols. You said yourself how strange it was he never asked what your father had to say about his company. So, he must have known your father was dead."

"Even so, it's a long shot," Jennifer said. "How long do you want us to sit here?"

"If I'm correct and the document is in that building it won't be too long."

"How do you figure that?"

"Simple. He knows what we've uncovered so far, from finding the documents in Israel and discovering and exposing the Golden Dawn in England—and now we've turned up at his office. He isn't going to risk leaving the document in the one place we'll come looking for it. He'll try to move it to a more secure location."

"And we follow him to that secure location. But what if he gets someone else to do the job for him?"

Bishop grinned as the waiter brought them their breakfast. "Have a little faith and enjoy your eggs."

Three hours later, the waiter had put up a parasol to protect them from the sun, Bishop was drinking iced tea and Jennifer was pouring herself another glass of water.

"This is madness, you know?" She waved her Kindle in the air. I just finished one book and if this carries on, I'll finish another today."

"It's good to brush up on your reading," Bishop replied. "If you want, I can upload some textbooks for your final year project. It could give you a head start."

"I suppose I could also spend my final year over here. I think that—"

"Wait a minute," Bishop interrupted, turning to watch a black Lincoln Town Car drive up to the entrance of Century Tower One.

"Blacked out windows. How exciting," Jennifer said smugly.

"Look at the driver," Bishop said and Jennifer saw that only the back windows were blacked out. "You see?"

"The redhead. What was her name?"

"Hartman. Alice Hartman. Have you remembered where you might know her from?"

Jennifer shook her head as Hartman got out of the car and walked up to the tower. At the entrance, she was met by Nichols and a man carrying a suitcase.

"I think this is our moment," Bishop said, quickly waving at the waiter. He took some cash from his money clip and placed it on the table. "Let's go."

The two of them headed straight for their rental car, a Nissan Rogue parked in front of the restaurant. As they got in, they watched the suitcase being loaded into the trunk of the Lincoln while Alice opened the back door for Nichols, who got in after a quick look around.

"Here we go," Bishop said, smiling.

"Could still be a weekend at the beach," Jennifer teased.

"Oh, ye of little faith."

As the Town Car drove away Bishop put the Rogue in gear, turned in the street and started following. From the Avenue of The Stars they headed west onto Santa Monica Boulevard and within ten minutes they turned onto the 405 north. Bishop zoomed out on the car's GPS.

"Where does this road lead?" Jennifer asked.

"Bel Air, San Fernando, Santa Clarita and all the way up to San Francisco."

Jennifer synced her telephone to the car stereo and opened Spotify. After a few seconds, the Talking Heads track Road to Nowhere blasted from the speakers.

"Very funny," Bishop said.

"Seemed fitting." Jennifer winked.

After twenty minutes or so they passed the Santa Clarita city limits and continued on into the hills.

"What do you think?" Jennifer asked.

"My bet would be San Francisco."

"San Francisco? That's quite a drive.

"About 400 miles."

"Do we have enough gas?"

Bishop pointed to the number 454 next to a gas pump icon on the dashboard.

"Well, if you don't mind, I could use some extra shut-eye," Jennifer said, reclining her seat and shifting onto her side.

"No problem. I'll wake you when something happens."

For more than four hours Bishop steered the Nissan along the I-5, following the Town Car. The only time Jennifer woke was when they left the road to park at a rest area.

"Hey, sleepy head."

Jennifer rubbed her eyes. "Where are we?"

"Somewhere near a place called Los Banos, still going north on the I-5."

"Are we there? Wherever there is?"

"Don't think so. They stopped to get gas about a mile back and I'm waiting for them to pass us again."

"Do you want me to drive?" Jennifer offered.

"That's okay, I can manage," Bishop said just as the Town Car passed the rest area. "There they go again and here we go again."

Once they were back on the I-5, Jennifer asked, "How long if we're going to San Francisco?"

"About two hours, I guess. But who knows. Maybe they'll drive all the way to Oregon."

"Not funny," Jennifer said, ignoring Bishop's grin as she turned up the volume on the radio.

For another two hours, they followed the Town Car passing places like Hamburg Farms, Ingomar and Crows Landing before reaching San Francisco's city limits at Castro Valley. Bishop inched nearer to the Town Car.

"Don't want to lose them now," he said.

"You better not," Jennifer threatened.

Passing Berkeley and Richmond, the Town Car continued travelling until it left San Francisco Bay.

"Oh my God," Jennifer muttered as she looked ahead at the looming woods and mountains.

Though Bishop was also wondering where the hell they were going, he didn't dare say anything.

For another fifteen minutes, they traveled in silence until the Town Car signaled to turn.

"Here we go." Bishop sighed in relief and pressed the GPS screen.

"What's over there?" Jennifer asked, pointing to the screen.

"Nothing much as far as I can see. Woods, woods and more woods, filled with huge Redwood trees. Interesting."

For another fifteen minutes, they snaked through the woods before driving up to a T-junction. The Town Car turned right onto Bohemian Avenue and Bishop braked to read the sign.

"Weaving spiders come not here," he said.

"What?"

"I think I know what the owl means." Bishop drove on. "Remember the owl on the business card holder with the words 'weaving spiders come not here?'"

"In Nichols's office," Jennifer said.

"Exactly. It's a quote from Shakespeare's *A Midsummer Night's Dream,* but I didn't connect it to this."

"To what?"

"To the grove." Bishop hit the brakes again and moved onto the side of the road as Nichols's car turned left to stop at a barrier leading to a track in the woods. "Hold on."

At the barrier a uniformed man walked out of a booth and up to the Town Car. Alice Hartman rolled down the window and handed him a piece of paper. After inspecting the paper, he peered into the car, checked the rear seats and then handed the paper back before returning to the booth. A second later, the barrier opened and the Town Car drove through, disappearing into the woods.

"What now?" Jennifer asked.

Without answering Bishop drove the car up to the barrier. "Just play along," he said before lowering the window. The uniformed man came out of the booth and walked up to him.

"Good day, sir. Can I help you?"

"Good afternoon," Bishop answered. "We're looking for the San Francisco Garter Snake."

"Excuse me?"

"The San Francisco Garter Snake," Bishop repeated. "A snake with a burnt orange head and turquoise body bearing thick orange and black stripes along its back. It's a very rare snake indigenous to this area. My daughter is writing a paper on them for school and we heard a small colony of them were spotted in this neighborhood."

Jennifer leaned across Bishop to give the guard a look.

"I'm sorry," the guard replied, unsure as to what to make of it all. "The road into the woods is closed this weekend."

"The whole weekend?" Bishop pretended to be disappointed and Jennifer pulled a glum face.

"I'm sorry," the man repeated. "The road will be re-opened on Monday for about a mile, but from there on in it remains private property."

"Are you sure you can't let us in?" Jennifer asked. "Only for an hour or so."

"I'm sorry. You need to go now," the guard replied as another car drove up behind them.

"All right, thank you." Bishop closed the window, turned the car around and drove back up Bohemian Avenue.

"What now?" Jennifer asked. "And what about the owl?"

"You saw that?"

"The owl above the guard's booth? Yes, I saw that. What about it?"

Bishop pulled up at the side of the road and took a deep breath. "Let's take a walk."

Once they were out of the car and walking along a footpath, Bishop turned to Jennifer. "Where to begin?"

"You connected the owl and the spiders to something," Jennifer suggested.

"Yes, 'weaving spiders come not here' is a line from Shakespeare's *A Midsummer Night's Dream*. In this case, it means something like, leave your business outside. It's also the motto of an all-male gentlemen's club called The Bohemian Club, a secret club that originated about 150 years ago and was founded by journalists who called themselves Bohemians. They met to talk about their work and the world. Today's members meet here, at Bohemian Grove, three weekends a year. While it is said that the club started with purist views, Oscar Wilde said he had never seen so many well-fed and well-dressed business-looking Bohemians in his lifetime. But anyway, the club grew and became more secretive over the years. Nowadays, it caters to the world's richest, such as prominent and influential business leaders, government officials, media executives and presidents. Nobody knows for sure who the real members are, though Ronald Reagan, George W. Bush, Herman Wouk and Jack London have been linked to it at some point in time. You know, the world is filled with more-or-less-secret societies like the Bohemian Club. There's the Freemasons, the Bilderberg Group and, of course, our own Skull and Bones at Yale. A lot of these organizations are associated with political decision-making."

"Like the fourth branch of government," Jennifer said.

"Something like that."

"Are you a member of any of these societies? Or perhaps were?"

"Now, it wouldn't be much of a secret if I told you, would it?" Bishop laughed.

Jennifer smiled back, but underneath the laughter she got the impression Bishop wasn't too keen on going down that route. "So, what about the Bohemian Club here at the Grove. If they leave their business outside, what do they do?"

Finding a bench to sit on beneath the huge redwood trees, Bishop invited Jennifer to join him before replying.

"Despite the motto, one theory is that they do, in fact, do business. More than that, it has been suggested that the Manhattan Project of 1942 that led to the first atomic bomb was planned right here. There are also a number of fairly credible rumors about secret ceremonies involving occult rituals and offerings taking place, which are carried out like theatrical plays. The problem is, no one besides members ever get in, and to become a member you have to be recommended by an existing member."

"So, what does this have to do with our case?" Jennifer asked while checking out the subject on her phone.

"I honestly have no idea. But if everything they say goes on in these woods does go on, then it would somehow seem to fit with what we're looking for."

Jennifer pointed at her phone. "It says here that only a handful of pictures, a few documented cases by former members and one blurry video are known to exist of what goes on in here."

She clicked on a link leading to an out-of-focus YouTube clip. On the bank of a small lake, a huge owl was surrounded by people dressed in white robes dancing and chanting to music while waving burning torches. "You think this is real? It kind of reminds me of the KKK."

"Well, I'm not sure about the reference to the KKK though, come to think of it, I don't know of any black members, but yes, I think it's real. I heard about a ceremony called the Cremation of Care. Apparently, the ceremony starts off the weekend and it's designed to banish all worldly cares from members. However, conspiracy theorists talk about human sacrifices. Still, I guess they would say that."

Jennifer grinned. "So I guess we're going to, uh...."

"We are," Bishop confirmed.

CHAPTER 42

The Owl

As Nichols's Town Car passed the barrier, driving deep into the woods, he opened a window and breathed in the forest air.

"It's so good to be here again," he said from the back seat.

"To be honest, sir, I already miss the sound of cars honking, sirens in the distance and the smell of the city," Alice replied.

"You know, I grew up under the trees. When I was born my parents lived in a trailer park until my father found success with his security firm. Only then did we move to the big city."

"I didn't know that. Los Angeles?"

"Chicago, the windy city. I moved to L.A. after school for an internship at Culver and I never left."

"We're here, sir."

Alice pulled into a parking space next to a large log cabin and a row of golf carts. She got out of the car and walked to the rear to open the door for Nichols as two young men in red uniforms emerged from a cabin. Alice opened the trunk and without a word the young men took the luggage from the car.

"This is where we part," Nichols said to Alice.

"I know, sir. Men only." She gave him a small smile, shook his hand, got back in the car and drove away. From the cabin, a man appeared and walked up to Nichols.

"Thomas," he said, offering his hand.

"George," Nichols replied, accepting the handshake.

George Moore was a tall, gray-haired, middle-aged man dressed in sneakers, a green sweater and khaki shorts.

"How was your trip?"

"Good. It gave me time to think and come to my senses. Thank you for meeting me here early. It's good to be here." Nichols raised his hands skyward, toward the treetops.

"No problem. As chairman of the Grove for nine years now, I'm quite familiar with the last-minute jitters some of our members have before their first active ceremony. I know from experience it's quite different from being in the audience. I also understand you made good use of Simpson?"

"I did. Thanks again for recommending him."

"Again, not a problem. I take it you brought it with you?"

Nichols nodded.

"Great. I'll have your luggage sent to your usual cabin. You remember the way?"

"Sure."

"Good. Take a cart, clean up a little, maybe rest or take a walk and we'll meet at dinner to talk about the ceremony tonight."

"Seven?" Nichols asked.

"I'll have you picked up."

The men shook hands again and Nichols climbed into one of the waiting golf carts. He then drove away slowly, deeper into the forest.

At Lucy's Lounge & Grill, Bishop pointed to a sign on the wall that read, "A woman's 'Be ready in 5 mins' and a man's 'Be home in 5 mins' MEAN EXACTLY THE SAME."

"True or false?" he asked Jennifer, who laughed.

"Have you never been married?"

"That took you a long time," Bishop replied. "No, never. Tried something like it a few times, but it never panned out. Not sure why, but I learned I needed a lot of time for myself, so I guess this is much easier."

"Or an easy way out?"

"Maybe."

"When did he say he was going to call back?"

Bishop looked at his watch. "Any time now."

"Do you think he can find us a way in?"

"If anyone can get us in or out of anything it's Monroe. I once involuntarily entered a heavily-guarded prison at the Algerian-Libyan border and he got me out again without anyone noticing. I'm sure that—" Bishop's cellphone rang on the table. "Speak of the devil."

"Just a moment," Bishop told Monroe before turning to Jennifer. "Let's go outside for some privacy."

Once outside they sat down at a picnic table at the edge of the forest. "You're on speaker," he informed Monroe as he placed the phone on the table.

"How are you doing?" Monroe asked.

"We're good, thanks. You found us a way in?"

"I'm good too. Thanks for asking. And the answer is maybe. As far as I can see the place is like a 2,700-acre fortress."

"But there's a maybe," Bishop noted.

"I figured a place that big had to have at least one or two vulnerabilities. I found one. Just north from you is a golf club called the Northwood that's separated from the Bohemian Grove by the Russian River. There's a place where members of the Bohemian Club cross the river by small boats to play golf. That place is cordoned off by a large fence and it's monitored by cameras, but just south of that there's an older crossing that was used until the eighties. It was sealed off when the new one opened. If my information is correct, the gates were locked, but kept intact, leaving a vulnerability."

"And how do we get through?"

"First, you have to cross the river. There are a few places where you can rent a kayak so that shouldn't be a problem. Just keep in mind that there's no kayaking allowed after sunset so you either cross in daylight or make sure you're not seen at night. The gate is hidden about a hundred feet into the woods. I'll send you the exact GPS coordinates. The fence should be easily cut open with a bolt cutter, but you need to look out because the fence is electric. The gate shouldn't be so if you only touch that you should be fine."

"Sounds simple," Jennifer said.

"I hope it is," Monroe responded.

"You hope?" Bishop asked.

"You'll be fine," Monroe assured him, chuckling.

"All right." Bishop picked up the phone. "Wish us luck and we'll see you in a few days."

"Good luck."

"So that's it," Jennifer said after the call ended. "We have our way in?"

"I guess so, which means we need to get some supplies and rent a kayak."

"I always wanted to go kayaking," Jennifer said as they walked to the car.

At dusk, Bishop and Jennifer kayaked along the Russian River, heading south.

"This is much easier than I thought it would be," Jennifer said, rocking the kayak as she spoke.

"Will you be careful?" Bishop half-shouted. "I came here to kayak, not to swim."

"Oh, don't be a baby. You should have brought a rod. You're a fisherman, aren't you?"

"That is correct, and the Russian River is actually well known for its steelhead and sturgeon fishing. Maybe next time."

"Next time," Jennifer said with a smile. "How far is it?"

Bishop checked the GPS on his phone and pointed into the distance. "Should be right around that corner."

"What do you expect we'll see or do when we get there?"

"To be honest, I've been asking myself that question for the past few hours and I truly have no idea. There's so little we know about the Bohemian Club and its members. What I do know is that females are only allowed in as workers and they're limited to the daytime, so whatever happens—"

"I know my place. I'll stay out of sight." Jennifer sighed. "And that, uh, cremation you were talking about?"

"The Cremation of Care. It's officially described as a theatrical production and in days gone by they would recite poems, but like I said earlier, conspiracy theorists claim that nowadays the ceremony has a more mystical feel. With a little luck, we'll know in a few hours." Bishop looked at his phone. "We're here."

Steering to the rocky bank, they climbed out, grabbed their backpacks and pulled the kayak onto the grass. Bishop then dragged it into the woods, out of sight of the river.

"Now let's see if we can find that gate," he said, holding his phone in front of him. "That way."

Walking into the woods it only took them a few minutes to find the steel fence securing the place they wanted to get into. Attached to the fence was a yellow sign showing a black lightning bolt and 'WARNING! LIVE WIRE, UNTOUCHABLE!' written in red.

"Let's not try it out," Bishop said.

"Do we go left or right?" Jennifer asked as Bishop fiddled with his phone.

"Not sure. If Monroe was correct it can't be far. You pick a side."

Jennifer shrugged before walking left, following the fence. Beneath the canopy of the trees, the last rays of sunshine struggled to cut through the leaves and darkness now fell swiftly over the grove. "It's getting hard to see," she said.

"We can't use flashlights," Bishop responded. "Wait! Over there."

Bishop pointed a little ahead of them to where the steel fence was interrupted for a few feet by a wire mesh braided with barbed wire across it.

"No!" Bishop shouted, grabbing Jennifer's arm as she reached to touch the mesh.

"What?" Jennifer yelped. "Monroe said the doorway wasn't electric."

"That's not what he said. He said the fence would be vulnerable here. But the mesh is connected by metal to the electric fence thereby conducting the power through it."

Jennifer sighed. "Thanks. So, what do we do?"

"Simple. We cut away the barbed wire using our isolated bolt cutters without touching anything metal with our bare hands. Then we cut through the hinges holding the mesh door and it should fall away allowing us to safely walk through."

From his backpack, Bishop took out two pairs of thick rubber gloves and two bolt cutters, handing a set to Jennifer. "You take the right side and be careful."

Cautiously, they started cutting, peeling away the barbed wire. Fifteen minutes later they were done.

"Now for the hinges," Bishop said, pointing to three hinges on either side of the door. "Start with the bottom two, then we'll cut the top two on my count."

With four snaps, the lower hinges came away.

"Now, on my count, cut the top one. When you're finished immediately step away to the side. Ready?"

Jennifer nodded.

"Three, two, one, go!"

After cutting simultaneously, Jennifer stepped away and Bishop positioned himself in front of the gate, putting his foot against the door to ensure it fell away from them. He turned to Jennifer, smiling. "And now we have a doorway."

Bishop bowed and invited her to cross the threshold.

"High five," Jennifer said as she raised a gloved hand, and Bishop responded accordingly.

"Let's gather our stuff and move on," he then said. "It's still a two-mile walk inside."

For half an hour they stumbled through the woods, with only Bishop's phone to light their way as they followed the coordinates sent by Monroe. Then they heard sounds in the distance and as they neared they saw flickering lights.

"We need to be absolutely quiet now," Bishop whispered into Jennifer's ear.

"That's not going to be easy." Jennifer pointed at the ground that was littered with fallen branches snapping under their feet with every step they took.

"Just walk as softly and slowly as you can," Bishop advised, carefully moving forward.

Some ten minutes later, Bishop stopped and kneeled, bringing Jennifer to an abrupt halt behind him. Through the trees, light from hanging lamps and small fires lit their path and the air was filled with soft haunting music.

"Look," Bishop whispered, pointing left toward a row of small log cabins where a man dressed in a red robe emerged. He walked along a path toward the light and music. "Let's follow him from a distance."

After the man turned a corner, Bishop and Jennifer joined the dimly lit path that took them slightly downhill. As the music became louder, they neared the end of the path and came to a clearing. Bishop pointed to raised bushes at the side of the path.

"There," he whispered and moved to squat behind the bushes.

Jennifer followed his lead. Once she was next to him they both raised their heads to take in the view, finding a small lake around which stood hundreds of people. At the far end of the lake they saw a forty-foot owl statue flanked by twenty men dressed in black and red robes, carrying torches.

"It's just like in the YouTube video," Jennifer whispered and Bishop nodded.

As the music grew louder, the robed men moved in front of the owl. Once in place, the music stopped and all was quiet, save for the loud croaking of tree frogs. After a pause in proceedings, two white-robed men walked onto a stage. One of them stepped in front of the owl to address the crowd, his voice amplified by speakers.

"The owl is in his leafy temple. Let all within the Grove be worshipful before him. Lift up your heads, oh ye trees, and be lifted up, ye eternal spires. For behold, here is Bohemia's shrine and holy are the pillars of this house. Weaving spiders come not here!"

Cheers and applause broke out among the waiting crowd. After a minute or so, the white-robed man raised his arms and the forest fell silent again until there was a loud drumroll.

"Hail, Bohemians!" As the man spoke, the drums stopped and the cast of red-robed men walked to the side. Using their torches, they lit a row of bowls sitting on the edges of the stage. "With the ripple of water, the song of birds; such music inspires the sinking soul. Do we invite you into Midsummer's joy? The sky above is blue and sown with stars. The forest floor is heaped with fragrant grit. The evening's cool kiss is yours. The campfire's glow, the birth of rosy-fingered dawn. For behold, here is Bohemia's shrine. And holy are the pillars of this house."

"What the hell is he talking about?" Jennifer asked softly.

"It's a kind of sermon," Bishop whispered back. "Don't take it too literally."

As the ceremonial music restarted, the crowd cheered. A minute or so later, the robed man addressed the crowd again. Once he finished, the music took over. It was a sequence that continued for thirty minutes before he finished his speech and walked to the side of the stage, accompanied only by the sounds of the forest's tree frogs.

"How long will this go on?" Jennifer asked.

"I have no idea," Bishop admitted.

At the sound of a bell ringing, the other white-robed man stepped forward to stand in front of the owl.

"O Great Owl of Bohemia!" he shouted. "We thank thee for thy adjuration. Begone detested care! Begone! Once more, we banish thee! Begone dull care! Fire should have its will of thee! Begone dull care! And all the winds make merry with thy dust. Hail, fellowship's eternal flame! Once again Midsummer sets us free!"

The bell rang three times.

"What is 'dull care?'" Jennifer asked.

"I believe 'dull care' is an obsolete form of 'worries.' The word 'care' actually comes from the old English word 'cearu,' which means sorrow."

The bell rang another three times followed by a drumroll.

"Look!" Bishop pointed to the other side of the lake where a tugboat stopped at the foot of the shrine.

"Behold, behold, an offering taken from our enemy is carried hither for our ancient rites."

"Is that...?" Jennifer pointed at the red robed man in the boat.

Bishop took a pair of Bresser 3×14 digital night vision goggles from his backpack. "I think you're right," he said after taking a look, and passed the binoculars to Jennifer.

"Wow, these are good. It looks just like daytime."

"Great, isn't it? It's also recording everything we see."

"So, it is Nichols," Jennifer said. "What's he doing?"

"We'll find out soon enough," Bishop replied.

After the boat was secured at the foot of the owl, Nichols was helped out. He carried a small box.

"What's that?" Jennifer asked and Bishop looked through his binoculars.

"It's a box."

"I can see that. But could it be...?"

"Why not?"

At the front of the owl, the white-robed man began speaking again. "Oh thou, thus ferried cross the ethereal tide. In all the ancient splendor of death. Dull Care, arch-enemy of beauty; not for thee. The gentle tribute and the restful grave. But fire shall have its will of thee. And all the winds make joyous with thy dust! Bring fire!"

With a loud *woosh*, flames lit up a large brass dish in front of the owl and Nichols carried the box to it while a drumroll sounded.

"They're going to burn it," Jennifer said aloud.

"Shh...." Bishop urged, quickly looking around to see if they had been discovered. "Thank God. Do you have any idea what would happen if anyone found us here?"

"Sorry, but they're going to burn the final document."

"There's nothing we can do," Bishop said, going back to the binoculars to watch Nichols walk up to the fire, open the box and take out an aluminum tube.

"Oh my God," Jennifer muttered as she saw Nichols throw something on the fire. Immediately, the flames rose a few feet higher as Chopin's funeral march played over the speakers. "He did it."

"Calm down," Bishop said. "He didn't."

"He didn't?"

"No, he didn't. Wait a moment." Bishop continued watching the spectacle for a minute or so more before lowering the binoculars and pressing a few buttons. He then handed them to Jennifer. "Take a look."

Jennifer looked into the binoculars to watch the recording. "They burned the box," she whispered.

"Keep looking," Bishop replied. Jennifer then noticed that one of the white hooded men took the aluminum tube from Nichols before taking it to the side of the owl. There, he opened what looked like a door before stepping inside and disappearing inside the owl, closing the door behind him.

"Where did he go?" Jennifer asked, handing back the binoculars.

"Don't know. Into the owl?"

"But...."

"You know as much as I do," Bishop firmly told her just as the white-robed man began speaking again.

"Well should we know our breathing flame. Of fellowship can sear. The greedy claws of care throttle his impious screams. And send his cowering carcass. From this grove. Begone, detested care, begone. Once more we banish thee. Let the all-powerful spirit of this lamp, by its purgative and ambient fire, girdle the mystic scene. Hail fellowship, begone dull care. Once again, midsummer sets us free."

From behind the stage, fireworks lit up the night sky, accompanied by Carl Orff's "O Fortuna" from *Carmina Burana.*

Bishop turned onto his back and looked to the sky. Jennifer joined him taking a deep breath. "Shall I say it?" she asked and Bishop frowned. "We need to get into the owl."

CHAPTER 43

The Archive

Two hours after the ceremony ended, the lake was still and the clearing was bare. It was now a warm and tranquil night. Moonlight shimmered on the flat water and all was quiet. Even the frogs were silent.

"Wake up." Bishop gently shook Jennifer by the shoulder.

"Huh, is it time?" Jennifer sat up straight, a little dazed from her brief sleep.

"Bad dreams?"

"I'm not sure. What time is it?"

"It's 2:00 a.m. You slept for almost two hours."

"What happened?"

"Nothing much. Everyone left."

Jennifer looked toward the lake.

"It's time," Bishop told her and grabbed hold of his backpack before standing. "You ready?"

"Sure," Jennifer said as she gathered her things.

"Let's go." Bishop walked onto the path. "Keep low and to the side of the path. You never know."

Almost crouching, they followed the path as it circled the lake heading toward the owl. A bird cried in the distance, but that was the only sound they heard. After a two-minute walk they arrived at the owl.

"It's bigger up close," Jennifer said as Bishop took a flashlight from his backpack.

"It's unlocked," he said, shining light onto the hasp and staple to find it was missing a padlock. "That's strange." He removed the hasp from the staple and opened the door.

"I can't see a thing," Jennifer said.

"Here," Bishop said as he directed his flashlight into the opening, revealing the top of a wooden staircase. "After you."

After a moment's hesitation, Jennifer descended the stairs followed closely by Bishop who closed the door behind him, still lighting the way. At the bottom, they stopped and took a deep breath.

"That explains the lack of padlock," Bishop said.

The room they were in was carved out of rock with two open old wooden doors, left and right of them, leading to what looked like storage rooms. Immediately in front of them was a heavy steel door, next to which was a code key panel illuminated by a bright red light. Underneath was another glass panel with the picture of a hand on it.

"It was way too easy," Jennifer admitted.

Bishop grunted and checked the rooms that had been left open.

"Nothing?" Jennifer asked.

"Just some empty shelves. I bet that whatever used to be on them in the past has been moved behind that steel door." Bishop walked up to the code key panel. "A biometric panel combined with a numbered key combination."

"What does that mean?"

"It means we need a key code, but we have no idea how many digits might be needed and the biometric panel scans a handprint. So, even if we did know the correct combination, we'd still need someone's hand."

"So, we're basically...."

"I think we are," Bishop agreed. "There's no way...."

From the top of the stairs they heard voices and Bishop put a finger to his lips. "Come," he whispered, quickly turning off his flashlight. Grabbing Jennifer by the shoulder, he dragged her into one of the old storage rooms and hid behind the door just as a single bulb on the ceiling of the hallway lit up the room.

"This happens every year," someone said. "A raccoon or a skunk triggers the alarm and I have to lose sleep over it."

"I'm very sorry, sir," someone else replied. "But you know the procedure."

While Jennifer stood stock-still, Bishop peeked through the small opening between the door and the wall. A security guard and two casually dressed men inspected the steel door. Bishop recognized one of the men as Nichols.

"I still don't understand why I have to be here, George," he said and the distinctive sound of his voice made Jennifer's eyes dart to Bishop, who nodded. "I thought you were going to show me around tomorrow."

"If you are to take over from me as caretaker next year, what better time to get acquainted with the job than the present?"

George Moore punched ten digits into the keypad before putting a hand against the biometric scanner. A soft rumble came from within the walls followed by a loud thump.

"You do the honors," Moore said, inviting Nichols to take hold of the large door handle.

"So, this is it," Nichols said and took a deep breath.

"It's really not that dramatic," Moore replied before turning to the security guard. "You can wait upstairs."

Once the guard had made his way upstairs, Moore turned to Nichols. "Now, if you don't mind I'd like to get some sleep tonight."

Nichols pulled on the door handle and the door easily swung open.

"It's hydraulic," Moore explained. "Shall we?"

Stepping through the doorway, lights switched on and Bishop turned to Jennifer.

"They've gone inside," he whispered.

"What should we do?"

"You wait here for a second and I'll go check it out."

Bishop left the storage room and carefully made his way to the steel door that remained open. He cautiously looked in and saw a short, narrow passageway with steel paneled walls. At the end of the tunnel was a red velvet drape. Somewhere behind the drape he heard indistinct voices. Looking back to Jennifer, Bishop waved at her to join him.

"You dare?" he asked in a whisper.

She looked into the passageway and faltered as every moment she had experienced in the last few weeks flashed before her eyes. It was all leading to this. She couldn't back out now. She had to know what lay at the end of the tunnel. She nodded.

"Follow me," Bishop said and stepped inside.

They slowly tiptoed through the tunnel, coming to a stop at the velvet curtain. The voices behind it were clearer, but still some distance from them. Bishop peeked behind the drape.

"I think it's safe to go in."

Holding the drape aside, they crept through.

"Wow," Jennifer whispered.

Behind the curtain was a room that could have been set in the future with stainless steel walls, ceiling and floor, upon which stood a number of free-standing, eight-foot tall, glass display cases. The room was designed as a labyrinth and the air felt sterile. Each display case contained one item and an LCD panel top front, displayed atmospheric conditions inside the room. Next, to each panel was a sign warning, 'Danger, case under pressure by flammable gas. No naked flames.'

"Is it a museum?" Jennifer asked.

"Of sorts," Bishop replied staring at a book inside one of the display cases. "I believe this is Nikola Tesla's manuscript on wireless-free electricity. In the late 1900s, Tesla claimed to have figured out a way to bypass fossil-fuel-burning power plants and power lines. His claim was that free energy could be harnessed using ionization in the upper atmosphere to produce electrical vibrations. The official story is that it didn't work, but rumors has it that his funder, J.P. Morgan, pulled the plug on the research under pressure from the energy lobby when they realized there wouldn't be any profit in free energy."

Bishop passed a few display cases before stopping again. On a folder was written 'PPD No. 29'.

"What's that?" Jennifer asked.

"Well, PPD stands for Presidential Policy Directive. Again, it's a rumor or conspiracy theory, if you like, that Obama, during his time as president, ordered thirty of these secret directives, all carefully administered and overseen by Congress. To the public, only the numbers are known. In 2014, he skipped from PPD-28 to PPD-30 leaving everyone speculating as to what happened to number 29."

Bishop moved on. "This looks like the plan to the secret rooms hidden beneath Grand Central's Terminal in New York, and"—Bishop pointed to a case at the other side of the aisle—"this looks like a translation of the Voynich Manuscript. You saw a copy of the original in my office."

"The book that no one has been able to translate?"

"Or did they?" Bishop asked. "And here, a Chronovisor, and here, a box full of documents regarding the Kennedy killing. This room is a conspiracy theorist's dream come true."

"But why?" Jennifer asked. "Why keep all of this secret?"

Bishop sighed. "It's no secret that the U.S. government wanted to control the release of new—and for that matter, old—technologies because they feared they might threaten national defense and the economic stability of the country. In the 1950s, the Invention Secrecy Act was passed, specifically designed for this."

"Another conspiracy theory."

"Nope. This one is fact."

"So, the government is behind all this?"

"I have no idea, but clearly there's a group of people who decide what the general public gets to know and see, and what they don't."

From the back, they heard voices getting louder.

"This way," Bishop whispered, moving to another aisle. "Let's try to find what we came for."

As Bishop made his way through the maze he headed in the direction of where he thought the voices had come from.

"What if they leave?" Jennifer asked, getting more anxious as she followed. "I don't want to get locked in here."

"Let's hope they stay a while then."

"That doesn't sound very reassuring."

"Listen," Bishop stopped to turn around and place his hands onto Jennifer's shoulders. "This is our only shot at finding the final document. If we leave now, there's no coming back here. But I'll leave it up to you. What shall we do?"

Jennifer thought for a moment. On the one hand, she felt that all their work had led up to this moment and there could be no turning back. On the other hand, her intuition told her this was probably the worst idea they had come up with so far. She took a slow, deep breath before stepping aside to allow Bishop to pass. As he did so, he grinned.

"There," Jennifer whispered, pointing to two display cases at the end of the aisle with open doors. Quickly, but quietly, they approached the cases, conscious of the other voices in the room moving further away.

"We need to hurry," Bishop said.

"There it is!" Jennifer stopped in front of the last case in the row. On a glass shelf lay the aluminum tube. "Now what? The case is sealed."

Bishop inspected the case with his hands, feeling the edges, left to right and top to bottom. No locks or levers. Only hinges on one side. With both hands, he pulled at the side opposite the hinges, like a door. Nothing happened. He pulled a bit harder, and harder again, but it wouldn't budge. *This doesn't make any sense,* he thought. He took a step back and looked at the display case. He then looked at the LCD panel. *6.2 PSIA* it read.

"Of course," he mumbled. "Stupid."

"What is it?"

"The sign says the case is under pressure by a flammable gas. It's very common to store specific goods in a gas-filled environment to preserve them. In the case of documents, there's another, better way for preservation: a vacuum. 6.2 PSIA stands for the measure of vacuum, the absolute pound-force per square inch. A vacuum exists anywhere between 0 and 14.7 PSIA. That's why the door won't open. It has been sucked closed. Look for a valve somewhere on the case."

"Nothing," Bishop said after a few seconds. "Wait."

He jumped as high as he could to look on top of the case. As his feet hit the floor with a thump, he lost balance and bounced into the case. The voices in the distance stopped.

"We're history," Jennifer whispered. "What now?"

"Quick, help me up there."

He pointed to the top of the display case.

"What?"

"Just do it!"

Bishop turned his back to the display case and signaled Jennifer to give him a leg up. Jennifer offered her hands and Bishop hoisted himself onto the top edges of the display case where he felt a thick rubber tube. With one forceful tug, the tube came out of its socket and Bishop fell to the ground as a loud hissing noise came from the top of the case as it filled with air.

"Who's there?" came a shout from the other end of the room.

Bishop pulled the display case door open and grabbed the aluminum tube.

"Guards!"

"I think that's our cue," Bishop told Jennifer.

"Guards? I thought there was only one!"

"Let's not wait and find out. Try to be quick, but as quiet as possible. Follow me."

Bishop quickly moved from one aisle to another, carefully looking into each row to see if anyone was coming as loud footsteps and shouts echoed around the room.

"This way! To the back! Check every aisle!"

Bishop stopped behind a case and peeked around it only to see a security guard in his way. "Damn."

Bishop turned to Jennifer and put a finger to his lips. He checked the other aisle only to find another guard. He gestured for Jennifer to come nearer and whispered, "We need to run."

Jennifer bit her lip before giving a wary nod.

"Now," Bishop said and sprinted past all the rows before hitting the end wall. A second later, Jennifer bumped into him.

"There they are! At the end of the aisle!" shouted one of the guards before giving chase.

Bishop looked ahead to see an empty pathway. He grabbed Jennifer's hand. "Come on!"

Running for their lives, they headed for the red curtain at the end of the aisle.

"Almost there!" Bishop shouted, just as a guard stepped out from behind a display case to stand right in front of them. Bishop and Jennifer came to an abrupt halt. Bishop glanced behind them wondering whether to retreat.

"Quick!" the guard in front of them shouted, holding out his hand "Give me the tube!"

"What?" Bishop said.

"Give me the tube. I'll distract them."

Bishop looked over his shoulder again.

"If you want to live, you have to trust me," the guard told him.

"Look," Jennifer said staring at the guard's arm. "Look at his wrist."

Bishop looked at the man's wrist and saw it: a bright scarlet string bracelet.

The guard nodded. "You have a friend. You've got to trust me."

Bishop glanced at the aluminum tube in his hand and bit his lip.

"Give it to him," Jennifer urged.

Bishop sighed and glanced backward only to see another guard now coming toward them at the end of the aisle. He looked forward, then backward and forward again, weighing his chances before finally handing over the tube.

"Go!" the guard ordered as he stepped aside.

Bishop and Jennifer ran past him.

The guard tucked the tube into his jacket and took a Zippo lighter from his pocket. He looked into the display case nearest him. On a label below a meal box it said "*Jan Sloot Digital Coding System.*"

"I'm sorry, Jan," the guard said before ramming his elbow into the glass panel, breaking it. He took a few steps back, sparked up the Zippo and threw it into the case before running toward the exit. With a loud woosh, a huge flame emerged from the case and into the aisle. Within seconds, the heat caused a chain reaction of fires quickly breaking out throughout the maze.

"We need to get out!" Nichols screamed, running toward the exit with Moore close behind him. "Everybody out!"

One security guard grabbed a fire extinguisher from the wall and Nichols knocked it from his hands. "Forget it! Get out, now!"

Bishop and Jennifer reached the stairs as more men arrived trying to get down.

"There's a big fire in there!" Bishop called out, but the men didn't pay any attention to him and continued to head toward the maze.

Running in the opposite direction, Bishop and Jennifer threw themselves out into the fresh air only to find the previously tranquil surroundings a hive of activity with sirens blaring and lights flashing through the trees. Bishop and Jennifer ran to the side of the lake, taking shelter behind a huge rock that looked like a sacrificial stone.

"Stay down," Bishop told Jennifer as he continued to watch the entrance beneath the owl. From his backpack he took out his hand sanitizer. A minute later, Nichols and a handful of guards emerged, followed by plumes of thick smoke and flames that quickly took hold to engulf the owl. The fire was fierce and as it lit the night sky, and men ran in every direction trying to escape the Grove. Jennifer joined Bishop to look over the stone, feeling the heat from the flames on their faces as the owl crashed to the earth.

"Such a waste," Bishop said and Jennifer shook her head. "We need to go."

Getting to their feet, they both walked up the path, toward the exit where a stream of luxury cars queued to get out as firetrucks and police cars tried to get in. The last police car passed them before stopping with a screech of tires. A door opened and they heard a loud voice with an English accent.

"Are you going somewhere?"

Startled, Bishop and Jennifer looked at the man in the car.

"Aren't you supposed to be in New Haven?" Bishop asked as Monroe got out of the car.

"And let you have all the fun?" the Brit responded as he closed the car door and the vehicle sped off toward the lake.

"Quite a coincidence finding you here," Bishop said.

Monroe chuckled. "Since when do you believe in coincidences? Are you both all right?"

"I guess I am," Jennifer responded.

Bishop cleared his throat. "It's been a long day, but I'm okay too." He shook his head. "So why are you here?"

Monroe took a deep breath "That's a long story. Maybe it's best we find you a place to rest and we can talk later."

A car coming from the grove stopped alongside them on the grass. A window slowly rolled down and they saw the guard who had allowed their escape from the maze.

"Everything all right?" he shouted.

"You!" Bishop replied. "Who are you?"

The man didn't respond and Bishop realized he wasn't addressing him or Jennifer, but Monroe. Bishop frowned in confusion.

"Like I said, this might take a bit of explaining," Monroe said. "Maybe this will help."

Monroe pulled up his sleeve to reveal a red string on his wrist. He then waved at the guard in the car who quickly took off.

Bishop's jaw dropped and Jennifer took Monroe's hand to look more closely at the red string. "You're Kabbalah?"

"You make it sound like a dirty thing," Monroe said.

"You've been lying to us all this time?"

"I never lied to you. I never told you I wasn't and you know I did extensive research on the Kabbalah. So, when you told me about your trip to Safed, the birthplace of modern Kabbalah, I simply had to join. When things subsequently became more serious, I felt compelled to inform some of my friends who told me they were already aware of something going on. They told me about the death of Father Matula in Poznań. I knew the man, and from there I took a special interest in this case. With the support of my friends, I followed your progress along the way. But"—Monroe laid his hands on Bishop and Jennifer's shoulders—"we're standing at the side of a small road in a forest in the middle of nowhere. I think we need to get out of here. The rest can wait. I have a car outside waiting. Come."

"And just who are your friends?" Bishop asked. "Other Kabbalistic believers?"

Monroe cocked his head and gave a throaty chuckle.

"But why didn't you say anything? Why didn't you say you're a Kabbalist?" Jennifer asked.

Monroe chuckled again. "Well, in the past I decided not to go public because it probably wouldn't go down well with my colleagues at the university. Then, when you got me involved in this whole John Dee case, I decided to join your crusade as a bit of fun. I was interested from a historical and Kabbalistic perspective, but still, my main reason was for the fun of it. But then one thing led to another."

"And what about the final document? Where is it now?" Bishop demanded.

"Yes," Jennifer aid. "What about all our work?"

"Enough with the questions." Monroe smiled. "It's safe for now. I promise."

As they left the Grove, Monroe pointed to a black sedan parked at the side of the road. "Just tell the driver I sent you and he'll take you anywhere you want to go."

"You're not coming?" Bishop asked.

"Later," Monroe responded. "I have to clean up some things before I go. But don't worry. Let's meet Monday evening at the university and we'll talk some more."

Bishop took Jennifer's hand and together they walked to the car. As they got in he glanced behind to see Monroe walking into the Grove. *Crazy*, he thought.

EPILOGUE

The gray-veined marble facade of the Beinecke library shone like gold in the early evening sun. On the streets outside, new students explored the campus where they would be spending the next five or six years at before earning their degrees. Inside the library, Walker Monroe stood beside an open glass display case housing the Gutenberg Bible. With a white, velvet-gloved hand he patted the book one last time before gently closing and locking the case. He returned to his desk, took off his gloves and wrote "Verse 5:27, the Book of Genesis" on a piece of paper that he then folded and placed in his wallet. He smiled to himself, thinking of the account of Enoch and Methuselah, and wondering whether his own secret would be blessed with their longevity. Or longer, he hoped.

"Reflecting on your sins?"

Bishop's voice echoed through the empty library and Monroe chuckled. After rubbing his face with both hands, he turned to see Bishop and Jennifer approaching.

"You came together?"

"We just met outside," Jennifer replied. "Seven, you said?"

"Yes," Monroe confirmed. "Take a seat." He pointed to two chairs opposite his desk. "How are you doing?"

"Still recovering, I guess," Jennifer admitted. "Still suffering from a mild case of sleep deprivation, but otherwise okay."

Bishop nodded. "And you? Everything 'cleaned up?'"

"I'm sorry," Monroe said, feeling a little uncomfortable. He tapped his fingers on the table.

"You're sorry for what?" Bishop asked.

Monroe paused for a moment. "About keeping you in the dark, I guess. I didn't see any other option at the time."

"Why not?" Jennifer asked.

"Well, you have to know we are a peaceful organization and we usually prefer to keep to ourselves. We believe that if we don't interfere in other people's business, they won't interfere in ours. We don't spread the word like others."

"So, what changed?" Bishop asked. "Why did you interfere in our business?"

Monroe smiled. "Two things, I guess. First, my work generally involves researching ancient texts and coming up with theoretical conclusions and evidence. As you were researching John Dee's texts that could actually lead to a hidden secret, who could resist?"

"And second?" Jennifer asked.

"I told you I knew Father Marcin Matula, the Polish priest you met in Poznań. We met years ago at a seminar and stayed connected over the years. He was very interested in my work at the university. After you visited him and introduced yourself as a professor from Yale, he called me to ask if I knew you and your research assistant. He also told me about your research into Uriël. He said he searched for your name on Yale's website and found the subject to be... um, peculiar for a professor of mathematics and philosophy. Then, when I heard he had been killed shortly after your visit—"

"You thought we killed him?"

"No, of course not," Monroe replied quickly. "Exactly the opposite. I thought you could use some help. I was worried about you. So, I decided to join you with the assistance of some of my friends in the Kabbalah network."

"And all the other moments like our rescue at Machpelah?" Bishop asked.

"Friends," Monroe confirmed. "I took the liberty to contact Rabbi Cohen before we got there."

"So, you're also the one who got us arrested afterward?" Jennifer asked flatly.

"That, I'm afraid to say, was a miscommunication on my part, for which I'm very sorry."

Bishop shook his head. "I still think you should have told me."

"Like I said, I'm sorry. I planned to tell you at the right moment, but I guess I didn't find the right moment."

"So, what about the Grove?"

"What do you mean?"

"At the Grove?"

Monroe looked at the huge glass box filled with ancient books before them. "You see all those books? Though they're part of the library here at Yale, they're also in the public domain. Anyone who's interested can look at them, read them and research them, if they like. When I entered what was left of the place hidden under the owl, there was evidence of dozens of secrets hidden over the years. You must have seen it yourselves. The place was a museum, a science exhibition of suppressed inventions, hidden not because they were a threat to humanity but because they were a threat to individual interests. Much like lobbyists in the United States who influence legislation to their advantage. Did you know the top twenty lobbying companies in the U.S. spent over $1.5 billion over the past few years lobbying for their cause? And those are only the official numbers. Healthcare being the top spender, by the way. As individuals, we think we are in control because we have the right to vote. But the truth is, that after the voting, the ones with money take real control. Not to mention their influence on elections through social media. Suppressed inventions are just another way of controlling our way of living, our health and the distribution of wealth and health all over the world."

"And you knew about this all the time?" Jennifer asked. "The Kabbalah knew about this?"

"Oh no," Monroe chuckled. "No. Like I said, I personally became interested when Matula died and you told me about Dee. I simply reached out to some friends who I know share the same interests as I do and they were all too eager to help. We never expected it to lead to something like this, but when it did...." Monroe fell silent.

"You took the final document," Bishop noted.

Monroe paused before carefully replying. "I did. Or rather some friends of mine took it."

"And where is it now?" Jennifer demanded.

Monroe hesitated. "I'm not sure." The only thing I know is what they told me, that it's somewhere safe."

Bishop shrugged. "And are your friends going to share it?

"Again...." Monroe shrugged.

"But why?" Jennifer said. "If they don't have any intention of sharing it, aren't they doing the exact same thing as the men at the Grove did—suppressing something that could be of benefit to mankind?"

"Maybe they're trying to figure out the implications of sharing it."

"And what about Nichols, Simpson and all the others involved?" Bishop asked. "What about the murder of your friend, Father Matula?"

"That's up to justice, I guess," Monroe replied. "I know they're tying the murder of Father Matula to Michael Robartés and he is in custody, so he'll probably be extradited to Poland where he will be tried. As for the others? I'm not sure, but I don't think they can be tied to any crime. I find it hard to believe that any of the prominent members of the Bohemian Club will be accused of anything, and even if they were, who would prosecute them? If anything about it becomes public, it will probably be put down to conspiracy theorists and reduced to a few blogs that no one will read."

Jennifer took a deep breath. "What I still don't understand is why Nichols gave up searching for the document we found at the British Museum after all he'd done to get the other documents? I mean, if he was just planning to hide the truth he could have simply hidden his part of the recipe at any time in the past ten years and nobody would ever have been able to reproduce the elixir."

"That's a very good question," Monroe said. "There must have been a time when he thought he could produce the elixir for himself, to his or to his company's advantage."

"But why stop when he was so close?" Jennifer pressed.

"He must have gotten nervous," Bishop said. "After all, for a time he managed to conduct his search without too much attention. Then things started falling apart, Robartés got arrested, the Hermetic Order of the Golden Dawn was dismantled by Europol and Simpson went on the run."

"He saved his ass," Jennifer concluded bluntly.

"The negative publicity and maybe even prosecution will even get a man like Nichols nervous," Monroe concluded. "And as long as nobody else had the recipe for getting rid of pain completely, his twenty-five percent of all sales on NSAIDs in the U.S. was safe and he would still make billions."

"I guess you're right," Bishop admitted. "But there's still something we don't know."

"Like what?" Monroe asked.

"Where did the recipe come from and who created it in the first place? The Aldaraia led us to a set of documents. If Dee indeed translated the Aldaraia someone else must have created the recipe and have hidden the documents before him."

"There's a lot we still need to wrap our heads around," Monroe replied. "In my opinion, it was probably Shimon bar Yochai. Remember, he told us it was time to reveal secrets?" Both Jennifer and Bishop nodded. "It was Yochai who was the one who studied the Torah and wrote the Zohar hiding for thirteen years in his cave and has several 'other' miracles tied to his name." He took a deep breath. "But there's no way to know for sure."

"That's it!" Jennifer almost shouted, suddenly slapping a fist on the table, and both men turned to her.

"I'm sorry," she said. "I'm on about something completely different. In my mind, I was rewinding the whole story, and that's when it came to me. Do you remember me telling you about Alice Walker, the red-haired lady I recognized but didn't know from where?"

Jennifer looked at Bishop who nodded.

"Well, I remember where I know her from now."

"Do tell," Bishop urged.

"Remember I told you about the game with the replica Krugerrands and that on my sixteenth birthday my father gave me a real one? Well, just after my father gave me the coin he was called away and I noticed him walking up to the front of the house with a face like thunder. After a few minutes I became worried and went looking for him. I found him at the end of the pathway talking very agitatedly to a woman, a woman with red hair."

"Alice Hartman," Bishop concluded.

"Yep," Jennifer said. "But what could they have talked about that agitated my father in such a way?"

"About ten years ago, you say?" Monroe looked thoughtful. "They must have been talking about the documents your father obtained from the auction. She must have wanted to convince him to work for them or maybe she just wanted to get the documents from him. Whatever the specifics, your father didn't agree with her in any way."

"How do you figure that?" Bishop asked.

"Well, and I'm sorry to say this Jennifer, I think it's safe to say your father made the mistake of taking the last document to be the only document and he experimented on himself with the recipe—with dire consequences."

"I had figured that one out myself," Jennifer admitted. "What I don't understand is why the doctors never made the connection with the toxins in his body?"

"Modern medicine doesn't always provide us with all the answers." Monroe replied.

Bishop leaned over the table. "And it's probably safe to say that if he did cooperate with Hartman he wouldn't have experimented on himself as Culver would have taken charge. Your father was a good man and it was just bad luck that the document he found was written in such a way he could never have known it was only a part of the whole. Maybe it was purposely written like that so whoever found it would stop there after realizing the recipe didn't work."

Bishop saw Jennifer's eyes widening as she took a deep breath.

"I just thought of something else," she said. "My father got sick after experimenting with the recipe on himself—very sick. But he was never in any pain, never in all the years he was sick. I mean, he lost control of his bodily functions, he collapsed during a speech and he was very uncomfortable, but he was never in any real pain."

"That's remarkable," Monroe replied. "So, there might be some truth to the recipe."

"So, is this it?" Bishop asked. "Is this the end of our journey, and we're still none the wiser?"

The three of them sat in silence for a while until Bishop spoke again.

"Of course, there's still one thing left for you to do, young lady. I believe you have a paper to write if you want to get your four-point course credit from the Linguistic Anthropology department."

Jennifer gazed at the men for a moment before rubbing her hands over her face.

"Don't worry, we'll help you," both men said together.

"But first"—Bishop rose from his chair—"I'm going home to get a good night's sleep."

"That's not a bad idea," Jennifer agreed.

"I'll close up here and see you around," Monroe said and Bishop tipped his hat in farewell before turning to leave while Jennifer moved to hug Monroe before following Bishop.

Once the clicking of the exit turn style echoed through the library, Monroe walked up to the case housing the Guttenberg Bible and stroked the glass. "Maybe one day," he whispered.

Outside, Bishop shook Jennifer's hand. "We'll see each other soon to get you started on that paper of yours."

"That would be nice," Jennifer said pulling him toward her to give him a firm hug. "Thank you for everything and especially for trusting me and my father's work in the first place."

"No problem. And if you ever find another tin box, you know where to find me."

Jennifer chuckled before wandering off into Yale's dark streets.

For a moment, Bishop looked up at the stars. Then, when he started walking to his car, he couldn't stop his mind from wandering as he searched for a meaning for everything that had happened to him over the past few weeks. As he put up his jacket collar, he remembered something Rabbi Naphtali Cohen once said to him.

If you wait until you find the meaning of life, will there be enough life left to live meaningful?

INTERMISSION

ACKNOWLEDGEMENTS

Another special thanks to Dan Brown, Michael Crichton, Stephen King, and Tom Clancy, for the pleasure they gave me reading their work, and for giving me the inspiration to write.

ABOUT THE AUTHOR

Dutch renowned author, Clinchandhill, had long-discovered his passion for writing at a young age. Despite past career detours, his love for worldbuilding and the written word were rekindled into a furious blaze. He has since penned his acclaimed political thriller, *Kursk*, and its equally compelling sequel, *47 Hours*, and will be releasing *The Mogadishu Encounter* in late 2020.

His irrefutable fascination for credible stories and true events is evident throughout all his fictional works, including this latest novel, *Aldaraia* [Evolved Publishing], and its upcoming sequel, *Lemuria*.

Clinchandhill now writes full-time in the Netherlands, with his beautiful wife of 20 years. In his spare time, he enjoys sipping tea with a good book and delving into his own adventures out on open waters.

For more, please visit Burt Clinchandhill online at:
Website: www.clinchandhill.com
Facebook: @Clinchandhill
Instagram: @Clinchandhill
Twitter: @Clinchandhill
LinkedIn: Burt Clinchandhill

WHAT'S NEXT?

Watch for the next (second) novel in this "Matthew Bishop" series of religious conspiracy thrillers, to release in the spring of 2021.

LEMURIA

The secrets of the past belong to the future.

When all over the world, the last isolated living tribes disappear, Professor Matthew Bishop is again, unwillingly, dragged into an adventure that will take him all over the globe.

His personal stake increases when his close friend Jennifer Porter disappears and seems somehow to be involved. Following the hidden clues, and with the help of the Vatican and old friends, Bishop uncovers the truth about the next step in evolution.

It's a truth that doesn't end on this Earth, but could very well mean the end of it, in a journey across three continents and into the heavens.

MORE FROM EVOLVED PUBLISHING

We offer great books across multiple genres, featuring high-quality editing (which we believe is second-to-none) and fantastic covers.

As a hybrid small press, your support as loyal readers is so important to us, and we have strived, with tireless dedication and sheer determination, to deliver on the promise of our motto:

QUALITY IS PRIORITY #1!

Please check out all of our great books,
which you can find at this link:

www.EvolvedPub.com/Catalog/

Thank you!

CPSIA information can be obtained
at www.ICGtesting.com
Printed in the USA
LVHW081143151120
671746LV00020B/1111